APOLLO

THE NAMELESS PRINCE

MICHAEL GEORGOPOULOS

Inks and Bindings
888-290-5218
www.inksandbindings.com
orders@inksandbindings.com

TABLE OF CONTENTS

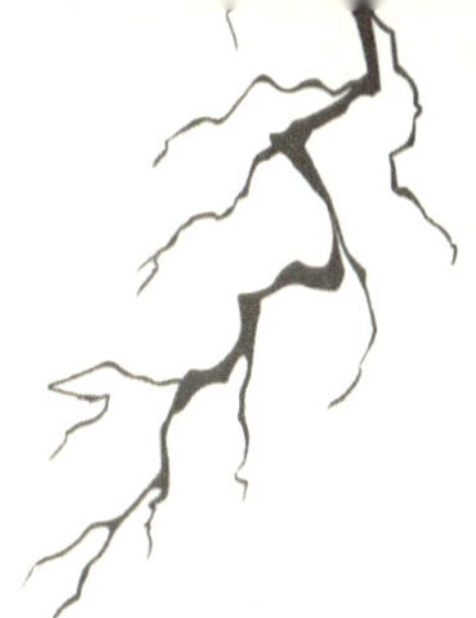

PROLOGUE

"Some destinies are forged in light. Others are hammered in shadow." — Eldersong, Verse XII

They say the Flow is life. It is the first breath of a newborn and the last sigh of the dying. It is the current beneath the soil, the whisper in the air, the pulse inside your blood. It binds the moons to their tides and the suns to their courses. It remembers the moment the first stars were kindled, and it will remain when the last one goes dark.

The Flow is not a god.
It does not love you.
But it will answer you and, in answering, it will change you.

To most, the Flow is invisible. They walk in it every day without knowing, like fish unaware of the ocean. But for a rare few, the Flow can be *touched*. These are the wielders. And for each wielder, the Flow shapes itself into a crystal a fragment of eternity given form. This is the Sunspear.

Every Sunspear crystal is unique, born the instant the wielder first touches the Flow. It does not merely choose you it is you.

Your doubts and convictions, your loves and hatreds, your courage and your fear all are etched into its core. When called upon, the crystal will take the shape your soul demands: a blade, an axe, a bow, a staff, even weapons the Order's forges have no name for. The form can shift over a lifetime, but its color is constant a pure reflection of the wielder's nature in the Flow.

Green for hope the kind that mends what has been broken, that binds wounds you cannot see.
Blue for calm resolve the steady hand in the storm, the unshaken heart when the walls close in.
Orange for unyielding will the flame that refuses to be snuffed out, even beneath the weight of worlds.
Red for wrath the fire that consumes without hesitation, burning until nothing remains but ash and memory.

And rarer still… there are colors no records speak of. Shades that do not belong to the visible world glints of silver like moonlight on still water, gold like the heart of a star, greens so deep they look like the first breath of creation. They are spoken of only in whispers, in the margins of forbidden texts, in the half-mad ramblings of those who walked too far into the Flow.

Such colors are not gifts.

They are warnings.
They mark wielders the Flow itself watches too closely not as favored children, but as pieces upon a board whose moves must be contained.

One truth stands, carved into the oldest stones of every temple from Elaris to the edge of the Umbers:
When a wielder dies, their Sunspear crystal dies with them.
The bond is severed.
The Flow turns its face away.

That is law.
That is balance.
That is truth.

Or it was.

In the known worlds, three great powers claim guardianship over that truth:
The Axis, who see the Flow as law and measure balance in obedience.
The Umbers, who see the Flow as trial and believe suffering tempers the worthy.
And between them the Order, sworn to walk the Flow and keep both extremes from breaking the world.

And then came the boy from Kaith.

Dragged from the smoking ruins of his village in chains, barefoot and bloodied, he clutched in his palm a broken Sunspear crystal his mother's. And though she was gone, the crystal still pulsed faintly with life. It should have been impossible. The Axis called it heresy. The Umbers called it a sign. The Order called it… dangerous.

No one could yet name what walked beside him. But some swore they saw it: a second shadow at his back too tall, too deep, moving when he did not. The same shadow said to have followed kings, conquerors… and monsters.

His name would become a legend a bad omen for the of the world .
But that was not the name he was born with.

And this is not the story of how he found it.

This is the story of how the Flow in all its beauty, in all its cruelty decided to give it back to him.

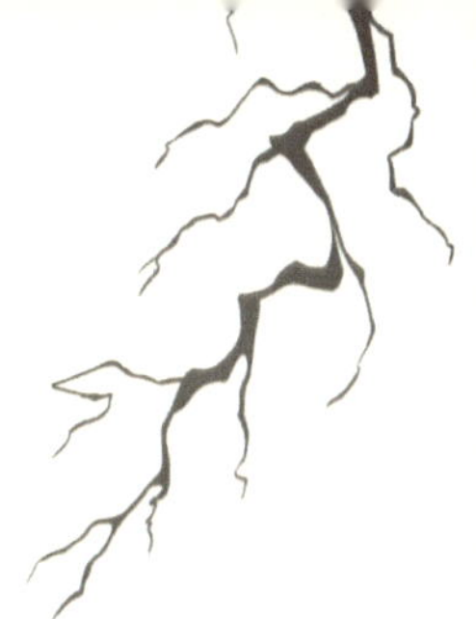

CHAPTER 1

*Kaith, the Shattered Vein — once a world of mines
and death, now a cradle of peace.*

Our story begins at the end. Valere sat alone beneath the silvered sky, where the moonlight spilled across the stones like a river of cold fire. The night was warm, but the breeze that wound its way through the quiet garden carried the scent of old rain and distant seas.

Her hair once the deep royal purple the galaxy had known and loved was now a crown of grey, each strand a thread spun from years of war, loss, and victories that never felt like triumph. It drifted softly in the wind, catching the light like fading silk.

Her body had grown old, brittle, a frame once honed for battle now wrapped in the stillness of age. The scars, half-hidden beneath her robes, were maps of a life carved into the bones of history. But her eyes… her eyes had not dulled.

They were still the sharp, unyielding steel of the warrior she once was the most elegant blade of the Order. They had called her the Purple Justice. The blade that could cut through the lies of kings and the darkness of the Umbers alike. The woman who could save any soul in the universe… except, perhaps, her own.

The garden around her was empty save for the rustle of leaves and the distant hum of the Flow through the old temple walls. In her lap rested a worn journal, its pages thick with the dust of years. Her fingers still steady despite the age in her bones turned the first page.

Kaith was no longer the planet she had first bled upon. Once, billions had died mining Flow ore from toxic caverns, their lives bought and sold in dust and heat. Now its valleys bloomed with crystal gardens, and its cities thrummed with music, laughter, and trade. The Flow here once thick with rage and agony — now shimmered with peace.

And yet… peace could be lonely.

She tilted her head back, gazing at the stars. A sudden flash broke the black a bright orange flare streaked across the heavens. Her lips curved into a trembling smile.

"Even in a perfect night, something comes to break it, you huge bastard giant," she murmured, her lips curling into the faintest smirk.

Her voice was half a growl, half a sigh. "I should be angry… but instead, I feel… joy." She shook her head, as if scolding a memory that refused to behave. "I missed you, you glorious idiot. Jaleon, the orange giant. The only man who could eat an entire barracks' worth of rations and still have room to steal my bread."

Her fingers tapped absently against her knee, as though keeping time to some long-lost barracks song. "I can still hear your laugh echoing in the mess hall, even when you were about to get us all executed. Gods, you were insufferable."

She paused, eyes drifting toward the horizon, where the silver sky bled into the darker edges of night. "But you never hesitated. Not once. Not when it mattered. Not even when the whole damned Order had their spears at our throats."

Her smirk softened into something almost tender. "I swear, if you walk through that gate right now, I'll call you an idiot to your face… and then I'll hug you until your ribs crack where is the other noble rat isn't he with you? Lux don't hide your aura behind this huge idiot."

Then the whole sky became the noble blue. "oh I missed you guys"

She laughed once, softly — but the sound cracked halfway, splintering into something fragile. The laugh broke into a quiet sob she hadn't meant to let escape.

Her hand went to her face, fingertips brushing the corner of her eye as if she could simply wipe the years away. But the ache stayed.

And then… the air shifted. It was almost nothing a faint change in pressure, the whisper of a breeze where there shouldn't have been one. Her breath caught.

For a heartbeat, she could swear she heard him. Not in the booming way Jaleon used to fill a room, but low, close, as though he were leaning on the table beside her.

"Even the strongest of us breaks from time to time," the voice said warm, tired, familiar. "We're just humans at the end of the day."

She froze, afraid that moving might scatter the moment like smoke.

And when the silence returned, she couldn't tell if he had truly been there… or if her heart had simply given his memory a voice, because it needed to hear him again.

Time stopped.

It was not the stillness of sleep, but the deep, soul-freezing silence she had not felt since her Mirrorwalk. The stars above seemed sharper, closer and in them, a shadow moved.
Her breath caught.

The stars above seemed sharper that night, like they'd been cut from glass and hung close enough to touch. Between their cold fires, a shadow moved slow, deliberate, patient.

Her breath caught in her throat.

She knew.

The weight in the air was the same as it had been on a hundred battlefields before the killing started. The same quiet she'd felt before the Flow bent itself toward one man.

Her voice was only a whisper, but in the stillness, it carried like a confession. "Now that you've come… I know" her voice steady as an iceberg "I will not wake to see another day."

The thought didn't frighten her. It warmed her, almost.

"I'm so happy you're with me," she murmured, her words trembling at the edges. "I missed you… Gods, I missed you. My body longs to be 'young again, just once more to fight at your side as we did before the world broke. I still love you" then Valere heard a voice carried form the wind like memory "if thought were seeds then for every moment you've lived in my mind , a garden would rise without end … and I would walk it until the stars forgot their names"… she froze and she remembered "my sweet Apollo."

Her eyes blurred, but she didn't wipe the tears away. They ran freely down her face, catching the starlight, falling like molten silver onto her hands.

For a moment, the years peeled away in her mind's eye she saw him as he was, Short and unshaken, the green fire of his Sunspear burning in the dark, the Flow itself bending around him like a cloak. She could almost feel the heat of him at her shoulder, the surety of his presence.

And then a voice.
Not his.
A small, warm one.

"Nana?"

Valere blinked. A child stood in the doorway of the garden, her wide eyes reflecting the starlight.

"Mama told me it's not good for you to stay out in the cold," the girl said. "Please, come inside."

Valere beckoned her closer.

"Come here, my sweet one. I want to show you something."

The child stepped into her arms. Even at her age, she could *feel* it the air thick with something ancient, an aura deep and intoxicating, like a god was standing just out of sight.

"Nana… why is the air so pure here?" the girl whispered.

Valere's smile was faint, almost wistful.

"Because my sweet Apollo is here."

The child froze.

"Nana… we don't say his name. It's forbidden."

"And do you know why?" Valere asked.

The girl shook her head.

Valere's voice grew low, almost reverent.

"Because once, he was only a boy small, wounded, forgotten. They laughed at his tears, carved pain into his skin, and left him in the dirt to die.

The Flow does not always send its gifts as light. Sometimes it sends the fire of suffering to burn away the servant, and forge a nameless boy into something the world will one day call a prince.

Now he is not merely a man. He is the hush that falls before the slaughter.

He wears no crown…" *(Axis)*
"…and carries no torch…" *(Umbers)*
"…yet when he walks into a city, kingdoms fall without a cry.

The girl swallowed hard, as if the shadows themselves had listened. Valere's gaze lingered on the horizon before she finally lifted her eyes to the sky. Stars blazed there in unnatural clarity, sharper and nearer, as if the Flow had drawn them close for her final night.

Somewhere in that vast stillness, something shifted. Not wind. Not sound. Just a presence, an unseen current that made the air feel heavier in her lungs.

The girl tilted her head, studying Valere with eyes too perceptive for her age.

"Nana… did you know this man before?" she asked, voice careful, almost afraid of the answer. "Mama never speaks of him. Or… of how great a warrior you are."

Valere's lips curled in a faint smile that was almost a wince. She chuckled softly, but there was no humor in it, only the brittle echo of a sound she hadn't made in years.

"So you've noticed?"

"I can see it," the girl said, the awe in her tone untouched by doubt. "Your purple Sunspear. I know you were with the Order. I know you fought."

Valere closed her eyes. The words pulled her backward like a hook buried deep in the past. She felt again the weight of her blade, perfect balance and perfect edge, in her younger hands. She heard the low, singing hum of the Flow filling her bones before a battle, the way the very air seemed to sharpen around her when her comrades stood at her side.

She saw flashes: Serena's green light cutting clean arcs through the void; Jaleon's orange flare roaring like a wildfire; Lux's disciplined strikes, precise as clockwork and… him.

Apollo.

The boy who walked into the Flow and came back with something no one could name.

Her chest tightened, the memories pressing against her like the tide against an old sea wall. She could almost smell the scorched metal of the Sunspears, the salt of sweat and blood on the wind, the electric tang of the Flow when it bent too close to mortal flesh.

When she opened her eyes again, the stars seemed closer still, and in their midst, a faint streak of green light passed silently across the heavens.

"Yes… I knew him. Not as a story or a legend — as a man. And I knew the boy he was before that. He carried a cracked green crystal, and a Red wound, the Flow itself could bend to him . They feared him. They called him cursed. But I…"

She paused, searching for the right word, her voice trembling.

"…I called him my friend."

The girl leaned closer, whispering as though afraid to break the moment.

"Is that why you cry?"

Valere's lips curved into a sad smile.

"No, little one. I cry because the world was quieter when he walked in it. And… even now, I can feel him near."

The breeze warmed again, curling around them. The child shivered, but not from cold.

"Nana… why does it feel like the Flow is watching us?"

Valere looked back to the stars, her voice a whisper meant only for herself.

"Because it is. And because he's watching too."

The child's voice was small, but it cut through the quiet like a silver blade through silk.

"Who was he, Nana? Why does everyone hate him?"

Valere's gaze stayed fixed on the stars above Kaith's gentle night. The constellations shimmered against the black canvas of space — ancient shapes drawn by the Flow itself — but to her, every star was a shard of memory, some sharp enough to cut.

Her voice came low, almost as if she feared the answer might wake the past.

"Because he came back from hell."

The girl's brow furrowed. Her small hands tugged at the edges of her shawl.

"How did he survive?"

Valere's lips tightened. Her back, though bent by age, seemed for a moment to straighten, as though she were again the warrior she once was.

"He entered the fire as a boy. The flames drank his fear, ate his weakness, and clothed him in their strength. But when he stepped out, all he had carried was gone — his name, his kin, his home… and the only thing left was his mother who had given him to the world."

The old warrior's voice softened, not in pity, but in something deeper — reverence.

"And that's what made him unstoppable. No chains around his neck. No law that could bend him. No master who could command him. He was his own kingdom, his own weapon. And the Flow itself seemed to fear him."

The girl hesitated, her voice trembling. But... what was he like? Was he beautiful?"

Valere's laugh came suddenly sharp and alive, yet weighed down with the years. It was joy and grief tangled together. "Hah! My sweet child... beautiful is the last word I would use." She leaned back slightly, her gaze turning inward.

"He was short a hundred and seventy centimeters at most but solid, built like a wall of obsidian. The kind you could crash a wave against and it would only get stronger. Jaleon, the great orange giant, used to tease him about his height... called him 'little blade.'"

A ghost of a smirk crossed her face. "But here's the thing even Jaleon, who feared nothing, feared him. Not for his strength, not even for his skill, but for his eyes. Those eyes... they didn't just look at you. They weighed you. Judged you. And when he was silent and oh, he was often silent the air itself seemed to thicken, as though the Flow was holding its breath."

"They trained together," she continued, "sweat and blood in the same dirt, bruises traded like coins. And still, that fear never left Jaleon." Even Lux with all his speed couldn't beat him, his eyes always watching"

The girl tilted her head, almost shyly.
"In the village… they say he never had a father. Is that true?"

Valere's expression shifted, sharpening. Her eyes narrowed as memories swept her far from Kaith's peaceful fields. "Nobody knows for certain," she said at last. "The records are… absent. But I know this, his mother, Elira…" Her voice softened, and for a moment, Valere's tone was almost reverent. "Elira was one of the greatest warriors the Order had ever seen. I can still see her in my sleep the way she moved, the way the Flow bent toward her without hesitation."

"She wielded the bluest Sunspear I have ever laid eyes on a blade so pure, so bright, it could blind the unworthy before it even struck. But she was more than her weapon. She was strong enough to carve her name into history… and kind enough to let her enemies live. That balance, child, is rarer than any crystal in the galaxy."

Valere's gaze drifted into shadow as her voice dropped lower, more intimate.

"When she was still sworn to the Order, she ventured where few dared to tread — to the Ancient Temple of Paradis, hidden deep within the living forest of Elaris. The forest itself was alive with the Flow, its roots humming softly beneath the soil, its leaves shimmering with colors that shifted in rhythm to unseen currents. Even the wind there carried whispers, as if the trees themselves spoke in a language older than stone.

Few who set foot in that place ever returned. Some said the Temple rejected the unworthy. Others claimed it simply swallowed them whole. But Elira… she did not go seeking glory. She went because the Flow had called her, and when the Flow calls, you answer.

Within the Temple's heart lay a chamber untouched by time, its walls carved from crystal older than the oldest records of the Order. And there, on a pedestal grown from the living rock, hovered a crystal unlike any the Flow had ever shaped. It was not bound to one color, nor even two. It was a living prism, its facets shifting and rippling with every color known and unknown green for hope, red for fury, blue for serenity, gold for devotion, and shades no human tongue could name. The light that poured from it bent the air, made the stone beneath her feet hum like a struck bell.

She reached for it.

The instant her fingers brushed its surface, the world collapsed. The ground beneath her feet dissolved into a sea of shadow, and above her, the sky ignited into sheets of fire. The air itself roared in her ears, though no wind touched her skin. And then — cutting through it all, more terrible than the silence of death came a voice.

It was not loud, but it filled her bones. A woman's voice, breaking with desperation, echoing through the void as though carried on the Flow itself.

'Run. Run, my boy. Please… run.'

It was not meant for her. She knew it, deep in her spirit. The words were meant for someone else someone who would not hear them for many years to come. And yet, they burned into her soul, a warning she could never forget."

The wind on Kaith shifted that day — warm and strange — as if the Flow itself had leaned in to listen. The kind of wind that does not belong to the hour, nor to the season, but to something greater.

"They found her in the forest three days later," I told you, my voice quiet enough that even the crickets seemed to pause.

"Her body was broken, her breath shallow, her eyes unfocused as though she'd been staring into something far too vast for a mortal soul to comprehend. Her Sunspear... the legendary blue blade that had once burned so bright it could sear the air itself... was shattered. Not broken like in battle or death, but fractured in a way no weapon of the Flow should ever be. It was as though it had resisted her — or something — until the last instant."

When they carried her back, the priests spoke of bad omens. They would not touch the fragments of her blade. The elders averted their eyes when she passed, as though the sight of her would invite ruin.

And nine months later... Apollo was born. No father. No witness to his conception. No record in the archives of the Order that she had ever even carried a child.

The punishment was swift. The Order stripped her of her rank, deleted her name from the archives as if she had never existed, tore the sigil from her robes. Every victory, every battle, every oath — erased. They sent her away not to another post, but into exile.

And not just anywhere. To Kaith.

Kaith the Shattered Vein. Once a bleeding wound of mines and death, now a dumping ground for misfits, murderers, and broken dreams. A world the Axis spoke of in whispers, as if the very mention of it might soil their tongues.

There, in the rust-colored dust of Kaith's valleys, among its fractured mountains and hollow-eyed exiles, she raised him. No longer Elira the Brightblade, champion of the Flow… but simply Elira. A mother.

And still… some nights, when the wind was just so, they said she would stand outside their home, broken spear in her hands, staring toward the distant forest of Elaris… as if she was waiting for something to return.

A single tear traced the wrinkles of her face, but Valere didn't wipe it away.

"And that… is where his legend began."

Her hands trembled now, not from age, but from the weight of memory.

"Apollo the Nameless Prince. The one who walked through hell and came back… not as a man, but as the silence before slaughter."

"You ask me who he was, little one, and I can see in your eyes you want the short, easy story. The kind that ends with a cheer and a hero standing tall. But nothing about Apollo was easy. Not his birth. Not his life. Not the road that made him what he became."

CHAPTER 2

Kaith… gods, I hated that place. It was where the Axis sent the unwanted thieves, deserters, rebels and the children of those they didn't dare kill outright. Above ground, heat shimmered off fractured crystal plains. Below, the mines breathed poison, their walls singing with Flow veins that could kill a man with one careless strike.

That's where Elira lived after the Order cast her out stripped her name, her rank. All she had left was a shattered crystal and a son in her arms.

That son was Apollo.

You'd think exile would break her but it didn't. She had nothing. No coins, no honor, no allies. And still, she gave to that boy more than many mothers give in palaces.

They lived in a one-room shelter carved into the side of a canyon, its walls patched with mech plating, its roof held together with prayer cloth so faded the gods themselves wouldn't recognize it. She worked in the markets, hauled freight for miners, and came home with bruises she never spoke about.

And yet she laughed. Every night, she wrapped Apollo in her old Order cloak, humming the battle-hymns of Elaris until they became lullabies. She always fed him first. Always made sure his belly was full, even when hers was empty.

"A warrior eats before the battle, my son," she told him once. *"And my battle is making sure you live."*

That broken Sunspear crystal was never far from her side. She carried it in a worn cloth pouch on her hip, like it was a living thing. Apollo used to take it in his hands and press it to his cheek.

"It's like a heartbeat," he told her.
"It is," she answered. *"It remembers."*

I think it remembered more than she ever said.

You ask me how I met him, child? How I came to know the one they call the Nameless Prince?

Patience, my love. This story is long, and it does not begin in light. It begins with fire.

"The Flow does not choose the strong.
It chooses the undone." Eldersong, Verse IX

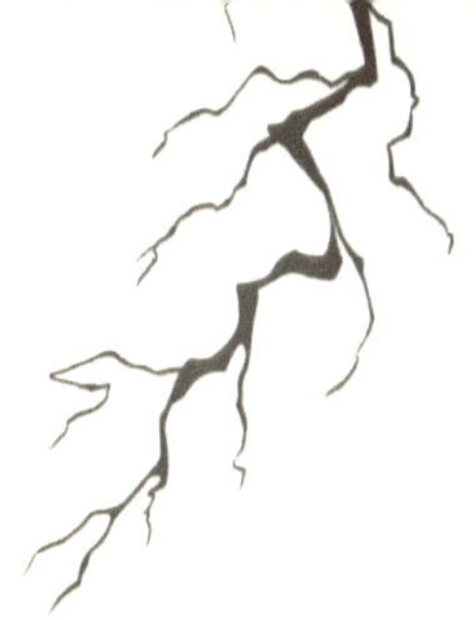

CHAPTER 3

The galaxy had forgotten Kaith long before I was born. A place the Axis cast aside, where miners bled into the crystal veins until they collapsed, where thieves and killers ruled the streets, and where children learned to run before they could walk. But the Order does not forget.

When the Flow stirs unnaturally when prayers are whispered to unapproved altars, when blood is spilled without doctrinal sanction the Order comes. And when we come, we descend like divine fire.

I was fourteen then, still an acolyte in blue and gold. My hands had never struck in battle. I was there to watch, to learn discipline from those older and stronger.

Our ships broke through the clouds in perfect formation, their anti-grav thrusters making the air shiver. Beneath them, the Axis seal burned bright an ouroboros cracked beneath a blinding sun. From the ship bellies spilled the enforcers of the Order, chanting mantras older than the stars:

"Harmony through Order. Cleansing through Flame. The Flow demands balance."

The sound was in my chest, my teeth, my skull. I thought I knew what we were here to do. I was wrong.

Kaith's people had no time to run. There was nowhere to go. Miners still caked in crystal dust, scavengers clutching rags and scrap, children with soot-blackened faces all already condemned. Declared Irregular. Diseased. The Flow, we were told, must be purified.

That's when I saw him for the first time.

A boy small, barefoot, clothes torn, eyes too old for his face. The others called him rat, stray, mine-child. No one could knew what this boy was.

His mother… Elira. Even in rags, she had the bearing of a warrior. Her arms were thick from labor, her back unbent despite exile. But that day she stood with nothing but her son… and a small cloth pouch at her hip.

When the sky turned red from our arrival, she pulled the boy to her chest. I was close enough to hear her voice low, cracked, smelling of sweat and copper.

"My boy, if I tell you to run… you run. And you don't look back."

He nodded, but his eyes never left her face.

At the front of our line stood Serena, one of the Order's commanders. Tall, wrapped in solemn blue, her green-crystaled Sunspear at her back, green the color of hope drawn through pain. I had admired her. That day she was only a blade.

Elira stepped forward, her boots barely whispering against the ground, though the air itself seemed to hold its breath. From the folds of her worn leather pouch, she drew it — the crystal.

It was cracked through its center, its surface scarred by years of battle and something deeper… something that no forge or blade could have made. The edges were chipped, splintered in places sharp enough to cut flesh, and yet it trembled faintly in her palm as if it still remembered what it was.

The light inside was no longer the pure, unbroken blue of its prime. Now, it flickered in slow pulses, a deep and melancholy azure, like moonlight spilling into a cavern where no wind could reach.

But within that tired glow, stubborn veins of brilliance coiled — reminders of a time when the blade had been the pride of the Order, feared and revered in equal measure.

And then… it ignited.

The air around her rippled, bending as if the Flow itself had turned its gaze upon her. That deep blue flame roared forth, imperfect and fractured, spilling shards of light into the air. It did not hum like the other Sunspears; it sang in jagged chords, each note carrying the weight of battles fought and victories won at great cost. The spear that formed in her hands was uneven, its length marked by hairline cracks that glowed like molten rivers, but it was beautiful — beautiful in the way storms are beautiful, in the way the sea is beautiful when it swallows ships whole.

I swear, my child, in that moment, even the wind seemed to bow to her

I remember the air shifting before they moved. It was the kind of stillness you feel right before a storm when even the dust holds its breath.

Serena and Elira stood facing one another, two pillars of the same Order, separated by choice, by command, and by the boy standing in the shadows behind his mother.

Serena's spear remained sheathed, but her aura shifted. I'd seen her in drills, always composed, precise, untouchable. Now she was different — the calm of someone who knows she's about to bleed.

They moved.

Serena raised a hand, halting the advance.

They moved toward each other like colliding storms. I remember the first step. Neither lunged. Neither shouted. They simply moved forward, closing the space between them as if the ground itself pulled them together.

Serena's hand moved to her spear hilt but she didn't ignite it yet. She waited, her breathing measured, shoulders squared, every inch the Order's champion. Even from behind her helm, you could *feel* her gaze assessing, calculating, waiting for the smallest opening.

Elira was different. She didn't stalk forward, she advanced like a mother shielding her child from wolves. Her grip on the fractured crystal was so tight that her knuckles whitened under the soot.

Serena's voice was low. I couldn't hear the words, but I could feel the rhythm of her tone coaxing, urging surrender.

Elira answered in the opposite rhythm, her voice hard, unyielding.

Then Serena ignited her spear. The green light bloomed smooth, steady, elegant the Flow's ideal form. It was the color of hope in pain, but that night, it felt like judgment.

The first clash came with no warning. Elira struck first a diagonal slash meant not to kill, but to drive Serena back. Serena pivoted, her spear snapping upward to parry. The sound was sharp, but beneath it I heard the hum of their crystals straining against each other, like two songs fighting for dominance.

They moved fast. Too fast for my eyes to follow cleanly. Serena's footwork was a masterwork each step precise, each turn a calculation that placed her spear exactly where it needed to be. Elira's was chaos. She moved like the ground itself was unsteady, like every strike might be her last, and that was why she threw her entire soul into each one.

Sparks of Flow energy spat off their weapons with every impact, scattering across the stone like burning petals. The ruins around them glowed in bursts of green and blue. I could smell the crystal heat sharp, metallic, and sweet all at once.

At one point, Elira hooked Serena's spear and wrenched, forcing her to step back. Gasps went through the soldiers around us Serena *never* lost ground. But she recovered instantly, reversing the momentum, twisting low to sweep at Elira's legs. Elira jumped not gracefully, but with sheer will and came down with a slash that almost caught Serena's shoulder.

They broke apart for a single breath, circling. Their auras swirled green steady as a heartbeat, blue jagged as a dying star. The Flow between them was thick, almost visible, like heat haze.

Then Serena shifted. I saw it the moment she decided. Her spear came up, her stance tightened, and she began to drive forward with relentless precision. Every strike pushed Elira back a fraction more. Every block cost her more strength.

The broken crystal flared brighter, its bursts uneven now, like it was fighting to stay alive.

Serena spun, her final strike sliding past Elira's guard. One clean thrust no anger, no malice and the green light passed through her chest.

Elira's face softened, not in pain, but in relief. She looked toward the boy. I couldn't hear her words, but I saw her lips shape them: *Run, my boy. Run.*

Her spear clattered to the ground. Her body followed, folding into the ash. The blue light flickered once… twice… and went out.

And the boy he didn't run

The boy saw everything.

He dropped to her side. Her blood pooled, thick and slow. She touched his face with a shaking hand.

"Please… my boy… run… run… run…"

The last word trembled into the air as her body stilled.

By every law of the Flow, a crystal dies with its wielder. But in his hands… it lived.

It pulsed once.
Twice.
Blue as oceans, bleeding into the red of blood.

Then he reached for it.

I had seen warriors try to lift the Sunspear of the fallen before. It's always the same the crystal dies with its wielder, the light gone, the Flow silent. At best, you get a dull shard. At worst, the crystal disintegrates into dust.

But not this time.

When his fingers closed over that shattered blue crystal, the world seemed to stop breathing. The color bled and shimmered in unnatural ways, and then gods help me it began to change.

It started as a deep ocean blue, pulsing like it still knew her heartbeat. Then, slowly, the edges darkened, thickened, and bled into crimson not the red of light, but the heavy, wet red of fresh blood. The two colors swirled together in the fracture lines, chasing each other like predators in a cage, until they formed something I had never seen in any codex or temple record.

The shards within the crystal caught the light like shards of ice, but their glow was alive red and blue locked in a constant, violent dance. Every pulse of light came with a faint sound, not a hum like a normal crystal, but something closer to a heartbeat.

The boy rose, still holding it, and for one impossible moment the broken crystal didn't just glow it ignited. The blade that burst forth was jagged and uneven, its edge alive with those same warring colors, spitting sparks where they touched.

The air turned cold enough to burn. Behind him, a black aura rose like smoke, curling into shapes I will never name.

I saw the soldiers hesitate. I saw Serena's grip tighten on her spear. And I saw a barefoot boy stand between his mother's body and an army, his eyes burning with pure, unyielding hate.

The Flow itself seemed to bend toward him.

"When the breath fails," a soldier whispered through tears, "the Flow begins anew…"

Everyone saw it. Soldiers. Civilians. Even the dying. It was the color of grief turned into a blade.

The Flow twisted around him in jagged pulses. Soldiers hesitated, weapons half-raised but unwilling to close the distance. Even the chanting had fallen silent.

Then Serena stepped forward.

She didn't come with her weapon raised. She didn't bark an order. Her movements were slow, measured, careful like someone approaching a wounded predator. Beneath the smooth curve of her helm, I could feel her fear.

She stopped just outside the arc of his weapon's reach and spoke softly, her voice pitched low so it would not carry.

"My child," Serena said.

It was not a command, not the clipped authority of a commander on the field — but an entreaty, a voice that reached for him rather than ordering him. The sound carried an unfamiliar softness, a quiet plea that cut through the clash and chaos that had filled the streets only moments before.

"You don't have to fight anymore," she continued, stepping forward as though any sudden move might break what little thread was holding this moment together. Her green Sunspear dimmed, the light drawing back into the crystal as if she feared even its glow might push him further. "Not now. If you stay here like this... more will die."

Apollo lifted his gaze to meet hers. It wasn't rage in his eyes now. Rage was loud, ragged, spilling over. This was quieter — far more dangerous. A still, glacial cold that sank into your bones. Looking into it was like staring into the depths of an endless well at night, knowing something down there was watching you back. If you looked too long, you'd feel it reaching for you, stripping you bare of every excuse, every mask.

The broken crystal of his mother's Sunspear was still in his grip, the blue fractured with veins of red that caught the dim light. He held it steady, fingers curled around it with the finality of someone who would sooner let his own bones break than release it.

His breathing was calm — too calm — each inhale measured, each exhale controlled. And yet, the air between them felt brittle, like frost stretched thin across black ice. One wrong word, one wrong breath, and it would shatter into something neither of them could call back.

I was watching from the edge of the ruined street, and could almost see it — not with her eyes, but in the way the Flow trembled. Serena was not just speaking to a boy. She was standing before a storm that had learned how to wait.

I couldn't tell if he heard her words at all.

From his own telling, later, he didn't.

The sound was far away. The cold was inside me now. I knew she was speaking, but the meaning slid off me like water. The Flow was loud — too loud — and I felt like I was drowning in it. My mother's voice was still in my ears, telling me to run. But my feet wouldn't move. I was afraid if I did, she would vanish forever. I just… stayed.

Serena took a slow, deliberate step closer. Her boots crunched against the rubble-strewn street, but her hand never drifted to her weapon. Instead, it hung loosely at her side, palm open — an unspoken promise.

"Please," she said, and the word wasn't command or caution. It was something smaller, more fragile. Almost a prayer.

For a long moment, he didn't move. He just stared at her, and in that stare was everything I couldn't name — grief that had curdled into something sharper, a cold that had nothing to do with winter air, and a weight that seemed older than he was.

The broken shard in his hand burned with that impossible storm — blue and red locked in a frantic dance, each flare like a heartbeat out of sync. But then… the light began to falter. It was slow at first, like a candle choking on its last breath. The colors bled together into a muddied, sickly ember. Then, with a shiver that seemed to ripple through the very air, the glow died entirely.

The jagged blade, once a weapon of defiance, unraveled into nothing — its edges scattering like dust in the wind.

No one spoke. Even the wounded and the weary, those who moments ago had screamed or cried, were frozen in the hush that followed.

Serena's shoulders eased — not fully, never fully — but enough for the rise and fall of her breath to steady. Beneath the shadow of her helm, her eyes never left his. She was watching not to judge, but to be sure… sure that whatever storm had been in him would not return before they reached the ship.

Finally, she lifted her hand in a small gesture. Two soldiers moved forward, their steps hesitant as they produced the crystal-forged cuffs. The sound of them locking around his wrists was unnervingly soft, a gentle chime that felt at odds with what it meant.

He didn't resist. Didn't speak. But as they turned him toward the waiting transport, his head shifted just enough to keep her in sight — like a tether neither of them had agreed to, but neither could sever.

In his grip, the once-living shard of his mother's crystal was no more than a dead stone now. Cold. Dull. As if it had never burned at all.

And no one could say why.

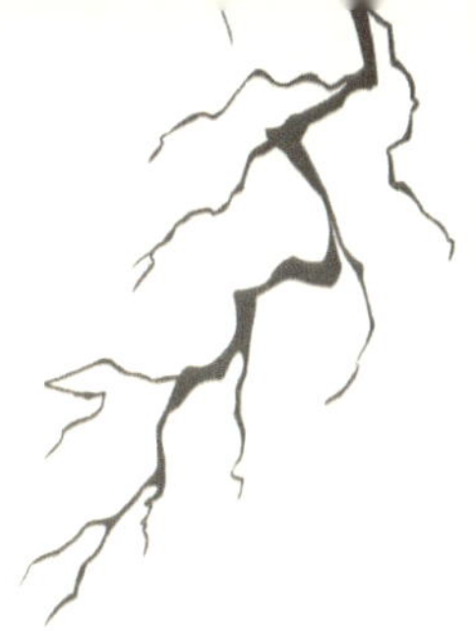

CHAPTER 4

At the ramp, he turned his head. His eyes met mine. And I knew, even as a sixteen-year acolyte, that the boy walking into that ship would never again be the same when he stepped out.

The hum of the transport engines became the only sound. No one spoke. Even the soldiers avoided looking at him.

I remember watching his hands. They were bound, but he still managed to keep the broken crystal in his grip, the way a drowning man might hold to a scrap of wood. It didn't glow anymore — it was just a dull shard of fractured blue streaked with dried blood — but it might as well have been alive, for how he held it.

I thought of the rules again and over again in my mind. *When a wielder dies, their crystal dies with them.* That was law. That was truth. And yet, I had seen it burn in his hand. I had felt it bend the air.

Now it lay still.

I wondered if he could still feel it.

The others on board kept their distance. Even the enforcers who had bound him seemed relieved not to meet his gaze. The air felt thicker around him, heavier, as though the Flow itself was circling warily.

My hair bound tight in the Order's braid, my training spear still nothing but wood. I knew I wasn't supposed to speak to prisoners. But something in me couldn't stand the silence.

I leaned forward in my seat until I was close enough for him to hear me over the engines.

"Does it hurt?"

His eyes lifted, slow, deliberate, and for the first time I saw them up close dark, unblinking, too old for his face. They didn't flare with anger. They didn't soften either.

"No."
His voice was rough, like stone dragged across stone. "It will be worse when it stops."

I didn't know what to say to that. My fingers tightened around my knees. I wanted to tell him I'd seen him stand over her body, crystal blazing in impossible colors.

I wanted to ask him what the Flow had whispered in his ears while it was holding her crystal. But I stayed quiet.

He lowered his gaze again, as if the conversation had never happened.

Hours passed in silence, broken only by the hiss of recycled air and the occasional cough of the soldiers. I think the others expected him to break, to cry, to shout, to beg. But he didn't. He just sat there, unmoving, eyes lowered, the faint rise and fall of his chest the only proof he was still breathing.

Maybe he was already somewhere else.

We descended through clouds the color of pale silver, the ship's hull vibrating under the strain of the upper winds. Then the light shifted brighter, warmer and I caught my first glimpse of the Temple of Elaris.

Ah… the Temple of Elaris," I told you once, didn't I? You've seen its likeness in hollos, but those are only ghosts.

From the sea below, it rises like a dream cut from black obsidian, its spires veined with living crystal that glows in slow rhythm, as if the Flow itself breathes through it.

The bridges between the towers are not stone, but light pure Flow shaped into narrow paths that hum beneath your feet. At night, they gleam with halos, so you feel as though you walk across the skin of the stars.

The High Dome crowns the heart of it all a sphere of crystal so flawless it catches both sun and moonlight, shattering them into a thousand rainbows that dance across the obsidian walls. Inside the Dome lies the Chamber of Still Light, where the great crystal sleeps and the Mirrorwalk begins.

Every tower has its purpose. The eastern spire holds the Initiates' Hall, where the sound of sparring spears rings from dawn until long after nightfall. The western spire belongs to the Codex keepers, the scholars whose voices echo like prayers in the crystal archives. The northern spire is the Sanctuary of Flow, where the oldest priests breathe in rhythm with the walls themselves. And the southern tower… the Hall of Crucible. That one is always quiet. Too quiet.

I tell you, child, when I first set foot there as a young acolyte, it felt like stepping into the heart of the galaxy itself. It was a place of promise, of discipline, of purpose. I thought it was a home. I thought it would make me into something greater than I was.

But that's not how *he* saw it.

Apollo looked at the same towers and saw spears aimed at the sky. The bridges were chains of light, not paths. The High Dome was not a crown, but a lid sealing something in. The shimmer in the air, which comforted me, made him flinch as if it were trying to press its way into him.

I saw beauty. He saw a cage.

Where I felt welcome, he felt measured. Judged. Even before he took a single step inside, he knew this place would try to shape him and he was already deciding how not to let it.

The ramp dropped with a hiss of pressure, letting in air heavy with incense and salt. The chains on his wrists rattled as the guards pushed him forward. Barefoot, head lowered, he stepped onto the polished black stone of the landing deck. I followed behind, just close enough to hear the dull scrape of his feet.

The landing decks stretched wide, inlaid with the Axis seal the ouroboros cracked beneath a blinding sun. Acolytes, priests, and guards stood in perfect ranks, their robes and armor catching the light so they gleamed like a single unblinking machine.

Every face was still. Every gaze fixed on him.

I caught one elder leaning to another and whispering a single word:

"Cracked."

Not as an insult as recognition. As if they were naming something dangerous.

Serena waited for him at the base of the main archway. Her helm caught the light, hiding her expression, but the way she stood told me she was studying him closely. She stepped forward, close enough that her voice wouldn't carry beyond us.

"You are safe here now," she said.

He didn't answer.

Her gaze dropped to the shard in his bound hands his mother's crystal and for just a moment, I thought I saw hesitation in her stance. The shard didn't glow anymore. It was only a dull fragment, fractured blue streaked with dried blood. And yet… the way he held it was the way a drowning man holds the last scrap of wood.

Serena said nothing else. She gestured for the guards to take him inside.

That was the first time I saw him walk beneath the shadow of the Order's walls. Even with the chains, he walked as if they were only an inconvenience.

I didn't know yet how much the Order feared him.
I didn't know yet how much they would try to control him.
And I didn't know yet… that they would fail.

The guards didn't take him through the Grand stairs like the honored initiates. No, they led him along the servant's causeway, a narrow path of black stone that clung to the outer edge of the Temple's foundation. The sea wind whipped against him, tugging at his torn clothes, the salt biting at the cuts along his arms.

We passed beneath shadowed bridges of Flow-light, their hum resonating in my ribs. I kept just behind Serena, close enough to see the way her shoulders had gone rigid as if she wasn't certain whether she was escorting a prisoner or something far more dangerous.

Inside, the air changed. The wind's roar was gone, replaced by the low, constant thrum of the Flow in the Temple's walls. Flame-crystals burned in tall sconces, their light bending around the obsidian columns. Statues of Sunspear warriors from ages past lined the hall eyes carved to follow you as you passed.

They brought him into the central sanctum.

The floor there was a perfect disc of polished crystal, so smooth it reflected every movement. He stood in the center, chains still on his wrists, the broken shard of his mother's Sunspear clutched tight in his bound hands. His eyes stayed low, fixed on the crystal as if the rest of the world had stopped existing.

Serena stepped forward, her armor catching the lamplight. For a moment, she only looked at him, her helm still hiding her expression. Then she removed it slowly as though deciding that this was a face-to-face moment.

Her voice was calm, almost gentle.

"Do you still carry it?"

He lifted his head just enough for their eyes to meet, then opened his hands slightly, revealing the shard. She didn't reach for it.

"The others may call you weak. Or cursed. But the Flow does not abandon the cracked it listens harder."

He said nothing.

Then she took one deliberate step closer.

What is your name? she asked like they were friends

He didn't say a word, but I felt it something was brewing in the shadows

"Fine then if you don't tell your name, i will name you… Apollo."

I saw him flinch. The reaction was small, but sharp as if she'd struck him harder than any blow could.

Apollo.

"You do not like the name?" she asked.

His voice, when it came, was low and raw.

"It's the name of fire."

Serena didn't look away.

"Then let it become the name of flame reborn."

He turned from her, but I could see the way the word had lodged in him a brand he would carry, whether he wanted it or not.

That was the moment the boy from Kaith the soot-faced child clutching a dead crystal became Apollo.

They didn't let him walk alone after the naming. Serena had already turned away to report to the elders, leaving the task of escorting him to me.

The corridors of the Temple were quieter here long, uninterrupted stretches of polished obsidian broken only by the faint, slow pulse of the crystal veins threading through the walls. The light they gave off was not the harsh glare of the outer halls, but a softer glow, breathing in a slow rhythm, like the heartbeat of something vast and ancient slumbering just beneath the surface.

The air was cooler here too, carrying a faint trace of incense and something older, harder to name the scent of stone that had stood too long and remembered too much.

My boots made no sound on the stone. His bare feet did. Each soft step was followed by the low, metallic rattle of the chain between his wrists, the sound carrying down the empty hall like a whispered reminder of why we were here.

He still clutched the shard. Even in the low light, I could see the jagged edges catch and scatter the crystal's pulse, as if mocking the perfect symmetry of the Temple's veins. His grip on it hadn't eased since we'd left the transport fingers locked tight enough that his knuckles were pale and bloodless.

We stopped outside a narrow door in the Initiates' wing. It slid open without a sound. The chamber inside was small no more than a cell, really a single cot against one wall, a stone shelf bare of books or ornament, a water basin that caught and reflected the wall's slow glow, and nothing else. The kind of place meant to strip a person down until all that remained was what the Order believed they should be.

It smelled faintly of cold water and dust. The air inside was still, the silence heavier than the hall outside.

And in that moment, I wondered if he saw it as a place to rest… or a cage.

"Hold still."

I took the key from my belt and unlocked the shackles. The metal fell away with a dull clink against the floor. He didn't rub at the marks they left on his skin just shifted his grip so the crystal rested more securely in his palm.

For a moment, neither of us spoke.

"You'll be given robes tomorrow," I said, keeping my voice steady. "White, for now — the color of unmarked potential. No crest, no color-thread in the seams. You'll earn those in time, if you stay."

He didn't answer, but I could feel his attention on me, even without him lifting his head.

"You'll be assigned a place in the training hall. Mornings are for drills spear forms, breathwork, Flow stances. The instructors will tear apart anything you think you know and rebuild it the Order's way. Afternoons… lectures. The Codex, the Balance, the history of the Ten Flames, the duties of a wielder. They'll test you on every word. Get them wrong, and they'll make sure you bleed for it."

We passed a high archway where sunlight spilled down through a lattice of crystal veins, casting shifting patterns across the floor. He glanced at it once, then looked away.

"Meals are taken in the mess hall. You'll sit with the other initiates. Don't expect kindness. They've already heard the whispers. Some will be curious. Most will be afraid. A few will try to make you prove yourself not in drills, but in other ways. The petty ways."

He didn't respond, but his grip on the shard in his hands shifted slightly. Even chained, he held it as though letting go would kill him.

"Once a week, you'll enter the meditation chambers," I continued.

"No weapons. No talking. Just you, the stone floor, and the Flow. Most initiates hate it at first. Some never stop hating it. But it's the only place in the Temple where no one can interfere. If the Flow wants to speak to you, it will speak there."

We turned into a narrower corridor quieter, the air cooler, the light dimmer. Through the windows I could see the lower bridges arching across the mist, the sapphire sea below. His eyes lingered there longer this time, like he was measuring how far he'd have to fall to disappear.

"If you last long enough," I said, my voice carrying in the stillness, "you'll earn privileges. The gardens. The upper bridges. And one day… maybe even leave these walls entirely. Travel wherever you please."

I didn't say the rest, but I knew it knew it the way you know when rain is coming.

He would go to Kaith. He would walk the jagged streets of the Shattered Vein, not for its markets or its towers, but for the scent of dust after rain, the scent she had carried home in her hair. He would find the places where her footsteps had fallen, press his palm to the worn stones, and try to feel the warmth she once left there.

He would stand in the wind, eyes closed, letting it pass over him in the hope that, just for a breath, it might be the same wind that had touched her cheek. And maybe if the Flow was cruel enough to allow it he would feel her there, just for a moment.

That earned me the smallest flicker of his eyes. Not interest, exactly. Something closer to… recognition

I stepped inside with him, closed the door behind us.

For a moment, we stood in silence. The faint hum of the crystal veins in the walls was the only sound.

"They'll tell you this place is your home now," I said finally. "But I know better. You didn't ask to be here. You didn't ask for any of it."

He looked at me then not angry, not pleading, just… steady.

I hesitated before speaking again.

"I was there. On Kaith. I saw what happened."

That steady gaze didn't waver.

"I'm not asking you to understand. But I am asking someday for your forgiveness."

He didn't answer. But I saw his grip on the shard loosen just slightly.

"My name is Valere by the way" and I chuckled.

He looked at me, and I could feel something, and he spoke to me, his voice was dimed and low, but his eyes fixed on me, "Thank you…" these two words was so important for me in that moment it gave me an instant smile.

I left him then, the door shutting behind me with a soft thud.

And for the first time since Kaith, I found myself hoping that the boy might survive this place not because the Order would shape him, but because he might shape himself in defiance of it.

CHAPTER 5

When the door shut behind her, the silence pressed in like a living thing. He sat there for a long time, still holding the crystal, until the ground beneath him creaked.

The room smelled of stone and faint incense from the hall. He hated it instantly. Too clean. Too still. Too far from the dust and heat of Kaith.

The crystal lay in his palm, cold as the deepest winter.
No pulse.
No light.
Just a dead shard, its once-vivid blue dulled to the color of ash, streaked still with the rusted stain of his mother's blood.

His thumb moved over its fractured edge, slow, deliberate — as though if he traced the lines long enough, he could piece it back together, could make it breathe again. The jagged ridges bit into his skin, but he didn't stop.

His breath grew shallow, his eyes unfocused, vision blurring until the room dissolved around him.

It came without warning.
Not a sob. Not a cry.
A sound so small it almost wasn't there — a soft, cracked whisper dragged up from a place deeper than the heart.

"Mama…"

It wasn't a plea. It wasn't even a word meant for the living to hear. It was the sound of something breaking in silence.

The first tear hit his knuckles. Then another. And then the dam broke. He curled over the shard, clutching it to his chest, the sobs shuddering through his body until his throat ached.

"Please… I don't know what to do, I am sorry for not fighting mama please come back…"

He saw her in the corner of the room as she was rags over strong shoulders, hands rough from work but gentle on his face. The way she laughed, low and warm, when he asked too many questions. The way she used to hum while they cooked scraps over a rusted stove.

And then, the other memory forced its way in the green spear through her chest. The way her lips had moved around words he couldn't hear until the very last one:

"Run… run, my boy…"

He pressed the crystal harder against his ribs, as if it might take him with it into the dark. But all it did was remind him of its silence.

When his breathing finally steadied, he rose. His body felt heavy, each movement dragging. He crossed to the small basin. The water inside was cool, clean foreign. He dipped his hands, scrubbing at the dried blood under his nails, on his forearms, on his face.

The red swirled away into pale pink, then nothing. It didn't make him feel cleaner.

He stripped and stepped into the narrow shower chamber, letting the water run over him until his hair clung to his face. He imagined the dust and smoke of Kaith slipping off his skin, but the memory of her touch clung stubbornly.

When he finally lay down, the cot felt too soft. Sleep came in pieces shallow, restless.

And then the world stopped.

The walls of the room dissolved into light, and he stood barefoot in a place he had never seen but somehow knew. The Temple of Paradis.

Crystalline trees rose around him, their branches hung with shards that rang like glass bells in the wind. The air was warm, heavy with the scent of something sweet and ancient. Light bent strangely here, making the shadows move as if alive.

And there at the far end of a marble path his mother.

Not as she was in her last moments, but younger, her hair longer, her face unlined by exhaustion, her armor flawless she looked like the perfect warrior. She was on her knees, hands gripping the earth, tears running freely.

He ran to her, calling out but the sound died before it reached her.

The shadows gathered behind her like a rising tide, long fingers reaching. She turned, staring into that darkness, she saw a small line of her Sunspear like a blue gentle thread forming around her and her lips formed the words he had already heard once.

"Run… run, my boy…"

The world shook. The light fractured. The shadows surged forward.

And he woke heart hammering, sweat cooling on his skin.

The crystal was still in his hand. Still cold. The room was quiet again.

Too quiet.

As Apollo slept, I found myself at rest or something like it. In my dreams, I felt him. I felt the tremor of his anger, raw and unshaped, the deep hollows of his pain. And yet… beneath all of it, there was a gentleness. A kindness that should not have survived what he'd endured. The same kind she had.

He looked like her. "oh my sweet child he was a spiting image of her untamed beauty"

That thought alone made my chest ache in ways I hadn't let myself feel in years.

When I woke, the room was still and dim. I lingered a moment before slipping into the baths, the steam curling around me, hot against my skin.

The water washed over me, but it couldn't drive away the memory of the smell copper and blood. It clung to my nose as if the air itself refused to forget.

I told myself I would try for four hours of sleep. That would be enough. I would have to wake him tomorrow, guide him down to the Hall.

When everything happened with Apollo, the sky had been dark the kind of dark that feels alive, that swallows the horizon until the world seems hollowed out. A darkness like death and void. The air itself had been thick with a strange bloom of cold, the kind that settles in your bones and makes the night feel endless.

It hadn't been a storm. It had been something else entirely.

The morning came slow, reluctant, as if even the sun feared to step inside these walls. The Temple bells rang their first note deep, resonant, a sound meant to carry through the spires and down into the sea.

I rose before the second bell. Habit. Training. And today, necessity.

His door was shut, but the air around it was strange — still, heavy. I knocked once, softly. No answer. I knocked again. Silence.

When I stepped inside, he was sitting on the edge of the bed, already awake. His eyes were fixed on the wall, unfocused, like he was looking at something far beyond it. The broken crystal was in his hands, resting in his lap.

"You should eat before the Hall," I said quietly.

He didn't move. Didn't even blink. It wasn't defiance — it was something colder.

"You'll be given robes today," I continued, stepping closer. "A place in the training hall. Meals in the mess with the others. It won't be home, but… it will be somewhere you can stand."

His gaze shifted to me, slow, deliberate. "Stand for what?"

I hesitated. "For yourself. For whatever the Flow hasn't taken from you yet."

He looked down again at the crystal, his thumb brushing over the jagged break. For a moment, I thought I saw it flicker — a brief pulse, too fast to be sure. But then it was dull again. Dead. Maybe my eyes were playing jokes on me,

I crouched so we were eye level, close enough to see the faint red veins in the whites of his eyes the residue of sleeplessness, of tears that had burned too hot to fall. "You should know…" I said, my voice low so it didn't echo in the small room, "I've seen hundreds come through these walls. Some lasted a year. Some didn't last a day." I let the pause stretch between us. "None of them had eyes like yours."

He blinked, slow, as if considering whether or not to believe me. "Eyes?" he asked, his voice almost a whisper, the sound so thin I might have missed it if I weren't watching his lips.

"Eyes that tell me you're still fighting," I said, "even when you don't move. Even when the worlds already decided you shouldn't be standing at all."

He didn't answer. Instead, his gaze dropped to the crystal in his lap, thumb tracing the jagged break again and again. I'd seen men polish their blades less reverently.

CHAPTER 6

We left his quarters without another word. The hallway greeted us with the cool stillness of early morning, its stone floors polished to a mirror sheen that caught our steps and threw them back to us. Each echo lingered a half-breath too long, as though the walls themselves were listening. The crystal veins running through the walls glowed faintly in the half-light, painting our shadows long and thin, making us look like figures caught in the stretched glass of memory.

The air grew sharper as we approached the outer cloisters. My breath misted faintly as we passed beneath the final archway and stepped into the training courtyard. The cold morning air bit at the skin, crisp with the scent of wet stone and faint incense curling up from braziers in each corner.

Acolytes moved in precise formations across the worn flagstones, their Sunspears flashing like molten glass in the sun's first touch.

The sound of their movements — the steady stamp of boots, the hiss of spears slicing air, the unison breath drawn for each strike — formed a rhythm older than any of us. Voices chanted the morning forms in low harmony, syllables rolling like the tide, calling the Flow into their limbs.

Beside me, I felt him pause. His gaze locked on the pattern of their movement, following each arc of a blade, each subtle shift in stance. His breathing slowed.

His fingers curled around the crystal in his palm, the way a soldier grips a hilt before battle.

This was where he would begin.
Or where the Order would try to break him.

We crossed the length of the training courtyard, the sound of spear hafts striking stone ringing in the crisp air. The rhythm of the drills didn't falter, but eyes followed us all the same.

It began with a glance from one of the younger acolytes, then spread like a ripple through the ranks. Whispers carried between sets of strikes words muffled but sharp enough to cut if you knew how to listen.

"That's him."
"…the one from Kaith…"

"…said he held a dead crystal, and it burned."

"Impossible. No one—"

"I saw it. Blood and blue fire, like it was alive."

"Then why is it dead now?"

"Maybe it's waiting."

They thought they were subtle. They weren't. Apollo didn't turn his head, didn't give them the satisfaction of a reaction, but I saw the way his jaw tightened — the single tell of someone who has learned to endure instead of lash out.

One of the purification squad soldiers from yesterday stood near the far wall, arms folded, his stance too casual to be anything but deliberate. As we passed, his gaze slid over Apollo, slow, assessing, like a man measuring a weapon before deciding if it should be locked away or put to use.

"He's smaller than I thought," he muttered to another. The second soldier's reply was almost reverent. "Size doesn't matter if the Flow bends for him. I saw Serena's face. She was afraid."

We kept walking. The great double doors of the mess hall loomed ahead — black oak banded with gold, carved with the same ouroboros-and-sun seal that had been on the belly of the ship that brought him here.

Inside, the world shifted.

Gone was the solemn rhythm of the training ground. The mess hall was alive with motion and sound — the scrape of benches on stone, the sharp clang of metal trays, the scent of steam and spiced broth hanging heavy in the air. A hundred conversations tangled together, punctuated by bursts of laughter or sharp retorts.

The ceiling arched high overhead its beams carved from black crystal that caught the light of the massive Flow-lamps hanging down on iron chains. Long tables stretched wall to wall, each crowded with acolytes in plain grey robes, some leaning in close to gossip, others devouring their food with the efficiency of soldiers on borrowed time.

Apollo hesitated just inside the doorway. His grip on the crystal tightened. I could feel his discomfort, as though the sheer press of voices and movement after so much silence was an assault in itself.

I didn't ask if he was hungry. I crossed to the serving line, grabbed a wooden tray, and filled it myself — thick slices of bread still warm from the ovens, a bowl of rice and broth, a handful of dried fruit. The servers looked surprised that I took the time, but none spoke. I was one of the temples prodigies after all.

When I returned, he was still standing where I had left him, eyes scanning the hall as if cataloging every threat, every exit.

I set the tray down at an empty table in the far corner, away from the worst of the noise, and gestured for him to sit.

"You need strength for what comes," I said simply.

He didn't move at first. Then, slowly, he sat. His hands hovered over the food for a moment, as though unsure if it was really for him.

"It's yours," I said. "No one will take it from you here."

For now.

"But Nana… what do you mean *for now*?" the child asked, her head tilting slightly, the lamplight catching in her wide eyes.

I almost answered — almost let the next part of the story spill into the open — but I stopped. The question lingered in the air like a note from a half-played song, and for a heartbeat my mind was no longer in this quiet room.

The cold of Kaith, the dark halls of the Temple — they melted away. In their place came a sky of deep amber and molten gold, the kind of light that wraps around you like an old blanket. It was warm — not the kind of warmth you fight for, but the kind that finds you without asking. A warmth steeped in the laughter of someone who never cared for titles, but made the world feel lighter just by standing in it.

A warmth of *love*.

It struck me so sharply that I felt my lips curve before I even knew they were moving. "Oh, come on, you bastard," I blurted, breaking the thread of the tale. "I'll get to you — wait your turn."

The child blinked in surprise. "Nana?"

"Yes, yes," I sighed, half-grinning, waving one hand through the air like I was swatting at an invisible pest. "I know you're listening. I know you want your grand entrance, you huge muscle-headed idiot. But you can wait."

I could almost hear him laugh — that booming, careless laugh that rattled the air and dared you not to join in.

The child giggled, the shadow of sadness lifting from her for just a moment. "You're talking about someone from the story?"

I smirked and leaned forward. "Oh, you'll know him when we get there. Nobody forgets him."

For a moment, the warmth stayed — rich and golden — but as quickly as it came, it drained away, leaving the old chill behind. The air was Kaith again, or the Temple's cold corridors, and the weight of the story settled back on my shoulders.

"Now," I said softly, "let's go back."

He'd barely taken his first bite when the peace shattered.

A voice boomed over the clatter of trays and the hum of conversation, cutting through the din like a spear slicing air.

"Well, look at this — they *do* feed the dangerous ones!"

I didn't need to turn. You never needed to, with Jaleon. He had a way of arriving like a storm front — loud, bright, and impossible to ignore. You could hear him before you saw him, and even when you saw him, you never knew if he was about to hand you a drink or throw you over a railing.

He came striding through the crowded mess hall like it was his personal parade route, weaving between tables with that long-legged swagger of his. Broad-shouldered, tall enough to make most men crane their necks, with a mane of orange-streaked hair tied back in a knot that somehow managed to look both deliberate and entirely lazy. His robe hung half-untucked, the sleeves pushed up to his elbows, and his boots were scuffed in a way that told you he hadn't been in formation all morning.

His tray—naturally—was piled high with twice the regulation serving. Bread, fruit, roast meat, something fried that was definitely not on the mess roster. Don't ask how he got it. Nobody ever asked Jaleon how.

I knew him before I knew Apollo. We'd bled in the same sparring pits, stolen wine from the same quartermaster, and gotten dragged to the same discipline hearings— usually with Jaleon doing the talking and me doing the apologizing. He was infuriating, irreverent, and the kind of friend who made enemies in your name before you'd even met them.

He dropped his tray on the bench across from Apollo with a thunk, loud enough to make the kid look up for just a second before returning to his food.

"So," Jaleon said, leaning forward with his forearms on the table, "you're the one from Kaith. The one who made Serena look like she'd swallowed a void eel."

Apollo didn't answer. Just kept eating, slow and deliberate, eyes on his bowl.

Jaleon grinned wider. "Not much of a talker, huh? That's fine. I can talk enough for both of us." He stabbed a chunk of bread with his fingers and pointed it at Apollo like it was a weapon. "I heard you held a broken crystal and it lit up like a war flare. That true?"

Silence.

He leaned back with a mock sigh. "Ah, the mysterious type. Good. We'll get along fine. I'm Jaleon, by the way. Jaleon the Magnificent, some say." He paused, tilting his head. "Well… only I say it, but still. Truth is truth."

Then—because of course he would—he reached over, grabbed a slice of bread from Apollo's tray, and tore it in half like it belonged to him.

"Jaleon," I said sharply, my voice cutting between them.

He froze mid-chew and raised an eyebrow at me, all mock innocence. "What? I'm just making friends."

"By stealing their food?"

"Sharing *is* friendship, Val," he said with a wink. "And if this kid's gonna be in the Order, he'd better get used to sharing with me."

Apollo finally looked up at him then. Not curious. Not impressed. Just… looking. An unblinking, cold-eyed stare that made even Jaleon falter for the briefest of moments before he leaned back with an easy grin, like nothing had happened.

"Yeah," he said after a beat, smiling like a man who'd just made a bet with himself. "You'll fit in just fine."

The noise of the mess hall swallowed the moment. Someone shouted for more tea, a chair scraped across stone, the scent of spiced bread drifted from the kitchens. Jaleon was already leaning into the next table over, trading some half-serious insult with a group of acolytes who knew him well enough to throw it back.

His laugh rang out — gods, I'd forgotten how big his laugh was. It filled the air like it didn't care who heard, like the world itself might as well laugh with him. He clapped one of the others on the shoulder hard enough to nearly knock them over, and when the poor boy retaliated by stealing a slice of Jaleon's meat, the entire end of the table erupted in noise.

Apollo stayed still.

He didn't flinch at the chaos, didn't scowl or frown. He just… sat there, shoulders slightly hunched, the empty space on either side of him like invisible walls. His gaze was fixed on the table, one hand still wrapped loosely around the bread Jaleon had left him, the other resting over the broken crystal tucked beneath his tunic.

It was strange — I could feel him listening. Not to the words, but to the *tone* of the room. Every burst of laughter, every clatter of dishes, every little flare of warmth between people who knew they belonged here.

He didn't belong here yet.

And though his face gave nothing away, I knew — *felt* — that he was measuring that space between himself and the rest of the hall. Weighing it.

Jaleon didn't notice, of course. He was halfway into an exaggerated retelling of some training match, describing an opponent as "built like a Flow ox but slower than a monkfish," his hands painting ridiculous shapes in the air. The others roared, and I caught the smallest, briefest flicker of movement from Apollo — a shift of his eyes toward the sound.

But no smile.

Not yet.

I remember thinking, *this one doesn't bend toward warmth quickly. The Order will try to break him before they learn how to reach him.*

But everything was cut short.

It started as background noise — a sudden bark of laughter from the far end of the mess, the scrape of a chair, the sound of boots crossing the stone. Then it hit.

A bowl of steaming oats cut through the air in a lazy, spinning arc before smashing into Apollo's chest. The mess splattered over his tunic, thick and gluey, dripping into his lap. The smell of overcooked grain mixed instantly with the faint tang of metal — his crystal was in his hand, and the heat from the food steamed off it like breath in winter air.

He didn't react. He didn't wipe it away. His hands stayed still, resting on the edge of the table.

Three men shouldered through the crowded hall like they were sweeping aside dust. They were already warriors — two, maybe three years out of acolyte training. Their armor was dented and worn the way some people wore jewelry, as proof of survival.

Smugness clung to their faces like another layer of plating. Their Sunspears not even in proper placement.

The first one—a broad-shouldered brute with scars crawling up the side of his neck—stepped right into Apollo's space and looked him over like a thing for sale. "So this is the Kaith rat," he said, voice pitched high enough to draw attention from the nearby tables. "Smaller than I thought. Guess they don't feed you much in the pits."

The second, wiry and sharp-eyed, leaned on the table with mock familiarity. "I heard about you. Whole village burned, and you were the only one they bothered to drag out. Not because you're special—nah. Just easier to clean up one body later than a pile."

The third—the mouth of the group—smiled wide enough to show the gap where two teeth should've been. "Kaith spawn. Bet your mother squealed like a stuck animal before she dropped. Did she look you in the eyes when she begged? Or was she too busy choking on her own blood?"

The brute chuckled, nodding toward Apollo's fist. "And you carry her crystal? What's the point? Everyone knows it's dead. Just like her."

The wiry one leaned closer, breath sour.

"Does it whisper to you at night, rat? Tell you how you failed her? Or does it just remind you she died for nothing?"

The laughter wasn't loud. It didn't need to be. It carried the cruel weight of knowing the whole hall was listening, waiting to see if the boy from Kaith would crack.

And then… I saw his eyes.

He lifted them slowly—not like a man ready to fight, but like a predator who had just decided the noise around him was worth noticing.

They weren't just red. They were deep, like molten metal at the heart of a forge, banked and waiting. The kind of red that didn't scream. It promised.

I felt it before I understood it—the air in the mess thickening, pressing against my ribs, each breath harder than the last. It was as if the Flow itself had decided to hover, watching.

The warrior didn't notice. Or maybe they did, and thought it was worth testing.

The gap-toothed one reached for Apollo's shoulder— and that's when the bench beside him scraped back violently.

Jaleon.

He didn't *enter* the scene so much as he exploded into it. Tall, broad as a siege gate, with his orange-streaked hair tied back in the messiest knot imaginable, his robe was half-unfastened and there was still bread in his other hand when he moved.

His first punch shattered the brute's mouth open, spraying blood and oat mush in equal measure. The man staggered, eyes rolling, before collapsing onto the table behind him.

The wiry one turned, but too late—Jaleon's shoulder rammed into his gut, folding him over. A fist rose and fell in the same breath, cracking nose cartilage with a sound that turned heads across the hall.

The gap-toothed soldier tried to pull his Sunspear—but Jaleon caught his wrist, twisted, and slammed his head into the table so hard the wood splintered. The food on it jumped, bowls clattering to the floor.

Blood pooled on the stone in fast, dark trails.

The mess had gone silent except for the ragged breathing of the three sprawled soldiers and Jaleon's low growl: "No one," he said, voice like a war drum under water, "talks about someone's mother like that."

The words hung in the air like smoke, daring anyone to argue.

And Apollo?

He hadn't moved. Not a muscle. He just sat there, eyes still glowing faintly, watching the scene as if the fight wasn't happening at all—as if something far worse was playing out in his mind.

The mess hall, for a moment, was nothing but chaos— overturned trays leaking broth into the cracks of the stone floor, boots slipping in spilled oats, and the sharp, ugly sounds of fists meeting flesh. Jaleon was a storm in motion, moving through the three warriors like they were practice dummies, his massive frame all blunt force and no hesitation. Each blow landed with a sickening finality, drawing gasps and winces from the onlookers.

The smell of blood rose fast, mixing with the steam of the morning porridge.

I saw Apollo stiffen—not flinch, not turn away—but stiffen like a blade being drawn. His head tilted just enough for me to see his eyes, and they... changed.

They weren't just angry. They *glowed.*

A hot, pulsing red, like fresh blood catching the light, and just at the edges—a flicker of something green. Untamed, unshaped, but alive.

It was then Jaleon came barreling in.

If Apollo's stillness was the gathering of a storm, Jaleon was the lightning strike.

And then—just as he was drawing back for another punch—Apollo's hand shot out and caught his wrist.

It wasn't a grip of strength, not really. But it *stopped* him.

I saw Jaleon's expression change in that instant—the wild, grinning fury draining from his face as he locked eyes with Apollo. Later, he would tell me he didn't see a small boy in that moment. He didn't see someone who needed defending.

He saw the Flow itself.

The rage, yes— molten and ready to pour over everything in reach—but also the weight of pain, the sharpness of loss, and buried deep beneath it, something that scared him even more: hope. A dangerous, impossible hope, flickering green like a small, defiant fire.

The air between them thickened. You could feel it, even from a distance — like standing too close to a forge's mouth.

"Please, stop that was more than enough" Apollo said.

No threat. No shout. Just a word that landed heavier than an order.

Jaleon's arm dropped without resistance. The warrior beneath him scrambled away, coughing blood, and the other two bolted for the far door, one clutching his jaw, the other limping badly.

The mess was silent.

Apollo released his grip, his hand falling back to his side.

Jaleon straightened, still catching his breath, and then—because he couldn't help himself—muttered, "Could've mentioned you had that kind of stare *before* I got oat mush all over my robe."

Apollo blinked. "...Thank you."

"You're welcome," Jaleon replied, rubbing at his wrist. "Next time, though, you throw a punch or two. I don't mind sharing the fun."

It was small, barely there, but I saw it—Apollo's lips twitching at the corners. Not a smile, not quite. But the first crack in his wall.

"I'm Jaleon," jerking a thumb at himself. "The Magnificent. Don't argue—it's true. And you're…?"

"Apollo."

Jaleon's brows rose. "Like the fire? Well, that explains it."

Before anything else could be said, the heavy doors at the end of the hall slammed open.

Serena entered, and the whole room shifted. Her armor—deep blue chased with gold filigree—gleamed in the mess hall's lamplight, and her cloak caught the air behind her like the shadow of something vast. The Sunspear across her back was dormant, but her presence burned hotter than any weapon.

Every acolyte, every soldier, straightened instantly.

Her voice rang out, sharp and absolute: "Attention!"

The mess snapped to it. Trays clattered down. Feet came together.

Her eyes landed on the two of them—Apollo, still in his ragged clothes, and Jaleon, still smeared with someone else's blood—and for a moment, I thought I saw the faintest trace of a smile tug at her mouth.

"Apollo. Jaleon." Her tone was firm, but not unkind. "Trouble finds you quickly."

Jaleon grinned, unrepentant. "We're… proactive in our relationships."

Serena's expression didn't change, but her voice softened in a way only those close enough could hear—like a mother who would scold but never turn away. "Enough for today. Jaleon, stand down. Apollo—you'll receive your robes. Valere will take you to the quartermaster."

Her gaze swept the hall once more, and silence followed her out the door.

The mess hall was still settling back into its rhythm when I jerked my chin toward the far corridor.

"Come on," I said, already turning toward the quartermaster's wing. "Time to make you look less like you crawled out of a smelting pit."

Jaleon fell into step on Apollo's other side without being invited. "Oh, this I've gotta see. You're about to get the full 'new acolyte' treatment. Robes, boots, a lecture about 'proper posture'—and that's before the part where the quartermaster sniffs you like a suspicious hound."

Apollo glanced at him but didn't bite. He just walked, clutching the dead crystal in his hand as if afraid someone would take it.

The quartermaster's wing was carved directly into the temple's inner wall, long and high-ceilinged, lined with crystal sconces that hummed faintly with Flow-light. We passed other acolytes and attendants along the way; some stared openly at Apollo, others whispered to each other. I caught the words "Kaith" and "cracked" more than once.

Jaleon didn't miss it either. He cupped his hands around his mouth and stage-whispered to one group of gawkers: "Yes, this *is* the dangerous one. Yes, he *is* prettier than me, but don't hold it against him."

One of the girls smirked; Apollo didn't even look up.

We rounded a corner, and there was the quartermaster's door—heavy oak, Flow-sealed with a pattern that shifted faintly in the light.

I pushed it open, and the familiar smell hit us: dust, old linen, and a hint of oil from the weapons racks in the back.

Quartermaster Berrin looked up from his ledger, squinting at us over the rims of his crystal lenses. He was built like a barrel wrapped in leather, bald as a moonstone, with a voice that always sounded like it was deciding whether or not to yell.

"Valere," he rumbled. "Brought me a stray?"

"Brought you a recruit," I said.

Berrin's eyes went to Apollo, and for a moment they softened—just a fraction. "Name?"

"Apollo," I answered before he could.

Berrin grunted and stood, moving to the racks along the wall. "You'll need standard robes, leather belt, boots, and a cloak for formal drills. Weapons come later, once Serena says you won't stab anyone important."

Jaleon leaned on the counter. "Better give him the good boots. Can't have him slipping in the courtyard and breaking that scary stare of his."

Berrin shot him a look. "And you. You're here why?"

"Moral support." Jaleon grinned. "Also to make sure you don't give him one of those itchy cloaks from storage. You know the ones—smell like old cabbage?"

Berrin muttered something about "bloody loud acolytes" and dumped a folded set of dark-grey robes on the counter, along with a belt and boots. "Try them. If they fit, they're yours. If not, I'll get the tailor to fix them."

Apollo picked up the robes carefully, as though they might vanish if he held them too tightly. I saw the way his fingers pressed into the cloth—how long had it been since he'd worn anything new? Since he'd owned *anything* that was his?

Jaleon clapped him on the shoulder. "Well? Go on, put 'em on. Let's see if the legend of Kaith cleans up nice."

Apollo gave him a flat look. "You talk too much."

"And yet," Jaleon said with a wink, "you're still listening."

Berrin jerked his thumb toward the curtained alcove at the far end of the quartermaster's chamber.

"Go on. Curtain's there. Boots on the bench. Don't tear the seams, or you're mending 'em yourself."

Apollo took the folded robes without a word. His wrists were still faintly red where the shackles had been, and he cradled the bundle like it might shatter if he held it wrong.

He stepped inside.

The alcove was small and dim, lit only by a single crystal lamp that pulsed faintly like a heartbeat. The air was warm and dry, carrying the faint scents of cedar oil, soapstone, and the faint metallic tang of freshly polished buckles. There was a bench for sitting, and above it a narrow shelf with a copper basin of still water, just enough to rinse the dust from one's face.

He set the bundle down and began untying it, slow and deliberate, as though every knot held a memory he wasn't ready to release.

The robe was a deep grey, woven with subtle threads that caught the light and shimmered faintly, like mist over black water. It was heavy, not in a burdensome way, but in the way that armor is heavy—a weight meant to anchor the one who wears it. The boots were soft leather, fitted to mold over time to the foot, soles reinforced with thin crystal plates to channel Flow in battle.

He ran his fingers over the seams, tracing the perfect lines of stitching. No frays. No patches. No torn edges sewn back in haste. He wasn't used to things like this. Kaith's clothes were born to die in the mines—scratchy, threadbare, already smelling of dust before they were even worn.

And then, the past bled in.

His mother, kneeling in front of him when he was no taller than her hip, helping him into a wool shirt she'd mended three times over. The elbows had been patched with a different color, the cuffs frayed, but she'd smoothed it on him like it was silk from Elaris itself. Her fingers had lingered on his shoulders, straightening the collar, and she'd smiled that tired but unbreakable smile—the one that said *you are mine, you are worth this.*

In the back of his mind, barely a whisper:

Run, my boy. Run.

It wasn't loud. It wasn't even urgent. It was just there, like a current under the surface, steady and inevitable.

He pulled on the robe. It fit as though it had been made for him, the belt cinching perfectly at his waist, the hem falling just at the top of the boots.

When he tied it, he felt the faintest brush of the fabric against his wrist, and it almost felt like a hand.

When he stepped out, the room shifted.

The robe caught the glow from the wall sconces and made him look taller, broader, his shoulders square and straight. There was a weight to him now, not just in cloth but in presence, like the room had to take him into account.

I forgot to breathe for a moment. I'd seen hundreds of initiates try on those same robes—some awkward, some smug, most looking like they were wearing someone else's skin. But not him. He didn't just wear the robe; he inhabited it. It was like watching a name being carved into stone.

And gods help me, he was beautiful. Not the polished, symmetrical beauty of noble portraits—no. He was the beauty of a storm on the horizon, of something raw and vast and uncontainable. The kind of beauty that makes you look twice, not because it's perfect, but because it feels like it *means* something.

I looked away before he caught me staring.

Jaleon, of course, didn't bother hiding it. He leaned against the counter, arms crossed, one eyebrow raised.

"Well, damn," he said with that lazy grin of his. "Didn't think they made these things in 'deadly.'"

Apollo gave him a flat look and said nothing.

"Seriously," Jaleon went on, "you look like the kind of guy they tell scary instructor stories about. You know the ones: *'And then the silent one turned, and—*" He made a dramatic slashing motion with his hand. "Whole squad gone. That's you."

Apollo's stare didn't waver.

Jaleon squinted at him, then smirked. "What's that? Are you the stoic type? Fine. I'll do the talking for both of us." He reached over, snatching a piece of bread from the tray on the counter and waving it like a pointer. "I heard you held a broken crystal and it lit up like a war flare. That true?"

Still nothing.

Jaleon grinned wider. "Alright, fine. Maybe you're mute. Or maybe you just don't like me yet. That's okay—everyone loves me eventually. I'm Jaleon, by the way. Jaleon the Magnificent. Well… only I say it, I think I have said again haven't i? but it's catching on."

I shot him a look sharp enough to cut stone when his hand drifted toward Apollo's belt to poke at the fabric.

He froze mid-reach. "Alright, alright. No touching. You're territorial. I respect that."

And then, without warning, the corner of Apollo's mouth twitched. Just barely. But it was there.

"Oh-ho!" Jaleon barked. "That was almost a smile! Careful—you do that too much, people might start thinking you're friendly."

And then it happened—short, rough, almost rusty from disuse—Apollo *laughed.*

Not much. But enough to make the air feel lighter. For the first time since I'd met him, he sounded like a boy his age.

Jaleon was still grinning like he'd just won a duel when I decided to turn the tables.

I tilted my head, eyes narrowing at him. "Speaking of uniforms…" I said, letting the words roll slow, "is that actually regulation issue, or did you wrestle it off a scarecrow?"

He froze, eyes darting down to his robe, which hung slightly lopsided over his frame. The belt was twisted, one sleeve cuff was rolled higher than the other, and the whole thing looked like it had been slept in for two nights straight.

"This?" he said, tugging at it. "This is tactical disarray. Keeps the enemy guessing."

I folded my arms. "Mm-hm. More like 'keeps the quartermaster crying.'"

Berrin, still behind the counter, actually snorted into his ledger.

Jaleon tried to recover with a grin. "Hey, the Flow doesn't care about neat folds, Val. It cares about results."

That was when it happened.

A sound burst from Apollo — sudden, sharp, completely unguarded. Not a chuckle, not a polite huff. A *real* laugh. It started as a short, almost startled bark, then rolled into something deeper, richer, and uncontrollable. He doubled over slightly, one hand braced against the counter, the other clutching at his side as if the very act of laughing was foreign and almost painful.

It was the kind of laugh that had weight behind it—the release of something that had been trapped too long. His shoulders shook, his eyes squeezed shut, and for a moment, his face was transformed. Gone was the guarded, expressionless mask; in its place was a boy who had forgotten, just for that heartbeat, the ash and blood he'd come from.

I… froze.

I'd heard his voice in fragments before—hoarse from grief, flat with silence—but never like this. His laugh was warm, alive, *young*. It was as if the walls of the quartermaster's room had tilted and let in a sliver of sunlight. I didn't realize I'd been holding my breath until I felt my chest ache.

Something inside me shifted—a quiet, aching relief I couldn't explain. It was dangerous, the way it made me want to protect that sound. To keep it alive.

Jaleon, for once, just stared at him, then broke into a slow, genuine smile. "Hells," he said, "that's the best thing I've heard all month."

Apollo tried to stifle it, pressing his knuckles to his lips, but another laugh slipped out anyway. And I swear, in that moment, if the Flow itself had been in the room, it would have paused to listen

Apollo was still coming down from the laugh—gods, that laugh—when the knock came.
Three sharp raps against the frame, clean and deliberate.

I knew before I looked that whoever stood there didn't belong in our little corner of the temple.

He stepped inside like the room was his. Tall for his age, with posture so perfect it looked rehearsed, hair dark and neatly bound at the nape. The white of his tunic was so crisp it almost hurt the eyes, trimmed in silver thread that caught the light when he moved. His boots shone like polished glass, and there was a faint scent of perfume—delicate, expensive—a smell from another life, another world.

His voice matched the rest of him. Smooth. Controlled. "Serena wants you. All of you. Now."
Jaleon leaned against the wall like he had all the time in the galaxy. "Careful, Apollo," he drawled. "This one probably polishes his spear before bed."

The boy didn't flinch. "Lux Tenvar. First son of House Tenvar, Crescent Sector." His eyes swept over us, slow, assessing—like we were items on a shelf. "And you are?"

Before Apollo could answer, Jaleon clapped him on the shoulder hard enough to make him sway. "This here's Apollo. Dangerous, broody, allergic to small talk. And I'm Jaleon—your new best friend or your worst nightmare, depending on how many desserts you leave unguarded."

I raised an eyebrow at Lux. "And I'm Valere. I keep these two from killing themselves. Mostly."

The noble boy blinked once. "If you're finished, we should move."

We followed him through the temple's high, winding corridors. The walls were alive with a faint crystal glow, every flicker catching in Apollo's hair, turning the black into threads of silver. I caught him looking— not around, but *through*—like he was walking in two worlds at once.

The air cooled as we climbed, the scent shifting from stone dust to burning incense. And then we stepped out into the courtyard.

I've walked that space a thousand times, but even now it can take your breath. The banners—blue, gold, and green—hung heavy in the wind, their edges frayed from years of storms.

And in the center, rising like it had grown from the earth itself, was the Mirrorwalk Temple.

Black obsidian walls laced with veins of milky-white crystal, each vein pulsing slowly, like a great sleeping heart. The twin spires rose so high they vanished into low clouds, connected by bridges of pure Flow energy—translucent, shifting with colors like oil across water. And the air here… it wasn't still. It was *listening*.

At the foot of the stairs stood Serena.
Polished armor. Blue-and-gold trim. Her green Sunspear at her back, alive with that rare light that seemed to warm the shadows around her. She has always looked like the Flow made her for war—but today, she was something else.

Beside her was High Priest Julius, robes layered in silver crystal, the sun bending around him as if even light was his to command. His eyes moved over us with the weight of someone who already knew our choices before we made them.

Lux went to his knee without hesitation, the movement crisp, practiced—the kind that's been drilled into noble-born acolytes since the day they could walk. His back was straight, his head bowed, his hands pressed just so against his thigh. The model of obedience.

Beside me, Jaleon groaned low in his throat—not loud enough to draw a reprimand, but just enough that I could hear the muttered curse that followed. He knelt anyway, joints popping, posture lazy, like a man bowing to a joke he didn't quite find funny.

I went down beside them, my own body moving with the muscle memory of years, but my eyes weren't on the High Priest or the temple doors. They were on the boy.

Apollo stood in the same place he had been a moment before, shoulders squared, chin lifted. The air around him seemed still—no, not still… waiting. I saw the flicker of something in Serena's gaze as she watched him. A silent plea, maybe. Or a warning.

He didn't look at the High Priest. He didn't look at the crystal spires or the guards or the crowd that had gone utterly silent. He looked only at Serena.

And he held there.

One heartbeat. Two. Long enough that I could feel the tension coil through the courtyard, the kind that makes even the birds stop their flight. Long enough that the elders shifted where they stood, and a few guards' hands twitched toward their weapons.

Then—without breaking that stare—he lowered himself. Not with the easy grace of Lux or the casual drop of Jaleon, but slow. Deliberate. Like a man deciding, in that moment, whether he would bow… or burn the place to the ground.

When his knee finally touched stone, it was not submission. It was a choice. And everyone there felt the difference.

The High Priest's gaze lingered on him a fraction longer than the others, but his face betrayed nothing. Lux kept his eyes down, disciplined to the last muscle. Jaleon shifted his weight like he was kneeling on a bed of nails, muttering something I couldn't catch.

But Serena… Serena didn't move.

She looked at him as if she were the only one allowed to see what he was really doing. Her expression didn't change, but I saw it—the way her eyes softened, just barely, as though she were telling him without words: *I see you.*

No approval. No rebuke. Just recognition.

Apollo didn't look away from her until the High Priest's voice filled the courtyard, deep and measured, drawing the attention of all.

Even then, I noticed it—the faintest tightening of Serena's jaw, the almost imperceptible shift of her stance. She was positioning herself between him and whatever might come next.

95

*"Beware the child the Flow whispers to first.
They carry storms beneath their ribs." Eldersong, Verse
XXXII*

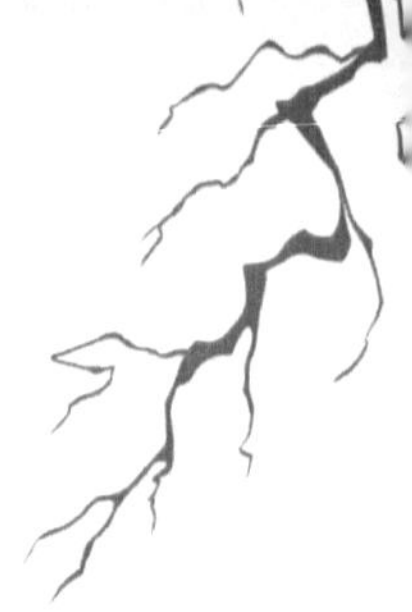

CHAPTER 7

And in that breath, I knew: if something went wrong, she would move before anyone else. "Before you walk the Mirror," Julius said, and the sound of his voice seemed to still the air itself.

It wasn't simply loud or deep—it *carried*. Every word felt like it had been spoken many times before, in chambers older than the Temple, in front of souls who had walked the same path for centuries.
The echo wasn't from the walls; it was from the weight of the ritual.

He stood beneath the great crystal arch of the Hall of Reflection. Above us, living crystal veins ran like rivers through the stone, pulsing faintly with the Flow—not in steady rhythm, but in something closer to a heartbeat.

His hand rested on his Sunspear, the darkened crystal at its head reflecting our faces in fractured pieces.

"The Mirrorwalk is not a test," he said. "It is not something you win. It is not something you fail. It is the first conversation between your soul and the Flow. You will go into the sanctum alone. You will place your hands upon the Heart Crystal, and it will reach into you in return."

He began walking the line of us—slow, precise steps that made not a sound, yet each one felt as if the floor itself acknowledged his presence. His robes brushed softly against the polished obsidian, trailing the faintest scent of resin and burning sage.

"The Mirror does not see your name, your rank, your bloodline," he continued. "It will strip you bare of the stories you tell yourself. It will show you what you are *when nothing else is left.*"

The words sank in like cold water. No one moved. Somewhere to the side, Jaleon's usual lazy grin was gone even he wasn't willing to break the spell Julius cast.

"For some," the High Priest said, his eyes narrowing slightly, "that truth is mercy. For others…"
He let the silence settle over us like a cloak before finishing: "…it is fire."

I'd been in this Hall before, but that day… gods, child, it felt *different*. The air itself seemed to hum, faintly resonating with the Mirror's pull. My chest tightened as though I were already in the sanctum, the crystal light reaching for me.

Even Serena—who could stand unmoved against entire legions—shifted ever so slightly. Her green Sunspear cast an almost living glow, and her eyes followed Julius with an intensity that wasn't fear, but respect of the kind soldiers rarely gave priests.

One by one,
Julius stopped in front of Lux, and for a moment, the hall seemed quieter. The High Priest's gaze swept over him—not the way a warrior sizes up an opponent, but like a craftsman running his hands over a blade, searching for hidden cracks.

"You carry the pride of the noble houses," he said slowly, each word measured like it was being weighed before release. "Your posture, your tongue, your eyes—they all speak of lineage. Of polished stone halls, of silken banners that never felt the dust of the battlefield."

Lux's chin lifted slightly, but Julius's gaze didn't waver.

"But pride is not strength. Strength is earned when the banners fall, when the marble cracks, and when you stand alone with nothing but the truth of your hands. Pride… will keep you looking backward at your own reflection. Strength will keep you alive when that reflection shatters."

Lux's throat worked once, a faint swallow. His eyes darted down for just a moment before finding the High Priest's again.

Julius leaned in the barest fraction, his voice lowering so that only we in the line could hear:
"You must decide whether you serve the Order… or only its image. One will demand your loyalty. The other will demand your soul."

Lux bowed his head then—not the quick, crisp bow of a noble greeting, but something slower. Less certain.

Julius stepped to Jaleon next. The shift in the air was subtle but real—his gaze was less cutting, more searching, like a man looking for the heart beneath a wall of noise.

"You hide your doubt with laughter," he said, his tone neither accusing nor indulgent, but certain. "It is a clever shield—one that has spared you more wounds than your spear has."

Jaleon tilted his head, grin already forming, the familiar one that dared anyone to take him too seriously. But Julius did not give him the chance to speak.

"Laughter can lift," the High Priest continued, his eyes never leaving Jaleon's, "or it can blind. There is a time to turn it into a torch that lights the way… and a time to set it down, so your hands are free to fight. You must learn when to stop hiding, before the moment comes when no one believes you can stand without the joke."

For just a heartbeat, Jaleon's grin faltered. His shoulders shifted, a fraction less relaxed, as if a weight had settled where none had been before. He didn't look away—he met Julius's gaze like a man taking a measure of something he couldn't yet name.

And then, almost too softly for anyone else to hear, he muttered:
"…Guess you've been listening more than I thought, old man."

Julius turned to me next.

For a moment, it was as if the room dimmed — not because his presence overshadowed everything, but because his eyes drew the world down to a single point.

He looked at me the way a father might look at a child who has returned from war — alive, but carrying pieces of the battlefield in her bones.

"Valere," he said, my name carrying the weight of memory. "You have stood longer than most. You have carried burdens not meant for one so young… and you have carried them well."

My throat tightened. I hadn't been called young in years.

"But endurance is not the same as healing," he went on, his voice lowering to something only I could hear. "You wear your strength like armor, yet I see the cracks you have welded shut with duty. You must decide whether you will let the Flow keep you standing… or let it teach you how to rest."

The words landed heavier than I expected. My mind tried to wrap around them, but part of me recoiled— rest was not a thing I knew how to trust.

I forced myself to meet his gaze. "And if I can't?"

Julius's expression softened into something almost— almost—like a smile. "Then the Flow will find a way to show you. It always does."

From the corner of my eye, I saw Serena watching me, her own face unreadable, though her grip on her green Sunspear tightened ever so slightly.

And then… he reached Apollo.

For a moment, the entire Hall seemed to narrow down to the two of them.
Julius studied him without speaking—not coldly, but as though weighing something beyond our understanding.

Julius stepped toward Apollo last.

I felt the air shift. It wasn't the hush of ceremony or the reverence the others got—this was heavier, as though the Flow itself was leaning closer to listen. Even the acolytes at the far edges of the courtyard seemed to sense it.

Apollo didn't flinch when Julius stopped in front of him. He held the High Priest's gaze like a man bracing for a blade.

"You," Julius said quietly, "are not here because the Order willed it. You are here because the Flow would not let you go."

Apollo's jaw clenched, but he said nothing.

Julius studied him, and for a moment his tone changed—softer, but in no way less powerful. "I have seen the records. I have heard the whispers. They call you cracked. They do not understand what that means."

He let the words hang, the silence drawing every ear closer.

"A cracked crystal lets the light through. But light alone is not enough. It will burn, or it will blind, unless you learn to temper it."

His gaze flicked, just briefly, to the shard Apollo still carried. The broken blue, still stained with a line of dried red.

"You may carry your mother's crystal today," Julius said, his voice deepening with a weight that felt almost ritual, "but know this—it will not be the one that answers you in the Mirrorwalk. There, the Flow will give you a new crystal. One that will be only yours. And when it does… you must decide what to keep of her, and what to let go."

I saw the faintest tremor pass through Apollo's grip. Serena shifted where she stood—protective, yes, but also wary, like someone watching a flame that might leap its brazier at any second.

Julius didn't step back immediately. His eyes stayed on Apollo's like a man measuring the depth of a well whose bottom he wasn't sure existed.

"You've walked through fire before, child," he finished. "The question now is… will you walk through it again?"

Apollo didn't answer. But I saw his fingers curl around the crystal, as if bracing it for the next burn.

Julius's gaze swept over us, lingering just long enough on each face to make it feel personal. When he spoke again, his voice had the calm rhythm of someone who had recited these words a thousand times, yet still believed every one of them.

"The Flow is not just power," he began. "It is life, and death, and all the currents between them. When you touch the Heart Mirror, it will not simply see you—it will *enter* you. Every thought you've buried, every wound you've hidden, every triumph you've cherished… the Flow will know them.

It will feel your joy and your rage, your mercy and your cruelty. It will walk through your past, and it will peer into paths you have not yet taken. And when it leaves, it will not truly leave—it will remain with you, a second soul."

He paused, his eyes settling on the green glow of Serena's Sunspear.

"You will become one with it, and it with you. From that moment, you will never again be alone. Some find comfort in that. Others… find it a burden they can never lay down."

The silence between us felt heavier now, almost physical.

"The color of your crystal is the Flow's reflection of who you are—and what it sees in you. Gold, the rarest, speaks of leadership born from sacrifice. Blue is clarity, patience, and an unbroken will. Green, as Commander Serena bears, is growth through pain, the triumph of life over loss. Crimson is courage, but also the willingness to burn everything in your path to protect what you love. White is purity of purpose. Black… black is not absence. It is the Flow's acceptance of the shadow within you, and the power to walk in darkness without being consumed."

Julius's tone deepened, carrying the weight of an old memory.

"The Conqueror, whose name still walks the stars, bore a crystal unlike any seen before—a flame of gold wrapped in white. The Ten Flames it birthed lit our galaxy into unity… and yet, unity came only after centuries of war. His crystal sang with every strike, but it also wept. For the Flow does not choose heroes or villains—it only chooses truth."

He stepped closer to us, his presence like a tide rising.

"When you step into the Mirror, it will not show you what you want to be. It will show you what you are. And when it places your crystal in your hand, you will know—without doubt—whether you are ready to carry the weight of that truth. And if you are not… it will break you."

His eyes moved to Apollo last.

"When your time comes, you may carry your mother's crystal into the sanctum. But you must understand— it will not answer to you as hers. It will remain hers, always. What waits for you in the Heart Mirror will be yours alone."

Serena's fingers shifted slightly on her spear, her green crystal catching the temple light. She was watching him—not as a commander watches a recruit, but as a soldier watches a storm forming on the horizon.

I remember thinking, child, that the Order looked like a single blade—perfect, sharp, and gleaming. But I had already learned, even at your age, that a blade's beauty hides its hunger. They polish the steel so bright you can see your own face in it, but that reflection blinds you to the truth.

The ceremonies show you discipline, harmony, banners snapping in the wind, and voices raised together as one. They tell you that the Order is the spine of the galaxy, that without it the Flow would twist into chaos and swallow us all. And maybe—maybe there's some truth to that. But truth, in the Order's hands, is a thing carved down until it fits neatly in their grip.

The Axis… ah, the Axis. They claim their hands are steady, that they keep the galaxy balanced, as a judge might weigh a scale. But the weight they place is never even—it tips always toward obedience. To them, balance means everything in its proper place, and if you step out of that place, they will push you back into it with fire, with steel, or with the Flow itself. They carve away what doesn't fit their shape. And if too much of you resists, they do not hesitate to break you entirely.

Then there are the Umbers. They do not care for law or neatness. Their doctrine is older, rougher—they believe the Flow was never meant to coddle. They say it tests us, grinds us down to our barest selves, and the ones who endure that suffering are the ones who deserve its deepest secrets. They wear their scars like scripture and call pain the truest teacher. I have fought alongside them, and I have fought against them, and I still cannot tell which is the greater danger.

Between those two powers—the Axis with its perfect scales and the Umbers with their crucibles of suffering—there is no safe ground. We, the rest of us, live in the space between their shadows. The common worlds, the lost sectors, the small orders that bend whichever way the wind blows… we survive in that middle place. Or we die beneath their boots, and the Flow carries our names away like sand in the tide.

Do not be fooled, little one. The blade may gleam in the sun, but it is still a thing made for killing.

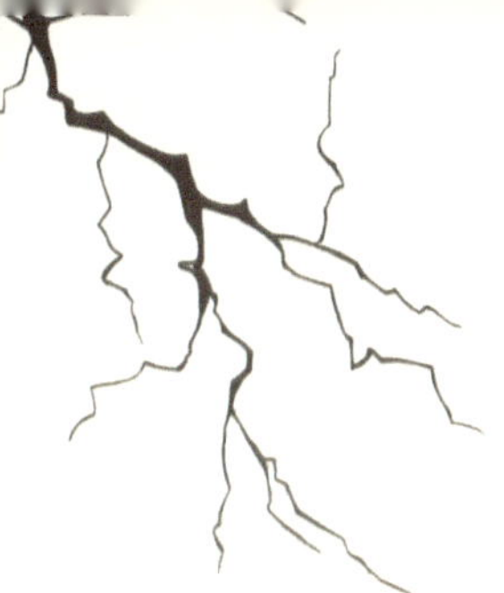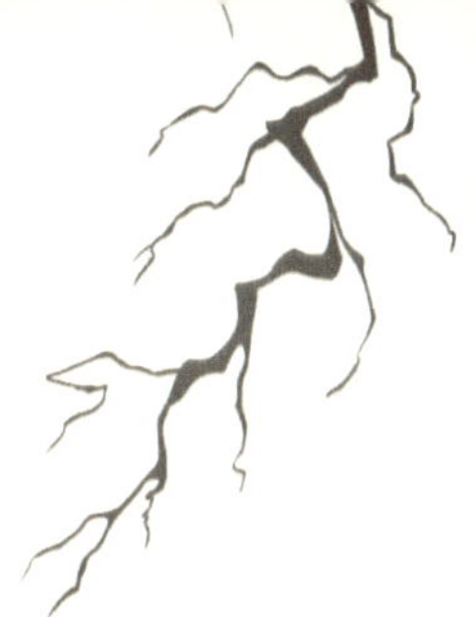

CHAPTER 8

Serena's gaze fell on Apollo. "Rise," she said, her voice steady, the green light of her Sunspear catching in her eyes. "You walk with me now."

We were nearly at the temple steps when Serena slowed her stride. Lux had already gone ahead, striding toward the crystal doors as though he could feel the Flow welcoming him. Jaleon lingered back, muttering something about the "fancy rock tunnel" to me, but my attention stayed on Apollo.

Serena's hand came up, resting lightly on his shoulder. It wasn't the grip of a commander—more like the weight of someone afraid to push too hard.

"Apollo," she said, her voice quieter than I'd ever heard it.

He didn't answer, but his head tilted slightly, enough to show he was listening.

"I know you think what happened on Kaith was nothing but loss," she began, and there was no steel in her tone now, only a careful honesty. "And I can't give you back what the Order took. I can't give you back her."

Her hand fell away. I saw her look down, just for a heartbeat, as if the stone at her feet was easier to face than his eyes.

"But you need to hear this—your mother didn't fall in vain. She stood in front of you knowing she could not win. She knew what it would cost her. She chose it anyway. That's not defeat, Apollo. That's a gift… the last one she could give you."

His grip tightened around the broken crystal in his hand. "A gift?" he said, the word sharp.

"Yes," Serena said, meeting his gaze again. "She gave you the chance to build your own path. Not hers. Not the one the Order sets for you. Yours. The choice to decide what kind of man you will become."

He looked away toward the sea below the temple, jaw locked. "And if I choose not to be the man the Order wants?"

Her voice softened further. "Then that will be your path. And I will not take it from you." She hesitated, then stepped closer, lowering her voice so only he could hear—or so she thought. "I should have found another way. I can't undo that. But I will tell you this—" she drew in a slow breath "—I will not stand by and watch you be broken. Not by them. Not by me."

For a moment, I could almost believe she was his mother speaking.

Then she straightened, her green Sunspear catching the light like spring leaves after rain. "Go," she told him, the faintest tremor in her voice. "Make me proud, I hope on day you will understand and forgive me"

Apollo didn't answer. But as we began to move again, I saw the smallest flicker in his eyes—something he was holding in, tight.

And though I know he didn't mean to. I think I heard him catch his breath.

Because somewhere in the back of his mind—and I swear I felt it too—another voice rose, her voice, younger and desperate, from a day drowned in fire:

Run, my boy. Run.

The doors to the Mirrorwalk opened with a sound like a sigh.

Inside, the chamber stretched out vast and round, its surface made of living crystal. Veins of pale, pulsing light spread across the walls like a heartbeat slowed to a patient rhythm. The air smelled faintly of rain after a long drought.

The four of us stepped in together—Lux at the front, Jaleon to his right, me between them, and Apollo at the rear, still clutching the broken blue-and-red shard. Serena stayed at the threshold, watching.

The moment the doors sealed behind us, the world changed.

The Flow was here. Not a force you could wield, but something that noticed you—*truly noticed*. It pressed in against your skin like warm water, slipped through your thoughts like smoke, sifted every memory you had ever locked away.

In the center of the chamber, the Sunspear crystal hovered above an obsidian pedestal. It wasn't solid— at least, not all the time. Its shape shifted every few heartbeats: a jagged shard, a flawless gem, a blade, a drop of water.

Its glow was neither bright nor dim, but perfect—the kind of light you felt in your bones more than you saw with your eyes.

The Flow didn't speak in words, but all of us heard it differently.

Lux stepped forward first, and from the way his chin lifted, you could almost believe the crystal had summoned him. He moved with the easy grace of someone trained for ceremony since birth—the same way his kind are taught to dance, bow, and bleed for the Axis without ever questioning why.

The pale, formless crystal above the pedestal turned in the air to face him. It slowed its rotation, as though the Flow itself was taking its time to weigh him. The air shifted—not colder, not warmer, but heavier, like the moment before a storm breaks.

Lux raised his hand, fingers straight, shoulders square. The instant his palm aligned with the crystal, light spilled outward in a wave, washing over the walls and crawling along the crystal veins like living frost. The illumination clung to him—silver threaded with soft blue, shimmering as if it had been pulled straight from the heart of a glacier.

And then we saw it.

It wasn't just a vision—it was as if the chamber itself became his memory, and we were forced to walk it with him.

The high marble halls of the Axis rose around us. Pillars of white stone lined with gold inlay. Ceilings painted with constellations older than history. And along those halls—portraits of his bloodline, men and women with expressions carved from discipline, their eyes fixed eternally forward as if daring the galaxy to challenge them.

Lux stood in the center, encased in ceremonial armor polished to a mirror sheen. Across his brow, a coronet— not a king's crown, but heavier somehow, because it carried not only authority, but the weight of generations watching.

In the stillness, I could feel it pressing into him. Duty as constant as gravity. Expectation wrapping around his ribs like iron bands. Never falter. Never show weakness. Never be anything but perfect—because perfection was the only thing his name allowed.

And beneath it all, there was… fear. Not fear of failure—fear of being *ordinary*.

The Flow spoke then, though not in words anyone's ears could hear. It moved through us like the echo of a voice in the blood.

Pride is not strength. Choose which you will serve.
Lux's breath shuddered—the first crack in his perfect composure.

The crystal drifted into his hand, and the light around it deepened, the silver falling away until only the pale, pure blue remained. It was the blue of open skies after storms, the blue of still water that hides unfathomable depths. It was honest, unflinching, unornamented—everything the halls of the Axis were not.

The blue light spilled from his fingers forming an elegant blue sword, flowing over his shoulders before it faded back toward the pedestal. For a moment, it looked as if the crystal didn't want to let him go.

When Lux stepped back into line, his face was unreadable—but his eyes betrayed something. Not relief. Not triumph. Something quieter. The look of a man who'd been given a truth he wasn't ready to face.

Jaleon went next, swagger in every step as though the Mirrorwalk was just another sparring match.
"Alright, magic rock, let's see what you've got," he muttered, rolling his shoulders.

It was a performance—the same one he gave at every meal, in every drill, every time he walked into a room.

The crystal at the pedestal rotated toward him, slow and deliberate, as if considering whether he was worth the trouble. Its inner light dimmed for a heartbeat— then flared, strands of molten gold and copper curling inside it.

When his hand touched the surface, the world around us shifted.

We were standing in the skeleton of a burned-out village. The air was thick with the acrid bite of smoke, the drizzle of cold rain mixing with drifting ash. Houses had been reduced to jagged black ribs; the ground was slick with mud and soot.

And there, in the middle of it, was a boy—smaller, thinner, barefoot. His hair was matted with rain, his hands trembling as they clutched the tattered remains of a blanket. From beyond the ruins came voices— cruel, mocking, accusing.
He didn't answer them.

Instead, he unwrapped the blanket just enough to reveal a single, precious loaf of bread—hard, cracked, but whole. Without a word, he broke it in half and offered the larger piece to another child huddled against the wall.

The Flow's voice—felt in the chest rather than heard—rippled through the chamber.

You hide your doubt with laughter. Laughter can lift… or it can blind. You must learn when to stop hiding.

For the first time since I'd met him, Jaleon's smirk faltered. Not gone—but changed. Softer. Honest.

The crystal in his hand bloomed into a deep, living orange—the color of late-autumn firelight, of embers that refuse to die. It wasn't Serena's sharp green or Lux's pale blue; it was a warmth that reached for others, even when the world was ash.

It pulsed once, a heartbeat of truth, before sliding free to hover above the pedestal once more.

When Jaleon stepped back, the grin was back on his face—but now, I could see the truth behind it. And maybe… so could he.

I hadn't expected to go in before him.

The thought of stepping into the Mirror again after all these years made my stomach knot—but there's no refusing the order of the crystal. When it turned toward me, I felt its pull in my chest like a rope I couldn't cut.

The others stepped aside. I moved forward, slow and measured, my boots silent against the black stone.

The pedestal stood waiting. The crystal's light shifted—not Lux's cool, regal blue, not Jaleon's fire-warm orange—but a deep, quiet violet that seemed to drink in the light around it.

When my hand touched its surface, the breath left my body. The chamber vanished.

I was back on Elaris. Not the polished spires of the Temple, but the war-torn outer valleys, the red soil wet with rain and blood. I was fourteen again—an acolyte in robes too big for my shoulders, my hands raw from drills. Around me, the Order's banners snapped in the wind, the chants of my elders pounding like drums in my skull.

Ahead, a burning ridge.
Bodies.
Too many bodies.

And in the center of it all, I saw myself—older, the woman I would become. Standing with a spear in hand, not in defense, but in execution. The look on my face chilled me more than the wind: detached. Efficient. My violet crystal shone bright, but it was cold.

The Flow's voice slid into me, soft and implacable.

You carry the discipline of the Order... and its blind obedience. You must choose which commands you will break, and which you will die for.

The younger me—the girl in the oversized robes—turned her head and looked straight at me. Her eyes were bright, wet with unshed tears.

Don't forget why you started.

When I blinked, the chamber returned. My hand was trembling against the crystal, and I realized the violet light had deepened—richer, heavier, as though it now carried the weight of both versions of myself.

I stepped back, breath slow, but my pulse hammering.

Lux stood still, unreadable. Jaleon gave me a searching look, like he wanted to ask but knew better. And Apollo... he was watching me in that way of his—quiet, unblinking, as if he'd seen more than he should have.

The crystal's glow faded back to neutral. And then…
it turned toward him

And then… Apollo.

When Apollo reached the pedestal, he didn't move
like the rest of us had.

For Lux, for Jaleon, even for me, it had been the same
a hesitant step forward, a trembling touch, and then
the visions came.
We'd walked toward the crystal as if approaching a
sacred relic.

But Apollo?
He moved as though the thing had called him by name.
Not with ceremony. Not with awe. But with the
inevitability of a man answering a debt he had always
known would be collected.

The broken blue shard of his mother's Sunspear was
clenched in his left hand, so tightly that the edges bit
into his palm. His knuckles were bloodless, the faintest
trickle of red slipping between his fingers where the
crystal had cut him.

The untouched crystal—the one meant for him—hovered above the black pedestal, spinning slowly in the air. Its light was pale, almost timid, the kind of glow that waits to be claimed.

The moment his right hand began to rise toward it, the chamber changed.

A tremor rolled through the obsidian floor, so deep it felt like it was climbing my bones. The crystal veins in the walls flared once and then dimmed, as if every thread of the Flow in the temple had turned to watch. The air between the two crystals thickened and warped, light bending around it like heat over stone.

The sound wasn't a shatter it was a deep, slow crack that rolled through the chamber like the breaking of an ancient seal. A light exploded from between them, so bright and violent it left streaks on my vision even when I closed my eyes.

The chamber's Flow veins pulsed wildly, the rhythm erratic, the walls themselves trembling like they were trying to contain something far too vast.

And then… they spoke.

Not in Axis canticles. Not in Umber chants. Not even in the lost prayers of the Conqueror's age. This was *older*. Words that didn't exist as sound, but as impact. Each one slammed into my mind, branding its meaning into the bone.

Blood remembers.
The wound endures.
The shard will not kneel.
Then it will burn.

The air vanished into blackness—not night, but *absence*, the kind that steals all sense of place or time. Shadows gathered around Apollo, circling him like a pack of silent beasts. Every time one leaned close, its outline broke apart into jagged, feral light—not blue, not gold… but a *green* unlike any that had ever touched the Flow.

It wasn't the soft green of Serena's Sunspear, or the leaf-green of the healers' light. This green was alive. It shifted and burned, as if it were forged from molten emeralds and lightning caught in a storm. It was the green of wild forests before the first axe, of seas in the eye of hurricanes, of stars that die and are born again in fire. It made my skin prickle, my lungs tighten, as if it could see through me and judge me wanting.

The untouched crystal fractured—a hairline crack racing across its flawless surface in a heartbeat. Gold veins bled through it like lightning trapped under ice. Then, with a sound like steel being drawn across stone, it broke apart into a blade.

A sword.

Long, uneven, jagged as if each edge had been bitten from it by rage itself. The green light roared inside it, spilling from every fracture, impossible to look at for too long yet impossible to turn away from. Gold lines threaded its length, trying to contain the fire, but the green kept breaking through, relentless.

It was not a weapon of ceremony. It was a rebellion made solid.
The Flow had not *given* this to him—it had been *wrestled* into existence.

The broken blue shard of his mother's spear still rested in his left hand, unchanged. Two crystals. Two histories. Both refusing to bow to the other.

Apollo stood still, his chest rising and falling slowly, the untamed green painting his face in something feral and unyielding. The shadows seemed to cling to him even after the chamber's light returned.

And for a breath no one moved. No one dared.

For a brief moment, in the very center of the chamber, I didn't see the young man standing before the pedestal. I saw the child from Kaith.

Barefoot. Clothes torn. Face smeared in soot and blood. His small hands clutched the broken blue shard of his mother's Sunspear the same way he had that day, knuckles white, eyes too old for their age. But this time... there was something else.

Behind him, out of the darkness, a blade rose.

Not just any blade a *sword*, massive and jagged, forged of that same impossible green. It hung in the air like judgment itself, its fractured edges dripping light that burned the floor where it fell. Every pulse from it sent shivers through the Flow veins in the walls.

The green was no longer only in his hand—it was *around him*, pouring off his shoulders like a divine storm. I could feel it pressing against my skin, my chest, my teeth. The air was thick, bending, and the scent of it was something primal the sharp tang of lightning after it strikes too close.

The Flow was bending to him.

No… it was *yielding.*

Every priest, every acolyte, every soldier in that temple felt it. The ground quivered beneath us, not from the stone, but from something deeper the very heart of the temple shuddered, as though the foundations of the Order itself were being reminded of a truth they had buried.

It was like an earthquake that shook not the floor, but the *soul.*

Some fell to their knees. Others pressed their hands to their chests as if to keep their hearts from breaking apart.

And still, in the middle of all that chaos, he stood there the same boy from Kaith but now shadowed by something vast and unnameable. The broken blue crystal in his left hand, the green sword burning in his right, and the darkness behind him whispering in a tongue older than the galaxy.

I couldn't breathe.
None of us could.

For that one moment, I swear, the Flow itself was holding its breath.

We all heard a soft voice saying
run my boy run….

When it was over, the ground seemed to breathe out—a deep, heavy exhale that rattled through the stone like the aftershock of some great beast settling back into sleep.

The light returned slowly, but it wasn't the same. It was weaker… or maybe it was that we had seen too much, and everything else felt pale in comparison. The crystal veins in the walls still pulsed, but their glow seemed wary, as though even the Flow had been reminded it could be broken.

I looked around and realized—we were all still upright, but every muscle in my body was trembling. Lux's knees had buckled at some point, though he stood again now, trying to mask it. Jaleon's hand was tight on his spear, but his eyes wouldn't leave Apollo. Even the priests, proud in their flowing robes, had their heads bowed slightly, as if instinct had pulled them toward the floor without their consent.

And then… he emerged.

Apollo stepped out from the pedestal's shadow, the green sword in his right-hand bleeding light like liquid fire. It wasn't a weapon so much as a wound made solid—jagged-edged, pulsing, alive.

In his left, he still clutched his mother's broken shard, its dull blue refusing to fade entirely, as stubborn as the boy himself.

There was no victory in his face. No smugness. No fear. Just that same slow, deliberate step he'd taken into the chamber, as though the walk back was simply the completion of some vow he'd made long before any of us had ever known his name.

The air around him bent faintly, warping the edges of the room as he passed—not from heat, but from presence. My breath caught, and I realized I wasn't alone; every set of eyes in the chamber followed him, but not one person dared to speak.

And, child… though I could not name it at the time, I swear the Flow itself leaned toward him as he left. Not to guide him. Not to test him. But to watch— like a predator circling the one prey it cannot quite understand.

The great doors of the Mirrorwalk chamber had barely closed when it began.
It started as a vibration—faint, like the distant roll of thunder—but it grew, heavy enough to rattle the crystal sconces along the walls.

CHAPTER 9

Then came the boots. Not the measured cadence of a ceremony guard. These were too fast. Too heavy. Too loud. Driven by something closer to panic.

A wedge of warriors forced their way into the sanctum corridor, their armor clattering like angry bells. The narrow hall seemed too small to contain them, the torchlight running like molten gold over their polished plates. Shields up, spears out—but it was their faces that caught me.

Every single one of them looked afraid.

They shoved past temple guards who dared to stand in their way, shattering centuries of ritual without a thought. No one marched into the Mirrorwalk armed. It was law. It was sacred. But in their fear, the warriors violated it without hesitation.

Behind them came the priests. Not the robed, soft-spoken ones who guided novices through rites. These carried Flow-spears tipped in blackened steel, their stance tight, every movement a prelude to violence. Their eyes fixed on Apollo like hawks fixing on prey.

One of the priests whispered—not quietly enough for it to be missed.
"This is not pure."

Another's voice followed, sharp and cold:
"An ill omen."

A third hissed through his teeth, his grip on his spear tightening, the blackened tip trembling as if hungry for blood.
"He's unstable. Dangerous."

And then the worst of them, the one whose eyes were fixed on Apollo with something more than duty—with fear disguised as righteousness: "Kill him."

The words spread like a poison through the ranks, each echo feeding the next. Armor shifted. Boots scraped against the stone. The chamber's light—already thin from the Mirrorwalk—seemed to pull back from him, leaving him alone in a faint halo of steam rising off the green-bladed Sunspear in his grip.

The weapon still bled heat from the trial, tiny threads of light curling from its fractured edges like smoke from cooling iron. In his other hand, the shard of his mother's broken blue crystal was clenched so tightly that his knuckles had gone pale. The edges bit into his palm, leaving small crescent marks, but he didn't let go.

He didn't even flinch.

The confusion in his face wasn't fear—no wide-eyed panic, no desperate glance toward the exits like prey surrounded by hunters. Instead, there was a quiet searching in his gaze, as if trying to understand why the air around him had suddenly filled with blades pointed his way.

It wasn't *what* had just happened inside the Mirrorwalk that unsettled him.
It was *this*.
The way they looked at him, as though he'd stepped out of the chamber carrying not a weapon, but a plague.

His eyes moved from face to face—the warriors, the priests, even the acolytes in the corners—as if asking a question none of them were willing to answer. And though his stance was still, I could feel it.

That slow, rising heat behind his silence.

Lux and I froze where we were.
The air was so heavy it felt alive—like moving through it might tear it apart, might be the one thing that made all of this shatter into blood.

Only Jaleon didn't hesitate.

One moment, he was leaning against a carved pillar at the edge of the chamber, that infuriating lazy grin still painted on his face. The next, the grin was gone, replaced by a tight, cold line. He moved without a thought, planting himself between Apollo and the ring of spears closing in. His stance widened, shoulders squared, and the entire room seemed to tilt toward him.

His hand dropped to the crystal at his hip. For the first time since I'd met him, he touched it like it was the most natural thing in the world—like it had been waiting for this.

The igniting burst came like the sun tearing through stormclouds. A roar of orange light surged from the weapon, flooding the chamber in a violent bloom of fire and shadow. It didn't form a sword like ours—no, Jaleon's crystal had always been different. It shaped itself into the brutal curve of a twin-headed axe, each blade catching the light as though molten metal had just been poured into it.

The heat rolled off him in waves, licking against armor and exposed skin. Warriors staggered back instinctively, their spearpoints wavering. The axe hummed, not with precision like Serena's green blade, but with the deep, bone-vibrating growl of untamed power.

"If you want him," Jaleon growled, his voice low but carrying through the chamber, "you go through me."

It wasn't a shout. He didn't need to shout. The promise in his tone—the unshakable certainty that he *meant it*—rooted men in place.

And then Julius moved.

I had only ever known him as the smiling high priest— the warm voice that could calm a hall with a word, the figure who moved like the Flow itself guided his steps. But what came forward now… wasn't the man I knew.

It was something else.

He crossed the space in a single, impossible leap, landing with the weight of a falling world. He didn't draw a crystal. He didn't need one. The air bent around him, folding like it had been told to kneel. The polished floor under his boots cracked, lines spidering outward from where he'd landed.

For a heartbeat, I forgot to breathe.

He wasn't carrying a weapon. He *was* the weapon.

With a flick of his wrist—no wind-up, no effort—Julius sent Jaleon flying. A man built like a mountain, wrapped in muscle and fire, was reduced to weightless debris in a storm. His body slammed into the wall hard enough to crack the marble. The sound was deep and splintering, like a tree trunk giving way in a lightning strike. Dust rained from the ceiling.

Jaleon's axe flickered, the vibrant orange glow shattering into dull embers before it blinked out entirely. He slid down the wall in a groan of breath and pain, one hand pressing against his ribs, but his glare toward Julius never broke.

And then Julius stood still.

The Flow around him was compressed so tightly that the air itself thrummed, a low and constant vibration that crawled up through the soles of my boots, into my bones, and into my teeth. I felt it behind my eyes—an invisible weight urging me to kneel, to bow my head, to *submit*.

Apollo didn't.

He didn't even flinch. His breathing stayed slow, steady. The green blade at his side, born moments ago from the Mirrorwalk, was still faintly steaming. And in those few steps Julius took toward him, Apollo's eyes never left the high priest's.

Then—Serena moved.

She stepped in front of him with no hesitation, her armor catching the torchlight, the green crystal of her Sunspear igniting with a sound that was neither spark nor flame but a clean, glass-like hiss, like the first edge of a blade leaving its sheath. The color burst into the air—not the wild, jagged green of Apollo's weapon, but something deep, pure, and alive. The green of new leaves after a long winter. The green of a dawn that promised survival.

But there was nothing soft in her stance.

Her body was coiled steel, her grip on the spear so tight the veins in her hand stood out pale against her skin. And then I saw it—tears, cutting two clean lines down her cheeks. Tears on Serena, the woman who could gut a man without blinking.

She spoke, voice steady but lined with something I had never heard in her before. Not fear. Not command. Plea.

"His life is mine. I will train him. I will forge him into an asset to the Order. You will not touch him."

A ripple went through the chamber. Priests shifted their weight uneasily, their spears wavering. Some of the warriors exchanged glances, unsure whether to advance or stand down.

Julius didn't move. Didn't even blink. He stared at her as if weighing not just her words, but her soul.

The air was still thick with his Flow, pressing against my lungs, until… it began to recede. Slowly, like a tide pulling back after a storm, leaving the taste of salt and iron in the air.

His voice, when it came, was colder than the stone beneath our feet. "These four are yours," he said. "Your responsibility. Your problem."

Then he turned his back.

And in that moment, Apollo's gaze shifted. Not toward Serena, not toward Julius, but to some far corner of the room—to *something* none of us could see.

Later, he would tell me he felt it then: a shadow at the edge of the Flow, watching him.

"But Nana," the child asked, her voice small, almost swallowed by the soft hiss of the fire, "what was that shadow?"

I didn't answer right away. I let the question sit between us like an uninvited guest. My eyes drifted to the flames, watching them bend and twist, looking for shapes I didn't want to find.

"I don't know, my sweet child," I said at last—but my tone betrayed the truth. "Or… perhaps I know more than I wish I did."

Her gaze sharpened. Children always hear the things you try to hide.

"There are whispers," I continued slowly, "passed from campfires to barracks, from priests to acolytes when they think no one's listening. They say the Flow speaks to all who can touch it—but not in the same way. For most, it is like a quiet river. A ripple in the mind. A voice you can ignore if you choose."

I leaned forward, lowering my voice until it was barely above a breath.
"But for some… the Flow does not whisper. It roars. And it is not alone when it does."

Her eyes widened. "Not alone?"

"No," I said. "There are those who walk with something else—something that is not cast by sun or moon or flame. A second shadow. It moves when they move, but it's not bound to their body. It is bound to their fate."

I saw the shiver run through her shoulders. "Like Apollo?"

"Yes." My words were quiet, but certain. "And even the Conqueror. They had seen him on the edge of battle, his cloak still in the windless air, and two shadows stretched from his feet. The first was his own. The second... bent wrong, like the light feared to touch it. And sometimes, when the camp was still, it moved even when he did not."

She swallowed hard. "What is it?"

I shook my head slowly. "Some believe it is the Flow itself, leaving its current to walk beside those who carry too much of its power—a guide, a guardian, a whisperer in the dark. Others..." My voice dropped further, "...believe it is older than the Flow. A thing the Flow cannot command. A thing that walks only with those destined to break the world or save it."

She hesitated. "And... is it good?"

I smiled faintly, though the warmth never reached my eyes. "That depends on whether it walks beside you to keep you standing… or to make sure you fall exactly when your time comes."

The fire popped then, sending a shower of sparks into the air.
For just an instant, I thought I saw a second shadow dance across the wall behind her.

Codex Fragment 27.14—*On the Second Shadow*
(Sealed under the Axis Proscription of 1137 A.F.)

It is written in the oldest record-stones, before the Axis, before the Flow had a name, that there walks beside certain souls a second darkness. It is not of the body, nor of the mind, but of the Path.

In the age of the First Flames, when the Flow was young and wild, the Elders spoke of the "Echo That Walks." It is not seen by all, only by those who stand where life and death grind against each other. To the untrained eye, it is only a trick of light. To the one who carries it, it is an unblinking companion.

This shadow moves with its bearer, yet its step is never quite the same. When the bearer stands still, the shadow may turn. When the bearer sleeps, it may lean close to their ear. Some have felt its hand—cold as the stone of the Void—on their shoulder before their greatest victory, or their final breath.

It is said the Conqueror walked with such an Echo. Witnesses in the battles of Reth-Gar and the Burning of Ollen swore they saw two shadows at his feet: the first his own, the second swaying to a wind no one else felt. When he spoke to his generals, his eyes sometimes shifted, as if answering a voice none could hear.

The Umbers claim the Second Shadow is the Flow itself given form—a guide sent to guard its strongest wielders from straying. The Axis claims it is a curse, a mark of imbalance, a thing born when too much power is drawn too quickly. But there are other records—older still—that call it neither blessing nor curse, but an ancient witness... a presence that walks only with those who will one day tear the pattern of the world.

And when the Second Shadow departs, it does not do so quietly. For when it leaves, so too does the soul it followed.

When the doors to the Mirrorwalk chamber finally closed behind us, I realized my hands were trembling. I don't think I was the only one. The priests dispersed quickly, muttering into their sleeves, while the soldiers kept their eyes averted from Apollo as if looking at him too long might call down bad luck.

The four of us were left in the hallway, the faint green glow of his weapon still clinging to the air like the taste of lightning after a storm.

Jaleon broke the silence first, rubbing his shoulder with an exaggerated wince.
"Next time," he said, loud enough for the priests down the corridor to hear, "I'll just let the boy get skewered. My ribs will thank me."

Lux's gaze was ice. "You shouldn't have interfered. You nearly made it worse."

Jaleon flashed him a grin. "And yet here he stands— unskewered. You're welcome."

Apollo kept walking. His blade was sheathed now, but the broken shard of his mother's crystal was still clenched in his other hand. He moved like the rest of us weren't there, his steps measured, his eyes fixed somewhere far away.

That didn't stop Jaleon. He limped ahead until he was level with Apollo. "You do know," he said, lowering his voice like he was sharing a secret, "you just scared the robes off half the temple, right? Even the statues looked nervous."

No response. Not even a flicker.

Jaleon leaned closer. "This is the part where you say 'thanks' for me playing human shield. Or at least grunt. I'll take a grunt."

Apollo's eyes shifted just enough to meet his. Not long. Not deep. But it was there.

Lux sighed from behind me, shaking his head. "If this is what the four of us are going to be, the Order is doomed."

That broke me. The laugh came before I could stop it—sharp and warm, the kind that feels like it's been trapped in your chest too long. And like a stone skipping across still water, the sound rippled outward.

Apollo's mouth twitched. Just a little, like a crack in a wall. But for the first time since Kaith, I saw a hint of a smile. Not joy—not yet—but the memory of it.

Jaleon caught it instantly. "There it is! Thought maybe your teeth had fallen out with your sense of humor."

I swear Apollo almost laughed. He shook his head instead, but that tiny flicker of light in his eyes was enough to make my throat tighten.

It wasn't much.
But it was a start.

We'd barely cleared the temple steps when Serena's voice sliced through the hum of the corridors.

"Hold."

We stopped like she'd yanked a chain. She strode toward us—boots clicking on obsidian, green Sunspear across her back, helm tucked under her arm. Her expression was calm, but her eyes… her eyes measured like a smith judging metal before the forge.

"You four," she said, her tone even, "are mine now. Starting tomorrow, you train under me. Every day. Every hour. Until you either rise to the Order's standard… or fall trying."

Jaleon raised an eyebrow, looking her up and down like he was deciding how much trouble he was in. "And here I thought we were gonna get a warm welcome. You know—'Congratulations, heroes of the Mirrorwalk,' maybe a fruit basket."

Serena didn't blink. "I'll make you a basket, Jaleon. Out of your own regrets."

"Oh, she's funny," he said, glancing at me like I should be taking notes. "You hear that? She's got jokes."

"I'm not joking," she said flatly.

"Even better," Jaleon grinned. "Deadpan humor. My favorite. Means I never know when I'm in trouble until it's too late."

Her gaze flicked to him again, just sharp enough to draw a bead of sweat. "Trust me, you'll know. I'll make sure your mouth gets as much of a workout as your arms."

He put a hand over his chest. "Serena, I'm flattered. You've noticed my arms."

"I've noticed you talk enough to tire them out," she said, already turning away.

Somewhere in the middle of that back-and-forth, Apollo—who'd been silent the whole time, green shard still clutched in his hand—let out this quiet, almost reluctant sound. It wasn't much, but I'd fought beside enough soldiers to know the difference between a scoff and a laugh.

Jaleon spun toward him like a hawk spotting prey. "Was that—? That was! You laughed!"

"It wasn't a laugh," Apollo muttered, looking away.

"Oh no, it was," Jaleon grinned. "It was a laugh, and I'm framing it in my memory forever."

The corners of Apollo's mouth twitched again before he smothered it. Lux didn't even blink. I kept my own face steady, but inside… there was this strange warmth, like I'd just seen a crack of sunlight in a storm that had gone on far too long.

Serena clapped her hands once, sharply. "Alright. Enough chatter. You've got food to find, sleep to get, and tomorrow you stop being strays and start being my acolytes."

Jaleon raised his hand. "Do strays get dinner before the training starts, or is this one of those 'eat after you collapse' kind of programs?"

"You'll eat," she said. "If you survive the morning."

He grinned wider. "See? She does care."

Serena ignored him entirely.

The corridor back to the dorms was long, lit by flickering crystal sconces and the soft hum of Flow threads in the stone. It should've felt heavy after everything—the Mirrorwalk, the confrontation, the weight of a new bond—but somehow, it didn't. Not for the others.

Jaleon kept the pace lively, hands behind his head, whistling an off-key hymn like he was marching to a tavern instead of sleep. "So what do you think the morning drills are like?" he asked. "Running? Punching? Screaming?"

"All three," Lux answered, tone flat as ever. "In that order."

"I call screaming," Jaleon quipped. "I've got range."

Valere walked just behind them, her arms folded, lips curled in a smirk she didn't bother hiding. "You'll scream when Serena drags you out of bed before sunrise."

"I prefer to be coaxed," he replied. "With warm bread and soft lighting."

Valere snorted. Even Lux looked vaguely amused.

Apollo followed in silence. The others laughed and bickered, and though he walked with them, he wasn't with them. His eyes never lifted from the floor. He still held the broken blue shard in one hand, knuckles pale from pressure, and even the hum of jokes couldn't shake the quiet fog surrounding him.

They reached their new chamber—a simple space with four beds, small footlockers, and narrow slats of window overlooking the high towers.

"Sleep while you can," Valere said, tossing her robe aside. "She'll be dragging us by the ears tomorrow."

Jaleon collapsed face-first onto his bed. "Can't wait."

Apollo said nothing. He moved to the corner bed, the farthest from the door, and began to remove the day.

His fingers worked slowly, undoing the clasp at his collar. The ceremonial robe slipped off his shoulders with a sigh of fabric, pooling around his feet. Beneath it, the standard tunic stuck to his skin—sweat, fear, dust. He peeled it away, exposing thin muscle and bruises half-healed from Kaith.

He unstrapped his belt, boots, shoulder guards. The Sunspear holster hung empty now—but still he checked it, as if unsure it hadn't vanished.

Then, finally, the broken crystal.

He sat on the edge of the bed, turning it over in his hand. There—just for a blink—a flicker. Faint blue light pulsed deep within the fractured gem. It lasted less than a breath.

His heart raced.

"…Mother?" he whispered. Nothing answered.

He lay down. Closed his eyes.

Sleep didn't come.

Not the kind he wanted.

CHAPTER 10

Darkness.

It started slow — a chill under his skin, like icewater seeping into his veins. He tried to shift, to move, but his body was sinking. The mattress beneath him had become liquid shadow, pulling him under.

He opened his mouth to call out, but no sound escaped.

Then he saw it.

A shape in the void. Towering. Vast.

A shadow not cast by light—but born of something older, deeper.

It loomed. Not evil. Not good. Just *present*—and watching.

Around it came the cries. Echoing. Distant.

Voices begging.

Screams breaking into sobs.

Then—

"RUN, MY BOY—!"

It was her voice. Elira.

He turned toward it and the world shattered.

He saw it again—the canyon on Kaith. The dust. The blood.

But he wasn't watching it happen.

He was *in it*.

He stood where Serena had stood, blade in hand, green crystal burning like wildfire.

Before him: Elira.

His mother.

No weapon. Just her hands up. Pleading.

He screamed. "NO—!"

But the blade moved. His hand. His crystal.

He drove it through her chest.

Blood sprayed. Her eyes widened—not in pain… but in recognition.

"My boy…" she whispered, not in fear, but in forgiveness.

He dropped the weapon.

Stumbled back.

And in the void beyond her falling body, the shadow loomed again—larger now. Leaning closer. Eyes like burning coals.

Apollo awoke screaming.

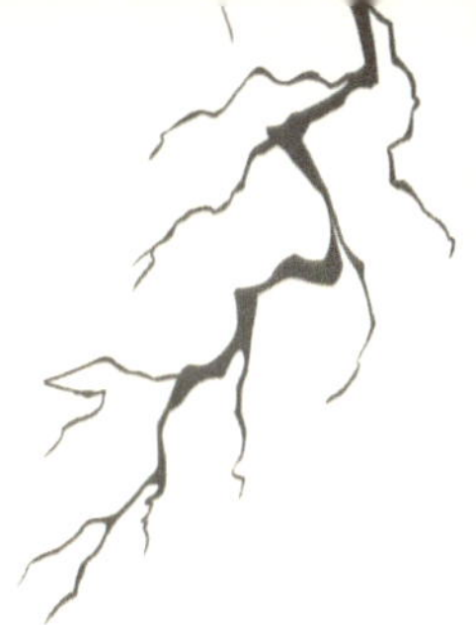

CHAPTER 11

The morning sun had just begun to spill through the high slats. Jaleon shifted on his cot, mumbling something half-coherent about food and glory, his heavy arm flopping over the side. Lux was still upright in his corner, spine rigid, a book balanced on his knee. The candle beside him burned low, its wax pooling and hardening in slow drips—he hadn't turned a page in some time. Valere stood by the open window, her silhouette framed in the thin wash of moonlight. Arms folded, chin dipped, she looked like a statue carved for watching—still, unblinking, yet holding a tension that never slept.

Apollo pushed himself upright, every muscle aching, skin damp and chilled despite the warmth of the room. The dream clung to him, heavy and acrid, like soot worked into the lungs. His breaths came shallow, uneven, as though he'd surfaced too quickly from a place he should never have entered.

In his palm, the broken crystal lay where he'd fallen asleep clutching it—fractured edges biting faintly into his skin. But now… faintly, barely more than a heartbeat, it pulsed.
Not with light, not entirely—but with a rhythm. A presence.

And in the deep of his mind, beyond waking thought, the voice remained.
No longer the panicked scream that had torn him from the void, but a low, aching whisper. A voice weighted with love and despair in equal measure.
Run, my boy… run.

The words didn't fade.
They settled into him, quiet and certain, as though the darkness itself had left its mark and would call to him again.

Our first morning together had finally come.
The Mirrorwalk was behind us, but the real test— Serena's training—awaited.

We dressed in silence, the rustle of cloth and the faint clink of crystal the only sounds in the room. The robes were simple: pale gray, bound at the waist, cut for movement rather than ceremony.

Each of us slid our Sunspear crystal into the pouch at our side—the weight of it both familiar and strange, as though it was already beginning to know us.

Apollo moved like the air before a storm utterly still, but charged. His eyes stayed ahead, fixed on nothing, yet seeing something far beyond the obsidian walls. He said nothing. Not to me. Not to Lux. Not even to Jaleon.

Lux, on the other hand, was muttering under his breath—probably reciting tactics, formations, and the lineage of every Axis champion since the founding of the Order. He adjusted his sleeves with obsessive precision, the way a duelist might check his blade before a duel.

I walked just behind them, watching, measuring.

And then there was Jaleon—our ever-burning orange flame of chaos—swinging his crystal in lazy circles until, with a flash of light, it sparked into the form of his double-headed axe. He twirled it one-handed, its edges humming, throwing faint glints along the hall walls.

"Alright," he announced with the confidence of a man who never considered losing, "I'll go easy on you all. Especially you, Valere—I don't fight girls before breakfast." I gave him a look sharp enough to cut leather.

He turned to Lux next. "And you, my royal friend—don't worry, I'll try to spill as little of your noble blood on those fancy robes as possible. Wouldn't want to upset the laundry staff."

Finally, his gaze landed on Apollo. "As for you, stone-face… let's make it interesting. If I beat you today, you're obligated to laugh at *all* my jokes for the rest of your life."

Apollo didn't blink. Didn't even twitch. The silence was almost comical.

Unfazed, Jaleon kept going, tossing out wisecracks about how Serena was probably going to have us polishing spears until our arms fell off, or running laps until we puked. His voice echoed in the hall, full of life and warmth—a sun that refused to notice the storm cloud walking among us.

The hall opened at last into the courtyard. The grass underfoot was short and soft, still wet with morning dew. Above us, the towers of the Temple rose like black glass spears into the pale light, their obsidian walls veined with slow pulses of crystal light. The Flow's hum was faint here, like the temple itself was holding its breath.

In the center stood Serena. No ceremonial armor today—just a plain tunic, her hair tied back, the green light of her Sunspear pooling like calm water along the blade's length.

Jaleon's grin widened instantly. "After I finish with these three clumsy idiots, I'll be ready for you, big scary lady."

Serena didn't flinch. "We'll see," she said—her voice neither amused nor offended, but something sharper.

The green light from her blade caught in her eyes, and I swear, for just a moment, even Jaleon stopped smiling quite so wide.

Today was the first day Serena would call us her acolytes. The first day we would move not as survivors of the Mirrorwalk, but as her students—her responsibility.

She stood in the center of the courtyard, her green Sunspear resting against one shoulder, the morning light catching along its edge. Around the perimeter, soldiers and commanders from the Axis stood in quiet ranks, their eyes sharp, their expressions unreadable. We were not just being tested for her approval—but for theirs as well.

"Today," she began, her voice cutting through the air with the precision of a blade, "is your first day as my acolytes. The four of you must prove yourselves—not only to me, not only to the Order, but to our allies in the Axis. Their military commanders are here, and they will be watching you."

She let that sink in.

Then she turned her gaze on each of us in turn. "First, let us begin with the basics. The three of you—Apollo, Valere, Lux—each hold a crystal that shapes itself into a sword. That means the Flow within you travels as energy—fast, precise, cutting. Your strength will come from speed and control. You will need to master both."

Her eyes shifted to Jaleon. The faintest smirk touched her lips. "And you, Jaleon. You carry a crystal that takes the form of a double-headed axe—which means your Flow translates into force. You have the advantage in one-on-one combat due to your raw power… but you lack stamina."

Jaleon grinned like she'd just complimented him. Serena's smirk sharpened. "And you are cocky. Cocky gets you killed."

She stepped back, her spear's tip tapping once against the ground. "Understand this—all of you. Your power comes from your crystal, and your crystal knows you. It feels how you feel, it learns how you act, it knows your fears. If you try to command it while lying to yourself, it will betray you… and that will cost your life. You must learn to fight controlling your hate, your rage, your love. The Flow must be channeled, not chained. Be like water—shapeless, able to take any form without losing yourself."

Then she pointed toward the training field beyond the walls. "Your first task is simple—run ten kilometers."

I thought she was joking. She was not.

We ran.

At the five-kilometer mark, Jaleon's breathing was ragged. By five and a half, he'd slowed to a walk. By six, he quit entirely, leaning against a tree, panting like an overworked forge. Serena didn't even need to mock him—the sight alone was enough—but she laughed anyway, that rare sharp laugh that carried more amusement than cruelty.

Lux made it to eight before collapsing in the grass, his fine noble posture crumpling like wet parchment. Serena strolled past him, not breaking stride. "What's wrong, my lord?" she called over her shoulder. "Do they not teach running in the noble palaces?"

I managed to finish—just barely—lungs burning, legs like stone, my vision blurring at the edges. I crossed the line and dropped my hands to my knees, gasping. Serena gave me a small nod, her voice warm despite her words. "Bravo, my little violet. Make me proud."

And then there was Apollo.

He ran.
And kept running.
And kept running still.

At first, I thought he was just stubborn—too prideful to stop. But there was something different in his stride. His eyes were distant, locked on some point far ahead, like he wasn't even here anymore. The way his feet struck the ground was almost too light, as if the Flow itself was lifting him forward.

Ten kilometers passed. Serena called for him to stop. He didn't hear her.

"You've passed the limit!" she shouted, half laughing, half in disbelief.

Still he ran, small but relentless, like the horizon was pulling him toward it.

the time Serena called him back, Apollo had already run a kilometer past the mark. His breathing was steady, his face unreadable, sweat barely beading along his brow. When he finally slowed, he walked toward us like nothing had happened.

Jaleon muttered something about "show-off" under his breath. Lux was too busy pretending he wasn't still winded to say anything.

Serena's green Sunspear hummed softly as she stepped forward, planting it in the grass.
"Not bad," she said, studying Apollo like a puzzle piece she hadn't decided where to place yet.
"But running will only carry you so far."

Her gaze swept over all of us. "A warrior must fight tired. Fight hungry. Fight when every muscle screams at you to stop. That is when the Flow decides whether it will carry you… or abandon you."

Before I realized what was happening, she flicked her spear toward Apollo. The green blade flared to life. "Draw your weapon."

I blinked. "Now? After—"

"Yes. Now."

The first she came for was me.

Her eyes locked on mine, no warning, no call to prepare—just the whisper of the grass under her boots before the green blaze of her Sunspear flared to life. I ignited my purple crystal, the light bursting into a narrow, uneven blade. It hummed in my hand, not yet fully formed—like it wasn't sure it trusted me enough to be whole.

She didn't wait.

The first strike came like lightning, forcing me to bring my weapon up fast enough that the clash of our crystals rang in my bones. I staggered back one step. Then another.

"Defending?" Serena's voice was sharp, cutting through the hum of our weapons. "If this was real, you'd already be dead."

Another strike. I barely turned it aside. Her flow was a river—smooth, steady, unstoppable—and mine was… scattered. Splashing against stone, bleeding into the dirt. I was reacting, not fighting. She pressed me hard, each movement unpredictable, forcing me to guard high one moment, sweep low the next.

Her blade was everywhere at once. I had no space to breathe, no time to think.

I blocked. I dodged. I kept my feet under me because falling meant losing, and losing meant hearing her tell me exactly how worthless my efforts were.

But then—between the strikes, in that blur of motion—I remembered. I remembered how Elira had moved when she fought Serena all those months ago. She never chased the attack. She waited for the moment Serena *expected* her to yield… and then she shifted.

I jumped back, letting her blade slice the air where my chest had been. My Sunspear pulsed in my grip, as though the crystal itself had felt my resolve. The purple flared brighter, surer—the blade now complete, humming with purpose.

I lunged. My strike sang with all the force I had, but Serena's guard slid into place like she'd been waiting for it. In a breath, I was locked again, her blade pressing mine away, her body angling to pin me.

I dodged left. She was there. I spun right. Her spear cut the path off before I'd even taken the step. No matter how fast I moved, she was already there—not guessing, but knowing.

My arms ached. My breath was coming hard. Every beat of my heart felt louder than the last.

Then her stance shifted. Her flow narrowed, all of it condensing into her left hand. I didn't see it coming until the force hit me like a wall—no weapon, just raw Flow crashing into my chest.

I hit the ground hard enough to see sparks. My weapon flickered and went out.

Serena stood over me, her blade dimming, her breath perfectly calm.

"That," she said, her voice flat as stone, "was pathetic."

Flat on my back, staring up at the cloudless sky, I caught movement just beyond the circle.

The Axis general stood there, not in armor, but in that crisp silver uniform they wear when they want to look untouchable. His posture was as rigid as the lines of the obsidian towers behind him, hands clasped behind his back. At first I thought he was simply observing… but then I saw the device in his palm.

Thin glass. Flow-woven metal edges. It pulsed faintly as his thumb slid across its surface, capturing numbers, symbols, shapes that flared for a moment before dissolving. He wasn't just *watching* us—he was *collecting us*. Every stance, every breath, every flicker of our crystals recorded and translated into neat data that would probably decide exactly how we were to be used.

His eyes didn't show approval. Or disappointment. Just calculation.

For the first time, the training ground felt less like a court and more like a forge—and we weren't the smiths. We were the blades.

After me, Lux stepped into the ring.
He moved like he'd been taught in marble halls—back straight, chin up, his light-blue crystal sparking to life in a clean, elegant line. For a heartbeat, it almost looked like he belonged there.

Then Serena moved.

She didn't just advance—she *closed* the distance, her green blade cutting through the air with a precision that felt personal. No flourish, no wasted motion. Every strike was a test, and every test carried an edge of malice that I hadn't seen her give me.

Lux's spear met hers, but only just. His footwork was polished, but his flow was shallow, brittle. You could feel it—a stream that had never been forced to flood or rage.

He tried to stay in defense, catching her strikes, blocking where he could, his breathing already strained.

"You will defend as well?" Serena barked, her voice slicing through the training court like a thrown blade. "You are a disappointment as well."

Something in him cracked then. I saw it in his shoulders, in the way his grip loosened. He stopped. The blue spear dimmed and vanished from his hands, falling into nothing.

For a moment, he just stood there, staring at the space between them as if all his years of careful training and perfect posture had been struck from him in an instant. Serena's eyes narrowed, and she said it without heat, without even a sneer—as if stating a fact written into the stone beneath our feet:

"It's easy to break a noble man."

Behind her, the Axis general didn't so much as shift his stance. His glass device shimmered once, marking whatever weakness Lux had just bared. His expression never changed, but I could feel the weight of his silent note: *unfit for the front lines.*

Before anyone could speak, Jaleon moved.
No ceremony. No stance. Just a sudden, explosive charge—the kind of reckless momentum you only see from a man who trusts his own body more than any plan. His orange crystal roared to life in his hands, shaping into the twin-headed axe that seemed almost too large for a human to wield.

The ground trembled under his boots. His flow hit like the first strike of a battering ram, flooding the court in a blaze of molten orange. It wasn't elegance. It wasn't measured. It was raw, untamed power—the kind you feel in your bones before you even see the swing.

Serena laughed—not mockery, but a bright, fierce laugh that carried over the clash of their weapons. "Now we are talking! Show me what you've got!"

They met in the center like colliding storms. His axe crashed against her green blade, sparks of Flow scattering in the air like burning leaves. Strike after strike, he drove forward, every blow rattling the obsidian tiles under our feet.

She didn't retreat. She *met* him, step for step, matching his force with precision. And yet… she was smiling. Her eyes gleamed with the joy of the fight, the thrill of meeting someone willing to give her no quarter.

Jaleon bellowed as he leapt high, the axe arcing above him. When it came down, it struck the court with such force that the Flow burst outward in all directions—a sunflare of orange that washed over all of us, humming in our chests. For a moment, it felt like he was shaking the very foundation of the Temple.

And then—blood.
Just a thin line across Serena's tunic, beading red against her side. But it was enough to make her laugh louder, sharper. "Bravo! That's my boy!"

Jaleon grinned through gritted teeth. "You're making it too easy, you old hag."

She only laughed harder, the sound ringing like steel on steel.

From the edge of the court, the Axis generals leaned forward. Their eyes weren't watching a student anymore—they were assessing an asset. A weapon. The kind you build campaigns around.

But even iron bends. I could see it—the faint hitch in Jaleon's breath, the way his shoulders dropped between swings, the fraction slower in his follow-through. The relentless blaze of his Flow that had once lit the court like sunrise now flickered at the edges, dimming as if the crystal itself was tiring with him.

Serena noticed before the rest of us. Her stance shifted, so subtle it might have been a trick of the light—a lowering of her center, the faint tightening of her grip. She waited, letting him spend the last of his strength in one final, desperate blow.

Jaleon roared, lifting the twin-headed axe over his head. It came down like a falling tower, the air around it screaming with the heat of his Flow. But it was too slow. Serena stepped in rather than away, her green blade gliding up and across in a perfect arc.

The tip of her spear didn't cut flesh—it kissed the haft of his weapon, Flow meeting Flow in a silent collision. The contact was brief, almost delicate, but it was enough. I felt the resonance shudder through the ground beneath us.

The orange blaze inside his axe flared once… then guttered out completely, vanishing like a candle snuffed by unseen fingers.

Jaleon's knees hit the grass with a thud that seemed to echo louder than any of his strikes. His chest rose and fell in great, ragged pulls of air. Sweat rolled down his temples and clung to his jaw, dripping from his chin.

Still, his grin stayed—stubborn, defiant, and alive. "You got me," he panted, voice rough but steady. Then, with a flash of the same reckless fire that had carried him into the fight, he added, "Next time, I'll destroy you."

Serena stepped forward, not as an opponent, but as a commander pleased with her soldier. She extended her hand, her grip firm as she pulled him back to his feet.

"We'll see," she said—and though her tone was calm, her eyes gleamed with something close to pride.

And then there was Apollo.

Serena's voice cut through the court like the first crack of thunder before a storm.
"Apollo," she called, her spear's green light flickering faintly in the breeze, "come. Show me what you've got."

But before the last word had left her lips, she was on him. No warning, no pause. She moved like the wind between heartbeats—her spear flashing, cutting the air with a hiss, striking from high and low in blinding succession.

He should have been overwhelmed, but he wasn't. Apollo moved in silence, his body slipping past each strike with a precision that was almost unnerving. No flinching. No wasted movement. Not a single word.

And still… his Sunspear remained dark.

Serena's tone turned sharp.
"You'll fight me without it? Are you so afraid of me?"

He said nothing—just kept evading, the grass bending beneath his light steps, the sunlight catching the edge of his worn tunic.

She pressed harder, the tempo of her strikes rising, her face shifting from command to something more feral. She wanted to break him open, to force him to ignite. And then… she made her mistake.

She stopped, only for a heartbeat, and let the words fall like a blade:
"That's why she died… because all you know is how to dodge and watch."

Everything changed.

I saw it—we all did. His eyes. Whatever warmth had been there vanished. The air around us grew heavy, cold, thick enough to press against the chest. Shadows stretched unnaturally, bending toward him. The Flow itself seemed to recoil and surge at the same time.

He stopped moving. He faced her directly.

And then it happened—a single, violent pulse of aura burst outward, ripping the air. His shattered green blade came alive, erupting in a wild, uneven blaze of emerald fire laced with streaks of gold. It didn't hum; it roared, like something ancient and untamed had been given shape.

For a heartbeat, he was gone—and then, impossibly, he was in front of her. The speed was inhuman, the space between them devoured in less than an eye-blink. Serena barely caught the first strike, her spear trembling against the impact.

He came again. And again. Each blow slammed into her guard with the weight of a world behind it. The grace was gone—this was raw, brutal, relentless force.

Serena's face changed. The playful light vanished from her eyes, replaced by something I had never thought I would see in her—fear. Fear for her life maybe.

She spun, trying to slip aside as she had with Lux. But when her blade brushed his, the technique failed—his aura tore through hers, flinging it away like cobweb in a storm. He struck again from the left, then the right, then above. My eyes couldn't follow.

The generals—the most seasoned commanders of the Axis—stood frozen, not in calculation but in awe. It was as if they were watching a god descend to the mortal plane, a god whose wrath had been chained too long.

And then it happened—a cut. Just a flick of the green blade across Serena's cheek, quick and deep enough to spill a line of red.

And then it happened.

A soundless shockwave burst from him—a single, violent pulse of aura so sharp it felt like the air itself was being ripped open.

The grass flattened outward in a perfect circle, the obsidian walls shivering as if they'd been struck.

She stepped back, her voice even, but her grip on the spear was tighter now.

"I think that's enough. Let's stop here."

But Apollo didn't stop.

His eyes were elsewhere—far, far away. His strikes came down again, a terrible rhythm that didn't falter, each blow forcing her backward, step by step, until the grass behind her lay flattened in his wake.

We shouted for him to stop. Our voices barely carried over the roar of his blade.

Something broke in the air between them. It wasn't the sound of impact—it was as if the tension itself cracked. In that moment, he saw her fear. And worse—he saw the pain he was about to inflict. Not Serena's alone, but something older, something burned deep into his memory.

His weapon still blazed, but his shoulders fell. The strikes ceased.

He stepped back.

The court fell silent. So silent I swear I could hear the echo of my own heartbeat. Even the Flow in the walls seemed to still, as if holding its breath.

Then Serena laughed. It wasn't the sharp bark of mockery she'd given us before. It was low, breathless, with blood glinting at her cheek and something complicated in her eyes—pride, yes, but also wariness. "I knew you were powerful… but not that much."

The crowd erupted in cheers as if it were nothing more than sport. The generals turned, speaking low to one another, their faces unreadable.

But I knew what I'd seen.
And so did Serena.

The court was still buzzing when Serena finally dismissed us. The generals were gone, the onlookers scattered.

We were alone again—just the four of us.

Jaleon was the first to break the silence. He slapped Apollo on the back so hard the boy nearly stumbled forward.
"By the Flow, green bean—I thought you were about to cut our dear teacher in half. Would've saved me a lot of trouble in training."

Apollo didn't even look at him, still lost in whatever place his mind had gone.

So Jaleon turned his attention to Lux instead.

"And you, noble boy—I've seen more fight in a loaf of bread. I think your crystal actually yawned during that match."

Lux straightened, brushing invisible dust from his robe. "At least I didn't collapse halfway through the run like you did."

"That wasn't collapsing," Jaleon said with mock offense. "That was a tactical power nap. You should try it—keep that delicate royal complexion from sweating."

I couldn't help it—a laugh escaped before I could swallow it.

"Don't encourage him," Lux muttered.

But Jaleon grinned wider, as if I'd just given him license to keep going.
"And you, little violet—you lasted longer than I thought before Serena swatted you like a fly. That's worth a drink in my book."

"We're not old enough to drink," I said.

"Details," he waved off. "Besides, if we're going to be Serena's personal punching bags, we might as well enjoy what time we have left before she breaks us completely."

Even Apollo smirked at that—just for a heartbeat, but I saw it.

We walked the long hall back toward the Initiates' wing, the obsidian walls glowing faintly from the veins of crystal running through them. Jaleon kept the jokes coming, his axe crystal still slung lazily over his shoulder.

"I'm telling you, one day I'm going to carve my name into those walls with this thing. Big letters, so everyone knows Jaleon was here. And survived."

"Barely," Lux muttered.

"I heard that, silk shirt."

By the time we reached our chambers, Serena's voice had already faded to memory—but the ache in my muscles was still fresh, a promise that tomorrow would be worse.

All except for Apollo. He moved quietly, as if his body remembered the fight but his mind was somewhere else entirely.

The crowd had scattered, their cheers still echoing faintly through the obsidian corridors. But above the training court, in a high chamber lit only by the veins of living crystal in the walls, the real battle was beginning.

Julius stood at the head of the blackstone table, his hands folded neatly behind his back. The glow of the Flow traced his profile, catching on the lines of a man who'd worn command for far too long. Around him sat six generals of the Axis—military minds sharp enough to cut, and twice as cold.

"You all saw him," the first general said, voice low but electric. "The boy's speed. The raw output of his crystal. I have never seen the Flow behave like that."

"Not just him," another said. "The orange one—Jaleon. Unrefined, but the force in his strikes… And the violet girl. Defensive instincts beyond her years. Even the noble brat—his control was weak, but his channeling was clean. Together, they—"

"—are a liability," Julius interrupted.

The chamber stilled. He paced slowly to the far end of the table, the hum of the Flow dimming with each step as if it, too, listened.

"They are undisciplined. Emotional. And in the boy's case…" His gaze sharpened. "Unstable."

"Unstable," the third general repeated, leaning forward, "or untapped? That weapon he carries—it's unlike anything in the archives. If we put him under the right command—"

"—he could tip the balance in our favor," another finished.

One of the older generals, his armor worn like an old scar, spoke for the first time.
"Then train them. Together. Push them until there's nothing left but the Flow and obedience."

"And if they resist?"

Julius didn't look at him when he answered.
"They won't resist… if we give them the right enemy."

The table fell into silence—not of disagreement, but of shared understanding. Around it, eyes met, plans formed without being spoken.

"They will be the spear we point where we choose," Julius said finally. "The Order will have its weapons. The Axis will have its war. Together will lay carnage to the Umbers"

The air in the high chamber was heavy with Flow, but colder now—as if the crystal veins themselves disapproved of the conversation.

General Markus leaned forward, resting his scarred forearms on the blackstone table. His voice was gravel, worn down by decades of war.

"You want them disciplined?" he said. "Then don't waste months drilling like the lower ranks. Put them through The Crucible of Silence."

Julius's brow lifted slightly. "Isolation?"

Markus nodded once. "The Isolation Trials are older than this temple. Older than even the Axis-Order pact. You take a promising acolyte, strip them of every comfort—clothes, food, warmth. Leave them with nothing but their weapon and the Flow in their bones. Seven days in the Silent Cells of the mind. No contact. No rest. No mercy. They either bond fully with their crystal… or the Flow breaks them."

Another general scoffed. "That's a relic of the Old Order. We haven't used it in decades."

Markus's gaze never wavered. "Exactly. Which means those who survive will be sharper than anything the enemy can imagine. The Hunger teaches you where your true strength lies. The Silence strips away fear. By the end, they'll breathe only for the fight. And if the boy—" he tilted his head, meaning Apollo "—is what we think he is… we'll know it by day three. Or he'll die with his crystal in his hand, either way no loss for us one orphan less"

Julius didn't move for a long moment. His eyes drifted to the glowing veins in the wall, their pulse steady, indifferent.

"And the others?" he asked finally.

"All four," Markus said. "We put them in together. If they bond as a unit in that darkness, they'll fight as one for life. If they turn on each other… we cull the weak."

A faint smile ghosted across Julius's lips—not warmth, but the satisfaction of a blade being honed.

"Arrange it," he said.

The generals exchanged glances — not of hesitation, but anticipation. Somewhere, in that silence, the future of four young lives was sealed without their knowing.

The last of the generals filed out, their boots echoing on the obsidian floor until only silence remained. The chamber seemed darker without them, the crystal veins along the walls pulsing faintly like the heartbeat of something buried deep.

Julius stood at the far end of the table, hands clasped behind his back. He didn't look at the door when it opened—he didn't need to.

"Serena," he said.

She stepped inside, her green Sunspear still strapped to her back, the tunic she wore in the fight stained with dirt and a thin line of blood across the cheek. Her jaw was tight.

"You called for me?"

Julius turned to face her, his expression unreadable. "You saw them today. The boy especially."

Serena's gaze sharpened. "I saw four acolytes who fought with everything they had. They are raw, unpolished— but they are mine now."

"That is precisely why I'm giving you this order," Julius said. "They will undergo **The Crucible of Silence**."

Her face hardened instantly. "No."

Julius's tone didn't change. "Yes."

"They're not ready. That trial is for hardened initiates, not children. You throw them in naked with nothing but their weapon for a week, you will not have four acolytes left to train. You'll have corpses."

Julius stepped closer, the air between them charged with the weight of his Flow. "And if they are to be weapons, they must be forged in fire. You think you care for them because you've spent two days by their side. That is weakness, Serena. A sword cannot love the hand that wields it."

Her jaw flexed, her hands curling into fists at her sides. "They are not swords. Not yet."

"They will be, we have a deal with axis sooner or later the Umbers will notice that we not unbiased any more" Julius said, voice like stone. "You will put them in the Isolation Cells tomorrow night. Seven days. No food. No water, except what they find in the dark. No warmth. If they bond with the Flow, they will be unbreakable. If not… we move on."

She held his gaze for a long, dangerous moment. Her mind screamed to refuse. To defy him. To take the four and run before the sun rose.

But the Order's chains were old and deep. And in the end, she bowed her head—a fraction, but enough.

"As you command," she said, her voice quiet but edged like a blade about to break.

Julius turned away, already dismissing her. "Good. See to it."

When she left the chamber, her steps were slow, heavy—not from fatigue, but from the weight of what she was about to do.

The fire crackled low in the brazier. Outside, the silvered sky of Kaith stretched endlessly, but the child's eyes were fixed on her.

"But, Nana… what is The Crucible of Silence?"

Valere leaned back in her chair, her old bones creaking. For a long moment, she didn't answer. She just looked past the child, past the walls, into places that no longer existed.

"The Crucible of Silence," she said finally, her voice slower now, "is older than the Order itself. Older than the Temple of Elaris. It was born in the First Wars, when the Flow was still wild and the world was not yet tamed. Back then, warriors were not chosen by rank, or family, or charm. They were chosen by survival."

"They would strip a promising fighter of everything. No light but the crystal's glow. No sound but the echoes of your own thoughts. No warmth but the heat of your Flow."

The child swallowed. "Why?"

Valere's eyes turned sharp. "Because in that darkness, your Flow hears you. It feels every fear, every doubt, every hunger. If you break—if you panic, or rage, or despair—the Flow turns against you. The crystal will dim, maybe even shatter. But if you endure… if you master your own mind when the world has abandoned you… your Flow will bond with you like it never has before. Your weapon will change. Sometimes into something greater. Sometimes into something… terrible."

She looked down at her own gnarled hands, remembering the weight of her purple Sunspear, how it had felt after her own week in the Cells.

"They call it **The Crucible of Silence** because no soul walks out the same as they walked in. Some walk out as legends. Others…" She shook her head. "Others never walk out at all."

The child's voice was small now. "Did you…?"

Valere smiled faintly, though it didn't reach her eyes. "Yes. And so did they. All four of us."

She didn't add what she was thinking—that only one of them would carry the shadows of **The Crucible of Silence** for the rest of his life

The doors to the Temple's strategy chamber slammed shut behind General Markus, sealing Julius in the darkness with his own thoughts. Markus did not look back.

The general's stride was long, deliberate—the kind of march that made lesser men step aside without thinking. The Flow veins running beneath the obsidian floor shimmered faintly as he passed, as if even the ancient currents recognized the weight of the decision now fixed in his mind.

He boarded his flagship without ceremony. No words to the dockmasters. No acknowledgment of the junior officers lined in rigid salute.

The vessel was a predator — its hull blacker than the void between stars, its edges lined with slivers of crystal that pulsed like a heartbeat.

As the engines roared to life, the Temple of Elaris shrank in the rear viewport, its glassy spires glittering in the last light of day.

Markus entered the war cabin, dimly lit by a single table of shifting holographic maps. "Activate the relay," he ordered.

The comm crystals flared, forming the spectral faces of distant Axis outpost commanders—battle-hardened men and women standing beneath the banners of their garrisons.

Markus didn't waste a breath.
"Signal every outpost. Arm every blade. Every spear. Every Sunspear bearer." His tone was carved from iron. "War is coming."

One of the commanders hesitated. "General... has the Senate declared—"

"I don't give a damn what the Senate has declared," Markus cut in, stepping into the light so they could see the resolve in his eyes.

"The Flow is shifting. I can feel it. It bends differently now, like a great river rising before a flood. Something is coming—and if we wait, it will devour us."

No one spoke after that. The message was sent.

The Axis capital rose ahead, a colossal tiered fortress-city built into the cliffs above the Sea of Mourns. Its black stone towers were veined with living crystal, pulsing in slow, steady rhythm. The highest spire vanished into low, blood-red clouds.

But tonight… the capital was awake.

Parade terraces overflowed with troops in burnished steel and Flow-threaded armor. Their ranks stretched down into the lower districts and spilled into the massive plazas beyond the city gates. Drums pounded like warhearts, their rhythm syncing with the march of thousands of boots. The air was thick with oil, metal, and the scent of bodies pressed shoulder to shoulder.

As Markus's flagship descended, the city's banners unfurled from the highest walls—vast crimson sheets stitched with the Axis emblem: a spear point encircled by a ring of unbroken flame. The banners caught the wind and snapped in unison like the cracking of a hundred whips.

The Senate waited for him at the Grand Dais—a balcony of black marble and silver railings that overlooked the mustered legions. Senators in gold-trimmed robes shifted restlessly, their eyes bright with greed. Conquest meant territory. Territory meant resources. Resources meant wealth.

Markus's boots struck the marble as he stepped down from the docking ramp.

The roar began before he even reached the edge. The soldiers stomped their weapons on the ground, the sound rolling up the terraces like the approach of a storm.

"Today," he began, "I stand before you not as a general… but as a leader."

A ripple went through the crowd, a shifting of stances, the tightening of grips on spear hafts and sword hilts.

"This day will be carved into the memory of the Flow itself. This day, we mark the *end* of the Umbers—those fanatics, those carrion-feeders, those shadows that have bled the galaxy for too long."

His voice rose, sharp and cutting, every word striking like a blade.

"They have *lived* long enough. They have *destroyed* long enough. They have desecrated our worlds, stolen our children, and defiled the Flow with their madness. And now—now, we will answer."

A murmur of fury swept through the soldiers, the sound of a thousand men gritting their teeth in unison.

Markus stepped to the very edge of the dais, looking down into the mass of armored bodies below.

"We will rain *pure justice* upon them. We will burn their temples. We will tear down their banners. We will grind every man, woman, and child who stands against us into the dust. The Umbers will vanish—not in exile, not in surrender—but in *erasure.*"

The roar rose again, but Markus lifted one gloved hand and it cut off instantly.

"Axis will prevail."
His voice was a blade now—short, clean, final.

He raised both arms to the night sky. The crystals in his armor flared brighter, catching the Flow's hum, and the banners above seemed to blaze in response.

"The Order stands with us. The Flow itself bends toward us. And together… we will be the true face of democracy! We will fulfil the Conqueror dream"

The crowd exploded. The roar was deafening, a tidal wave of voices shouting, stamping, hammering weapons against armor. The sound struck the marble walls and came back doubled, until the whole capital shook beneath its weight.

Markus let the fury build until the soldiers were no longer a disciplined force, but a single, raging heartbeat. Then, with the precision of a commander who knew exactly when to strike, he thrust one fist into the air and gave the final word.

"WAR!"

Tens of thousands answered, the chant rolling like thunder:

"WAR! WAR! WAR!"

Above, the banners of the Axis whipped violently in the wind, painting the night sky red. Below, the Senate watched in silence—not in disapproval, but in the quiet, calculating joy of men who knew war would make them rich.

And at the center of it all, Markus stood unmovable, a dark silhouette against the firelit heavens, a leader crowned not by gold, but by the will of an army that was ready to burn the galaxy for him. We didn't know what was happening. We had no idea.

We were just children, pieces on a chessboard whose game had been set long before we were born. The Axis didn't see us as people—we were lines in their ledgers, blades in their vaults, weapons of destruction waiting to be sharpened.

And all we wanted… was to leave.

The war began with a whisper. It always does.

But when it struck, it struck like the end of the world.

Grith—the City of the Black Flame—was the first to burn.

From the void above, the Axis fleet blotted out the sun. Dozens of colossal black warships drifted into formation, each one a fortress carved from shadow and steel, their flanks veined with rivers of crystal conduits. Those conduits pulsed like the veins of a living thing, bleeding light into the storm clouds they tore through.

The sky over Grith changed—not just darkening, but bruising, as if the heavens themselves recoiled. The high towers of the city, once proud and defiant, were suddenly dwarfed beneath a wall of descending death.

And then the first blow fell.

A silence hit first—deep and unnatural—as the Flow around the fleet tightened, compressed into a weapon. Then, in the space of a heartbeat, a column of searing white light erupted downward.

It was not lightning. It was not fire.
It was *pure Flow*, crushed and funneled into a single, merciless beam.

The center of the city became a sun. Towers of black obsidian shattered in perfect unison, bursting outward in rings of shrapnel. Streets that had been lined with markets and homes simply… ceased to exist. The shockwave rolled like a living thing, tearing through every alley and courtyard, hurling bodies into the air as if the ground itself had betrayed them. Roofs tore away. Bridges splintered. The heat was so intense that stone warped and glass ran like water.

The screams began before the light even faded.

They called it *pure justice.*

But justice does not scream like that. Justice does not set fire to children's beds. Justice does not leave the air so thick with ash that breathing tastes like swallowing blood.

The first breach came with a sound like a mountain splitting. The outer gates of Grith, once carved with the symbols of the Black Flame, crumpled inward under the force of the Axis siege engines—hulking constructs that glowed from within, as if molten crystal beat like hearts in their cores.

Through the smoke, they came.

The Axis soldiers moved in tight phalanxes, blackened steel plating their bodies, crimson banners snapping from their spears. Among their ranks some flow wilders their Sunspears blazed with every color but mercy—red for wrath, orange for will, green for conquest. They did not advance like men. They advanced like a tide.

Where the tide touched, life ended.

The Umber defenders fought as best they could—thin lines of warriors wielding blades wrapped in their city's sacred black fire. They met the invaders in narrow alleys and on the steps of their shrines, but the battle was over before it began. The surprise had gutted them, and the Axis knew it.

There was no quarter.

A woman with a screaming infant in her arms ran from the market square. An orange spear found her before she cleared the steps. An old man stood in a doorway, clutching a kitchen knife. They split him from collarbone to hip without breaking stride. A boy, barely past his first year of training, raised a wooden practice sword at the oncoming soldiers—and was trampled before he could swing.

You see, the Umbers… they never had an army. They believed they didn't need one.

After the First Break of the Ten Flames, when the galaxies burned and the treaties were carved into the marrow of the Flow, the Umbers trusted in words. Their planets—their homes—were to remain untouched. The Axis swore upon the Flow itself to honor that pact, and with the protection of the Order, balance would endure.

That was the promise.
That was the illusion.

But promises rot. Treaties decay. The Order—the very guardians meant to preserve equilibrium—was bought and sold long ago. The ink of justice had been drowned in gold.

And even in this era, even in the time of the Flow, where color and essence command the cosmos… gold still remains the true god.

The Umbers never raised legions, never forged fleets. Why would they? They believed in balance, in oaths, in the sanctuary of law. But law without honor is only parchment, and balance without truth is nothing more than a mask.

And so when the Axis came—the Umbers had nothing but faith to defend them. Faith, and the bitter realization that faith cannot stop fire.

The slaughter was not random. It was methodical.

They moved street by street, room by room. They set fire to every home. They killed every shadow that moved. Even the animals—hounds, sky-birds, the massive draft-beasts of the northern stables—were butchered where they stood, their bodies left in the open to rot under the crimson glow of burning banners.

By nightfall, Grith was not a city.
It was a wound in the world, still smoking, its streets carpeted in ash and blood.

It was Kaith all over again.

I remember the stories from my own homeworld—how the Axis claimed to bring order and unity, but left nothing but ash. How they left *silence* in their wake.

In Grith, the silence came slowly, dragged out by the screams.

The black flame of the Umber temple was extinguished when the high spire fell, crushed beneath the legs of Axis siege walkers—great four-legged beasts of armor and crystal that spat molten light into the ruins.

The river that ran through the city turned red, then black, choked with the dead.

From the balcony of his command ship, General Markus watched Grith die.

The ship hovered in perfect stillness above the city, its crystal conduits casting a pale, hungry glow across the burning streets below. Markus stood with his hands clasped behind his back, his black coat stirring only when the heat rising from the inferno below reached him. The flames painted his face in flickering shades of gold and crimson—not enough to hide the faint curl of satisfaction at the edge of his mouth.

Behind him, a court scribe worked in silence, stylus scratching against a thin slab of crystal. Every detail was recorded in precise, clinical lines: population estimates, casualty tallies, number of Sunspear ignitions, the exact moment the outer wall fell. Each entry was not written as tragedy, but as achievement. A ledger of victory.

Below, the last of the Umber resistance collapsed. The final defenders—a knot of warriors backed into the shadow of the central spire—were swallowed in a blaze of green and orange light. Their bodies fell without ceremony.

The screams dwindled. The clash of weapons fell silent.

Markus did not look away until the only motion in the city was the slow drift of ash, swirling in the updraft like snow in a winter storm. The once-proud towers of Grith, black flame sigils still etched in their scorched stone, stood gutted and hollow.

Only then did he give the order.

"Raise the banners."

From the broken walls, the red flags of the Axis unfurled, their fabric snapping in the hot wind. The sigils—black sun and twin spears—caught the firelight until they seemed to bleed into the smoke-choked sky.

In the streets below, Axis soldiers stood at attention among the corpses, their weapons still lit, their armor slick with blood and soot.

To Markus, this was not cruelty.
This was order.

The Senate back in the capital would cheer when the news arrived. They would rise from their seats and call it victory. They would dress it in the language of democracy, of justice, of a safer galaxy. Speeches would ring across the chambers like hymns—not of truth, but of convenience.

For they feared him.

Magnus Throne, General of the Axis, had become more than a man. To some, a tyrant. To others, a savior. But to the Senate? He was neither. He was a threat. His victories, his power, his very name bent the galaxy's balance away from their grasp. And power they could not bend—they would break.

So the daggers were already drawn. Not on the battlefield, but behind velvet curtains. Senators whispered in the shadows, their lips silvered with promises, their hands dripping with gold. They schemed not for justice, not for peace, but for survival of their own rule.

You see my child all this is a game , a wheel of time that never changes , you win and you kill and then you get killed or you kill long enough that even your family your friends want you dead .

But on the ground, in the ruins of Grith, there was only the smell of burning flesh, the groan of walls collapsing, and the whisper of the Flow—faint, almost inaudible, as if it had turned its face away.

We did not know then… that the path from this slaughter would lead straight to us.

And that we—unknowing, unwilling—would be the next pieces they moved on the board.

"When the Flow trembles, kingdoms fall silent."

The Great Conqueror.

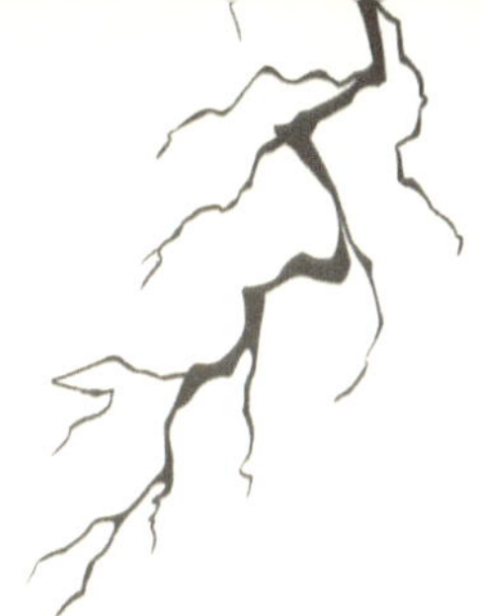

CHAPTER 12

Back in the Temple, we were clueless about the storms gathering beyond its walls—about the generals whispering to Julius, about cities burning.

All we knew was the echo of our own laughter.

The obsidian corridors caught it and threw it back at us, making it sound like the whole Temple was in on the joke. Jaleon, our walking disaster of an orange giant, had somehow—and I truly mean *somehow*—stolen an entire iron pot of mashed potatoes from the kitchens. Not a bowl. Not a plate. An *entire pot*. He had the wooden spoon in one hand and his axe crystal in the other, swinging it lazily like a toy as he marched down the hall.

"Gods, Jaleon, you're going to get us all killed," I told him.

"Don't worry," he said through a mouthful of potato, "if the guards come, I'll defend us with the Spoon of Destiny."

Lux rolled his eyes, the very picture of noble disdain, but I caught him sneaking bites whenever Jaleon offered the spoon his way. Even Apollo, quiet as a shadow, had cracked the smallest of smiles—the kind you might miss if you blinked, but that meant more than any laugh.

For a moment, we weren't acolytes. We weren't soldiers. We weren't pawns on anyone's board. We were just… people.

Then Serena came.

At first, I thought she'd just finished sparring. Her tunic was plain, unarmored, her braid a little loose. But then I saw her face. It wasn't the sharp, hawk-eyed expression she always wore when training us. It was softer… no, not softer. *Weighed down.* Like she'd been carrying something all day and had finally decided to set it down.

She didn't speak right away. She stepped up to each of us, one by one, and hugged us.

A *real* hug. Tight. Firm. Warm. The kind that leaves the scent of the person in your clothes.

She started with Lux, murmuring something too low for me to hear. Then me—her hand lingered on the back of my head like she was memorizing the shape of it. Apollo didn't move at all when she took him in her arms, but his eyes changed—for a moment, I swear, he looked like a boy instead of a blade.

When she reached Jaleon, he smirked and said, "If this is about the potatoes, I can explain—"

"I'm sorry," she whispered, cutting him off.

He blinked. "Sorry? For what?"

She straightened, her voice steady, but I could hear the fracture underneath. "The Council has decided. You're going to the Crucible of Silence."

The joke died in Jaleon's throat. Lux frowned, brows drawing together. Apollo just stared at her, the faint smile gone.

"What is that?" Lux asked.

Serena looked away from us, toward the crystal veins that ran through the obsidian walls. The light from them painted her face in shifting green and gold, and for a heartbeat she looked… ancient.

"This is older than the Order," she said. "Older than the Temple itself. The Crucible strips you to nothing. You will be taken into the Black Chamber—no food, no water, no light. No comfort. Nothing but the weapon in your hand."

Her gaze swept over us. "You will be naked—not just of cloth, but of the self you know. The Flow will find you there. It will test you. It will break you. It will show you things you were never meant to see."

She took a slow step toward me, her hand settling on my shoulder. Her grip was warm, but her voice was ice. "No one knows exactly what happens inside. Those who return never speak of it. Those who don't… are not spoken of at all."

For a moment, the only sound was the faint hum of the Flow in the walls.

"If you survive," she said, "greatness awaits. But survival is not promised. And if you make it through…" she hesitated, "…never speak of what you saw. Not even to each other."

Something in her voice made it clear this wasn't just an order—it was a plea.

The hallway felt smaller. Colder.

Even Jaleon didn't have a joke.

That night, the Temple was too still. The walls seemed to hold their breath. Even the faint crystal pulse in the stone felt slower, dimmer, like a heartbeat on the edge of stopping.

The others tried to settle.
Jaleon sprawled across his cot, arms behind his head, mumbling something about the mashed potatoes he'd stolen earlier. Lux sat cross-legged on his bed, eyes closed, whispering quiet prayers to whatever gods nobles keep. I leaned by the narrow window, watching the glow from the veins in the walls fade in and out.

Only Apollo didn't try.

He sat on the edge of his bed, his mother's shattered crystal turning slowly in his fingers. No words. No movement but that. And then he lay back, the shard pressed to his chest.

Sleep took him fast.

The void was waiting.

It was always the same—endless black, cold as the space between stars. But tonight it was sharper. The darkness seemed to breathe.

His armor was in pieces, jagged edges of broken plates hanging from his frame. Blood dripped from somewhere—his blood—vanishing into the nothing beneath him. In his right hand, the Sunspear was ignited, but it wasn't whole. The emerald blade was cracked, its light laced with furious gold, pulsing as if it had a heartbeat of its own.

The shadow was there too. Huge. Towering over him. It didn't move. Didn't need to. It only watched.

From the dark ahead, a figure began to take shape. At first, it was Elira—her presence cutting through the black like dawn through fog. Her hair loose, her blue eyes steady, the same warmth she'd given him as a child.

He tried to speak, but his voice didn't exist here.

She smiled—and her face began to shift. Bone bent. Skin reshaped. The eyes turned sharper, greener. Her jawline changed. And suddenly it wasn't Elira at all.

It was Serena.

She mouthed something to him. Words he couldn't hear.

And then—chaos.

The black around him erupted with cries for help, screams tangled with the clash of steel, the wet sound of blades in flesh. Blood poured from the darkness itself, splashing at his feet. He turned and saw flashes—soldiers in Order armor falling, Serena's spear striking, his own hands cutting down shapes he couldn't name.

Then one body fell at his feet.
Elira.
But as he looked, the face flickered between hers and Serena's, over and over, until he couldn't tell them apart.

The Sunspear in his hand burned deferent—almost red now—and still the shadow loomed behind him, closer, reaching—flashes of green and red everywhere, blood and dirt everywhere .

The world shattered.

The door to our chamber burst inward. Wood splintered, shards bouncing across the floor.

Soldiers in black armor and with dark black sinister ceremonial masks poured in, silent, efficient.

Apollo woke gasping, his hand still wrapped around the crystal. But he said nothing. Not now. Not ever.

They pulled us from our beds, ripping away our robes without hesitation. The cold hit like icewater. My skin prickled under the crystal light. Lux turned his head away, jaw tight. Jaleon fought—kicking, cursing, his voice booming in the small room—until they twisted his arms behind his back and drove him forward.

And in the doorway, Serena stood watching. Her face was unreadable. Her hands were clenched into fists so tight I thought her knuckles might break.

Jaleon met her eyes and stopped struggling. "…It's time," he muttered.

Barefoot, stripped of everything but the crystals in our hands, we were marched into the silent corridors. The sound of the soldiers' boots echoed ahead of us, pulling us toward the dark.

Apollo never spoke of what he saw in his dream.

But the way his eyes stayed fixed on the shadows ahead… I think he still saw it.

The air grew colder the deeper we went.

The Temple's polished obsidian halls gave way to older stone—rough-hewn, slick with moisture, veined not with glowing crystal but with hairline cracks that seemed to drink in the light. The torches here burned low, their flames shivering in unseen drafts.

We were barefoot, the stone biting into our feet. The only thing we carried was the crystal each of us had been bound to. I was naked with one hand I was holding my crystal with the other one my chest.

The soldiers said nothing. Their armor clinked in rhythm with our steps, the sound bouncing back from the walls until it felt like a second, heavier heartbeat.

I'd heard stories of this place—fragments spoken in whispers between Initiates. The Crucible of Silence. No one ever said what happened inside. No one who returned spoke of it.

The passage twisted down and down until I lost all sense of direction. At times it felt like we were walking in circles. At others, like we'd crossed into somewhere that wasn't under the Temple at all.

Jaleon broke the silence first.
"Bit chilly for a midnight stroll," he muttered, his voice cracking against the stone. "Next time, old hag, you could at least tell us we're going for a walk."

No one laughed. Even he sounded like he didn't expect anyone to.

We came to a door—if you could call it that. A slab of black stone wider than three men, carved with symbols like some forbitten runes so old the edges had worn to almost nothing. A low hum pressed against my skull, as if the rock itself were breathing.

The lead soldier raised a hand.
The slab split down the middle. Not with the creak of hinges, but with a sound like stone shattering underwater. Beyond was only darkness—not the kind you get in unlit rooms, but a deeper thing, the kind that seemed to reach out and taste the edges of you.

Serena stood there waiting.

No armor. Only a tunic. And her green Sunspear strapped across her back. She looked at each of us in turn. Her gaze lingered on Apollo.

"This is older than the Order," she said quietly. Her voice didn't carry far the dark seemed to drink it. "Older than the Axis. Older than the Umbers. The Flow itself watches what happens here."

Lux swallowed. "And… what happens here?"

Serena's eyes didn't waver.
"You survive. Or you don't."

With that, she stepped aside.

One by one, the soldiers pushed us forward. The darkness took the light from our crystals within moments. Behind us, the stone slab closed without a sound.

And the silence began.

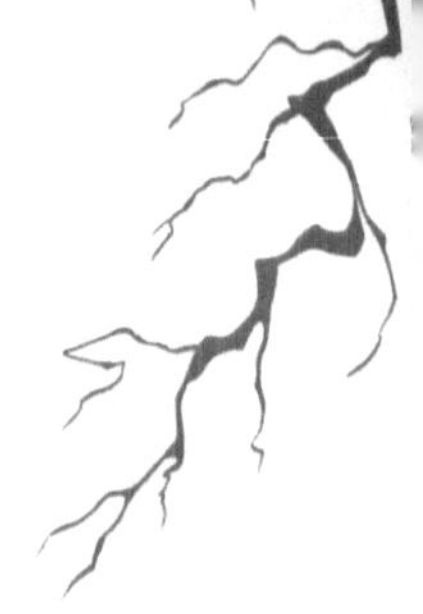

CHAPTER 13

It wasn't the absence of noise. It was a living thing, pressing against your ears, crawling under your skin. My breath sounded too loud. My heartbeat felt exposed, like it didn't belong to me anymore.

Somewhere in that black, Apollo's shadow split—two shapes now followed him. One small. One impossibly tall.

He didn't speak. None of us did.

We had stepped out of the world we knew. And the Crucible had taken us.

The door closed behind us without a sound.

No light.
No draft.
Just the sudden, crushing absence of the world.

Even our own breathing seemed swallowed.

The first sound came from Jaleon—a low, dangerous growl.
"Not playing this game."

I heard the snap of his crystal, the flare of ignition. Orange erupted into the dark like a sunrise in hell. For a breath, we could see one another—Lux wide-eyed, Apollo utterly still, and me clutching my crystal as if it could anchor me.

The light made the walls glisten like wet stone… but there were no walls.

Then it came—not an echo, not a sound I could place. A deep concussion that rattled my bones, like the world itself had slammed shut.
The orange blaze was gone.
And so was Jaleon.

No footsteps.
No shout.
No trace.

Lux's voice cracked. "Jaleon?! Jaleon!"

And then the void moved.

I swear it moved—not like mist or shadow, but like a slow tide, deliberate and patient, rolling over the spot where Jaleon had been.

Lux's panic broke into motion—a stumbling, desperate sprint into nothing. I heard his bare feet slap stone, then multiply, as if the sound was bouncing wrong from unseen shapes. His voice trailed with him. Then silence.

Just me.

Apollo didn't move.
Didn't speak.
Didn't even shift his stance.
And though my eyes were useless, I knew—he was watching something I could not see.

The pressure in my chest grew until I thought my ribs might snap. I clutched my crystal, forcing the Flow through it. For a moment, violet light burst from my hand—a thread of safety—and then it died. Not extinguished… consumed. Sucked into the void as if the darkness itself drank it.

The silence thickened.

I could feel Jaleon's rage somewhere—not seen, but in the Flow. A storm of will, slashing, bellowing, refusing to submit. But nothing struck. His battle cries had no echoes. No blows landed. The void devoured even his defiance.

I tried to move, but my knees buckled. I was cold, trembling, unsure if seconds or hours had passed. My own breath began to sound foreign. I whispered to myself just to know I was still there.

And Apollo…

I reached for him in the Flow, but he was gone. Not just hidden—*gone*. No breath, no step, no thought. It was like he had been erased from the same reality I stood in.

I was lost.

Not in a room. Not in a tunnel. Lost *inside* of nothing.

I think days had passed… but there was no sun to rise, no night to fall. Just the same endless, lightless expanse pressing in from all sides. I think I was wondering in the vast darkens yet I was in the same place,

At first, I could still *sense* them. Jaleon's stubborn rage flaring like a bonfire, Lux's frantic energy fluttering like a trapped bird's wings. But that was gone now. No more Jaleon. I think even he had stopped fighting. His defiance—that unshakable force that filled a room—was gone like breath in winter air.

There was nothing left to hold on to.

We will die here.
I knew it.

All I could hear was the void. And something deeper beneath it… not words, not voices, but *chaos*. A sound like the grinding of mountains under an ocean, a storm you could never escape. It didn't just echo in my head—it lived there now, coiled in my skull like it had always been waiting for me.

I tried my crystal once more. My violet flame—my anchor. I poured what was left of my strength into it, begging it to light. A flicker answered me… then was sucked away, consumed like it had never existed. The cold in my hand was worse than the darkness.

I think Lux was somewhere ahead of me… or maybe behind me. The way sound twisted here, the way the Flow bent, I couldn't tell. He could have been a thousand steps away or only inches.

Or maybe… maybe we weren't standing anymore. Maybe we were floating in nothing.

My legs didn't work right. My knees shook every time I tried to move, like gravity was shifting against me. My body felt wrong, hollow, like the void had scooped pieces of me out without asking.

If this is power… I don't want it.

The thought tore something inside me. My breath came fast. My teeth clenched.

Please, Serena. Please stop this.

The words came out ragged, broken, tears cutting hot trails down my cheeks. The moment they left my mouth, I hated myself for saying them—but I couldn't take them back. I wasn't a warrior here. I wasn't anything.

And then…

A voice.

Soft. Warm. *Hers.*

"My Valere… I love you."

I froze. My whole body shook.

Tears blurred my sight—not that there was anything to see. "I love you too, Mom." My voice was small. The words hurt to say.

Why is this happening to us?

The question hung in the void like a stone sinking into black water. No answer came—just that shifting, endless silence, thick with something I couldn't name.

And for a heartbeat, I swore I felt her hand on mine. My mother. Warm, gentle, the way she had held me as a child.

But it wasn't her.

The realization tore through me, and I broke. I wasn't myself anymore—I was something hollow, something unhinged. Panic rose like poison in my throat.

"Please… please kill me, Mom!" I screamed. My voice cracked, half a sob, half a howl. I clawed at the air like a drowning man, desperate for release, desperate for her to end it.

The crystal was in my hand. My own blade, my own light. I pressed it against my chest, hard enough to feel the bite. My hands trembled as I tried to ignite it, to end myself in fire. One spark, and I would be gone.

But nothing came. My will faltered. My flesh betrayed me. I was too weak. Too cowardly to even die.

Tears blurred my vision. My voice dropped to a ragged whisper, choked and broken.
"Please… if anyone hears me… end this."

Jaleon was defeated.

The orange glow that had always seemed to follow him, like he carried a second sun in his chest, was gone. His axe—the great, two-headed beast he'd swung like it was an extension of himself—lay cold and dead in his hands. No flare. No hum.

And Jaleon… Jaleon was on his knees.

Not grinning. Not throwing some stupid joke to make us roll our eyes. He sat there like a child who had lost something he could never get back, head bowed, shoulders slumped. I couldn't even hear his breath.

It was wrong. Everything about it was wrong.

I *think* I was hungry, but hunger here didn't make sense. My stomach was hollow, but my body felt… full. And empty. At the same time. Like I had been fed nothing but air, and the air itself was turning to stone inside me.

Lux was worse. He wasn't in the void anymore—not really. He'd gone somewhere else entirely, trapped in his own mind. I couldn't hear his voice. I could just *feel* the spiral of his thoughts, circling tighter and tighter, crushing him.

I knew what he saw.

Failure.

Failure to his training. Failure to the noble house whose crest he wore with such stiff pride. Failure to the family that now, in his mind, had already erased him from their name. Dead to them in every way that mattered.

And that's when I felt it.

It came first as a tremor—not in the ground, because there *was* no ground here, but in the Flow itself. A ripple that slid through the darkness, so sharp it burned against my skin.

Then I *knew*.

It was Apollo.

But not the Apollo I'd walked the halls with, not the quiet boy who carried his mother's broken crystal like it was the only piece of the world worth holding onto.

This was something else.

Something older.

Something ancient and vast, the kind of power you don't find—the kind that finds *you*.

It was cold, but not like winter. It was the cold of deep water, of endless night, of a place where no sun had ever risen. And wrapped around that cold… was something sharp, something that felt like the edge of a blade held just against my throat.

The void didn't feel empty anymore. It felt like it was watching.

Apollo had not moved.
Not once. Not since the darkness swallowed us whole.

But now… something changed.

We all felt it.

The shadows drew close, folding into shapes that were not shapes—forms you could only see from the corner of your mind. Faces emerged and vanished. Elira's face. Then Serena's. Then both, shifting into one another until the difference was gone.

Blood in the air.
Her blood.
Their blood.His hands holding the Sunspear.
His hands delivering the killing blow.

It was not memory alone. The Flow was showing him *what was, what is, and what could be.*
But the visions tangled together like broken threads—they could not be separated without cutting the weave itself.

It wasn't an image.
It wasn't even a thought.
It was like looking through cracked glass.

A field… or many fields… he couldn't tell.
Black soil, fractured stone, and something like ash drifting from a sky that wasn't really a sky.
Sounds—metal tearing, voices crying out—then nothing.

Shapes moved.
Bodies, colorless, lay still.

And among them… someone.
Maybe him. Maybe not.

In his right hand burned a blade of green—jagged, uneven, alive. It did not shine like a weapon forged, but breathed, as though the Flow itself had been trapped inside and was trying to escape.

In his left… something heavier. Quieter. A crystal made flesh, its light red, but not like fire. Not warmth. Not life. It was the color of an open wound, of a scar that would never close, bleeding forever into the world.

Two crystals. Two powers, alive at once in the hands of a single man. Impossible. The law was clear—one crystal, one soul, bound until death. Anything else was heresy, collapse, death for both wielder and world.

Yet here it was.

And in that chamber, where the Flow bent and broke, where all sense of truth was torn apart—impossibility lived.

Figures fell around him, but he couldn't tell if they were enemies or friends.
Maybe there was no difference.

Far away, banners hung from shattered towers—but whose they were, Axis or Order even the Umbers, he couldn't see.

The sky itself seemed torn—green and red bleeding together like two rivers that should never meet. Every breath tasted of iron and smoke.

And in the middle of it all, the figure—or perhaps himself—stood unmoving, as though waiting for something that would never come.

There was no end.
No beginning.
Only this.

And still, the voice came.
That same voice he had carried from the night his mother died.

"Run, my boy… run."

But he did not run.
Not this time.

He did not raise his voice.
He didn't need to.

When Apollo lifted his head, the void seemed to lean closer, as if the Crucible itself had been holding its breath for him.

"You know…" he began, and the darkness swelled around his words, carrying them to every corner of this endless place.

"If you gaze long enough into the abyss…"

The pause was not for effect—it was the weight of inevitability.

"…the abyss will gaze back at you."

Something shifted in the black. The silence deepened, so heavy it pressed against my chest like stone. Even without eyes, I *felt* the stare of something vast, ancient, and patient.

"I understand you now," he said, his voice cutting through the dark like the edge of a blade.

"They say you are everything—that all is Flow. That you are the god who lets us breathe, who gives us life.

My mother believed that. She was a great warrior, and even with so little in her hands, she held more faith than anyone I've ever known. People called her fallen, broken, but not me. In my eyes, she was my god. My Flow.

She was the spoon that fed me, the arms that held me, the world itself—and she asked for nothing in return.

And you… you let her die. Betrayed by the very crystal she trusted.

So here, in this silence you use to break us, I dare to ask you one question: Why? Why did she have to die? Why take her, when I had so much left to learn, when I still needed her?

I want to believe that death is mercy. That it's a doorway to reunion with those we've lost. But I know the truth. I know I will never see her again.

And if you can hear me—then hear this: I hate you. I hate you for leaving her."

The shadow moved, slow and deliberate, like the tide crawling over a shore. Not in anger. Not in fear. But in recognition.

"But I've learned something," Apollo said, the words sharper now, coiled with power. "Power does not belong to those born the strongest. Or the fastest. Or even the smartest. No. Power belongs to those who will do anything to take it."

The void stirred like a great beast awakening. Every hair on my arms stood on end.

"And I…"

He exhaled slowly, and it was less a breath than a vow—a blade honed on the edge of defiance.

"…am done with you. Do you hear me? I will guide my fate—not you. Not the void, not the Flow, not even the gods. It will take more than shadows to break me. I will forge the course of my life… and my death."

For a heartbeat, silence. The temple itself seemed to hold its breath.

Then the darkness moved.

It did not strike. It did not surge.
It folded.

The air bent inward like reality itself had flinched, collapsing upon itself, reshaping. Walls rippled as though made of liquid shadow, the floor cracked with lines of green and black light colliding.

And in that fracture, we saw it—the truth, naked and terrible.

The void was not merely his weapon. It was alive. Watching. Waiting.

The shadow had never stood behind him.
It had never been in front of him.

It had always been inside him.

The Crucible screamed. The sound was like metal rending, stone fracturing, the bones of the world snapping one by one. Green light exploded from Apollo's shattered blade—not the gentle glow of the Flow, but a violent, uneven blaze that clawed its way into the dark, streaked with veins of molten gold. Each flare of light struck like a hammer blow, cracking the blackness open in jagged fractures.

The pressure slammed into us, nearly driving me to my knees. The void itself seemed to flinch.

And then… he was there. Standing before us.

The green blade in his hand wasn't merely alive—it was ravenous.
Its jagged edge dripped with embers of raw, living Flow, each droplet hissing like acid as it vanished into the void beneath. Sparks scattered, but they were no sparks of light—they fell like burning promises, each one heavy with danger, each one whispering of ruin.

And his eyes—gods, his eyes.
They burned a dark, fevered emerald, glowing as if he had devoured not just the Flow, but the very shadows around him. It was as though Apollo had become the

vessel of everything—light and dark, order and chaos—a man no longer containing the Flow, but consuming it.

He looked at each of us, his eyes calm, the storm contained but not gone.
"Come," he said, his voice the stillness after the breaking of a storm. "Let's get out of here."

Our crystals didn't just ignite—they *roared* to life, answering not my will, not Jaleon's or Lux's, but Apollo's.
It was as if the Flow itself had bent its knee.

Jaleon became the fury incarnate—his axe swelled in size, its twin heads spinning with molten orange arcs, each strike of its pulse like a thunderclap in the void. He moved with the raw, unstoppable rhythm of an avalanche, no longer a man but a force of nature.

Lux was lightning given form—his sword thinned to a needle of blinding azure, vibrating so fast it sang in the air. He moved in flickers, here one heartbeat, gone the next, his strikes carrying the elegance of a noble duelist and the cold precision of a predator.

Mine… mine burned violet and pure, but no longer the gentle glow of a hopeful apprentice. This was *judgment*. Every flare from the blade felt like a verdict being passed, every swing a sentence delivered. It was the justice I had once feared I had lost, now flooding my veins like fire.

We were alive.
No—more than alive.

The void itself seemed to *fear* us.

And Apollo… he didn't just move—he *commanded*. The shattered green blade in his hand blazed so brightly its light tore shadows from the walls. Gold veins ran through the cracks in its surface, leaking power in great, violent bursts. He didn't even need to look at the rift he made—one swing, and the darkness screamed as if it were a living thing, torn open from crown to root.

The wound in reality bled blinding light, pouring over us, swallowing the last taste of hunger, fear, and despair. Ahead, the door began to form, a colossal merging of shadow and gold, its surface rippling like molten glass.

We didn't hesitate.
The four of us stepped through in perfect unison—not the same frightened children who had entered.

Something had been forged in the dark.

And it wasn't human anymore.

We walked out of the Crucible not as survivors, but as weapons the world was not ready for. As we crossed the threshold, I swear the Flow itself *shuddered.*

The light from the Crucible's door swallowed us whole, and then it was gone—leaving us standing in a place so different from the void that it hurt to look at.

Cold stone pressed against bare feet.
Real walls rose around us—black obsidian polished to a mirror sheen, lit by torches that burned low and steady. The air reeked of incense and oil.

We were back.
And we were naked.

Not stripped just of clothes, but of everything.
The Crucible had taken the warmth from our bones, the weight from our pride, even the memory of who we were before we entered.
Our skin was ghost-pale, streaked with dirt and sweat and thin cuts we didn't remember receiving. The torchlight caught on every bruise like it was marking territory.

Jaleon stood with his shoulders rolled forward, not in shame but in something heavier—as if the fire inside him was banked to embers. His eyes burned still, but it was a quiet burn, the kind that smolders in the dark before it finds fuel again.

Lux didn't meet anyone's gaze.
He kept his chin up, his face composed, but the rigid set of his jaw betrayed the way the humiliation bit into him. His noble bearing was intact, but barely—his dignity stitched together with pure defiance.

Me… I felt hollow and full all at once. My violet Sunspear crystal was still deep inside me, but I could feel it thrumming like a second heart, pulsing with a slow, deliberate rhythm. I didn't ignite it—not yet— but I knew it was changed, and so was I.

Apollo…
Apollo walked as though he hadn't just returned from the Crucible, but had brought some of it back with him. His eyes were fixed ahead, unreadable. His hair clung damp to his face, and in his right hand he still held the shattered green blade—its edge faintly steaming in the cool air, as if it refused to cool.

We crossed the floor together, our bare feet silent on the stone.

Every gaze followed us. While we bled in the dark of the Crucible, Elaris fell without a single blade drawn.

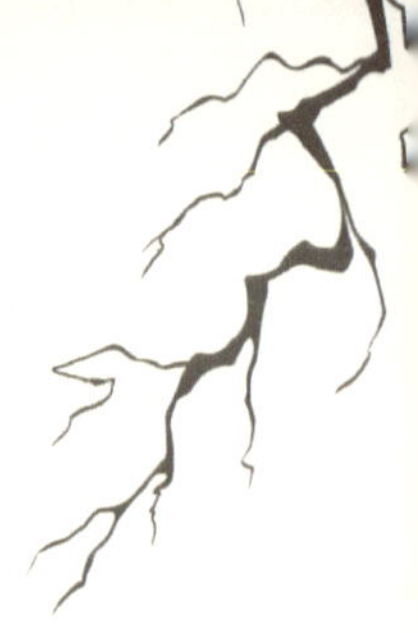

CHAPTER 14

The Axis fleet came at dawn—a slow-moving wall of black metal and crystal, each warship as large as a temple tower. They didn't fire a shot. They didn't need to.

The Temple bells rang once… then fell silent.

Julius stood at the great gates of the temple, his robes immaculate but his hands clenched behind his back. He had called no banners, rallied no guard. The Order's defenses stayed sheathed in their scabbards. Not because the Axis had broken them—but because he'd ordered it.

A thousand black-armored soldiers marched through the streets in perfect formation, their crimson banners unfurling to replace the silver sigils of the Flow. Citizens peered from windows, too afraid to speak. The great bridges of light between the spires dimmed as the Axis took control of the crystal conduits, severing the Temple's independence strand by strand.

Markus rode at the head of the column, helmet under his arm, eyes fixed on the horizon as if the conquest was beneath his notice. Behind him came the "observers"— not scouts, but occupation troops. They took posts at the gates, on the bridges, in the halls where the Order's council once met.

By midday, Elaris belonged to the Axis. The change was total, surgical.

In the central plaza, Markus mounted the steps of the Flowspire and spoke to the gathered citizens, Priests and even the acolytes:
"This is not conquest—this is protection. The Axis and the Order are one now. Together, we will bring justice to the galaxy."

His words were swallowed by the silence of the crowd.

High above, in his private chamber, Julius watched it all through the window. His reflection in the glass looked older, smaller. He told himself it was to protect the Temple. That resisting would bring only fire and blood to the streets.

But in the Crucible below, we knew nothing of this. The darkness hid the sound of boots on stone, the banners being torn down, the quiet surrender that would change everything.

When we emerged, we would no longer be walking into our Temple.

We would be walking into an occupied temple.

Council members stood in robes so heavy they seemed carved from stone, their rings catching the light. Order warriors lined the walls in ceremonial armor and roaring our names then they stop all of the Sunspears crystal ignited and a chants came for us "ou ou ou ou ou". And above, in the balcony shadows, the Axis generals leaned forward. Markus. Julius. Others I didn't know by name, but whose presence made the air feel thinner.

They didn't see us as people.

They saw us as the result of an experiment.

Four weapons fresh from the forge. Naked. Tempered. Ready to be shaped.

Serena stood apart from them.

Her arms were crossed, her tunic plain, but her eyes told another story. She didn't look at us like prey or tools—she looked at us as if she was counting the wounds the Crucible had left that no one else could see.

The doors behind us shut with a heavy hiss, like a blade sliding home.

The sound echoed far too long in the chamber.

We had survived.

But in the way they looked at us, in the way Markus' eyes lingered on Apollo's blade and Julius' gaze swept over all four of us… I knew.

Survival wasn't the end of this.
It was the beginning of something worse.

the blinding gold fading into the dull gray light of the temple hall.
We were standing there—naked—in front of the entire council, and the warriors, and more than a few dignitaries who clearly hadn't been warned about… this much exposure.

No one spoke.
The silence was suffocating.

Then Jaleon glanced down at himself.
Then at us.
Then at the crowd.

"Well," he said slowly, "this is… intimate."

Lux groaned immediately. "Don't start—"

But Jaleon stepped forward like a man taking the stage. "Friends, generals, distinguished perverts… this is a proud day for the Order. Not because we survived the Crucible. Not because we came out stronger, faster, better. No." He spread his arms wide. "Because today, for the first time in history, the Order has paraded four champions into the grand hall… without pants."

I bit my lip hard, trying not to laugh.

"And let me tell you," he continued solemnly, "there's a breeze in here, and it's doing *wonders* for morale."

That was it—I cracked. A laugh burst out of me, sharp and unrestrained.
Lux muttered something under his breath, but his shoulders were shaking.

And then—*miracle of miracles*—Apollo spoke.
"You do realize," he said, voice calm as ever, "you've now given the Council enough material to have you arrested for public indecency."

Jaleon nodded gravely. "Exactly. This is political theater."

Apollo tilted his head. "Your politics are… small."

The room froze.
I blinked.
Lux choked.

Jaleon stared at him for a full two seconds—then broke into a wide, proud grin. "Ladies and gentlemen, he *joked*. Somebody write this day down."

And just like that, we were laughing—all of us, even Apollo, even some of the soldiers at the walls. The tension bled out of the air, the shadows of the Crucible slipping a little further away.

But while we laughed in the lower halls—naked, exhausted, still tasting the strange victory of survival— something was shifting far above us.
Something that had been waiting for this moment.

The Grand Council Chamber of the Temple was not as I remembered it. Once, its walls had been draped in pale silk and lit by the soft pulse of Flow-crystals, the air heavy with incense that whispered of old traditions. Now, the silk was gone, replaced by towering banners of Axis red, their black sigils catching the light like oil on water. The familiar fragrance of the Temple's incense was choked beneath the metallic tang of armor and the faint, oiled scent of war machines.

At the far end, beneath the great mosaic of the Flow's first forging, Julius sat in the high seat. His robes were immaculate, his posture unshaken—but his hands gripped the carved arms of his chair as though he could anchor himself against the storm in the room.

Before him stood General Markus. He did not bow. He did not need to. The man carried the weight of command like a crown, his black-plated cuirass veined with molten crystal, the Axis crest burning on his breast. Behind him, six senior commanders stood shoulder to shoulder, helms tucked beneath their arms, silent and unmoving. The chamber felt smaller with them in it. Smaller, and no longer safe.

"This," Markus began, his voice a low, deliberate hammer, "was a greater success than I dared predict." His eyes swept the room, not to invite agreement, but to make sure none dared to deny it.
"I was certain at least two would fall in the Crucible. But four… four emerged. Alive. Stronger. Tempered. That, Julius, is not chance. That is proof."

Julius's gaze didn't falter, but his words carried the edge of resistance.
"They survived. Yes. And you will have your weapons." But this is a all about the theatrics and the hidden politics the temple was bought and the council with Julius had there purses full of stolen and bloodied coin.

Markus smiled then—not with warmth, but with the satisfaction of a predator watching prey realize it is cornered.
"This is not a democracy anymore. The Axis will prevail. You are our warriors now, Julius. All of you.

And the Temple…" His gaze traveled up the columns, across the sacred carvings older than the Axis itself. "… belongs to us. My soldiers will remain here—to ensure there is no confusion."

The murmur that followed from the other officials was quickly silenced by the glance of one of Markus's commanders. This was no negotiation. This was a declaration.

"They will have their first mission immediately," Markus continued. "Serena will prepare them. They will be placed under the command of a seasoned officer and a battalion. One of our outposts in Tessara has gone silent. The Umber dogs may be behind it—retaliation for Grith. They don't have the strength to face us directly, so they will claw at the edges. Your four will assess the damage."

He stepped closer to Julius's chair, voice lowering until it was almost a whisper—intimate, poisonous.
"And if they find any Umber survivors… leave none alive."

For a moment, the silence was absolute. Not the peaceful kind—the kind before a noose tightens.

Julius's jaw tensed. I could see it even from my place at the chamber's edge. He was the Temple's voice, but here, now, he was speaking under the weight of someone else's will. When his answer came, it was not the voice of the man who had once spoken for the Order.

"…Very well."

Markus's smile was thin, victorious. His officers turned sharply on their heels, boots striking the stone in unison as they left. Their red banners stirred in the draft, as if they could already smell blood in Tessara.

The heavy chamber doors had barely closed behind Markus before Julius sent for Serena.

She came quickly, as she always did—boots striking the polished floor, her green Sunspear resting against her back. But when she stepped inside and saw the Axis banners hanging from the walls and the armed soldiers standing where Temple guards should have been, her pace slowed.

Julius was alone at the table now, though the room still felt poisoned by Markus's presence.

"What's happened?" she asked, her tone tight, wary.

"Close the door," Julius said. When she did, he hesitated—a dangerous thing for a man like him. "The Axis is taking command of your acolytes."

Her eyes narrowed. "Command? For what?"

"Tessara. An outpost we've lost contact with." Julius's voice was flat, mechanical. "They'll go there under Axis authority to assess the situation and eliminate any Umber forces they find."

Serena's grip on the strap of her spear tightened. "Then I'll go with them."

Julius shook his head slowly. "No. That's… part of the arrangement. Markus insisted they go without you. He wants a commander of his choosing in charge."

For the first time, Serena didn't hide the anger in her face. "You're sending them into an Axis operation without me? After the Crucible? Do you have any idea what they've just been through—"

"This isn't a request," Julius cut in sharply, though his voice cracked under the weight of it. "The Temple is no longer neutral. Axis troops will remain here as 'observers'—" he spat the word like poison "—and if you refuse, they'll be reassigned to someone far worse than Markus."

She stepped closer to the table. "They're children, Julius."

"They're weapons now," he said quietly. His eyes didn't meet hers. "And you know as well as I do—weapons don't get to choose where they're aimed."

Silence. The words hung between them like a sentence already passed.

Finally, Serena turned toward the door. At the threshold, she paused, her shoulders rigid. "Tell Markus this," she said without looking back. "If they come back broken, I will put my spear through his heart. Axis or not."

Then she was gone, leaving Julius alone with the knowledge that, this time, he had not just failed the children—he had given them to the wolves.

We were finally back in our quarters.
No darkness. No void. No whispers in the Flow. Just the four of us—flesh, bone, and breath.

Jaleon was sprawled across his cot like a warlord in his throne, arms behind his head, bare feet up on the trunk at the end.
"I'm telling you," he said, "if I had five more minutes in there, I'd have *conquered* the Crucible. Made it beg for mercy."

Lux groaned. "You were crying at one point."

"That was strategy," Jaleon shot back without missing a beat. "Tears confuse the enemy. Makes them think you're weak, and then—" he slapped his palm for effect, "BAM! You hit 'em with the axe."

Even Apollo was smirking in the corner, pretending not to listen.

I just shook my head. "Pretty sure the Crucible doesn't have an enemy to confuse."

Before Jaleon could come up with another masterpiece of self-praise, the door slid open.
Serena stepped inside, her expression unreadable—but her eyes softer than usual. She took a moment to look at each of us, like she was committing our faces to memory.

"You survived," she said simply. "Good."

"That's it?" Jaleon asked, sitting up. "No 'bravo, my little champions'? No feast in our honor?"

Serena's lips twitched, but she didn't bite. "No feast. Not today. You've got work to do."

The room went quiet.

"You're to visit the quartermaster," she continued. "Get fitted for new armor. You'll need it for your first mission."

Lux straightened in his seat. "Mission?"

"Yes. Orders from the council." She didn't elaborate, but I caught the way her gaze lingered on us—especially Apollo—just a second too long. "The quartermaster's expecting you. Don't waste his time."

With that, she left, the door sliding shut behind her.

Jaleon leaned back, grinning. "New armor, eh? Bet mine's gonna have spikes."

I didn't say it out loud, but as we headed toward the armory, the air in the hallways felt… wrong.
It wasn't just the silence—the Temple had always been quiet, but this was a different kind of stillness. A watching stillness.

Axis soldiers lined the walls now, standing like statues in their jagged black armor, helmets sealed, visors reflecting the glow from the crystal veins in the floor. Their presence carved the corridors into narrow lanes of power and submission.

The white stone of the Temple, once bare and clean, now carried shadows from the blood-red Axis banners that draped over balconies and doorways. The silk caught the light, shimmering faintly, each one stitched with the sigil of the double-headed spear.

The glances from the people we passed—servants, younger acolytes, even some of the instructors—were not the same as before. There was no recognition, no warmth. Only careful avoidance, eyes flicking away too quickly, as if to acknowledge us was to draw the wrong kind of attention.

Somewhere deep inside, the Temple's pulse—the faint, steady thrum of the Flow that had always been there—felt thinner, weaker, like a song played in the wrong key.

We were going to get new armor.
But we weren't walking into the same Temple we'd left.

The quartermaster's forge smelled of hot oil, hammered crystal, and leather cured so long it had grown a kind of dignity. The air shimmered with heat from the great braziers set into the walls, their orange glow catching on racks of half-forged weapons and plates of armor that hung like the shed skins of some great metal beast.

Every clang of hammer on crystal rang through the chamber, sharp and pure, as if the weapons themselves were singing in their sleep.

Jaleon got there first—of course he did—striding in like he owned the place and planting both hands on the counter with a grin that could sell bad wine to a sober man. "Alright, old man," he said, puffing his chest out, "give me something that makes me look dangerous."

The quartermaster, a wiry fellow with skin weathered like old parchment and eyes like a fox peering from a den, looked him up and down. His gaze lingered on Jaleon's broad shoulders, the faint scars peeking above his collar, and the easy arrogance in his stance. "You already look dangerous," the old man said dryly, setting down the crystal rod he'd been polishing. "I'll give you something that makes you look competent."

The room erupted—Lux snorted, I choked on my own laugh, and even Apollo's mouth twitched like he was fighting to keep it in.

Jaleon clutched his chest in mock injury, staggering back a step. "Competent? Old man, I'll have you know I'm a *legend* in the making. The bards will sing of me."

"Mm," the quartermaster muttered, reaching under the counter, "if they survive hearing you talk that long."

The quartermaster waved Jaleon aside with all the ceremony of brushing crumbs off a table.

"Next."

Lux stepped forward, every inch the nobleman—back straight, chin lifted just enough to suggest he had somewhere far more important to be. He placed his crystal on the counter like it was a priceless relic, not the battered weapon it truly was.

"I'll require something *functional*," Lux said, "but also dignified. Nothing gaudy. And absolutely no orange. I'm not trying to look like a festival lantern."

"Dignified," the quartermaster repeated, as though tasting the word and finding it faintly ridiculous. "You're here to fight, boy, not host a banquet."

Lux adjusted his cuffs—even in training robes, the man found something to fuss with—and gave a thin smile. "One can do both."

Jaleon barked a laugh from the side. "Oh, sure. Maybe the Umber warlords will be too busy admiring your fancy new armor to stab you in the face."

Lux didn't even look at him. "I'd rather be stabbed looking like a prince than live looking like *you*."

That got another round of laughter from the rest of us, though Jaleon muttered something about "royal twigs" under his breath. The quartermaster rolled his eyes, then ducked into the back, muttering about "damn peacocks" as he went to find whatever "functional dignity" looked like.

When Lux stepped aside, I moved up to the counter, trying not to grin too wide.

"Alright," I said, "I want something fast. Light. Something that says 'I'm already behind you before you even knew I was here.'"

The quartermaster gave me a slow look, the kind that measured more than just my height. "Fast, huh? Then you don't want armor. You want to be naked."

From the corner, Jaleon nearly choked on his own laugh. "Oh, please, *please* take that deal. The Umber will surrender instantly."

I shot him a look sharp enough to cut crystal. "Careful, or I'll make *you* surrender instantly."

Lux, ever the instigator, smirked. "Don't worry, Jaleon. She'll need a running start."

"Alright, children," the quartermaster cut in, pulling out a sleek set of violet-trimmed plates. The metal was thin but strong, each piece edged with crystal lines that caught the forge light like liquid starlight. "Fast enough for you?"

I ran a hand over the smooth surface, feeling the Flow hum faintly beneath. "Yeah," I said softly. "Fast enough."

Then it was Apollo's turn.

He stepped forward without a word, the laughter from before fading around him like it knew it had no place here. The quartermaster's sharp eyes softened, almost imperceptibly, as he studied him.

"What do you want?" the old man asked.

Apollo didn't answer right away. His gaze roamed the racks—not greedily, not like Jaleon's bravado or Lux's pride—but as if he were listening to something only he could hear. Finally, he said, "Something that doesn't get in the way."

It was a simple request, but the way he said it… it sounded like he meant more than armor.

The quartermaster reached under the counter and brought out a set unlike the others. Deep green plates, uneven in their crystal veins, as though they'd been grown rather than forged. They caught the forge light differently—not with a gleam, but with a quiet depth, like a forest at dusk.

Apollo touched the breastplate, and for the briefest moment, the uneven veins pulsed. The green deepened, streaks of gold glimmering in its heart.

And that was when I saw him—truly saw him. Not the quiet boy. Not the survivor of the Crucible. But something else entirely. His eyes, catching the forge light, seemed too old for his face, too certain for fifteen. In that second, it wasn't armor being fitted to a boy… it was the boy claiming something that had always been his.

When the quartermaster began to fasten the plates, Apollo simply nodded. No smile, no joke, no show. But the room felt smaller around him.

The quartermaster cinched the last strap, and Apollo stepped back from the counter.
For a moment, no one said a thing. Lux adjusted his new gauntlet like he had somewhere else to look. I was still watching him—not the armor, but the way it seemed to fit him too well, like it had been waiting for him.

Then, predictably, Jaleon couldn't help himself. "Well," he said, grinning wide, "looks good, little guy. Shame they didn't have it in your size."

A ripple of laughter passed through the room—even mine—though it came out softer than I expected. Apollo didn't rise to it. He didn't even glance Jaleon's way. Just shifted his weight, rolled his shoulders in the armor, and murmured, "It fits well enough."

Something about the way he said it made Jaleon's grin falter—just a touch—before he barked another laugh to cover it. The forge's heat pressed in again, the moment of humor melting into the heavy, restless air.

The smell of hot crystal and oiled leather still clung to my hands when the door to the quartermaster's forge slammed open.
A soldier stepped in—not one of ours. Axis black plate, polished to a mirror sheen, visor shaped like a predator's snout. His voice came through the helm like gravel dragged over steel.
"You four. With me. Now."

The warmth of the forge seemed to drain away as we followed him into the corridors.
I'd walked these halls my whole life—but now, they felt like someone else's home. The bright banners of the Order, once hung like sunlight caught in cloth,

were gone. In their place, Axis colors: red like blood, black like scorched stone. Soldiers lined the walls shoulder to shoulder, spears grounded, eyes unreadable. Even the air felt different—thicker, heavier, as if the Temple itself had forgotten how to breathe.

We came out into the Court.
The same Court where Serena had beaten us into the dirt on our first day.
But it wasn't ours anymore.

Axis pennants draped from the obsidian towers, their silk snapping in the wind. The training sand was gone, replaced by ranks of soldiers standing in perfect formation. In the center of it all, like the eye of a storm, was a man I didn't know but could not mistake for anything other than a commander. His armor was plated in black and gold, his shoulders marked with the insignia of an officer whose word moved armies. This, I learned quickly, was Axel—our new commander.

And behind him…
A battalion, all on one knee, heads bowed to us.
To us.

At the far end of the Court stood General Markus, his hands clasped neatly behind his back, expression carved from something colder than stone. His gaze swept over us like a craftsman inspecting tools.

"Heroes," he called us, and the word rang too sharp, like it had been hammered into the air by force.

He began the briefing—voice deep, steady, and far too pleased.
"Our mission is simple. You will accompany Commander Axel and his men to the outpost at Tessara. We have lost contact. I believe the Umber rats have struck back—not openly, they lack the strength—but through sabotage and infiltration. You will assess the damage. And if you find any trace of them…"
His eyes hardened, and the soldiers around him seemed to lean forward as one.
"Leave. None. Alive."

Beside him, Julius stood rigid, not meeting our eyes. A man trapped between duty and something else.
And by his side… Serena.

Not in her training tunic.
But in full formal armor, the deep green plates polished. She looked every inch the warrior who had first terrified me—and yet her eyes, when they found mine, were something else entirely. Something softer, edged in guilt.

I felt my jaw tighten. The Court smelled of oil, dust, and the faint copper tang of old blood. The banners overhead snapped in the wind.

And though Markus's voice kept speaking, laying out orders and consequences, I could feel the shift inside me.

The Temple was no longer the Order's.
And we… were no longer free.

Markus's voice rolled on, a drumbeat of orders and victory talk. But I wasn't listening anymore.
I was watching Serena.

She stood perfectly still beside Julius, shoulders squared, chin lifted—every inch the dutiful soldier she was supposed to be. The green of her armor caught the torchlight in glints that reminded me of sun through forest leaves. To anyone else, she was a statue of discipline.

But I knew her.
I'd seen her laugh, curse, bleed, break. I'd seen the way she hugged us before the Crucible, like she was holding on for the last time.

Now, she wouldn't move her lips, wouldn't risk a sound—but her eyes… her eyes spoke.
A warning.
A plea.

They flicked to Markus, to Julius, to Axel, then back to me. As if she was telling me to remember who was giving the orders now.
As if she was telling me to be careful.

I swallowed hard and gave the faintest nod, hoping she'd see it.

The moment shattered when Markus barked, "Arm yourselves and prepare to depart!"
The soldiers around us straightened like blades being drawn. The sound of boots on stone filled the Court.

When I looked for her again, she had already turned away, her face once more the perfect mask of an officer loyal to the Axis.

We were led from the Court with Commander Axel at our head, his black-and-gold armor gleaming like the edge of a guillotine.
The gates of the Temple closed behind us, and I realized—maybe for the first time—that we might never come back the same way we'd left.

The Court's echo still clung to us when the Axis soldier at Markus's side barked, "Move!"

We fell into step behind Commander Axel, his black-and-gold armor clicking with every stride. The man walked like he owned the stone beneath his boots, and I suppose, in a way, he did now.

The gates loomed ahead, high and carved with the old sigils of the Order—once a promise of unity, now half-draped with Axis banners. The red cloth swayed in the wind, covering history with conquest.

The hallways had changed since we'd gone into the Crucible. Axis soldiers lined the walls in rigid formation, their armor swallowing the Temple's white light into a dull, merciless gleam. Some stared straight ahead, others let their gaze slide over us, measuring, judging.

Jaleon caught one staring too long and grinned.
"What? Never seen perfection before?"
The soldier didn't flinch.
"Perfect target, maybe," he muttered back.

Lux snorted. "You're really going to insult armed men in full armor while you're still polishing your own?"

"I'm just giving them a preview," Jaleon shot back. "This way, when they see me fight, they'll know it wasn't a fluke."

I shook my head but couldn't help the corner of my mouth twitching. For a moment, it almost felt like we were back in the mess hall, not marching into whatever this was.

Apollo said nothing, his steps quiet, measured. I noticed his hands flexing once, twice, like he was testing the weight of the air itself. His eyes stayed forward—but not on Axel. Not on Markus. On the gates. Always on the gates.

The hum of the transport ship was constant—low, steady, like a giant heartbeat in the walls. Our quarters were barely more than a metal box bolted into the hull: four bunks, no windows, a single flickering light that made everything look tired.

Jaleon flopped onto the lower bunk with all the grace of a falling boulder.
"Well, I gotta say," he sighed, folding his arms behind his head, "for people calling us 'heroes,' they really know how to give us the royal treatment."

Lux, sitting on the opposite bunk, arched a brow. "Royal treatment? You're in a room with me. That's the closest you'll ever get to royalty."

Jaleon grinned. "Yeah? Well, remind me to ask the Umber assassins if they're impressed before they stab you in the face."

"Not if I stab them first," Lux shot back, but the corner of his mouth was curling.

I sat cross-legged on my bunk, polishing my Sunspear crystal out of habit. The hum of the ship made my bones itch. "You two gonna spend the entire trip measuring egos, or should we maybe talk about the mission?"

"That's easy," Jaleon said, waving a hand. "We get there, smash some skulls, look amazing, and go home. Preferably in time for dinner."

"Right," Lux said dryly. "Because outposts go silent for friendly reasons."

Jaleon pointed at him. "That's the spirit. Keep thinking positive."

I glanced at Apollo. He hadn't moved since we'd come in. He sat on the edge of his bunk, elbows on his knees, staring at the floor like it might tell him a secret.

"You're quiet," I said.

He looked up, and for a moment, I almost wished I hadn't asked. There was no anger in his eyes—no fire—just a stillness so deep it felt like the hum of the ship stopped for it.

"Thinking," he said simply.

"About?" Jaleon leaned forward, chin in his hands like a gossiping child.

Apollo didn't smile. "What's waiting for us in Tessara. And what's waiting for us after."

Lux tilted his head. "You mean Markus?"

"No," Apollo said, gaze dropping again. "Worse."

The room went quiet. Even Jaleon didn't have a comeback. The hum of the ship filled the space between us again, louder than before.

After a moment, Jaleon sat back and forced a grin. "Well… if it's worse than Markus, I'm definitely bringing my bigger axe."

I chuckled despite myself. Lux rolled his eyes. And Apollo… Apollo just kept looking at the floor, as if he could already see Tessara burning.

And in that moment, I remembered the Crucible—
the way the shadows had bent toward him, the way
something had *looked back* when he stared into the abyss.

And I wondered if maybe he was still there.

"What is given is sweet.
What is taken is heavy.
What is born is dangerous." Umber Poet

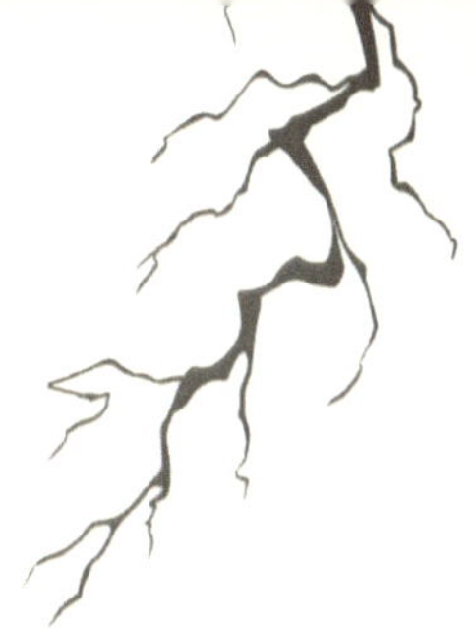

CHAPTER 15

The ship's engines hummed in that low, steady way that could either lull you to sleep or drive you insane. The quarters were dark except for the faint red glow of the emergency strips along the floor. We'd all claimed a bunk, the air heavy with that mix of oil, metal, and stale recycled air that never quite leaves a transport.

Lux was already half-asleep, his breathing slow and measured. Apollo sat on the edge of his bunk, still in that same motionless posture, like he wasn't entirely here with us. Jaleon had tossed himself onto his mattress with his arms behind his head, staring at the ceiling like it owed him answers.

"Ehmm… guys," Jaleon said suddenly, his voice breaking the quiet.

Lux groaned. "If you're hungry again, I swear—"

"No, no," Jaleon said, holding up a hand as if Lux could see it in the dark. "Important question."

Lux cracked an eye open. "You have *important* questions?"

"Yeah," Jaleon said, sitting up, his messy hair casting long shadows across the wall. "Where exactly is Tessara? And also… what kind of planet is it? 'Cause I've never been there."

Apollo looked at him like he'd just asked where the sun was. Lux had the same expression—equal parts confusion and disbelief.

I sighed, rolling onto my side so I could see them. "Alright, I'll bite. I've been there. Went with the Order when I was younger."

Jaleon leaned forward like a kid hearing a campfire story. "And?"

"Tessara…" I began, my voice softening as the memories surfaced. "The Green Flame. They call it that because the heart of the planet glows emerald at night—the Flow there runs pure and bright, and in the right season, you can see it under the soil. It's the reason the place became the center of agricultural innovation. For centuries, Tessara fed the Ten Flames. Wheat taller than your shoulders, orchards that stretch further than you can ride in a day, rivers that glitter like liquid glass.

When the wind blows through the valley fields, it's like watching a green ocean in motion."

Jaleon whistled low. "So… we're going to farm-world? What's the big deal, then? Worst case, we get in a fight with some angry cabbage."

Lux smirked. "If it's so peaceful, then why did the Axis lose contact?"

My words caught for a moment. "Because Tessara's more than farmland. The planet's mostly open plains, but it's ringed with thick greenstone ridges—full of deep valleys and caves. Perfect places for someone to disappear… or for an army to hide."

Jaleon grinned in the dark. "Alright, so angry cabbage *and* caves. Sounds like a party."

I shook my head. "It's not a joke, Jaleon. If the Umber took Tessara outposts, they didn't do it head-on. They're there for a reason—and they'll fight to keep it."

Apollo hadn't said a word the whole time. He just sat there, elbows on his knees, staring at the floor like he could already see the planet in his mind. When the silence stretched too long, Jaleon tried to lighten it.

"You know," he said, "I was expecting a mission with a bit more… excitement. Giant monsters, exploding cities, Serena yelling at us. But no—we're going to go weed someone's garden."

Lux rolled over with a groan. "Go to sleep, Jaleon."

I settled back into my bunk, but even as my eyes closed, I could feel the heaviness in the air. Tessara might be beautiful. But something was waiting there—and if the Axis wanted *us* to deal with it, it wasn't going to be angry cabbage.

The night was deep, and through the narrow porthole above my bunk, the galaxy stretched forever—a thousand pale fires scattered on a sea of black. Somewhere out there were worlds burning, others blooming, and we were just a small dot between them. The hum of the ship wrapped around me like a lullaby, and for a while, I slept.

Apollo lay in bed, waiting. He knew what was coming. The shadows always came. They did not pounce—they crept, slow and patient, until sleep delivered him back into their arms. This time, he did not resist. He let them take him.

Darkness. Then flashes.

Red. Blinding red, streaking like torn veins across the void. The sounds of Flow colliding echoed like war-drums—deafening, endless. Trees split and toppled in silence, their falling muted by some unseen hand. Shattered Axis banners drifted through the abyss, weightless, dissolving as though the memory of war itself was unraveling.

Then silence. The silence of a graveyard.

Apollo floated in the void, his body lost, no horizon to ground him. His breath left him in ragged clouds, yet even that sound was consumed—eaten by the dark. He tried to speak, his voice barely a whisper: "What do you want from me?"

But nothing came. His words did not echo. They were stolen, dissolved, as if the void itself hungered for sound.

Then it came.

The shadow. A mass so vast it was less a figure and more a wound cut into existence. Its edges bled into infinity, its size beyond measure. The mere thought of its shape made Apollo's chest tighten, like something in him wasn't meant to comprehend it. The void pressed heavier, bending him toward it, and he reached instinctively for his crystal.

Dead. Cold. Lifeless in his palm.

His heart seized. Here, in this abyss, the Flow was gone. The only thing that answered him was his own trembling fear. But as he shut his eyes and pressed deeper into himself, something shifted. Emotion. Raw, festering emotion. Rage. Not his own, not entirely. The shadow's.

It poured over him, suffocating, unbound. Rage like the sun collapsing. Rage so pure it stripped him bare. His chest heaved, his body shaking as if the emotion itself was clawing inside him.

And then—behind it.

In the distance, blurred, flickering like a dying star, he saw something else. A figure. Tall. Unmoving. Its outline rippled, indistinct, yet in its hand it held a sword. Not black. Not green. Gold. A blade of justice, radiant against the abyss. For a fleeting breath, Apollo felt warmth. Hope.

But the rage twisted. Corrupted. The golden blade blackened, bleeding from hilt to tip. Its brilliance drowned in shadow until only jagged darkness remained, thrumming with malice.

The figure blurred again—and was gone.

Apollo's pulse thundered in his ears. His teeth clenched. His chest burned.

And then he woke.

CHAPTER 16

Morning—if you could call it that in the void—came with the soft hiss of the cabin lights warming to life. I was the last to stir.

Apollo was already up, standing by his bunk with the same deliberate movements as always, fastening the straps of his armor. The pale light caught the edges of his green crystal, making it flicker faintly as if it were aware. Lux was ready too, of course—his uniform immaculate, his hair perfectly in place, that noble posture making him look like he was preparing to address a court rather than step into the unknown.

And then there was Jaleon.

He wasn't in the quarters at all. A muffled clatter came from down the hall, followed by the unmistakable smell of fresh-baked something.

When he returned, he was in full uniform… except for the bulging pockets and the crumbs dusting his chestplate. A croissant hung from his mouth like a cigar.

He caught me looking.

"You want one?" he mumbled through a mouthful, holding another pastry out to me like it was a peace offering from a guilty child.

I took it—warm, buttery, flaking in my hands—and shook my head. "You know, there's this thing called discipline."

"Yeah," Jaleon said, swallowing. "I'm disciplined enough to never start a mission on an empty stomach."

Lux rolled his eyes but couldn't hide a smirk. Apollo didn't say anything, but I saw the faintest twitch at the corner of his mouth.

We traded a few more jokes—Jaleon declaring himself the "Official Morale Officer" of the team and threatening to duel anyone who refused breakfast—before the commander's voice cut through the intercom.

"Prepare for landing."

The mood shifted just slightly—not enough to break the joking outright, but enough to make the silence between words feel heavier. It was like a ripple disturbing still water; you couldn't see the cause, but you knew something beneath the surface had moved.

We fell into formation without needing to be told, muscle memory taking over. Buckles clicked into place, the soft rasp of leather straps tightening across armor filled the cabin. Lux adjusted the angle of his crystal blade in its clasp as if even a fraction off would insult the weapon. Apollo's hands moved slower, more deliberate, each strap tested twice. I checked my own gear, feeling the subtle vibration of the ship's hull beneath my palms as the engines shifted pitch.

The low hum deepened into a resonant growl, and the floor tilted ever so slightly. We were descending.

Out the narrow window, the infinite scatter of stars began to melt away, swallowed by a swelling, luminous green. At first it was only a haze, like light caught in mist, but as we fell lower it grew sharper—the curve of Tessara filling our view.

She was beautiful. Vast continents draped in emerald forests, rivers gleaming like veins of silver, clouds spilling lazy shadows across fields so wide they seemed without end. But there was something strange about the light—richer than sunlight, warmer than firelight—as though the world itself breathed Flow into the air.

Jaleon leaned over, his shoulder bumping mine. Another croissant—where he kept finding them, I had no idea—was wedged between his fingers.

"Last chance," he said, voice low but still carrying that unshakable grin. "Planet's probably full of killer lettuce."

Lux groaned softly from across the cabin, muttering something about agricultural worlds not being warzones. Apollo didn't react, but his gaze didn't leave the window.

I almost laughed. Almost.

Instead, I kept my eyes fixed on that green glow—the endless forests, the strange warmth in the light. Tessara was beautiful, yes. But beauty like that always hid something sharp underneath.

We were here for a reason. And reasons like this never came without blood.

The landing was smoother than I expected—too smooth.
I'd felt this once before, in Kaith: that uneasy stillness just before you step into a place that has already decided to swallow you. But this time, Apollo was beside me. Somehow, that steadied me.

The cockpit doors hissed open, and Tessara's light spilled in.

It wasn't sunlight. It was warmer, thicker, as if the air itself carried the heartbeat of the Green Flame. A vast, living forest stretched in every direction, the green so deep it almost shimmered, swallowing the horizon. The scent of wet earth and blooming flowers hit first, intoxicating in its richness, almost enough to mask the unease coiling in my chest. Almost.

We descended the ramp in full formation. Boots sank into soft moss that clung to each step like it wanted to hold us there. Shafts of emerald light cut through the canopy, painting our armor in fractured patterns. Even the air felt alive—each breath tasting of sap and pollen, heavy in the lungs.

The commander gave a sharp hand signal, and we began moving.
The forest closed around us like the walls of a cathedral, the canopy so thick that even the ship vanished behind a curtain of leaves. The sound of our movement—boots on roots, the faint creak of leather—was the only thing breaking the hush.

And then the air changed.

It was so subtle at first, just a faint note beneath the green scents. Metallic. Rotten.
The warmth of Tessara's light seemed to fade as we went deeper, swallowed by something colder, older.

Then it hit in full—the stench of blood and dead meat. It wasn't just smell. It clung to the back of the throat, coated the tongue, made each breath taste of copper and decay.

The first body appeared slumped against the trunk of a great silver birch tree—or what was left of it. Half a torso, armor shattered, the crystal at its core dark and cracked this was a warrior probably from Elaris. The moss beneath it was black with dried blood.

Then another. And another.

The deeper we went, the more there were. Axis soldiers—dozens at first, then scores. Some impaled clean through on long, jagged stakes of crystal jutting from the earth like the bones of the forest itself. Others torn apart, limbs scattered like discarded tools.

Formation! the commander barked, his voice snapping through the green gloom like a whip.

Lux's gag came first—sharp, wet, and then he was doubled over, vomiting into the roots. Jaleon's grin was gone, replaced by a grim set to his jaw, his knuckles white around the haft of his weapon.

We passed a fallen standard—the black and red of the Axis—its sigil soaked and dark with old blood. Around it, the ground was littered with hands, legs, and severed heads, the faces frozen mid-scream.

There was no pattern to the dead. No neat line of battle. It was chaos—a massacre—the kind you don't come back from.

And yet, as we moved deeper, I noticed something worse: not all of the armor belonged to soldiers. Some were scouts. Some… were civilians. Their bodies lay among the military dead, stripped of weapons but still bearing the marks of execution.

The commander said nothing after that. None of us did. But I saw the way Apollo's eyes moved over each corpse—not fast, not lingering, but with that steady, cold awareness that said he was counting them.

We kept moving, leaving the dead behind us. But I could feel them following in silence, a warning left to rot in the green heart of Tessara.

The forest had been suffocating us for hours, but now every step felt heavier, slower.
The smell of death was still in my nose, in my mouth, in my lungs. My fingers twitched around my weapon, but they weren't steady. I told myself to breathe, to

focus—but this wasn't training anymore. This wasn't sparring under Serena's watchful eye.

This was war.
No, worse—this was slaughter waiting for us to join it.

I turned my head, my voice low so the commander wouldn't hear.
"Hey, Lux… how are you holding up?"

He looked pale, but he still managed a smirk, tilting his head with that noble arrogance that never quite left him. "Even now," he started, "I look better than Jale—"

The rest of the word never came.

It happened too fast for my mind to keep up. A flicker of movement. A thin streak of red slicing the air. The sound—like glass breaking underwater.

Then impact.

The dagger hit dead center, right through the polished crest of his chestplate. The force staggered him back into me, and then—warmth. Thick, hot, metallic. My violet hair clung wet against my face, soaked in his blood before I could even scream.

The blade was gone a heartbeat later, yanked back the way it came as if the air itself had returned it to its master.

And then I heard it—the voice.
Not a shout, not a battle cry. Just one word, dripping with finality:

"Death."

The trees shifted. Shadows peeled away from the trunks. Shapes stepped forward, dozens of them, their eyes catching the green light like embers in ash. The Umber warriors moved as one, their weapons black-flamed and humming with the Flow's darker edge.

And in the center, he stood—the Red Wielder.
His armor was scarred and jagged, his helm crowned with streaks of crimson crystal. His Sunspear burned the color of fresh blood, and when he lifted it, he didn't need to shout.

The signal was clear.
Attack.

I dropped to my knees beside Lux, my hands pressing hard over the wound, feeling the blood seep hot between my fingers. His eyes were glassy already, his breaths shallow.

"Mama…" he whispered. His voice cracked. "…please… I'm sorry."

Something in me broke at that, but before I could speak, the forest erupted.

Jaleon roared like an animal, his axe flaring with a blinding burst of orange Flow. He didn't wait for orders, didn't care about the numbers. He charged headlong into them, swinging like a man possessed, each strike shaking the ground.

The Umber line tightened, and the air filled with the clash of crystal on crystal, the smell of ozone, and the scream of the dying.

Jaleon didn't hesitate.
He didn't even breathe before charging, his axe igniting with a violent orange blaze that lit the canopy above us like wildfire. His roar split the forest, and then he was among them—hacking, cleaving, cutting Umber soldiers down as if they were made of paper.

But it wasn't mindless rage. Not this time.
Every swing had precision, every step was calculated. He moved with the confidence of a predator who knows the kill is his—axe high, then low, twisting with his shoulders, momentum rolling through him like the tide.

Blood—red, black, and something stranger—spattered the green ferns in his wake.

For a moment, it almost looked like pride made flesh.

I turned—expecting Apollo to be beside him—but he wasn't.

Apollo stood still, his hands loose at his sides, his eyes locked on Lux's crumpled form. His face was unreadable, but I could feel something deep beneath the calm—a pressure, a heat, as if he were staring at a memory only he could see.

The forest screamed around him, and he didn't move.

I couldn't stop shaking. My hands were still on Lux's wound, but my tears blurred everything. I could barely see through them—until movement in front of me snapped everything into sharp focus.

Our commander.
Axel had been rallying what was left of the formation, barking orders over the chaos. Then a shadow swept past me—too fast to register—and the world seemed to slow.

A streak of red carved the air.

And just like that, his head was gone.

One moment, Axel's voice was rising above the din; the next, his body stumbled forward, blood spraying in a dark arc across the grass before collapsing in a heap. His helm rolled once, twice, before resting against a root, visor staring at nothing.

I froze. My breath caught in my throat. The sound in my ears was just a dull, empty hum.

The Umber line surged forward.
The Red Wielder's spear gleamed in the chaos, dripping crimson that wasn't his own.

Somewhere to my right, Jaleon roared again, carving a path straight toward him.

Jaleon saw the Red Wielder.
And in that instant, there was nothing else.

The battlefield blurred away—the screaming, the smoke, the stench of blood—all of it drowned beneath the pull of the Flow surging between them. It rippled through the ground, through the air, through the space between their eyes—two warriors bound in the same current, but crashing toward each other like rival tides.

Jaleon lowered his stance, his double axe blazing with orange light so bright it bled into the edges of the world. His aura roared outward, the Flow pouring through him in raw, molten waves, the kind that didn't hum or sing but *bellowed*. He charged, and every footstep cracked the earth beneath him.

The first swing was meant to kill. A perfect arc, the Flow concentrated along the edge like a compressed sun. But the Red Wielder slipped aside, the currents bending around him unnaturally. The Flow didn't flare for him—it *coiled*, as if the very air feared touching him. In his hand was no spear or heavy blade, but a crimson dagger, the kind of weapon meant for killing up close, where the Flow could slip inside your ribs and stop your heart.

"So…" his voice cut through the noise, deep and even. "Now they send *child giants* to fight their war? Begone, boy… or perish."

Jaleon didn't answer. His aura flared brighter, and the Flow bucked like a living thing. Every swing of his axe tore through Umber soldiers like dry twigs, scattering sparks of orange light with every impact. He was a force of nature, his Flow pouring freely, feeding on his pride.

The Red Wielder moved differently—never fighting the Flow, but *riding* it, stepping where currents eddied, striking where resistance was weakest. The dagger slashed upward, trailing red light like liquid flame, grazing Jaleon's ribs with a line of heat.

"You fight with arrogance, boy," the Red Wielder said, his words calm but sharpened with contempt.

Jaleon's reply was not words at first—it was a sound torn from deep within him, a primal roar that shook the Flow itself.
The air rippled, and the orange blaze of his aura surged higher, flaring so violently that the ground beneath his boots cracked and spat molten shards. The Flow lashed outward in all directions, wild and unrestrained, like a storm tide breaking its banks.

His axe became a living sun in his hands.
He brought it down in a cleaving arc—sparks bursting on impact with the Red Wielder's dagger—then reversed, sweeping across with the weight of a mountain. He spun with the momentum, the head of the axe screaming through the air, then brought it up again in a brutal uppercut strike meant to split the man in half.

The Flow *answered* his rage, forming a halo of molten arcs around him—heat shimmering in the air, dust and ash lifting as though gravity itself bent before his will. For a moment, he wasn't just a warrior—he was a furnace, a beacon of raw force made flesh.

And then... came the opening.

The Red Wielder slipped into it like water into a crack. His movement was a blur—no wasted effort, no grand flourish—just lethal precision. The dagger in his hand seemed to *drink* the Flow around its edge, stealing the orange light until it shimmered with a hungry, blood-red glow.

The strike was small. Clean. Precise.
It cut deep into Jaleon's arm—and the sound was more than the wet crunch of bone breaking. It was the *Flow snapping*—the invisible channel between weapon and wielder jolting, sputtering like a candle in a gale.

The axe dipped. The orange aura faltered, its once-blazing arcs collapsing inward.

But Jaleon did not step back.
One-handed now, the muscles in his neck and jaw straining, his arm bleeding freely, he lifted the axe again. The Flow around him was no longer smooth or radiant—it was jagged, savage, whipping in violent

surges as if it wanted to tear the world apart just to match his fury.

The Red Wielder moved through it untouched. His dagger darted in and out of the chaos, always finding the smallest gaps in the current, sliding past the wild surges as if the Flow itself bent to his will.

Then, with the precision of a butcher choosing his cut, he swept low. The dagger moved like it had always been meant for this one motion, and the Flow around it *tightened*, guiding the blade as if the world itself wanted to see it land.

It slashed cleanly across both of Jaleon's knees.

The giant fell. His knees hit the earth with a heavy, final sound, his axe slipping from his fingers to crash into the dirt. The aura that had once blazed like a miniature sun now guttered, flickering like the last embers of a fire.

The Red Wielder stepped forward, slow and unhurried. Each step seemed to pull the Flow toward him, shadows bending in his direction, the air growing colder with his presence. He stopped just close enough that Jaleon could see the reflection of his own battered face in the crimson blade.

Jaleon's breath came ragged, each inhale scraping like gravel in his throat. Sweat and blood stung his eyes, but through the haze he stared up at the Red Wielder.

The dagger hovered inches from his neck, close enough that he could feel the cold Flow it radiated—that suffocating, merciless stillness.

And then… he smiled.

A broken, blood-slicked grin.

"You said I fight with arrogance, boy?" he rasped, his voice rough but steady.

He spat a glob of blood into the dirt. "Is that supposed to be an insult?"

The Red Wielder tilted his head ever so slightly, as if waiting.

"That's not arrogance," Jaleon said, his grin widening through the pain. "That's *pride*. Pride in the warrior I am. Pride in the fact that even now—with my knees cut, my arm useless, and your pretty little blade at my throat—I'm still here, staring you dead in the eyes."

He leaned forward just enough that the tip of the dagger pressed into his skin, a single bead of blood welling up.

"I will be the greatest warrior who ever lived. And if you kill me now, you'll *never* be more than the man who couldn't stop me until I was broken."

The words hung heavy, vibrating through the Flow itself—defiance made manifest.

The Red Wielder's gaze hardened. No amusement now. No smugness. Only the tightening of his grip, the subtle twist of his wrist as the Flow coiled around the dagger like a snake ready to strike.

I looked at Apollo through the blur of tears. Lux's blood was hot in my hands, soaking into my robes, his breaths short and shallow—each one sounding like it might be his last.
Beside us, Jaleon was on his knees, his once-mighty aura flickering like a candle about to die.

My voice broke when I said it.
"Please… do something. Our friends are dying."

Apollo's head turned slowly, his gaze falling first on Lux—pale, trembling, and fading—then on Jaleon, broken but still staring up at the Red Wielder with that stubborn fire in his eyes.

Something in the air shifted.
The Flow itself *tilted.*

Then it came.
A surge of power so massive it drowned out every heartbeat, every scream, every clang of steel. It was not smooth. It was not perfect. It was *uneven*, fractured—but it was alive. Alive in a way that made the very ground tremble.

The shattered green blade in Apollo's hand erupted in light, jagged and unbalanced, each flare cutting the shadows around him into wild shapes.

One moment, he was standing beside us.
The next, he was in front of Jaleon—moving so fast the air cracked in his wake.

The Red Wielder's dagger descended—and Apollo's blade intercepted it with a *ring* so sharp it froze the battlefield for an instant. Sparks of green and red Flow erupted from the clash, streaking out like shooting stars.

The dagger was knocked away from Jaleon's throat. The Red Wielder staggered back, surprised but silent.

Apollo knelt for just a moment, his eyes meeting Jaleon's.
"You've made me proud," he said, his voice low and steady despite the chaos. "I'm sorry I was too late."

Then he stood—and charged.

The ground *shuddered* under the force of his first step, the Flow around him tearing into jagged streams that trailed his movement. The green blaze of his shattered blade flared unevenly, like a storm barely contained, while the dagger in the Red Wielder's hand glowed a deep, blood-tinged crimson, its edge whispering with lethal intent.

Green against red.
Dagger against sword.

The first clash rang out like a crack of lightning, the sound carrying far beyond the circle of their fight. The second was heavier, a rolling *boom* that rippled through the soil and bent the grass flat around them. The third was faster—too fast to follow—and left a flashburn of green and red streaking in the air between them.

Every strike was a storm in itself. Apollo's blade was uneven, fractured in shape, yet every swing carried the force of an avalanche. The green light deepened with each blow until it didn't just illuminate the air—it seemed to burn *holes* into it, leaving afterimages like ghosts of his fury.

The Red Wielder's movements were sharp, precise, and merciless—the dagger drinking in the Flow with every parry, its edge always seeking a gap in Apollo's guard. But Apollo wasn't just defending, and he wasn't just attacking. He was *pressing*, step by step, forcing the red light backward.

Each time their weapons met, the impact wasn't just heard—it was *felt*. A deep, bone-vibrating shock that traveled through the earth, making even the most hardened warriors falter in their footing. The Flow rippled in visible waves, bending like water struck by boulders.

Around them, the battle began to slow. Umber and Axis soldiers alike turned from their fights, drawn in as though gravity itself had shifted toward this duel.

Sunspears dimmed. Voices fell silent. Even the dying seemed to hold their breath.

Red clashed with green again and again. Sparks—not just of steel, but of pure Flow—cascaded around them, falling like rain that hissed and vanished before it touched the ground.

The air between them grew heavier with every heartbeat, not just with power, but with meaning. This was no mere contest of blades.

It was the meeting of two fates—one written in blood, the other in fire—and whichever broke first would shape the course of everything that came after.

Apollo's strikes began to change.
At first, I thought it was exhaustion, the falter of a man pushed beyond his flesh. But then—no. It was something else.

He stopped. Drew back. For a heartbeat he stood still, crystal in hand, shoulders trembling as if the weapon itself resisted his grip. And then I saw it.

It was not one shadow that held his blade—but two. His silhouette seemed split, layered in impossible shapes, as though something greater pressed through him. The green flame that always burned jagged and wild upon his crystal began to shift, streaked now with flecks of gold. Not bright, not pure—but fractured, like sunlight bleeding through a storm.

And then we felt it.

The air turned violent. The Flow itself shuddered, as though recoiling from what it had birthed. Rage poured from Apollo—not tempered, not disciplined—but raw, unbridled, primal. It surged out of him in waves that rattled the stone, made the banners whip like screams in the wind.

Even his eyes betrayed him. Once sharp, human—now drowned entirely in emerald light, rivers of green aura spilling from them like smoke, like fire. They weren't eyes anymore. They were wounds in the world, windows into fury unbound.

At first, they had been measured—deliberate—but now, each swing came harder, faster, with less space for breath. The jagged green light pouring from his sword grew so bright it painted the battlefield in its uneven glow, swallowing the colors of banners and blood alike.

The Red Wielder's dagger still moved with precision, but there was a hitch now—the smallest delay between parry and counter. Apollo noticed. He *pressed.*

Another blow sent a shockwave that tore grass from the ground in a ring around them. Another forced the Red Wielder back a full step, boots grinding furrows into the dirt. And then another—so violent it nearly wrenched the dagger from his grip.

The Flow itself seemed to rebel against the red aura, twisting away from it and funneling toward Apollo instead, wrapping his blade, his shoulders, his very breath in raw power. The air crackled as if lightning were trapped inside it, waiting to strike.

The Red Wielder tried to circle, to break the rhythm, but Apollo moved with him—no, *through* him—every step forward closing the space before the man could breathe.

Then came the moment.

A feint high, a sweep low, a sudden twist of the wrist—and the Red Wielder's defense faltered. His dagger caught the strike, but the force behind it buckled his stance. Apollo followed, the green light flaring so violently it blinded half the watching soldiers for a heartbeat.

Steel screamed against crystal. Sparks scattered like meteors.

The Red Wielder stumbled back. And in that instant, something in the air shifted.

The battlefield—Axis and Umber alike—began to realize they weren't watching a fight anymore. They were watching a hunt.

The hunted was bleeding red light.
The hunter's blade was drinking it whole.

And Apollo…
Apollo was no longer fighting to win.

He was fighting to *end*.

The Red Wielder's breath came in sharp bursts now, his stance faltering under the relentless onslaught. His dagger still pulsed with that deep, murderous red—a glow that twisted the very air around it—but every time green met crimson, the red dimmed a little more.

"You fight like a beast," he growled, trying to circle. Apollo stepped in, blade low, voice steady. "No. I fight like someone who's done running."

The next strike came heavy and fast—green fire lashing forward. The Red Wielder caught it, the clash throwing up sparks that burned where they landed on skin.

"You think the Flow favors you?" the man spat, twisting his dagger to push Apollo off-balance. "It devours men like you."

Apollo's eyes narrowed. "Then I'll devour it right back."

He shifted, feinting high—and the dagger rose instinctively to block. But instead of retreating, Apollo drove his entire weight forward, green blade screaming as it carved down through the crimson edge.

For a heartbeat, the world held its breath.

Then the dagger snapped.

It wasn't just steel giving way—it was the very Flow screaming as it was torn apart.
For an instant, the world held its breath.

Then came the rupture.

Green and red detonated together, not as light but as raw, living force. The blast tore outward in a sphere of violence, ripping the air to ribbons. Trees bent and splintered under the shockwave the ground split in jagged scars. Soldiers—were hurled from their feet as if the battlefield itself had rejected them.

The explosion carried no sound at first, only a white-hot roar inside the skull, the kind that drowns every thought. Then came the echo—a rolling, bone-deep thunder that chased the blast into the horizon.

When the haze began to clear, the scene was unrecognizable.
Leaves and ash swirled together in the air, drifting down like a rain of green fire and black snow. The once-solid tree line now stood broken, a jagged wound through the forest.

In the center of it all lay the Red Wielder, sprawled in the churned earth. His dagger was gone—not broken, not discarded, but reduced to glittering shards of nothing, its Flow extinguished like a candle drowned in the sea. His aura, once sharp and defiant, had bled away into the dirt.

And above him stood Apollo.

The jagged emerald blade in his hand bled power in uneven surges, every flare sending ghost-light crawling over his armor and skin. It was imperfect, unstable — and more dangerous for it. The green fire burned brighter than before, but along its edge shimmered faint threads of red and gold, as if the weapon had devoured part of its enemy in the breaking.

His breath was steady. His eyes were fixed not in triumph, but in something colder—something that made even the victorious hesitate to look at him for too long.

The Flow did not surround him now.
It bowed to him.

"Rest in eternal light" he said quietly, the words carrying through the silence. "Go with the flow, as the flow goes with all things."

The Red Wielder's eyes darted—not toward his own soldiers, not toward any chance of rally—but toward the shadows between the trees.

It wasn't the look of a man thinking of victory.

It was the look of a man deciding how to live long enough to see another dawn.

Apollo stepped forward once, his jagged green blade still spilling that uneven, searing light, and the ground itself seemed to lean away from him.

The Red Wielder faltered. His heel caught in the churned mud, splattering black earth up his greaves. He backpedaled another step, then another, each one faster, less sure, until his form blurred into the tree line and was gone.

The forest exhaled a long, cold silence.

Then—the break.

One Umber dropped his spear and bolted, eyes wide as if the light itself were chasing him. Another followed. Then ten more. Panic spread like oil on water.

They had seen it.

They had seen a warrior tear the Flow from another's weapon—unmake it with sheer will—and no banner, no oath, no chain could hold them now.

The red haze of their auras guttered out one by one as they fled into the deep green, weapons tumbling from their hands to the blood-soaked soil.
Some ran without looking back.
Some didn't run far enough.

In less than a minute, the battlefield was empty of everything but the dead, the dying… and the victors.

The jagged emerald light still clung to Apollo's blade like a living thing, refusing to dim even though the fight was done. It pulsed slow and uneven, painting the haze of dust and smoke in ghostly greens that shifted with every shallow breath.

No one spoke.
Not yet.

Only the rasp of exhausted lungs and the slow drip of blood from armor to earth marked that they were still alive—that they had survived him.

Apollo stood still.

Not breathing hard.
Not swaying.
Just… still.

The battlefield moved around him—cries, the shuffle of boots, the groan of the wounded—but none of it seemed to touch him. The jagged green blade in his hand still dripped light, each ember hissing as it fell into the churned mud, burning for a moment before fading.

We broke before he did.

The cheering began as a murmur, a ripple of disbelief in the aftermath of carnage—then it surged, swelling into a roar that shook the battered trees and rolled over the blood-soaked ground. Warriors who had doubted him, who had spat the word *broken* like a curse in shadowed corridors, now screamed his name like it was salvation. They called him savior. Hero. Champion.

The sound should have been triumphant, but in my ears, it rang hollow.
Because the man they praised wasn't celebrating.

Lux lay pale on a stretcher, his once-gleaming noble armor torn open like foil, the blue crest of his house drowned in blood. Crystal shards from his shattered chestplate glittered against the wrappings they'd bound him in. His breath came shallow, uneven, as if each inhale was a battle in itself.

Jaleon came next, limping heavily, his massive frame sagging under the weight of his wounds. One arm hung useless, shattered in multiple places; the bandages on his knees already seeped through with crimson. His jaw was set tight, but his eyes—the eyes that had always been quick to mock, quick to laugh—stared forward, empty, fixed on nothing.

And around them… the field.

Bodies everywhere, tangled in death's embrace. Axis soldiers lay face-down in churned mud, their armor split, their weapons snapped like dry branches. Some were sprawled as if they'd simply fallen asleep, others frozen mid-reach for comrades they'd never touch again. The air was thick with the metallic bite of blood, the smoke of discharged crystal weapons, and something worse—that sweet, rotting stench that meant the heat was already working on the dead.

There would be no rites. No names carved.
No hands left to carry them home.

The dirt would swallow them whole, nameless and forgotten, their final resting place marked only by the crows circling above.

I wanted to look away. I couldn't.

Not because I wanted to remember—but because I was afraid I already would, for the rest of my life.

And still, the crowd roared.

They didn't notice that Apollo wasn't moving. Didn't see the way the jagged green light dripping from his blade fell into the mud like dying stars. Didn't see the way his shoulders didn't lift with the pride of victory— only hung heavy, like something in him had broken along with the Red Wielder's weapon.

He hadn't just won.
Something inside him had been pulled apart, piece by piece, and none of them seemed to realize it.

Apollo.

He stood over the Red Wielder's corpse, the dead man's shattered dagger lying in the dirt like a broken fang. His jagged green blade still burned, casting fractured light across his armor, making every dent and smear of blood look like a war mark carved by the gods themselves. Shadows bled from him, long and thin, bending in strange angles across the churned mud.

The wind shifted, curling around us, bringing with it the copper sting of fresh blood, the acrid bite of scorched soil, and something else—something heavier. The smell of Flow, raw and unshaped, like the air after lightning strikes but before the thunder breaks.

And then the world slowed.

Not the sluggishness of fatigue. Not the stunned haze after victory.
This was deeper. Stranger.
The noise of the cheering crowd didn't stop—it stretched, warping into long, hollow echoes that seemed to come from another place entirely. The smoke rising from the battlefield moved like molasses, every wisp curling in slow spirals. Even my heartbeat felt like it had been pulled into another rhythm.

It was just him.
Alone in that stillness.

That's when I saw them—the tears.

Not the kind that come from relief, when you realize you've survived. Not the kind that follow exhaustion, when the weight of your body wins over your will.
No—these were the tears that come from something being carved out of you while you're still breathing. Something you can't get back.

Regret.

His jaw clenched, but it wasn't anger that tightened it—it was the strain of holding something back. His gaze stayed locked on the corpse at his feet, but I knew he wasn't seeing the Red Wielder anymore. He was somewhere else entirely. Somewhere far darker.

And then I felt it.

We all did.

A surge of Flow—not pure, not steady, but warped, jagged, and full of a pain so deep it was almost a voice. It was coming from somewhere in the trees, just beyond sight, heavy as a storm you can feel in your bones. And with it… eyes. Watching. Waiting.

They did nothing.
For now.

I moved to him before I could stop myself. My hands were still slick with Lux's blood as I wrapped my arms around him. "Thank you," I whispered, and I meant it in a way I didn't know how to explain.

He looked at me then—the most broken smile I have ever seen. Tears cut through the grime on his face. "I would die for you," he said, his voice almost a ghost.

Then he turned away, blade still burning, and began walking toward the ship.
I stayed frozen where I was.
Because for the first time, I wasn't sure if we had won anything at all.

But I knew better.

The cheers, the shouts of victory, the stomp of boots against the churned earth—it was all noise meant to cover a truth no one else seemed willing to feel.

Somewhere in the tree line, beyond the bodies and the broken banners, that presence still lingered. Not just watching, but *studying*. Not just waiting, but *measuring*. I could feel it in the Flow like a cold fingertip running down my spine—patient, deliberate, ancient.

It didn't move when Apollo's blade struck.
It didn't flinch when the Red Wielder fell.
It didn't need to.

And in that moment, I understood something the others didn't.
This—all of this—wasn't the end of a battle.

It was the opening move.

The war—whatever it truly was, whatever had been hidden behind missions and orders and banners—had only just begun.

The roar of the battlefield was gone, replaced by the low, steady hum of the transport's engines.
We left Tessara the way we'd come—in formation—but now it was a different kind of march. No proud strides, no cocky smirks. Our steps were uneven, slowed by stretchers and the stiff, deliberate gait of the wounded.

Lux was laid out in the medbay, his once-pristine armor peeled away in ragged pieces. His chest was swaddled in crystal-thread wrappings, each faintly glowing to mend the damage beneath. He was pale, sweat beading on his forehead, but his breathing—thank the Flow—was steady.

Jaleon sat across from him, his right arm encased in a heavy Flowsteel brace, knees bound so tightly they looked carved from stone. He stared at the bindings like they were an insult, his jaw clenched as if daring them to heal faster.

Apollo hadn't sat since we boarded. He stood at the starboard viewport, armor still battered, shoulders squared but not tense—just… still. The green glow of his sword was gone, but the faint reflection of starlight across the glass clung to him like it didn't want to leave.

I kept to the rear bulkhead, arms crossed, watching the cabin. The hatch sealed with a deep *clang*, the vibration rolling through the deck. Slowly, Tessara's endless green vanished beneath the clouds, swallowed by the black. The planet shrank into nothing.

It was quiet.
Too quiet.

Then Jaleon's voice broke it—rough, but laced with that stubborn humor that even pain couldn't kill. "Alright… so which one of you geniuses was gonna tell me we were fighting *killer salad people*? No? Just me?"

Lux groaned without opening his eyes. "Even now, you're an idiot."

"Not an idiot," Jaleon shot back, "just *surprised*. Lettuce shouldn't stab you back."

I smirked despite myself. "Pretty sure it wasn't lettuce, Jaleon. You might've just been hallucinating."

"Hallucinating?!" Jaleon scoffed. "I *know* what I saw. There was definitely a cabbage with a knife."

That finally got a weak chuckle out of Lux, though it ended with a hiss of pain.

Apollo hadn't said a word, but I caught the faintest twitch at the corner of his mouth in the viewport's reflection.

I nudged him. "Careful, commander. If you smile, your face might crack."

He finally glanced over his shoulder, voice low and dry. "If I wanted comedy, I wouldn't be on a ship with you three."

Jaleon grinned wide. "Ha! He's talking again. Look at that—our mighty green hero *can* speak."

Lux muttered, "Don't push him, Jaleon… he might decide the cabbage was right."

That broke us.
We laughed—loud, unrestrained, ridiculous.
And for a moment, the smell of blood and the weight of death slipped away, replaced by something lighter.
Something almost like home.

But in the reflection of the viewport, Apollo's eyes still looked somewhere else—far away, and much, much darker than the jokes could reach.

The laughter died slow.

Like embers cooling after a fire, each chuckle left a little more quiet in its place until only the ship's hum remained. Lux drifted back into uneasy sleep, Jaleon finally slumping against the bulkhead with a grunt, his good arm draped over his knees.

Apollo hadn't moved. He was still standing at the viewport, watching the streaks of light stretch past as the ship punched through the dark.

I slid out of my seat and crossed the short distance between us. My reflection joined his in the glass, small compared to his still, unyielding frame.

"You're not gonna sit?" I asked.

"No." His answer was clipped, but not unkind.

I studied him for a moment, the faint starlight tracing the line of his jaw, the way his hand rested against the glass as if he could feel the cold of space through it.

"You scared me back there," I admitted.

His eyes didn't leave the view. "Scared you?"

"Yeah. You were..." I searched for the right word. "Gone. Like you weren't even there with us anymore. Like the Flow had swallowed you whole."

He was silent for a long beat. Then:
"Maybe it did."

I frowned. "Apollo—"

"Do you know what it's like," he said, still not looking at me, "to hold something in your hands that could destroy everything in front of you... and still feel powerless?"

The question hung heavy in the cabin.

"I know what it's like to lose," I said quietly.

"Loss is simple," he replied. "You grieve. You hurt. You carry it until it gets lighter... or until it crushes you. But this..." His hand flexed slightly against the glass. "This is different. The Flow doesn't care if you're ready. It doesn't care if you want it. It gives... and it takes. And when it gives too much, you start wondering if it's *you* holding the blade... or the blade holding you."

For a moment, I didn't know what to say. His voice wasn't angry, wasn't even bitter—it was... tired. Like each word had been carried a long way before it reached me.

"You saved us," I said finally.

His gaze shifted just enough to catch mine in the reflection. "You could not see what I saw—and that is all right.

My vision was never meant for you; it is mine to bear, mine to forge.

I was not born with tools in hand; I must carve them from pressure, pain, and persistence

While others speak, I fear losing myself.

I fear that when the moment comes again… I will fail you all."

I held his eyes, even through the glass. "Then we fall together. That's the point of 'us'."

Something flickered there—not quite a smile, not quite a surrender—before he turned back to the stars.

The others had gone quiet again—Lux breathing in shallow pulls, Jaleon snoring like a saw through stone. The cabin lights were low, the kind of dim that made space outside look endless.

Apollo hadn't moved from the viewport.

"You know what, Valere…" His voice was low, like he wasn't talking to me so much as to the glass.

"What?"

"I still see her."

"Who?"

He swallowed once before answering. "My mother."

I stayed still, afraid that if I moved, he'd stop

"I still feel her," Apollo said again, slower this time, as if repeating it might make me understand. "It's not just memory—it's… *presence*. Like she's in the room, in the Flow, in the air I breathe."

He didn't look at me. His gaze stayed locked on the stars outside, and for a moment, they reflected in his eyes like fragments of some broken constellation.

"And I can't shake her last words. *Run, boy, run.*" He let the phrase linger in the air, heavy as stone dropping into deep water. "It's not just words, Valere. I *know* it's not. It's… something else. Like they carry weight I haven't figured out yet. Like the more I think about them, the closer I get to something I'm not sure I want to see."

His knuckles whitened as his hand curled into a fist against the glass. The faint vibration of the ship hummed under our feet, but it felt distant—like we were the only two people left in the galaxy.

"I can't take it anymore."

The tears came then, not sudden but creeping, slow, trailing down his face in the silver light of the viewport. He didn't wipe them away. "I feel pain… all the time. Not the kind you can cut out or stitch shut. This… this *stays*. It's like it's etched into me. And it's making me lose myself."

He finally turned his head toward me, and the look in his eyes hollowed my chest. "Sometimes I think her crystal talks to me. Sometimes I think I'm not even here—like I'm standing in another place entirely. Somewhere cold. Somewhere… someone is watching me. Judging me. Waiting."

I didn't move. I didn't breathe. I'd never heard him speak like this, never seen him so stripped of the walls he carried into every fight.

In that moment, Apollo wasn't the unshakable warrior from the battlefield. His eyes were wide, wet, searching—not for answers, but for something solid to keep him from breaking apart.

"I almost let Jaleon die," he said, voice cracking like it hurt to speak. "I almost… let him die."

My throat felt dry. I opened my mouth, but the words that should have come—comfort, reassurance, anything—were gone before they formed.

All I could do was step closer, my hand finding his shoulder. He didn't pull away. The warmth of him felt fragile, like if I let go, he'd disappear into whatever shadow haunted him.

I don't know what came over me.
One moment, we were just sitting there, the hum of the transport ship filling the silence. The next, I was leaning closer—close enough to feel his breath, to hear the unsteady rhythm of it. My lips brushed his, hesitant at first, like testing the edge of something dangerous.

It was my first kiss.
I could still smell the coppery tang of blood in my hair, feel the grit of dust clinging to my skin. My hands trembled as they found his, the ridges of old scars under my fingertips. His palms were calloused, warm, rough from the fight—and yet the way he held me back was almost… delicate. Like I might shatter if he forgot himself.

The taste of him was not sweet—it was salt and ash, battle and breath—but it was real. For the first time since Tessara, I felt alive in a way that had nothing to do with the Flow.

When I pulled back just enough to look at him, I saw something shift in his eyes. The usual sharpness was gone, replaced by a fragile sort of wonder, as though he didn't know whether to believe what was happening. The green light from the galaxy beyond the viewport spilled over his face, catching on the tear tracks that still lingered there.

He cupped my cheek, his thumb tracing the curve of my jaw like he was memorizing it. And for a heartbeat, the weight he carried—the loss, the rage, the regret—seemed lighter.

We stayed like that, suspended between stars and silence. I could feel his heartbeat through our joined hands, steadying against mine.

The war, the wounds, the dead we'd left behind—all of it faded for just that moment.

I didn't want it to end.

I kissed him again—deeper this time, letting the moment swallow us both.
It wasn't rushed. It wasn't desperate.
It was like trying to breathe for him, to draw the weight from his chest into mine and scatter it among the stars outside. His lips were warm and steady, but there was

an ache beneath them, a quiet surrender that made me want to hold on tighter.

For the briefest heartbeat, the pain in his eyes eased. Gone was the shadow of grief that seemed welded into his gaze.
In its place was something… softer. Something that scared me in its own way, because it felt real, unguarded—the kind of look you don't get twice in a lifetime.

We stayed like that, close enough for our breath to mingle, foreheads pressed together. Outside, the galaxy poured itself through the viewport, streaks of blue, silver, and faint green painting our skin. His hand stayed on my cheek, the calloused pad of his thumb gliding along my jawline in slow, careful passes, like he was engraving me into memory.

I could feel the steady rise and fall of his breathing, each inhale a slow tide, each exhale brushing warm against my lips.
The hum of the ship wrapped around us like a quiet lullaby, low and constant, as if the galaxy itself was holding its breath.
The war, the blood, the acrid sting of scorched earth— all of it dissolved into the background, stripped away until nothing remained but the small, shared space between us.

In that moment, it was as though the stars beyond the viewport leaned closer, their cold light spilling over our skin in rivers of silver and pale blue. His shadow merged with mine on the wall, two shapes inseparable, swaying slightly with the ship's gentle drift.

It was the first time I had ever seen him without armor—not just the steel plates, not just the jagged green light of the Flow—but without the unyielding fortress he'd built around himself. The relentless warrior, the untouchable blade… now just a man, raw and unhidden before me.

And the realization struck me like a blade between the ribs, sharp and irreversible:
I would give anything—my breath, my strength, my place in the stars—to keep him like this.
To keep this fleeting, fragile version of him that the galaxy would never see again.

The thought scared me almost as much as it warmed me. Because somewhere deep down, I already knew… moments like this don't last

For a moment, the weight of everything we had been— warriors, survivors, fractured souls—simply fell away. The blood on my hair, the bruises blooming beneath my tunic, the ache in my bones from running and killing and nearly dying—none of it mattered.

We weren't champions or weapons or pieces on someone else's board.
We were just… two people.
Two people clinging to each other in the thin space between heartbeats, in the quiet that exists only after the screams have faded and before the next order comes.

His warmth bled into me, steady and grounding, as if he could anchor me to this one perfect sliver of time. Beyond the glass, the stars turned in their patient arcs, galaxies curling like distant brushstrokes, slow and eternal. Every second that passed felt stolen, delicate—like if I breathed too deeply, the universe might notice and take it back.

I wished—with everything in me, with a desperation I could barely contain—that the night would never end. That the engines would hum forever, that the ship would drift endlessly through the starfields, that no orders, no alarms, no war could reach us here.

But somewhere in the back of my mind, I knew the truth: the galaxy never lets moments like this live for long.

"But Nana… why this? Why tell me all that now?"
The child's voice was small, curious, but there was a slight tremor—like they weren't sure they wanted the answer.

I leaned back in my chair, feeling the old wood creak beneath me. The firelight painted the walls in gold and shadow, and for a moment I just looked at them. So young. So certain the world was still as simple as the stories in the books.

"Because, my sweet one…" My voice was softer than I meant it to be. "I want you to know my legacy. I want you to know *their* legacy. All these great heroes I've told you about—the ones who bled, who fought, who carried the world on their backs—they're dead now. History won't write their names. No one will ever remember them."

The child frowned, confusion flashing in their eyes. "But… Apollo—"

"Apollo?" I almost laughed, but it came out as something heavier. "They will say he was a bad man. That he was filled with rage and despair. They'll strip away his victories, paint over his truth, and give him nothing but a title: 'Nameless.'"

"But… Nana, history is always right, isn't it?"

I smiled sadly and shook my head. "Oh, my young one… what is history?" I leaned forward, my hands curling around theirs. "It is the lie everyone agrees on. The powerful write it. The weak accept it. And the fools defend it."

They blinked, their small fingers tightening in mine.

"They erase the guilty," I went on, my voice hardening, "silence the truth, and call it 'education.' You weren't taught history. You were fed a script."

The child shifted, uneasy, but didn't pull away. I could see the questions fighting behind their eyes.

"No one will tell you the crimes of the Axis," I continued, my tone now low, steady, deliberate. "The children who lost their lives for a peace that never came. The Order—they were mercenaries in robes. Whoever had the coin could wield them like a weapon. And the Umber fanatics? They thought they were chosen, blessed by some divine will… but they let people die to prove a point."

I paused, letting the words settle. The fire popped in the hearth, and the shadows on the wall seemed to lean closer.

"Apollo didn't continue the wheel," I said finally. "He came, and slowly—*slowly*—he broke it. He took the power of the people and wielded it with fairness. For once, someone did not serve the throne, the creed, or the coin—he served *them*. And yet…"

The child's eyes widened. "Yet what, Nana?"

I leaned back, my gaze drifting to the fire. For a long time, I didn't answer. The silence between us grew heavy, the kind that makes you aware of your own heartbeat.

"We will get to that, my love," I said at last, my voice almost a whisper. "But when we do… you'll never see the stars the same way again.

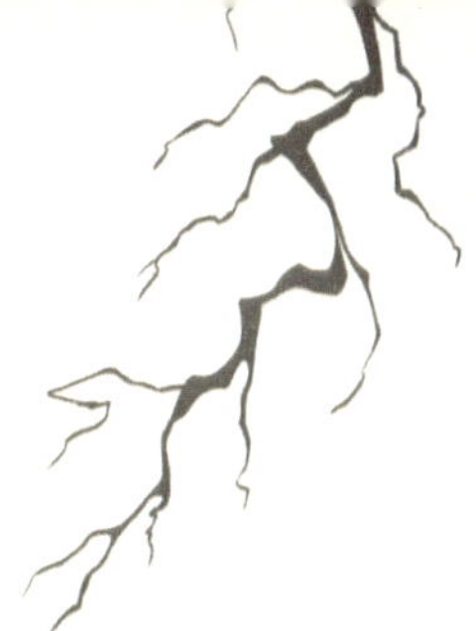

CHAPTER 17

We were ready to land on Elaris. The transport's descent rattled through the hull, but it was nothing compared to the weight in my chest. Through the narrow viewport, the great obsidian towers of the city rose to meet us, their black glass spines catching the pale light of the sun. They shimmered like frozen lightning, beautiful and cold—monuments that remembered every war they'd outlived.

I could hear noise even before the landing struts touched the platform—not the clang of industry or the murmur of the marketplace, but voices. Cheering. Hundreds of them. It was strange… after what we'd just lived through, the sound almost felt wrong in my ears.

What success?
We were almost killed.
Axel was dead—lying seven feet under foreign soil, along with more than half the battalion that had followed him into Tessara's forests.

Lux could stand now, but his movements were slow, stiff. His chest was still wrapped, the bandages hidden under a hastily polished uniform. Apollo, silent as ever, lifted one end of Jaleon's stretcher while Lux took the other. Even Jaleon's usual thunderous voice was quiet his eyes darted toward the exit, as if unsure what waited for us out there.

The gate began to open with a deep mechanical groan. Light spilled inside, warm but sharp, revealing the figures outside—a sea of people, packed shoulder to shoulder. Soldiers in ceremonial armor, acolytes in flowing white, civilians draped in the colors of the Axis. Some carried banners. Others threw flowers.

They were cheering us like heroes.

The petals rained over the ramp as we stepped forward, brushing against my boots. I wanted to feel proud— to believe this was for us—but all I could see behind my eyes were the faces of the dead we'd left unburied in the dirt of Tessara.

And then, at the far end of the reception, I saw him.

General Markus. Formal uniform, polished medals gleaming like captured suns, his posture radiating that effortless pride that could almost make you forget the blood on his hands. Beside him stood Serene, unbent and unbowed, her armor immaculate, her face the same unshakable mask it had always been.

Apollo and Lux shifted the stretcher to lower Jaleon for a moment. Lux smirked.
"You know, you're a lot heavier when you're unconscious."

Apollo glanced at him, lips twitching just barely. *"He wasn't unconscious—he was pretending, so he didn't have to walk."*

Jaleon lifted his head from the stretcher, managing the ghost of a grin. *"You're both just jealous. That's what real muscle weighs."*

Lux rolled his eyes. *"If that's muscle, then I'm a Flow prophet."*

"You'd have to stop talking for that," Jaleon shot back, and for a brief moment—despite the flowers, the towers, and the hollow cheering—I felt the faintest flicker of something that almost resembled home.

Two Axis soldiers in ceremonial armor stepped forward, clearly sent to take Jaleon's stretcher from Apollo and Lux.

They each grabbed a side, grunted, and lifted—or at least, tried to.

Nothing.
The stretcher barely moved.

One of the soldiers adjusted his grip, the other braced his legs and gave it another go, both of them straining as if they were trying to uproot a tree. Jaleon, of course, didn't help. He just leaned his head back and smirked like a king on his throne.

Apollo raised an eyebrow, deadpan. *"Careful. That's not dead weight—that's ego."*

Lux broke into laughter, nearly doubling over. *"No, no—it's all the food he's been hoarding. You could feed a whole battalion with what's in there."*

Jaleon grinned wider. *"Muscle, boys. Pure muscle. Don't be jealous just because your bones rattle in the wind."*

The two struggling soldiers looked at each other, clearly mortified. That's when another pair arrived, jogging up in formation.

With four of them now—grunting, shuffling, and muttering under their breath—they finally managed to lift Jaleon's stretcher and start carrying him toward the infirmary.

As they disappeared into the crowd, Jaleon called back over their shoulders, *"Tell the healers not to fix me too much! I'd hate to be prettier than Lux."*

Lux rolled his eyes, but there was no hiding the smile tugging at his mouth. For the first time since Tessara, the air between us felt a little lighter.

That's when the noise from the gates swelled—not just louder, but deeper, like the city itself had drawn breath to greet us. The sound rolled down the great avenue in a wave, striking us full in the chest. The crowd outside Elaris was a living tide, packed shoulder to shoulder, spilling into the balconies and rooftops above.

Flower petals drifted through the air in great arcs, catching the sunlight so that for a heartbeat it felt like we were walking into a storm of slow-burning embers. The acolytes were a vision in their spotless white robes, their hands raised in blessing. Axis soldiers lined both sides of the street, black and crimson armor polished to a mirror sheen, halberds held like iron columns.

And in the spaces between — citizens in their brightest silks, the golds and reds of celebration, faces alight with the thrill of seeing living legends return.

Above it all, the obsidian towers of the Tempe rose like silent sentinels. They caught the morning sun in their black glass faces, throwing back fractured light. Every mirrored flank reflected banners—Axis crimson and Order white—draped from arch to arch, each one rippling in the same breeze that carried the perfume of crushed flowers and the distant scent of burning incense.

The roar of the crowd grew with every step we took into the open. It wasn't simply welcome. It was ownership. Their cheers were not just joy—they were a declaration: *you are ours now.*

And at the far end of the parade line, framed by the arch of the Grand Gate, stood Markus. His face was set in the perfect expression of pride, carved into him like it belonged on a coin—but I knew the steel underneath, the readiness to turn that warmth to command in an instant.

Markus stepped forward. He didn't need to raise his voice—the crowd bent to hear him.
"You return to us as heroes." The word *heroes* rolled over us again and again as the crowd echoed it, their voices layering until the sound filled every space in the

street, until it was impossible to tell where one voice ended and the next began.

"You have served the Axis—and the Order—with honor," Markus continued, his gaze sweeping over us like a commander inspecting his troops. "And now, the people see you for what you are: the shield that holds back the darkness."

More petals swirled through the air. One landed in my hair; another caught on Apollo's shoulder, pale against the black of his armor. Lux, still stiff with injury, straightened, every inch the noble scion even with his bandages peeking from under the plates. And though Jaleon was somewhere ahead of us—probably still giving the stretcher bearers grief—I knew he would have loved this. The roar, the spectacle, the people calling our names.

But standing there, beneath the banners and the flowers and the roar of the crowd, I could see what no one else seemed to notice.

This was not just a greeting.
This was a claiming.

The crowd's roar still clung to me as we crossed into the inner courtyard of the temple. The banners and petals gave way to stone corridors where the cheers could not follow. Here, the air was cooler, quieter—but no less heavy.

We were told to wait near the colonnade while Markus, Julius, and Serena stepped through a side archway into a small chamber. The heavy door didn't close all the way.

I wasn't trying to listen.
But the echo in this place carried their voices like threads through a loom.
"…losses… acceptable," Markus's voice—sharp, clipped.
A pause. Julius, lower, harder to make out: "…children… not soldiers."
Then Serena, not raising her voice, but cutting clean through the space: "…your banner does not command my loyalty."

Shadows shifted on the wall beyond the doorframe—Markus's stance all forward weight and squared shoulders, Julius stiff as carved marble, Serena still and unyielding, arms folded like a locked gate.

I leaned back against the column before anyone could notice me watching.

The cheer of the parade already felt like another world.

When they emerged, their faces were masks again. Markus, the picture of triumph. Julius, a diplomat's smile. Serena… unreadable, but her eyes found mine for a fraction longer than they needed to. And in that look, I caught it—not pride, not relief, but warning.

We went back to our rooms.

The corridors of temple felt strangely hollow after the parade—like the cheers had been stripped away the moment the gates closed behind us. I couldn't shake what I had overheard earlier, the fragments of Markus, Julius, and Serena's conversation echoing in my mind. Words like *acceptable losses* and *your banner does not command my loyalty* tangled in my thoughts. But the exhaustion was heavier than my questions, and I let it pull me along.

When I stepped inside, I saw him.

Apollo sat alone on the edge of his bunk, elbows on his knees, hands loosely clasped. The dim light caught his hair, painting it in silver lines. I didn't think—I just crossed the room and threw my arms around him. He stiffened for half a second, then laughed—low and surprised—before his arms came around me.

Then he kissed me.

Each kiss felt like it was pulling something out of him—like I was drinking fragments of pain straight from his chest, one heartbeat at a time. His hands lingered against my back as if reluctant to let go. For those few breaths, I forgot about Markus, about the war, about the shadow of the Axis.

That night was short, restless—a shifting thing.
Yet in Apollo's arms, I slept in peace.

In his embrace, my dreams were made of light: a kiss without end, a hug that I wished would last forever. I thought it was love's purest gift, that simple warmth. I didn't know what was happening inside his dreams at that same moment. Not then. When I learned, it was already too late.

You see, fate is cruel. Sometimes it whispers warnings, lays hints before our feet. But we—all of us—were blind. While I dreamed of eternity, Apollo struggled once more in the void.

Every time he closed his eyes, it came for him. It wanted to speak. To claim him.

Again, he floated in the endless dark.
In his left hand—his mother's crystal, shattered and lifeless. Yet from its ruin sparked a single thread of

blue, a flicker of her prime. And from that light, he heard her voice:

Run, my boy. Please… run.

Then the shadow appeared. The blurred figure he had seen before, clearer now, closer. It held a child in its arms—a baby—and for a moment, Apollo felt happiness radiating from it. A vision of peace, of what might have been.

But peace was fleeting.

The shadow shifted. Its form convulsed. Rage poured from it—boundless, uncontrollable, flooding the void with its weight. The golden crystal in its grasp twisted black with fury. And then it ran at him, sprinting through the void, the blurred figure raising its blade toward Apollo.

Before he could see the face, before he could know the truth, he woke.

And I was there.
In his arms. Safe.
He held me tighter, as if anchoring himself in my warmth.

I thought he was only clinging to love. I did not yet understand he was clinging to survive.

But the truth sat behind us like an uninvited guest—a great game being played upon the board, and we were only pawns. Pawns in a match where everyone screamed the rules weren't fair, and no one could leave the table

You see child every morning a war begins before your feet hit the floor not with the world but with your self with your doubts your fears that quet voice that wishpers stay in bed you will fail anyway

"But Nana… why did no one see the truth?"

I had asked the question a thousand times in my heart, but now it broke free in trembling words.

Old Valere's eyes narrowed, their violet sheen glimmering in the firelight. He breathed deep before answering, as though the Flow itself weighed on his tongue.

"Because we were young… and too blind."

The words hung heavy, and as they did, the very air of Kaith shifted.

It grew colder—not the clean chill of winter, but a dense, suffocating cold, as though the world itself held its breath. The night deepened. The shadows stretched. And in that stillness, I felt it: the weight of being watched.

Not by soldiers. Not by spies. By something older.

The Flow stirred uneasily, ripples running through me like a drumbeat beneath the skin. It was as if Kaith itself listened, remembering the truth we had denied, the truth we had buried beneath laughter and bravado.

Valere's voice lowered, softer now, but sharper, each word slicing the silence.
"We mistook our courage for clarity. We mistook our victories for wisdom. And so the truth walked beside us unseen—patient, waiting—until it was too late."

The fire guttered low. Somewhere in the darkness, a bell tolled. Not near. Not far. But there, all the same.

And I understood then what it meant.
The truth had never been hidden. It was the blindness of youth that refused to look.

"When five destinies collide, the Flow remembers in sorrow." Axis Senator "Luxius Varon"

CHAPTER 18

The morning came too early.

Markus summoned us to the courtyard before his departure. We stood in a neat line as he strode forward, gleaming in formal armor, the picture of Axis pride. To each of us, he awarded a medal—his voice smooth and practiced, the kind of praise that felt more like a politician's handshake than a commander's thanks.

When he reached Apollo, he didn't step back.

"Come, child," Markus said, voice carrying enough weight to silence the courtyard. "I have one more gift for you. But you must come with me to the capital to receive it."

Apollo's reply was instant. "I don't want gifts for actions of death."

Markus's lips curved into something between a smile and a command. "You will want this gift."

I wish I had known what he meant. I wish someone had stopped him. But no one spoke. No one moved. And Apollo agreed.

For the first time , I thought, I won't see him again

Jaleon clapped him on the shoulder with his good arm. "Don't get soft in the capital, boy. And don't come back wearing noble boots."

Lux grinned, leaning on his cane. "Try some ale for me. Proper Tessaran brew, not this watery Elaris swill."

Apollo managed a smile for them, the kind of smile that reassured everyone else—but when his eyes finally found mine, the mask slipped.
There it was: the sadness. The unspoken weight. It made my chest tighten as if I already knew the words he wouldn't say.

He stepped close, so close the noise of the others dimmed, as though the world had decided to give us a moment alone. His arms came around me, not in triumph or comfort, but in a desperate gentleness that made everything else fall away.

His eyes—gods, his eyes—warm, honey-colored, glowing faintly in the light, yet heavy with something I couldn't name. His gaze intoxicated me. In his embrace, I was not a wielder, not a warrior, not a fighter forged in hardship—I was butter melting against his heat, undone by the simplicity of his presence.

"I will never get tired of holding you," he whispered, and his voice trembled between vow and confession. "Because holding you… is my happiness."

The air stopped. My breath stopped. Even my heart stopped, just to hear it.

And then—Jaleon's voice shattered it.
"What about me, huh? No hugs? No flowers? At least take me out to dinner, bro!"

The spell cracked like glass.

Lux burst out laughing, nearly choking on his own breath as he added, "Dinner? Please. He's not nearly rich enough to feed *you*."

their laughter rolling through the space, filling the air with warmth again. The jokes bounced back and forth, light and clumsy and ridiculous, but I barely heard them.

All I could feel was the weight of Apollo's arms still around me, the steady beat of his heart against my chest, and the strange, sharp certainty that lingered in the back of my mind:

Something was about to change.

And it would not be for the better.

The courtyard felt colder after Markus spoke.

The medals still gleamed against our chests, but they might as well have been stones. I watched Markus turn toward the landing platforms with that commanding stride of his, every movement calculated, every step declaring the world would bend to him. And Apollo followed.

He didn't look back right away.

The transport ship waited at the far edge of the platform, its hull catching the pale morning light. Axis banners draped along its flanks, snapping in the wind like the wings of some waiting predator. Soldiers in black and crimson lined the walkway, their boots clicking in perfect unison as they saluted. It wasn't an escort. It was a claim.

When Apollo finally glanced over his shoulder, it was only for a heartbeat—but in that heartbeat, I saw it all.

The reluctance.
The weight.
The quiet acceptance.

I raised my hand without thinking. He didn't mirror it. Instead, he gave me that same broken smile from the night before—the one that made my ribs ache—and mouthed something I couldn't hear over the engines.

Markus put a hand on his shoulder then, steering him toward the open ramp. Apollo didn't resist.

The hiss of hydraulics filled the air as the ramp began to rise. I caught one last glimpse—the green of his eyes, the line of his jaw, the faint shadow of exhaustion that never seemed to leave him. Then the metal sealed shut with a final, hollow clang.

The ship lifted, slow at first, then with a roar that scattered the flower petals still lingering from our arrival. They swirled in the air—white, red, and gold—before falling into the cracks of the courtyard stone.

Jaleon muttered something about the capital turning him into a "fancy boot-wearing peacock," trying to coax a laugh. Lux smirked faintly, but I didn't.

I just kept staring at the sky until the ship was nothing but a black speck swallowed by the horizon.

And for the first time since Tessara… I felt truly alone. I didn't know what became of that ship when it vanished into the clouds.
None of us did.

We stood there at the gates of Elaris until it was only a speck, then nothing at all. The air seemed quieter without him, though the streets still buzzed with Axis banners snapping in the wind. I remember thinking it felt wrong—as if the very Flow in the temple had shifted, tilting toward the direction he had gone.

For days, the capital was just a word on our lips. Distant. Untouchable. A place where power lived behind walls of black stone and silver gates, and where people like us had no say.

But later, when the whispers started trickling back, I learned the truth.

Markus had received Apollo as if welcoming a long-lost heir. There had been a procession—golden carriages, soldiers in perfect formation, flower petals tossed from balconies as they rode through streets lined with thousands. He was taken straight to the high halls of the Axis Palace, where ceilings soared higher than the spires of our temples and crystal light poured from chandeliers the size of warships.

They dressed him in armor forged from blacksteel and inlaid with veins of emerald Flowglass.

Every word Markus spoke to him was honeyed. Every toast a promise. Every banquet a performance. And all the while, subtle chains were being fastened around him—not of iron, but of loyalty, of debt, of unspoken bargains.

Markus knew exactly what he was doing.

He wasn't honoring a hero.
He was binding a weapon.

And the worst part?
We did nothing to stop it.

When Apollo left, he was still the boy who had bled beside us in the Crucible. The boy who had carried Jaleon through the mud of Tessara while his own armor was cracked and burning. The boy who still woke with shadows in his eyes but laughed anyway when Lux teased him.

When he returned…

He came back a man.

But not the same man I knew.

There was a weight in him now—not just the scars, but something sharpened and honed in the dark halls of power. His eyes didn't just look at you anymore; they measured you, like he was already playing out the moves you might make. The green fire was still there, but it had been caged, directed.

Markus had forged him into something else. Something neither of us fully understood.

It was night when it started.
I didn't know why, but my dreams had turned restless— shadows bleeding into them, a cold that didn't belong creeping under my skin.

I jolted awake, heart hammering. The room was dark except for the thin stripe of moonlight cutting across the floor. Something was wrong. I could feel it—not just in the air, but deep in the Flow, like a string being pulled taut far away.

I swung my legs out of bed and crossed to Jaleon's bunk, shaking his shoulder.

"Wake up."

He grumbled, half-asleep. "Unless you've got food in your hand, this better be life or death."

"I'm serious," I said, my voice sharper than I intended. "Something's happening."

He smirked, still half in a dream. "Yeah. What's happening is you're paranoid and I'm trying to sleep."

But somewhere far from us, in the heart of the Axis Capitol, the night was anything but quiet.

The Hall of Kings loomed in shadow, its pillars soaring into the darkness like the trunks of some ancient, petrified forest. The great crystal braziers that lit it by day now burned low, casting the chamber in long, jagged shadows. Their light caught on the black marble floor, making it seem like they were standing over a mirror that reflected only night.

Markus stood at the center—not in the polished armor of ceremony, but in his simple general's tunic. He was flanked on either side by guards who looked more like executioners than escorts. Before him, the semicircle of the Senate waited, their seats rising in tiers like stone thrones.

The air was heavy with the scent of old incense and something sharper—the metallic tang of political blood about to be spilled.

The heavy doors at the end of the hall creaked open, and Apollo stepped through. His boots rang against the marble, the sound echoing far too loudly in the vast chamber. His shoulders were squared, but there was no mistaking the fact that he was walking into a den of predators.

The first voice came from somewhere to the left—sharp, dismissive.
"Is this your prodigy, Markus? This short little boy?"

A ripple of mocking laughter passed through the chamber.

Another senator leaned forward, the silver chain of his station catching the dim light.
"Markus, you fool. We named you Great General of the Axis Army, and yet you return with nothing worth

the title. You destroyed Grith—a city we might have held—and still the Umber scour our borders. They attack us through shadow, they cut down our soldiers, and you bring us a boy with a shattered crystal?"

Markus didn't move, didn't flinch. But I could imagine the iron behind his stillness.

A third senator's voice, colder than the rest, cut through the noise.
"The Senate will strip you of your command. You are weak. The Axis bleeds, and you offer us nothing but… this."

Their gazes turned on Apollo then—weighing him, dismissing him, underestimating him.

And far away, lying awake in the dark, I felt it.
The pull in the Flow tightening

The chamber had been tense before.
Now, it was a storm.

The air was hot with too many bodies in one sealed place, the scent of oiled armor mixing with the sharp tang of old stone and incense burning low in the braziers. The floor beneath Apollo's boots was polished marble, its surface so perfect it caught the faintest reflection of torchlight—and the flicker of faces twisted in fury.

A senator—broad-shouldered, silver hair plastered to his sweat-slick brow—slammed his fist against the marble rail so hard the sound cracked through the room like a whip. His voice broke with grief, but every word was honed to a blade's edge.

"You lost Axel! One of our best commanders… and my son!" His eyes shone wet, but there was no softness there—only blame, sharpened by loss. "My boy is dead because you started a war you could not finish!"

The words still hung in the air when another voice cut across them, slicing the moment clean.

"Our soldiers are dying while you sit here in safety, Markus! You—" the man jabbed a finger like a spear "—are nothing but a mistake!"

A third senator didn't bother with insults; he bellowed like a judge reading a sentence. "Execute him!"

It started small—one voice in the chamber's echo—but the cry grew, picking up others like a fire catching dry leaves. Within moments, the entire Senate was on its feet, silk robes brushing the rails, gold ornaments clinking as fists pounded wood and stone. "Kill him! Kill him!"

Markus had once been the most feared general in the Axis. The same mouth that once barked orders no soldier dared disobey was now the target of their jeers. To them, he was already dead—all that was missing was the formality.

Apollo stood beside him, still as carved stone. He didn't understand the intricate weaving of power in this room, the centuries-old grudges hidden beneath their words. But he understood their eyes. Every glare was the same—the look of someone who wanted him gone, who wanted him erased.

Markus didn't flinch. He didn't even seem to hear the roars.
When he finally moved, it was only to square his shoulders, turning to face the entire chamber. His voice cut through the chaos without effort, not by volume, but by weight.

"You speak of the dead?" His tone was cold iron, stripped of ceremony. "At least I kill my enemies—not my own." The words hit like hammer blows. "You call yourselves wolves, but you are sheep. Fat. Weak. Feeding on the flock you swore to guard."

The noise faltered, but only for a breath. Markus stepped forward, each footfall echoing like a drumbeat.

He pointed at Apollo, his arm steady, his eyes never leaving the senators.

"This boy—this man—has more honor in his shadow than you will ever have in your entire bloodline." His voice sharpened further, each word precise and deliberate. "And do you want to know why?"

Markus's gaze hunted down the faces of the loudest dissenters, pinning them like prey.

"Because the Order you command… the Order you used like a dagger in the dark… murdered his mother. You burned his home until nothing remained but ash. You made him suffer."

A hush settled for a moment—the kind that comes before lightning strikes—and Apollo felt the space around him tighten, as if the Flow itself had gone still to listen.

A senator leaned forward, the golden chain across his chest clinking faintly as he rested his weight on the rail. His lips curled into a sneer that showed too many teeth. "This is your great plan?" he spat, voice thick with disdain. "To parade a child into this hall and tell us we're guilty of killing his bastard mother?"

The words seemed to hang in the air like smoke—foul, heavy, impossible to ignore.

Another voice cut in before the first could fade, sharp and final.
"Kill the boy as well."

The order hit the chamber like a bell tolling.

The guards moved immediately—black armor scraping against marble as their boots thundered forward in unison. The heavy weight of their presence closed the space between them and Apollo with frightening speed. Their hands hovered over hilts, the smell of leather and steel growing stronger with each step.

And then… it happened.

The air didn't just shift. It *collapsed.*
Every sound, every movement seemed to sink under a crushing weight as something bled out from Apollo's skin—something black and unnatural, like shadows made tangible. It rolled across the floor in tendrils, curling up the senators' thrones, clinging to the walls.

It wasn't just darkness. It was cold.
A deep, marrow-freezing cold that bit into the lungs with each breath, turning every inhale into a sting. The temperature plummeted so fast that frost began to spiderweb across the polished marble under his boots.

And the smell came with it.

Not the sharp freshness of winter snow—but the metallic, choking tang of blood left to freeze in the dead of night.

Apollo's eyes lifted—slow, deliberate—and the room seemed to narrow, pulling everything into the space between him and the ones who called for his death.

He didn't speak.
He didn't *need* to.

Because his sword spoke for him.

With a sound like a scream muffled by iron, green light erupted along its length—jagged, uneven, alive with rage. The flame was wrong, fractured, spilling in uneven bursts that made the shadows themselves recoil. Its glow crawled up the walls, painting the senators in sickly green as if their skin had been lit from within.

The guards faltered mid-step. One's boot slid slightly on the thin sheen of frost now creeping toward their toes.

The senators leaned back as the light swelled, their eyes darting but finding nowhere safe to land.

"Kill him!" the Senate roared again — but this time, there was a thread of fear braided through the sound.

The first soldier swung.

He never reached Apollo.

One motion—one strike—and the man folded to the marble floor, armor split clean through from collar to hip. Steam hissed from the wound as blood spilled onto frost, the red spreading in a jagged halo beneath him.

The next came from behind, blade already raised. Apollo didn't turn so much as *flow*, the air bending with him like water around a prow. His sword carved a green arc, catching the man mid-step. There was no cry—only the dull clatter of a helm rolling across the marble.

Then panic bloomed.

It spread like wildfire through dry grass—the shouts breaking, steps faltering, the coordinated advance dissolving into a scramble. Apollo moved through them like a storm let loose in a cage, his uneven green blaze slicing through steel and flesh alike. Each swing was punctuated by the shriek of splitting armor and the bone-deep thud of bodies hitting stone.

The Hall of the Kings became a slaughter pen.

In one hand, his sword—burning jagged, too bright to look at directly. In the other, the crystal that had once belonged to his mother, its light beating in time with his heart. Every pulse fed the fire in him, each beat a fresh wave of rage that pushed him faster, harder.

He didn't see soldiers.
He didn't see senators.

He saw executioners.
Murderers.
Wolves fattened on the corpses of his kin.

The crystal's glow deepened, bleeding into the green blaze until it was no longer just light but *heat*—oppressive, suffocating. The scent of scorched flesh mingled with the metallic tang of blood, curling into the cold air until the Hall stank of death.

Then came the end.

A single, shattering surge of Flow erupted from him—raw, unchecked, carrying the scream of his grief in its wake. It tore through the chamber like a green lightning storm, splintering marble columns, shredding silk banners from the rafters. The blast blew the breath from every chest, rattled the iron thrones on their foundations, and snuffed the torches against the walls.

When it faded, there were no senators left. Not whole ones. The floor was a sprawl of broken bodies, the marble slick with blood and littered with fragments of armor. The banners lay torn and trampled, the royal crests smeared red.

The surviving guards broke and ran. They didn't get far. Apollo followed—silent, relentless—cutting down those who fled through the side passages, his blade finding them no matter where they turned.

And Markus?

He hadn't moved.
He stood in the center of the carnage, hands folded behind his back, boots untouched by the blood pooling around him.

There was no shock in his face.
No horror.
Only the faintest curve of satisfaction—the kind a sculptor might wear when a masterpiece finally takes shape.

This was no accident.
This was the man he had been building all along.

They say when Flow users remain together long enough, they begin to feel the faint undercurrent of each other's emotions—like threads tugging at the edge of the mind.

When it happened, I was dreaming.
Or… I thought I was.

A sudden spike of dread lanced through me, so sharp it yanked me from sleep with a gasp. My heart was already hammering before I knew why. I threw the blanket off and went straight to Jaleon's cot, shaking his shoulder. "Something's wrong."

He blinked blearily at me, tried a half-smile, tried to make it a joke—but his eyes betrayed him. Wet already. Shining in the dim lamplight.
"I know," he said softly, voice unsteady. "I felt it too. Something terrible's happening."

A movement by the doorway—Lux, standing pale as snow, his skin almost translucent in the cold light spilling from the hall. His irises, an impossible blue, seemed to catch and hold something distant. His voice was hollow when he spoke. "I feel death," he said simply. "I feel Apollo. And… whatever it is, it's bad."

We didn't wait.
The three of us moved fast down the corridor, bare feet on cold stone, the unease twisting tighter with

every step. When we reached Serena's quarters, I didn't knock. I shoved the door open.

She wasn't asleep.
She was on her knees in the center of the room, hands pressed to the floor, tears streaming down her face in heavy, silent drops. The strongest soldier I had ever known looked up at us—and she was broken.

"I failed." The words barely carried across the space between us. "Something is happening, and we can't stop it. Fear… imbalance… it's spreading everywhere."

Her breath caught, and her voice cracked open into confession.
"I started it. I was the one who killed his mother." She looked away, shame curling her shoulders inward. "I felt the Flow in him, even then. And I was a fool. I should have let them live. Now… if what I sense is true… we may have unleashed something far worse than we can imagine."

Her tears didn't stop. They clung to her jaw, fell into the fabric pooled at her knees. I stood frozen, staring at her—at the woman who had murdered the mother of the man I loved. The rage that rose in me was sudden and hot. My fingers curled into fists, nails biting my palms.

But before I could speak, Jaleon stepped between us. "No matter what's happened," he said firmly, "he's still our friend. The same man who saved our lives. That hasn't changed." He turned to look at me, his voice softening but holding its edge. "There's a reason for this. When he comes back, we'll hear it from him. Then we'll have our truth."

His words cooled the fire just enough for me to breathe again.

We left Serena there, the weight of her guilt still pressing against the walls. And though Jaleon told us to go back to sleep, I knew none of us truly would.

Somewhere out there, Apollo was changing.
And I didn't know if the man who returned would be the one I loved—or a stranger.

Apollo stood in the center of the throne hall.
His armor, once polished to a mirror sheen, was now drenched in blood—some black and oily, some still crimson and wet. It streaked down the ridges of his pauldrons, pooled at the joints of his gauntlets, dripped onto the marble until each drop rang in the silence. His hands were no longer the hands of a soldier. They were the hands of a butcher.

Around him, the air shifted. Not with sound. Not with motion. But with the pull of something vast and cold. The edges of the room bled into shadow until even the banners were swallowed.

The void crept inward, swallowing the light, swallowing the smell of blood, swallowing the world.

Time froze. The marble under his boots no longer held weight. The bodies around him were gone, replaced by nothing but black. His breath echoed against an emptiness that wasn't air.

And then—movement.

A figure emerged from the darkness. Not the towering, formless vastness he had faced before. This was smaller. Closer. Human in scale, human in shape. It stepped near enough that the shadows peeled back just enough for him to see... her.

His breath caught. His eyes widened.
"...Mama?"

The woman smiled—the same gentle, impossibly warm smile he remembered from Kaith

"My son," she said softly, her voice breaking like sunlight through a storm. "I told you to run."

His throat closed. The words scraped out like stone against steel.

"What… what have I done?"

She stepped closer, cupping his cheek with a hand that was cool but steady. Her eyes searched his face, and for a heartbeat, there was only her, only the comfort of her presence.

"I told you to run," she whispered again.

His voice trembled. "What am I supposed to do now?"

Her smile faltered. Her hand slipped away. The shadows wrapped around her form like black water. Her voice dropped—lower, harsher, twisting into something sharp.

"I told you to run!"

The cry shook the void. Her face flickered—not his mother's, but something wearing her shape. The shadow's fingers became claws as it shoved him backward, and the darkness folded in on itself, pulling him out of that impossible space—

—And he was back.

The marble hall returned in a rush of sound and light. Markus stood before him, smiling like a man watching a prophecy fulfilled.

"My boy," he said, his voice almost reverent. "You and I will forge a new universe."

The great bronze doors shuddered before they opened— an ancient groan that echoed off the blood-streaked marble. The sound was almost a warning, a reminder of the centuries those doors had guarded this hall, and of the weight of the history about to change inside it.

They swung wide, spilling harsh torchlight from the outer corridor. Shadows stretched across the ruined chamber, cutting over broken thrones and torn banners.

Soldiers flooded in. Their boots struck the marble in perfect rhythm until they reached the threshold… and then all movement died.

They saw it.

The bodies. The torn red-and-gold banners sagging from shattered poles. The green-stained cracks where Flow had burned into the stone.

And in the center—Apollo.

Blood dripped from the plates of his armor, tracing the grooves of its design until it fell in slow, deliberate taps to the floor. His face was unreadable, jaw locked tight, eyes fixed somewhere far beyond the walls. Beside him stood Markus, immaculate, untouched by the carnage, his hands folded behind his back like a king surveying his court.

A single heartbeat passed. Then another.

And as if bound by some unseen force, the soldiers dropped to one knee—the sound of metal gauntlets slamming the marble ringing through the hall like the clash of a thousand shields.

From somewhere deep in the formation, a voice broke free, raw and loud enough to shake the rafters:
"LONG LIVE THE KING MARKUS THE UNBROKEN! THE TRUE KING OF AXIS!"

The cry spread like fire through dry grass.
"LONG LIVE THE KING! LONG LIVE THE KING!"

The chant became a living thing—rolling over the chamber in waves, each repetition pounding like war drums, each word hammering the truth Markus wanted written into the bones of history.

Markus did not raise his voice. He didn't need to. He lifted one hand, and the noise bled away into silence, the kind of silence that feels like the moment before an arrow is loosed.

His eyes never left Apollo.
"Summon the banner," he said, each word a decree carved in stone. "At dawn, we begin. We will forge a new universe."

Markus didn't move for a moment. He simply watched, as if measuring the boy—no, the man—who had just slaughtered the Senate. Then, slowly, he stepped forward.

"You feel it now, don't you?" His voice was low, stripped of the public thunder he'd shown moments ago. "The weight. The clarity."

Apollo's gaze flicked up, but he didn't answer. His breath was slow, deliberate—the way someone breathes when they're fighting the urge to shake.

Markus stopped a few paces away, his boots tracing clean arcs in the blood pooled on the marble. "The world has always belonged to those willing to take it. You took it tonight. Not for them"—he gestured to the empty thrones—"but for yourself."

Apollo's jaw tightened. His voice, when it came, was quiet enough to vanish into the vastness of the hall. "I killed them all."

Markus stepped closer, his shadow cutting over Apollo's. "You ended a rot. You burned out a disease. And now…" He let the pause stretch, the torchlight glinting in his eyes. "…now you will build what comes after."

"Tomorrow, the banners rises" Markus said. "Tonight, you rest. When the sun breaks over Axis, the universe will know our names."

CHAPTER 19

Apollo didn't move. Didn't answer. Only the steady drop of blood from his armor broke the silence as Markus turned and walked away, leaving him in the middle of the throne room—alone with the ghosts he'd made.

Two soldiers walked on either side of Apollo, the rhythmic *clack* of their boots echoing down the gilded corridor. They kept their distance, as if proximity itself was dangerous.

They thought they were whispering quietly enough that he couldn't hear.
"Stronger than any of us…" one murmured.
"Stronger, yes—but if he snaps? Gods help us all."
A short pause. "If he turns on Markus… we'd never stop him."

Apollo didn't look at them, but their words coiled around his mind like smoke.

They stopped before a towering set of golden doors, inlaid with delicate engravings of Axis victories—battles won, empires bent to the knee. The gold was polished to a mirror sheen, mocking in its perfection.

"This is your room," one soldier said, his voice stiff, almost ceremonial.

Apollo reached for the handle. The golden metal radiated a strange, unnatural warmth, as though it had been waiting for his touch. His reflection warped across its surface—a face smeared with blood, eyes ringed with exhaustion.

With a slow push, the massive doors swung inward on whispering hinges, revealing a room so lavish it might have belonged to a god.

A bed dominated the center, impossibly large, its silken sheets blindingly white under the flicker of torchlight, like snow unbroken by footprints. Along the walls, banquet tables groaned under the weight of excess—roast meats glistening in their own juices, citrus fruits split open to reveal jeweled flesh, golden bowls spilling over with berries, cheeses soft enough to melt at a touch. Wine decanters, cold to the touch yet dripping with condensation, breathed the faint perfume of fermented grapes.

At the far end lay a marble bath carved from a single piece of stone, its edges etched with curling motifs of dragons and tides. Steam rose in lazy tendrils from its surface, carrying with it the heady scent of oils— sandalwood, rose, and something darker, almost like myrrh.

This… was the price of killing.

The thought struck him with more weight than any sword blow.

He crossed the threshold slowly, each step dragging as if the air itself resisted him. His armor seemed heavier now, not with steel but with guilt. He reached for the clasps, fingers clumsy from fatigue, and the metal groaned as if in protest. One by one, each plate came free and dropped to the floor with a resonant *clink* that echoed in the vast, hollow room. Dried blood cracked where it had fused to the steel, flaking away in dark rust-colored shards. His undershirt, stiff with gore and sweat, clung to him like a shroud.

The bath called to him.

Without ceremony, he stepped into the water. The heat bit into his skin, a shock that became a slow burn, loosening the crusted blood until it bled into the water in crimson threads.

The scent of steel and death lifted into the steam, mingling with the perfume of the oils until the room smelled of a battlefield disguised as a sanctuary.

He sank lower, until the water covered his mouth and nose, until the world above became muffled and far away. For a fleeting moment, he imagined staying there—letting the heat and silence take him whole. To drown not in water, but in the hope of forgetting.

But when he emerged, steam rolling from his skin, he was no cleaner inside than when he had entered. The blood was gone. The shame remained.

When Apollo finally rose from the bath, the water was almost black — a grave for all the blood he had carried in with him. His skin was scrubbed clean, but the stain beneath the skin remained, an invisible rot threading through every vein.

He dried himself in silence. The feast on the tables called to him with the sweet scent of roasted meat and wine, but he turned away. No taste could cut through the metallic ghost still clinging to his tongue.

The bed received him like an open grave—soft, consuming, white sheets gathering around his body until the world blurred. Sleep came quickly, dragging him under. But it was not rest that found him.

The golden light of the chamber dimmed to a sickly glow, then bled away entirely. The walls dissolved first, their edges curling into nothing. The floor and ceiling followed, until he was suspended in a black so deep it felt wet, pressing in on his skin. This time, he didn't flinch. He knew this place now—the abyss. And the abyss knew him.

Shapes began to bleed through the dark. Not vast, endless things like before—these were closer. Human. The first was bent and frail, its form trembling as though a stiff wind might scatter it to ash. Beside it stood another, smaller but coiled with strength, its silhouette sharp as a drawn blade.

The voices came before their faces.

"But Nana… why didn't he run?" The words were a whisper, fragile, yet threaded with accusation.

Vals reply floated back, steady but weary: "Flow works in mystery. Flow is harsh, yet beautiful. It gives with one hand… and it takes with another."

Apollo's breath caught. That voice, worn down by time yet unmistakable, was Valare's—older now, weathered by decades he had never seen.

She spoke again, not to him, not even to the smaller shadow, but to something beyond them both.

"Flow is everything. It is our past, our present, our future. Sometimes… I see what will come before it happens. Sometimes I see what has already happened—but I cannot stop either."

The smaller shadow shifted, head tilted, silent.

"I have tried to understand it," Valare's voice hardened, the tremor replaced by something colder. "But Flow feels like a sinister child. A child with the eyes of a jester… laughing at us all, knowing the punchline before we do."

The black began to fold in on itself, swallowing the shapes, leaving only their voices. Then the voices thinned, stretched, and vanished into the suffocating dark.

Apollo opened his eyes to find the golden room restored, silent and still, the feast untouched. Yet the air seemed heavier. The whisper clung to him like smoke he could not breathe away:

It gives with one hand… and it takes with another.

Morning came for all of us—but it was not the same as the one before.

The sun did rise, but its light felt pale, stretched thin, as if it had passed through too many clouds before reaching us. We woke still tangled in the grip of our dreams, those fractured, uneasy things that left a sour taste in the mouth. The echoes of the night—the silence, the memories we couldn't name—clung to us like damp wool.

Jaleon was the first to break the quiet, tugging on his boots with a crooked grin.

"Anyone else feel like they've been kissed by a troll and lived to regret it?"

No one laughed at first. Then he added, "If I die today, I want you all to know I'm still not paying back my gambling debts." That earned him a few chuckles, though the sound was thinner than usual, like music played on a cracked flute.

We dressed, checked our gear, and headed toward the training grounds.

The sky above was the color of burnished steel, the kind that gleams just before a storm. Clouds hung heavy, their bellies swollen with unspent rain. The air felt thick—not quite choking, but dense enough to make every breath feel earned.

Serena was already waiting for us, standing with arms crossed, her hair tied back in a tight braid.

"Line up," she ordered, her tone brisk. Her movements were precise as clockwork, each strike of her practice blade an example we were expected to follow. But I noticed it immediately—the way her eyes kept drifting toward the horizon, lingering there for half a heartbeat too long.

"Careful, Serena," Jaleon called while ducking under her strike, "if you keep staring out there, you'll start to miss my pretty face."

Her reply was flat, almost distracted. "That assumes I've noticed it before."
This time the laugh was genuine, brief though it was.

We went through the motions—drills, counters, footwork—but the rhythm was off. Each clash of wooden blades carried an undercurrent, a pulse we couldn't place. I watched Serena closely. Her stance was flawless, her corrections sharp, but the set of her jaw told a different story. She was somewhere else entirely.

Once, between drills, I caught her murmuring something under her breath—too quiet to hear. When I asked, she shook her head. "Nothing. Just… the wind's wrong today."

We all felt it, even if we didn't say so. The air was wrong. The morning was wrong. Something was coming.

Apollo's morning began differently. His armor, scrubbed and polished to a mirror sheen, waited for him by the bedside—the work of silent servants who had labored through the night. Every trace of the slaughter, every crust of dried blood, was gone. The shine was perfect, but its perfection felt hollow, almost obscene.

He dressed slowly. The clasps whispered shut, the buckles slid into place, and the steel seemed to remember his shape as if it had been forged for his very bones. It sat perfectly on his shoulders, and yet—it weighed more than it ever had before.

Stepping into the corridor, the light of the wall torches splashed across him in molten gold. The marble floor caught his reflection in long, broken shards. Guards he passed stiffened and averted their eyes; not out of protocol alone, but because they remembered what those hands had done yesterday.

The great hall loomed ahead, its massive bronze doors yawning open on silent hinges. Inside, the pulse of empire beat strong.

Generals leaned over sprawling tables drowned in maps, charts, and shifting star projections. Commanders moved counters across regions like pieces on a grand, deadly game board.

Routes were traced in red ink, crisscrossing entire systems. Naval deployments glittered in tiny metallic markers, fleets poised like coiled serpents.

The air hummed with tension — the smell of hot wax from map lamps, the faint tang of steel polish, and the charged energy of men and women plotting the reshaping of worlds.

And then, Markus.

He stood at the head of the table, one hand resting on the edge, the other swirling a glass of dark wine as if this were a dinner party rather than a council of war. His gaze found Apollo instantly, a smile flickering across his lips.

"Oh… good morning, sunshine," Markus said with disarming ease, as though they had met in a garden instead of a war chamber. "Sleep well?"

Apollo's voice was firm, even. "Mission? I thought I was to return to the temple."

Markus laughed—a rich, knowing laugh that carried just enough warmth to hide the steel beneath. "Not yet. You've got one more thing to achieve for me."

He gestured, and the nearest general unfurled a new map. "Today you ride with one hundred of our finest—and with Commander Zack of House Vermilian. Your first task: keep him alive."

Apollo's brow furrowed. "That's all?"

"That," Markus said, leaning forward, "is just the start. From there, you will proceed to planet Thyrix—the Flame of Truth. The holy planet of the Umbers. They think us too cautious to strike there, too fearful to desecrate their sanctum." His smile sharpened. "They are wrong."

He traced a finger over the map, stopping at a small, glowing marker. "You will find a temple. Not like Elaris—no… this one is worse. A nest of lies. A forge of heresies. They are building weapons there, feeding them with their so-called truth. I want it cleansed. I want every stone broken, every soul extinguished. When we are done, there will be nothing left but ash. This will be our declaration of war."

Apollo stood his ground, his jaw tight, eyes like steel. He did not raise his weapon, but his words cut sharper than any blade.

"If you want a massacre," he said, his voice calm, steady, unflinching, "then go and do it yourself."

The hall froze. Soldiers who moments before had cheered victory now stood silent, as though the air itself held its breath.

Markus turned toward him, slow, deliberate, his crown catching the torchlight like fire. His gaze was cold, carved from the stone of power itself. When he spoke, it was not loud—but it carried the weight of command, of a man who had already claimed the world as his own.

"You think you have a choice?" Markus hissed. "I gave you justice. I gave you purpose. You will obey my orders… because if you do not, others will pay the price."

The words sank deep. Everyone knew what "others" meant. Elaris. His home. His family. His brothers and sisters in the Flow.

Apollo did not flinch, but something in his eyes shifted. The fire of defiance dimmed into something colder, harder. He lowered his gaze for a breath, then lifted it again—and when he spoke, his voice carried not defeat, but understanding.

"Yes."

One word. A surrender not of spirit, but of necessity.

For in that instant, he understood the truth. He could strike Markus down where he stood. He could unleash all the fury, all the Flow, all the pain he carried. He could bring the entire chamber crashing down in fire and ruin.

But if he did… Elaris would burn for it. Every friend. Every child. Every soul who had ever looked to him for hope.

His hands clenched, and his chest ached with the weight of it. The boy who could defy kings… bowed to protect the only home he had left.

And Markus smiled.

You see, my little one Valere said to the child… never trust a gift freely given. Nothing is ever free. The moment it touches your hand, you are already paying for it.

Do you know the oldest trick in the human mind? Reciprocity. Give a man anything—a coin, a smile, even the justice he has hungered for—and his heart will twist into debt. It will not weigh the value. No. The mind does not calculate cost… it records the gesture. And once the mark is made, it binds you.

You will defend them. Fight for them. Kill for them. Not because you want to… but because to refuse feels like betrayal. That is how the game is played. Not with swords. Not with laws. With favors.

Power is not built on thrones or speeches. It is built on debts you never knew you owed. And they… they will make sure you keep paying.

The moment you accept, you are already bought.

And Apollo—in that single breath of silence— understood the true price of his rage.

The generals bowed their heads. The commanders murmured their praise. The council chamber echoed with their loyalty.

But Apollo… Apollo stood still.

Around them, the generals bowed in unison, their polished armor catching the torchlight like a ripple of molten bronze. Commanders, cloaked in the colors of their houses, raised their voices in praise.

"Markus the Unbroken!"
"Savior of Axis!"
"The True King!"

Each title struck the air like the pounding of a ceremonial gong. The words rolled over the gathered warriors, heavy and resonant, like the first distant rumble of thunder before a storm. It was the sound of history turning, of an empire holding its breath before the plunge into blood.

From the far reaches of the hall came the sound of war drums—deep, deliberate, echoing from the courtyard beyond. Banners unfurled from the upper balconies, their silk snapping in the updraft from the torches, each emblazoned with the sigils of conquest. The scent of burning oil thickened the air, mingling with the iron tang of steel.

Markus saw it all—and smiled wider.

It wasn't just a smile of victory. It was the smile of a man who saw the next three moves in a game no one else realized they were playing. He turned slightly, letting the adulation wash over him like warm rain, yet his gaze never truly left Apollo.

"See?" Markus said lightly, his voice almost lost beneath the chanting. "They already know. And soon, so will the rest of the galaxy."

He stepped closer, the din of the hall dimming as if the air itself bent toward his words. "You stand still, Apollo… but the universe moves. You'll have to decide whether you move with it—or get buried beneath it."

While we laughed in the courtyard, chasing the morning's chill away with half-serious jabs and clumsy jokes, Apollo was somewhere else entirely. Not in body—his boots still touched the same ground as ours—but in soul.

He was alone, locked in a war he had never chosen. A life thrust upon him like a sword shoved into unwilling hands. A destiny that, in time, he would learn was never his to decide.

We saw him and thought we understood. To the common soldier, he was the chosen one, the wielder of greatness—the boy who carried the green flame as if born from it. They whispered his name like a blessing, a promise that Axis could not fall so long as he stood.

But life, like the Flow, has two sides.

There were others who saw him differently—not as a hero, but as a killer. The senators whose kin would never rise from the marble. The guards whose brothers lay cold in the hall of judgment.

The widows who would curse his name when the drums of war faded and the truth crawled in to take their place.

And between those two truths, he stood alone. Not in the golden light of destiny, not in the shadow of condemnation—but somewhere in between, where no one's eyes could follow.

That was Apollo's war. Not the battles we saw… but the one inside, tearing him apart long before any blade could.

Apollo stood at the very edge of the embarkation platform, the cold wind from the carrier's engines tugging and snapping at his cloak like impatient hands. The air tasted of iron and oil. His armor gleamed in the pale morning light—polished to a warrior's perfection—but its weight was heavier than steel. It was the weight of what Markus had commanded… and the blood he already carried on his soul.

Below him, the army stretched in faultless formation, ranks of steel and shadow, their banners rippling like the black wings of crows. At the front stood Commander Zack of House Vermilian—tall, broad-shouldered, the kind of man whose stance alone commanded obedience. Beside him, a young woman lifted her voice in song.

It was not a battle hymn. It was older, softer, an echo from a time before war had names. Her voice wove through the air like smoke from a dying fire—haunting and slow, yet unyielding. She sang in a language older than Axis itself, a tongue few understood, yet all felt in their bones:

"Through the night we sail,
With no star to guide the way,
Carry me home on the river's breath,
Before the dawn takes my name."

As Apollo descended toward them, the world itself seemed to shift. The shadows along the walls leaned toward him. The air grew heavy, tasting faintly of copper. The soldiers' eyes followed him, their postures tightening not from parade discipline, but from something instinctive... a primal recognition. Behind him trailed an almost tangible pressure—a quiet, sinister aura, as if the Flow itself had coiled around him like a living thing.

Step by step, he crossed the platform, the woman's voice stretching each moment into slow motion. One by one, the ranks turned toward the yawning bay of the carrier. The song followed them, refusing to fade.

"If the wind forgets my face,
And the tide swallows my name,

Tell my mother I am only sleeping,
And the river carried me away."

Inside Apollo's mind, another voice slipped into the melody. His mother's voice. Soft, desperate.
Run, my boy… run.

The massive bay doors closed behind them with the finality of a tomb sealing. The engines roared, vibrating through steel and bone. Then—silence. The kind of silence that made a man aware of every breath he took.

Apollo stood at a narrow window, watching the sky fall away as Axis shrank beneath them. His reflection in the glass looked like a stranger—pale, unreadable, with eyes too old for his age.

A soldier approached, young-faced but battle-worn, a faint crack in his voice. "Sir… thank you for being here with us."

Another voice came from behind, deeper, warm but cautious. "Yes, sir. These Wilders can be tricky. Having you with us… it means something."

Apollo turned, expression unreadable. "I'm not a 'sir.' I'm younger than both of you."

The first soldier grinned sheepishly. "Maybe so… but you're still the one we'd follow into hell."

Apollo didn't answer. The song still lingered in his ears. And hell… was exactly where they were going. For some for some others this hell was called home like Kaith

CHAPTER 20

The descent burned the heavens.

From the carrier's viewing deck, Apollo stood silent, hands braced against the glass as the planet swelled in the viewport. Thyrix revealed itself in stages—first the endless sweep of pale-gold deserts, their dunes rippling like an ocean frozen in mid-tide. Then came the cliffside cities, sprawling tiers of white stone carved straight into the rock, their balconies glittering with banners of deep crimson and gold. Vast rivers of molten sunlight wound through the land, catching the sun like blades of glass, until they spilled into the sapphire sea.

And there, on the far edge of the coast, the Temple of the Flame rose.

It dominated the skyline—a masterpiece of white marble and sun-gilded bronze. Its spires climbed toward the heavens like the fingers of a hand in eternal prayer, each tipped with a beacon-fire that had burned, it was said, for a thousand years. Bridges of carved stone connected its towers, and at its heart stood a great dome, inlaid with fireglass mosaics that shimmered with every breath of wind.

As the carrier plunged through a veil of thin, silvery clouds, the light seemed to change. Softer. More reverent. It touched the temple like a blessing, setting its spires aglow. Even Apollo, hardened by war, felt the stillness of the moment. This was holy ground. The kind of place where voices lowered and footsteps slowed.

But the engines of war did not slow.
The shadow of the carrier spread over the city like a black tide, its shape bending over the temple's steps, swallowing the light it had just kissed.

The landing was an act of violence. The massive steel belly slammed into the earth with a bone-deep thud, the shock rolling through the marble streets. Dust burst upward in choking clouds, smearing the horizon. The bells of the Temple of the Flame began to toll—slow, heavy peals that were meant to summon the faithful but now rang as a warning.

The great bronze gates at the temple's entrance shuddered under the sound, their embossed flames seeming to flicker in the shifting light. From the high terraces, robed priests and acolytes looked down in stillness, their expressions caught between disbelief and dread.

When the boarding ramp of the carrier groaned open, the first sight to meet them was Axis steel. Banners of black and gold unfurled into the wind, snapping like war drums. The army poured forth in perfect formation, boots pounding in unison against the marble. Commander Zack of House Vermilian led them, his armor reflecting the temple's firelight as if mocking it.

Beyond them, the Temple of the Flame stood untouched—for now. Its doors were shut, its relics still safe within. But Apollo knew the order. Knew what Markus had commanded. The sanctity of this place would be torn apart stone by stone, until nothing remained but ash.

The bells tolled again.
And the holy ground trembled under the boots of an empire.

The Axis army stood like an iron wall before the Temple of the Flame. The morning sun lit their armor in blinding gold, their banners whipping in the wind — but all that light only cast longer shadows upon those who stood to defend the holy ground.

They were not warriors.
They were the women and children of the temple, robed in colors that spoke of devotion rather than bloodshed. Every acolyte, every priest, every keeper of

the sacred flame had come to the steps — not because they thought they could win, but because they would rather die here than see their faith burned away.

They clutched their crystals—green, blue, red, orange— each a shard of the sacred prisms that lit the temple halls. In the rising light, those gems cast their glow across the faces of their bearers. The colors should have been beautiful. Instead, they trembled with fear, glimmering in the eyes of children who had never seen battle.

Apollo's gaze swept them, and his stomach turned. Some were no older than seven or eight—younger even than the novice acolytes of Elaris. Their small hands gripped Sunspears too large for them not yet fully developed weapons, the shafts shaking as they tried to hold them upright. These were defenders in name, only to the trained soldiers of Axis, they were no threat at all.

And yet… they stood.
Not out of strength, but out of belief.

A silence gripped the courtyard, the kind that doesn't just fall—it crushes. The only sound that dared to live in it was the low, steady hum of the great crystal heart within the temple, its resonance seeping through the marble underfoot. It was an ancient sound, deep and alive, as if the stone itself was breathing.

And then… it broke.

From among the line of defenders, a small figure stepped forward. No one called him back, though every eye followed him. He was no more than nine years old, his temple robe too long, the hem frayed and stained from years of use. In his hands, gripped so tightly his knuckles whitened, was a Sunspear crowned with a crystal of pure blue—it caught the light in a trembling blaze, scattering shards of color across his frightened face.

He ran.

The boy moved awkwardly, his stride uneven, the small body of a child not yet accustomed to the weight of a weapon. Yet there was no hesitation in his intent. Each step slapped against the marble stones of the courtyard, sharp and hollow, echoing like the beating of a frightened—but unbroken—heart.

The blue crystal flared brighter with every stride, fragile but resolute, as if the boy's memories themselves breathed life into it. Apollo felt the Flow surge faintly around him, and in that moment he knew—the boy carried no rage, no hatred, no malice. What flowed within him was something rarer, purer. Love. Love for the temple, for the people behind him, for the laughter and warmth he refused to let die.

A soldier stepped forward, armor clattering, blade already drawn. A grown man facing a nine-year-old child—a fair fight, in the twisted eyes of the Axis. The soldier swung hard, the edge meant to end the boy in a single stroke.

But the child moved.

His body ducked low, slipping past the arc of steel like water slipping through fingers. In one clean motion he thrust the Sunspear forward, the crystal edge grazing the soldier's chest. The man staggered, shocked, but not slain. For the boy's spear was not sharp enough, not fully grown into the weapon it would one day be. And because—even here, facing death—he had struck not with the intent to kill, but with the intent to protect.

It was an act of pure love.

The boy stood before the entire army of Axis soldiers, his tiny form trembling but unbroken, blue light humming against the backdrop of blood and banners. His voice rang out, high but clear, cracking with emotion yet carrying with it the weight of truth:

"This is a place of peace—not war! I thought... I thought we had peace!"

Silence fell like a curtain. Hundreds of soldiers froze, their weapons lowered, their breaths caught. The echo of the boy's words seemed louder than any war cry.

Apollo's heart twisted. In the boy's defiance, he saw himself—Kaith reflected back at him. The same eyes, the same unshakable will. But unlike Apollo, this child carried no rage. Only hope. Only love.

The boy took another step forward, closer to Commander Zack. His small hands tightened around the Sunspear, the glow trembling but unyielding. His sandals scraped the stone, steady now, as though with each stride he grew taller in spirit.

And in that moment—for a fleeting heartbeat—it felt as though the entire Axis army held its breath, waiting to see if innocence could stand against the weight of empire.

Commander stood unmoved at the head of the Axis line. His armor gleamed like forged midnight, his hand resting on the hilt of his sword as though the boy's approach were nothing more than a formality. When the child reached striking distance, Zack moved—a flash of steel, swift and precise.

The blade passed cleanly.

The boy's legs buckled, his spear clattering against the marble, the crystal at its tip shattering into a spray of fractured light. The shards danced and spun across the white stone before settling in silence, the blue glow fading to nothing.

A single cry tore from the defenders—not a battle shout, but a raw, human sound of loss. And then there was stillness again. No one else charged. The courage of one had not stirred the rest; it had shown them the truth.

The truth that this would not be a fight.
It would be an ending.

Apollo did not move.
His boots felt rooted to the marble, his breath lodged somewhere high in his chest. Around him, the courtyard was alive with color—but he saw none of it. All he saw were faces. Faces that could have been his friends back in Elaris, boys he'd trained with in the temple's gardens, girls who'd laughed with him in the quiet hours of dawn. Faces that belonged to brothers and sisters he never had but now imagined. They blurred, overlapping with the present until he could not tell if he was looking at the defenders of Thyrix or the ghosts of a life before Markus, before the war had stripped him bare.

Zack's voice broke the illusion like a hammer through glass.
"Charge! Leave none alive!"

It was a command sharpened on steel—and the Axis soldiers obeyed with a roar that rattled the air.

They surged forward as one.
Boots thundered against the sacred steps, drowning out the hum of the crystal heart. The defenders' robes—green, blue, red, orange—flashed once, twice, before being swallowed by the silver sheen of blades and the black crush of advancing armor. The bright, jewel-like colors became streaks on the marble, indistinguishable from the splintered light of shattered acolyte crystals.

The first clash was not a clash at all. There was no exchange, no parry and counterstrike—only impact. The Axis ranks broke through like a flood bursting its dam, cutting down the untrained wielders as if they were reeds in a field. The air filled with the brittle, ringing snap of crystal weapons shattering, with voices crying out in prayer and pain until both were lost under the grind of steel.

For the Axis, it was not a battle.
It was the efficient, methodical ending of a people's faith.

And for Apollo… it was the moment his armor stopped feeling like protection and became a prison. Every plate, every strap seemed to press tighter, as though it knew it was holding him in place while the slaughter unfolded around him.

The courtyard of the Temple of the Flame was no longer a sanctuary.
It had become a furnace of screams and steel.

The perfect white steps of the temple ran red. Blood pooled in the channels carved into the stone for rainwater, carrying away petals from the ceremonial gardens, now crushed underfoot. The air was thick with the smell of copper and burning oil from overturned braziers.

Apollo stood in the midst of it all—motionless, a single figure in a storm of slaughter.
His sword remained sheathed at his side, the green crystal at its hilt faintly pulsing, as though even it hesitated.

Tears stung his eyes, blurring the carnage into streaks of color—crimson on white marble, gold from fallen banners, black shadows of soldiers moving through smoke. Heat pressed in from all sides, but in his chest, a deep and unnatural cold had settled, crawling into his bones. Each breath was shallow, tasting of copper and ash, scraping his throat like sand.

Every scream, every clash of steel, every body hitting stone clawed at something deep in him. And then— unbidden—another image cut through the chaos. Not Thyrix. Not now. Kaith. Another massacre. Another courtyard painted in blood. The same smell. The same helplessness.

The same truth: *If I act now… Elaris will burn. Jaleon will die. Lux will die. Valere will die.*

The choice was a chain around his throat.
He could not move.

Then, the temple's great doors erupted outward in a thunderclap of sound and force.

From the shadowed interior, she emerged.

Zeri.
Grand Master of the Temple of the Flame.

Her very presence bent the air around her.
Her crystal—pale orange—blazed like a muted sun, the color of harmony now warped by grief into something fierce and unstable. The light it cast danced across her features, revealing not the calm, stoic master her people once knew, but a warrior raw and stripped of restraint.

Her eyes swept across the courtyard with deliberate slowness, drinking in every detail:
The still forms of children she had once guided through morning meditations.
The women who had shared her meals and prayers, lying in unnatural angles on the blood-slick stone.
The few survivors pressed against the temple steps, their crystal charms clutched tight to trembling chests, too afraid to move.

The sight burned into her, and something inside her broke—not quietly, but like a dam shattering.

When she exhaled, it came out as a sound closer to a growl than a breath.

Her hand went to her weapon, and the moment her fingers closed on its hilt, the blade came alive, orange fire racing the length of steel, crackling with the energy of her rage. The ground seemed to tense under her feet. Her stance was low, coiled—a predator poised to strike.

And when she moved, it was with the unrelenting speed of grief turned to fury.

With a roar that cracked the still air and rattled the carved pillars, Zeri drew her blade. The weapon answered her fury instantly—its edge erupting in a blaze of pale orange fire, the light dancing across her armor and casting jagged shadows across the blood-slick marble. The crystal set in the hilt pulsed in time with her heartbeat, each throb feeding the flames until they hissed and spat like a living thing eager to kill.

She launched herself into the Axis ranks without hesitation.
Her movement was not reckless—it was precise, honed from decades of discipline—but it carried the ferocity of a storm that has broken its restraints.

Each slash tore through steel plate as if she were cutting cloth. The soldiers, armed and trained for war, were nothing before her fury. Their cries were drowned beneath the roar of her blade meeting armor, the wet crack of shattered bone, the hiss of scorched metal.

"You came here to kill children?!"
Her voice carried over the din, breaking like a whip in the air.
"This is your honor?!"

Her strikes fell like judgments from the heavens. A soldier raised his spear—she stepped inside the thrust, severed the shaft in one clean arc, and cut him down before his scream could fully form. Two more tried to flank her; she pivoted, her flaming blade carving a blazing half-circle that sent them both crashing lifeless to the marble.

The temple's sacred courtyard—once filled with the colors of crystals and prayer cloths — now became a killing ground. The light from her sword painted the walls in wild, dancing fire, turning the faces of the fallen into ghostly masks.

Then her gaze found him.
Commander Zack of House Vermil

ian.

He stood tall at the head of his troops, barking orders with the calm of a man who had seen this before — as if this massacre were merely another line on a campaign ledger. The sight of his composure against the backdrop of slaughter ignited something deeper in her. Her rage narrowed into a single, burning point.

Zeri broke into a sprint, feet splashing through pools of blood, her path a straight line over the bodies of her fallen acolytes.

The smell of iron filled her lungs. Her hands gripped the hilt so tightly her knuckles whitened beneath the firelight.

Zack stepped forward, meeting her charge with a raised steel blade. The world seemed to slow as they closed the distance. Her strike came first—a downward cut backed by the full force of her grief and fury.

The impact was like a forge hammer on brittle metal. Sparks erupted in a blinding spray, and a sound like a bone snapping echoed across the courtyard. Zack's weapon sheared apart under the blow, the steel snapping in two, each half clattering at his feet.

The soldiers around them faltered. Even the Axis banners seemed to shudder in the sudden silence after the strike. Zeri stood before Zack, her blade still burning, her chest heaving—the only thing between her and his life was the thin air that carried her next breath.

Apollo saw it.
Saw the shattered remains of Zack's blade at his feet.
Saw Zeri standing before him, her weapon aflame with orange fury, every muscle in her body tensed for the killing stroke.

And with it came the echo.

Markus's voice from days before, smooth as steel drawn from a scabbard:

Your first mission is to protect him.

It wasn't just an order—it was a chain wrapped around his throat. A single, brutal truth stabbed through his mind: if Zack died here, so would Elaris. Markus had made sure of it.

His breath caught. The air around him felt heavier, as though the world itself was waiting for him to move.

He did.

Apollo's fingers closed around the hilt of his sword, the motion as inevitable as the pull of gravity. The weapon roared to life with a violent hum—a jagged green light sparking unevenly along its fractured edge, hungry, unstable, alive.

Then he was in motion.

To the soldiers, it was as though the wind itself had turned predator. Apollo cut between them with terrifying precision, his movements a blur of steel and emerald fire. Armor scraped against stone as they stumbled out of his path, their eyes wide at the speed they could not follow.

In the space between one heartbeat and the next, he was there—between Zeri and Zack.

Their swords met with a sound like the sky tearing in half. Green flame clashed against orange fire, and the collision sent a shockwave ripping through the courtyard. The very air bent under the force, warping with heat and pressure.

Flow erupted from the impact in violent, crackling waves—jagged arcs of energy snapping across the marble, scorching banners, shattering loose stone.

The ground beneath their feet trembled as if the temple itself were recoiling.

The air grew hotter, each breath burning in the lungs. The scent of ozone and scorched crystal filled the courtyard, mixing with the metallic tang of blood.

From deep within the temple, the great crystal heart began to pulse faster—a slow, rhythmic beat turning into an urgent drum, as if it recognized the duel now unfolding. Its light spilled out through the cracks in the temple doors, bathing the combatants in shifting hues of orange and green, as if the Flow itself could not decide which of them it belonged to.

Apollo's jaw clenched. His arms shook under the force of her strike, the heat of her blade searing close enough to blister skin. Zeri's eyes, burning with grief and righteous rage, bored into his—and in that look, he saw that she understood.

Not why he fought her.
But that he didn't want to.

The first clash had already shaken the courtyard, but now the world seemed to draw inward.
The noise of the slaughter dulled to a distant, muffled roar, as though reality itself wanted to hear what would happen next. The Flow surged between them—not passive, not invisible—but a living current, like a river deciding whether to flood or recede.

Zeri's breath misted in the heat radiating from her blade. "You… protect *him*?" she spat, glancing at Zack over Apollo's shoulder. "Elaris should be neutral and yet you are here defending a monster. COWARD"

Apollo's jaw tightened. "I don't have a choice." His voice was low, almost drowned by the whispering of the Flow around them. "You think I want this?"

"Want or not," Zeri growled, "you will die here."

She moved first. Her blade swept low in a burning arc, the orange Flow spilling from its edge like molten silk. Apollo pivoted sideways, his green, jagged sword intercepting hers in a flash of opposing light—orange and green meeting with a crack that sent spiderweb fractures racing across the marble.

The Flow reacted violently. Each strike sent shockwaves spiraling through the air, carrying flecks of light like embers in a gale. The banners above the temple tore loose, carried upward on the current, their colors twisting in the turbulence.

Apollo countered, stepping in with a diagonal slash meant to drive her back. She caught it at the midpoint, their weapons locking. Flow coursed between them— not just heat and light, but a pressure that pressed against skin and bone, testing their resolve.

You're strong," Zeri hissed, her voice tight with both strain and awe. Their blades locked, her orange fire flaring against his jagged green blaze. Sparks showered the courtyard, sizzling as they struck the shattered marble.

"But your Flow…" She faltered for the briefest instant, her eyes locking onto his. And in that flicker of time, she saw something she could not name. Two currents. Two forces.

It wasn't just Apollo standing before her—it was as though two selves warred within the same vessel, each vying for dominance, each striking at her through him.

Her chest tightened. She had seen eyes like that once before—not in a duel, not in any battlefield, but in the whispers of prophecy, in the stories told of those who were touched too deeply by the Flow. Eyes that were not singular, but fractured. Eyes that burned with something more than mortal will.

"My Flow is what?" Apollo's voice cut through her thoughts, sharp as his blade. He wrenched upward, forcing her weapon back.

Green light erupted between them, jagged and violent. It wasn't a clean surge, not a noble blaze like the flames of her own crystal—it was raw, uneven, chaotic, as if the Flow itself strained to remain inside him. The eruption sent a ripple through the ground, cracks spiderwebbing outward from their feet, dust exploding upward in a ring.

The temple's crystal heart pulsed in answer, its resonant hum shaken into a trembling wail, as if the very sanctum recoiled from what it felt within Apollo's strike.

Zeri used the opening to spin away, her footwork a dance of precision learned over decades. She came back in with a high slash, then a low feint, her blade carving orange trails through the air. The Flow shimmered like heat-haze in her wake, each motion tugging at Apollo's own current, trying to unbalance him.

Apollo met her head-on, his movements sharper, less graceful—but relentless. His blade's edge howled against hers, sparks spitting in every direction. Every time their weapons connected, the Flow bent around them, condensing into visible rings of force that burst outward, knocking nearby soldiers off their feet.

The temple's crystal heart pulsed faster, its light now flickering erratically between green and orange, as if it were caught in the duel's rhythm. Cracks began to crawl along its base, glowing like veins under skin.

"You can't win this," Apollo warned, driving her back a step. "I won't let you."

Zeri's eyes blazed. "You've already lost."

With a cry, she poured everything into her next strike —the Flow in her blade roaring like a wildfire. Apollo braced, letting his own energy surge upward from his core, into the jagged heart of his weapon. When they collided this time, the sound was not steel on steel.

It was thunder.

The courtyard exploded with light. The ground split beneath them, molten energy searing upward from the cracks. Soldiers shielded their eyes as the force tore through the air, scattering dust and crystal fragments like shards of a shattered star.

When the light faded, they stood locked together, blades trembling, neither giving ground. The Flow raged between them, wild and uncertain, as if deciding in that instant which one it would break—and which one it would crown.

The duel was no longer just combat—it was a storm. Green and orange light tangled in the air like warring comets, whipping the banners into flames and cracking the temple's crystal heart with each clash. The marble beneath their feet spiderwebbed under the force of every blow.

Zeri moved like a dancer forged in grief. Her footwork was tight, coiled, each step drawing Apollo into her tempo. Apollo countered with raw force—sweeping arcs of jagged green light, the hum of his Sunspear grinding against the shriek of her crystal blade.

They circled.
Strike. Parry. Clash.

The Flow surged with each collision, bending the air into heat waves that rippled out across the courtyard. Crystals embedded in the temple walls flickered and dimmed in time with their strikes, as though the building itself was holding its breath.

Apollo (through clenched teeth): *"Stand down, ! This doesn't have to be—"*
Zeri (cutting him off, voice like thunder): *"Doesn't have to be what? A massacre? A graveyard of children? You made your choice!"*

She feinted left—Apollo pivoted to intercept—and that's when she saw it. A breath too long in his stance. A half-inch drop in his guard.

Her eyes narrowed to a razor's edge, the pale orange of her crystal flaring until it seemed to burn with the light of a dying sun. The heat of her rage rolled off her in waves, bending the very Flow around her like molten air over desert stone.

She stepped once—twice—then lunged. The orange blaze of her blade split the air, a lightning bolt condensed into steel and fury.

Apollo saw it too late.

The world tilted.

The point of her sword found the seam in his guard and punched through his chest with a wet, tearing sound that seemed impossibly loud and yet… instantly devoured by silence.

The courtyard's chaos—the screams, the clash of steel, the pounding war drums of boots on marble—all vanished as if someone had torn the sound from existence. Even the deep mechanical thrum of the carrier's engines above became nothing more than a memory.

Only one sound remained.
His heartbeat.
Slow. Heavy. Deafening.

The blade was buried deep, the fire of it scorching the edges of the wound until it felt as though molten glass had been poured into him. The heat radiated outward in cruel pulses, each one stealing more of his strength.

His breath caught mid-inhale, tasting of copper and ash. Every swallow was a struggle, each drop of air a thread that refused to stay in his lungs. His fingers twitched on the hilt of his green Sunspear, but the grip faltered, the weapon dipping toward the ground.

Somewhere beyond the void, Zeri's face hovered inches from his, her breath hot against his cheek. The orange light of her blade painted her features in fire and shadow, every line carved by fury and grief.

Far away from Thyrix, the wound rippled through the Flow like a crack through glass.

Jaleon stopped mid-step in the training yard, the practice blade slipping from his fingers to clatter against the stone. His face twisted, the air stolen from his lungs as though an invisible hand had closed around his heart. He clutched at his chest, knuckles white, eyes darting to the horizon without knowing why—only feeling the strike as if it had landed in him.

I—Valere—staggered against the temple wall, the world narrowing into a tunnel of pain. My vision flashed white, breath shattering into ragged gasps. My fingers curled into the stone, clawing for something real as a phantom spearpoint punched through me from breastbone to spine. In that moment, I could taste the metallic sting of Apollo's blood in my own mouth.

Lux was the worst of all. In the sparring circle, his knees buckled beneath , his sword falling with a dull thud. The yard spun in a sickening whirl of sky and earth. he gritted hir teeth, refusing to scream, but his hands trembled violently as if the Flow itself was tearing them apart from the inside. His breath came in short, panicked bursts, his heartbeat thundering in his ears like a war drum out of sync with the world.

None of us could see the battlefield, but we felt it—the exact point where orange fire tore into Apollo's chest, the soundless rip in the bond we didn't choose but could never escape. It wasn't just pain. It was fear. It was the certainty that something in him, something in all of us, had just been broken.

Zeri held him there, the orange fire of her blade buried deep in his chest, the heat searing muscle and bone. Her breath was ragged, her face so close he could feel the tremor in it, smell the iron tang of blood on her skin. Her voice, though quivering, struck like a blade of its own.

"You could have been our savior," she hissed, her eyes wet but unyielding. "You could have stood with us—with the innocent, with the ones who needed you. But you… you stand with them. With butchers. With killers." Her grip tightened, forcing the blade an inch deeper. "This is the only end you deserve."

And then, the world around her blurred.
The edges of her face melted into another—softer, gentler, framed by hair the color of dusk, wild and unbound in the wind. Eyes glistening not with rage, but with fear.

His mother.

He heard her before he fully saw her, the sound slipping through the roar of pain, threading between the pounding of his heartbeat.
Run, my boy… run.

It was the same voice from the nights of his childhood, when storms shook the roof and she would hold him close. The same tone she had used the day she'd told him to flee and never look back. But now it was fainter, as though carried on the last breath of a dying wind.

The battlefield dimmed around him. Zeri's weight, the heat of her weapon, the screams, the clash of steel—all receded, drowned beneath the echo of that voice and the sight of those familiar eyes. For a moment, there was no war, no Markus, no Thyrix. There was only the boy she had told to run… and the man who had stayed.

Something inside him ruptured—not just in body, but in soul. It was as if a sealed chamber deep within had cracked open, releasing something that had been caged for lifetimes.

The green flame of his Sunspear flared violently, spitting sparks like a dying star, before collapsing inward as if consumed by its own hunger. The light did not fade—it deepened. From the bright emerald of life, it sank into a green so dense and saturated that to look at it was to feel your eyes strain, your mind recoil. This was not light that illuminated—it devoured. It drank the brightness from the air, swallowed the color from the world, leaving the edges of everything dim around it.

The Flow itself reacted. The air thickened as though the atmosphere had grown heavy with stormwater. Invisible currents twisted and bucked like wild beasts, the very fabric of reality writhing away from him before snapping back in violent waves. It was no longer the gentle river of life and fate—it had become an ocean in upheaval, roaring with an ancient, predatory rhythm.

It was not merely power. It was something *remembered*— an echo of a force the galaxy had once feared, awakened again in him.

Dust swirled in frantic spirals at his feet. Crystals embedded in the temple walls flickered in distress, some shattering outright, unable to withstand the vibration in the air. Even the blood pooled on the marble rippled outward, forming circles that trembled in time with his heartbeat.

And then there were his eyes.
They blazed that same deep, consuming green—so bright they seemed not to glow, but to burn holes in reality itself. In the haze of battle, they cut through the dust like twin beacons, cold and unblinking, the gaze of a god who had decided what must live and what must be destroyed.

Zeri staggered back a single step, the orange light of her blade trembling in her grasp. Her breath came fast, but not from exertion—from something older, deeper.

Her voice, once a battle cry, broke into a whisper. "What… are you?"

The words tasted of fear.

It wasn't the wound she feared—it was him. The way the air bent around Apollo now, the way the Flow recoiled and then coiled tighter, like a predator circling its prey. The deep green of his eyes was no longer just a color—it was an abyss, swallowing all light, all certainty.

Her heartbeat pounded in her ears, each thud dragging memories to the surface unbidden.

She was a girl again, kneeling on the temple's sun-warmed marble, swearing the Oath of the Flame. She felt the joy of her crystal's awakening, the day it first burned orange in her hand, filling her with the certainty that she would protect Thyrix until her last breath. She saw the faces of the other acolytes—the ones who had laughed with her in the cloisters, who now lay lifeless at her feet.

And now… now she saw her end.

It came not as a single image, but as a flood—fragments of her life flashing too quickly to hold. Her first sword. Her first kill. The scent of temple incense in the morning. The sound of bells in the rain. All of it compressed into the single, inescapable truth that stood before her: she would die here, and it would be by his hand.

The inevitability of it was more crushing than the fear. It wasn't death she resisted—it was the knowledge that she had never faced anything like this. Not a man. Not a soldier. Not even a killer.

Something beyond human.

And in his eyes, the Flow itself stared back at her…
and it was laughing.

The air seemed to pause, holding its breath.
Then—Apollo moved.

It was not the speed of a warrior lunging. It was the inevitability of an avalanche breaking loose, the silent promise of destruction that nothing could halt. His boots struck the marble with such force that the stone spider-webbed beneath him, sending hairline cracks racing outward like fleeing serpents.

Zeri pivoted, drawing on the last surge of her strength, her orange crystal burning with a defiance that defied reason. She swung—a perfect guard born of decades of training, every muscle and memory committed to this one desperate block.

Green met orange.
Not as color, but as worlds colliding.

The deep green light of Apollo's blade did not cut—it consumed. The moment they touched, Zeri's weapon did not simply break. It *ceased to be*. The edge of her sword dissolved into motes of glowing dust, vanishing into the air as though the Flow itself had decided her weapon no longer had the right to exist.

And then the shockwave came.

It tore through the courtyard with the voice of gods in wrath. Soldiers were flung backward as if struck by invisible giants, their armor screaming as buckles snapped. Banners ripped free from their poles, vanishing into the storm. The marble tiles of the temple steps shattered and peeled away, curling like paper in a flame.

Deep inside the Temple of the Flame, the crystal heart—centerpiece of its sacred power—split down the middle with a sound like the sky breaking open. The crack glowed for a heartbeat, then dulled, its song silenced forever.

When the dust finally began to fall, the world revealed itself again. Zeri lay on her back, her body slack, the pale orange of her crystal dimming to nothing. Her eyes, once fierce, now stared glassy into the heavens, reflecting only the empty sky.

And standing over her… Apollo.

His eyes still burned with that abyssal green, but in his pupils, you could see a gold statue a light that seemed older than war, older than any king. He looked like a warborn God—something not made, but unearthed from the bones of the world, brought forth to decide the fates of nations.

Silence fell. Not the uneasy pause before more violence, but the true silence of the world recognizing something it could not name.

Then Apollo moved again—but slowly. He knelt beside Zeri, the weight of the moment pressing even heavier than his armor. His gauntlet reached forward, fingers brushing her face with a gentleness that jarred against the devastation surrounding them. He closed her eyes with care, as though sealing away the fury that had burned in them.

His voice cracked, the words carrying not to the soldiers, not to the generals, but only to her.
"Your fight is over."

A tear cut down through the dust on his cheek.
"Rest in eternal light" Apollo said with respect in his voice "May we meet again, Zeri."

He had never heard her name. And yet, somehow, he had always known it.

Apollo's breath rasped in his throat as he pushed himself upright, the pain radiating through every nerve like molten lead. He had been wounded before, yes—but never like this.

This time the Flow had not healed him fully.

Instead, it had left him marked.

The scar was black, deep as a chasm, cutting across his chest. It seemed to drink the light, swallowing it into its depths. To look at it too long was to feel as though the world tilted beneath your feet, as though it were not merely a wound, but a door into something cold and endless.

He staggered, nearly falling before a soldier caught him under the arm. The man's grip was strong, but there was a tremor in it. His eyes flickered toward the scar and quickly away again.

Apollo's gaze shifted past him.
The soldier who had thanked him earlier lay sprawled nearby, eyes glassy, lips parted as though still trying to form his last words. His blood soaked the marble in a slow, widening pool. The other—the one still breathing—was caked in gore that was not his own, his armor dented and his breathing ragged.

"Holy shit, boy," Zack's voice cut in, thick with that careless bravado only killers carry. He strode over, his grin wide enough to be mistaken for joy. "For a moment, I thought I lost you! You are something amazing."

Apollo did not answer.

His eyes never met Zack's.

Instead, he turned toward the temple.

Its massive bronze doors stood agape, as if left yawning in shock at what had just happened on its steps. The blood of the defenders streaked the white marble stairs, flowing into the grooves between the stones.

He walked forward, each step deliberate, boots clicking on stone in the deepening quiet. The shadow of the temple's entrance swallowed him, and the world outside faded into muffled echoes.

Inside, the air was cool and heavy with the fading scent of incense—faint, but still lingering, like a memory refusing to be forgotten. The light filtered through shattered skylights above, dust motes drifting in golden shafts that cut across the floor.

The marble beneath his boots was white as bone, veined with gold. It reflected his image back at him, fractured and broken where the tiles had been cracked by battle. Blood was smeared here too, tracked in by the boots of men who had no reverence for the ground they trod.

He looked up.
Golden pillars soared toward the ceiling, their surfaces etched with intricate carvings of flame and water

intertwined—the cycle of creation and destruction, the sacred balance of the Umber faith.

It was… nothing like Elaris.
Elaris had been obsidian and shadow, lit by firelight and the soft glow of crystal lamps. It had been a place of solemn whispers and steady resolve.

This temple had been a beacon of light. Warm. Open. Alive.

Now it was silent.

Apollo's steps echoed between the pillars. Each one felt like an intrusion.
His eyes caught on the statues along the walls—serene figures, hands outstretched in eternal blessing. The same calm expressions carved into the statues of Elaris. The same posture of guardianship, the same gaze that seemed to follow you through the room.

The Umber people… these so-called fanatics… had prayed under the same gaze, whispered to the same silence.

Different names. Different banners.
But every side had its devil.

He walked deeper. The vast central chamber opened before him, dominated by the temple's crystal heart—a towering shard of pale orange light, now cracked through the center. It pulsed weakly, as though each beat cost it more than it could give.

Around its base lay offerings that had been untouched for centuries—bowls of sand from sacred dunes, carved wooden effigies of the Flame, strings of crystal beads. Among them were smaller things—a child's toy carved from stone, a faded ribbon, a copper pendant engraved with a name.

Ghosts began to stir in his mind.
Not real, perhaps—but the Flow whispered them into being. He could see the courtyard alive again: children chasing each other between the pillars, their laughter spilling like sunlight; acolytes sweeping the marble floors with quiet devotion; the Grand Master Zeri walking among them, her presence a calm tide.

And then the vision cracked.
The sound of steel. The smell of blood. The vision children falling. The offerings overturned.

The ghosts faded, and Apollo stood alone in the hollowed heart of the temple.

The wound in his chest ached, but the ache was not from Zeri's blade.

It was from the knowledge that this place would never be what it once was.

He turned back toward the entrance, his shadow stretching across the white marble like a stain.

Apollo drifted deeper into the temple's wounded heart, his boots whispering over marble streaked with soot and blood. The air was heavy here, the scent of burning oil mixing with something older—incense baked into the stone over centuries, clinging stubbornly despite the violence around it.

From the outer halls came the sounds of desecration.
Boots on marble.
Metal on marble.
A deafening clang as a statue was dragged from its pedestal and shattered against the floor. A wooden altar cracked open with a dry, splintering scream. Soldiers' voices rang out in sharp, vulgar bursts—laughter, orders, curses—all of it echoing off the soaring vaults that had once carried only prayer.

But Apollo moved apart from them.
His steps were unhurried, almost reverent, as though he were walking in a place that belonged to a memory, not a battlefield. Every line of his body was tense, but

his eyes traced the details—the archways engraved with rivers of gold leaf, the murals depicting saints of flame, their paint chipped but still luminous.

This was not his victory.
He could feel it in his bones—this had been a place of peace. And even now, beneath the stink of blood and smoke, that peace clung to the air like the faint note of a song that refused to fade.

Then his gaze caught on something in the shadows ahead.

A doorway, partially hidden behind a fractured pillar. Its frame was a marriage of contrasts—rich gold chasing the edges of black obsidian, the light of the former catching the torchglow, the latter swallowing it.

Two marble guardians flanked it.

The one on the left was decapitated, its great bow still gripped tight in sculpted hands, aimed eternally at an enemy that would never come. The missing head lay in ruin at its feet, shattered into a dozen sharp fragments. Some soldier's careless strike had reduced a century of artistry to rubble. Yet even without a face, the statue's posture radiated the silent, stubborn authority of a protector who had not yielded, even in death.

The one on the right was untouched—and perhaps untouched for a reason.
The sculptor's craft was so flawless that the face felt alive. The eyes had depth—the kind of depth that caught you off guard, that made you feel seen in a way that stripped the skin from your thoughts. They followed him as he stepped closer, unwavering, not hostile, but coldly assessing.

Apollo slowed, the hairs on his arms rising.
This was no passive relic.
This statue was judging him.

The conqueror.

The figure's hands gripped a weapon unlike any Apollo had ever seen in life—a golden Sunspear, rendered with such obsessive precision that he could imagine its balance in his palm, the cool weight of its haft, the blinding heat of its point. The gold shimmered strangely in the dim light, as though the spear's likeness remembered the touch of its real counterpart and resented being trapped in stone.

Apollo lingered there, staring into the conqueror's unyielding gaze. The world outside the doorway felt far away.

The soldiers' shouts dulled to a distant thrum. All that remained was the silent weight of the two guardians and the chill that seeped into his bones as he stepped into their shadow.

There, behind the conqueror's feet, in the dimness of the alcove, stood a girl.

At first, Apollo thought she was a carving—a small stone figure left forgotten in the shadows. But then she moved, the faintest tremor running through her limbs. Her breathing was shallow, uneven, as if every inhale was a decision, she wasn't sure she wanted to make.

She was tiny. Seven years old, perhaps eight at most. Thin arms, too frail for the weight she carried in them—a small crystal, its fractured surface flickering with a weak, wavering light. It trembled in her hands like a dying star.

Her white acolyte's robe was torn and soaked in blood. Some stains were dry and brown, others fresh enough to glisten in the dim light. He couldn't tell how much of it was hers.

The girl's face was streaked with dirt and tears, but her eyes… her eyes burned with the raw defiance of someone who had seen the world end and refused to bow to it.

She didn't see a man in front of her. She saw the killer who had brought the storm to her home.

Apollo froze.
The memory slammed into him—Kaith.
That same unflinching stare, the same mixture of terror and rage. He had been on the other side of it once, a child looking up at a warrior and wondering if the next breath would be his last.

Slowly, deliberately, he reached for his weapon—and then stopped halfway. The girl's grip on the crystal tightened, her knuckles paling.

Instead, he let the spear fall back into its harness with a muted click.
"My child," he said, his voice low, the tone neither command nor threat. "You don't have to fight anymore."

She didn't move. Her shoulders shook, but her stance didn't break.

"Please," Apollo said again—but this time, the word carried something deeper. Not the voice of the Axis's weapon, not the voice of Markus's soldier... but the voice of a man begging the universe to give him one mercy in this place. It was almost a prayer.

The girl's breath hitched. A tear slid down her cheek, cutting a clean line through the grime.

Apollo stepped forward, the sound of his boots echoing off the cold marble. When he reached her, he crouched until his eyes were level with hers. For a moment, they simply looked at each other—two survivors, staring across a gulf neither of them had asked to cross.

Then, slowly, he reached out and pulled her into his arms. She resisted for a heartbeat, then sagged against him, her small frame trembling so violently he could feel it through the steel of his armor.

"It's over," he whispered, though he knew it wasn't. Not for her. Not for him. Not for anyone here.

Carrying her, he turned back through the ruined temple. Soldiers paused to stare as he passed, their looting briefly forgotten at the sight of the blood-covered girl in his arms.

He found a soldier near the courtyard's edge. "Take her to the ship," Apollo ordered.

The man nodded and reached for the chains at his belt.

Apollo's hand shot out, gripping the soldier's wrist hard enough that bone creaked. His voice was iron. "No. No chains. She is our guest."

The soldier hesitated, about to argue, but Apollo stepped closer until his green-lit eyes were the only thing the man could see.

"If something happens to her," Apollo said, each word a blade, "I will make sure everyone pays the price."

The soldier swallowed hard and nodded, taking the girl with unsteady hands and far more care than before.

Apollo stood in the doorway's shadow, watching as the soldier carried the little girl away.

She clung to him only because she was too exhausted to resist, her small hands knotting in the fabric of his blood-stained uniform. Her eyes—wide, luminous, and wet—locked on Apollo's face even as the distance grew.

They didn't blink.
Not once.

She was silent, but her gaze spoke in ways words could never reach.

Fear, yes—but also something deeper, rawer. The kind of look that comes when the world you knew has been ripped away in an instant, leaving you weightless and untethered.

Her head turned slowly over the soldier's shoulder as they passed through the temple's great hall. He kept walking, his boots echoing in the blood-slick marble, until the crowd of Axis soldiers swallowed her small frame entirely. The last thing Apollo saw was the faint glint of her crystal, clenched tightly in her fist like the last piece of herself she still owned.

Silence seemed to settle in her absence.

And then, Kaith.
The memory rose unbidden, unmerciful.

He saw the faces from that day—younger versions of himself and his friends—the smell of ash, the hollow ringing of screams in empty streets. The way the light had dimmed when the Flow burned through the city. The helplessness that had lodged deep inside his chest and never left.

It pressed against him now.

The weight of his armor—usually a familiar burden— felt suddenly different. Heavier. Not just on his shoulders, but sinking into him, pressing down on his ribs, making every breath a conscious effort. The plates clung to him like a sentence he could not escape, every clasp and buckle binding him tighter to choices he hadn't wanted to make.

He exhaled slowly, but it did nothing to ease it.

The sounds of soldiers shouting orders and looting the temple filtered back into his awareness, but they were muffled, distant—as though he stood underwater. He lingered there in the shadow of the conqueror's statue, feeling the gaze of its carved eyes on him still.

For a moment, Apollo wondered if it was judging him… Or simply recognizing what he had become.

Apollo's hand pressed against the cold white marble. The stone groaned, the sound echoing up into the high arches above him like the slow protest of something ancient being disturbed.

The seam between the doors widened, spilling out a breath of air unlike anything outside—cool, unnaturally so, as if it had never been touched by the warmth of the sun. It carried with it a faint hum, not a sound exactly, but a vibration that curled along his skin and burrowed deep into his bones. It resonated with him, stirring something half-forgotten, half-feared.

He stepped forward, and his breath faltered.

The space beyond was a mirrorwalk—but not like the black, light-drinking obsidian halls of Elaris. This was its reflection, its antithesis. White marble walls climbed high into the air, streaked with delicate veins of gold that caught and fractured the light into warm halos. The ceiling arched overhead like the nave of a cathedral, carved in flowing lines that guided the eye forward.

Every step he took was answered by the floor beneath him—a hollow, ringing echo that seemed to linger a beat too long, as though the room itself were listening to him. Watching him.

And there, at the far end of the path, it floated.

A crystal. Untamed. Untouched. It hovered in the still air like a drop of frozen sunlight, turning slowly on an unseen axis. The glow it gave off was faint yet impossibly pure, pulsing in a slow, steady rhythm—the heartbeat of something alive, and old. Older than Axis. Older than Elaris.

It felt like it had been waiting. Not for *someone*. For *him*.

The doors behind him swung shut with a final, resonant thud. It was a sound that did not belong to mere wood or marble—it was the sealing of a fate. The lock of a choice.

No guards followed. No witnesses remained. There was no way back.

Without thinking, Apollo's left hand slipped to his pocket. His fingers found the small shackle he carried always, and the crystal bound to it. Her crystal.

It was cool in his palm—smooth as glass, but carrying a weight that no gem should have. His thumb traced its familiar edges, every contour etched into his memory as if it had been carved into him along with his scars.

It was the one fragment of his mother he still possessed. The last piece of her that had survived the fire, the war, and time itself.

For a moment, he didn't look at the crystal ahead. He looked only at hers.

And for the briefest breath, the room's cold, humming air seemed to warm—not by the golden light ahead, but by the memory of her voice, of the way she had once said his name.

Then the hum deepened, the pull of the untamed crystal ahead growing heavier, drawing him down the path like the undertow of a black tide.

He gripped his mother's crystal hard enough for the metal shackle to bite into his palm, and began walking.

This path was not unknown to him—he had walked it before in Elaris. But then, it had been different.

Now… there was only blood on his hands and the ghosts of children in his eyes.

The white-and-gold marble seemed to stretch endlessly ahead, the golden veins in the stone pulsing faintly as if the very walls felt his approach. With each step, the air thickened, the hum of the untamed crystal growing louder—not like music, but like a warning siren buried in the marrow of his bones.

The Flow shifted.

Not in welcome.
In rejection.

It wasn't a shove, not a physical force—but it was there, an invisible pressure at his chest and shoulders, pushing back, slowing him, making every step feel like walking through deep water. His breath grew shallow. The weight in the air was a message.

No.
You are not meant to touch this.

But Apollo's stride did not falter.

The hum in the air became a growl, the kind that makes prey animals bolt and the sky itself seem to tighten. Every part of him felt the truth: this was forbidden. This was wrong. But he kept going, the shackle in his left hand anchoring him to the only reason he still had to move forward.

When he reached the end of the path, the crystal floated there, spinning lazily, its glow too perfect to be natural.

He raised his right hand.

The instant his fingertips brushed the surface—
—the world went black.

Not shadow. Not darkness. Absence. The white marble, the gold, the air itself—gone.

Only the crystal remained.

And it was changing.

Hairline cracks split across the crystal's surface with slow, crawling inevitability, each fissure glowing faintly from within as if something ancient and terrible were trying to breathe through the prison of its shell. The sound was sharp and high, a crystalline scream, like ice breaking on a winter lake under unbearable weight, echoing in the infinite emptiness that now surrounded him.

The fractures multiplied, racing toward one another in jagged lines, converging like predators on prey. The glow spilling from them was no longer the calm, noble gold it had once been—it was restless, violent light, flickering as though it despised being contained.

The perfect symmetry of the crystal warped before his eyes. Its smooth surface twisted, points and planes contorting into unnatural angles until it no longer resembled anything born of purity. The form hardened, edges serrated like shards of broken glass, every contour screaming of imbalance.

And then came the glow.

It was not the living warmth of fire. It was not the healing green of the Flow. This was something else— deep, cold, and merciless, a red so heavy it seemed to pull heat from the air. It was the color of a heart that had stopped mid-beat, of the last light leaving a dying sun.

Looking at it made his breath shorten.
Looking into it made him feel seen in the worst way—as though death itself had turned its head, met his eyes, and acknowledged him.

The silence thickened, yet within it came a voice—distant at first, but growing clearer, each syllable trembling with urgency.

"Stop, my boy… stop."

It wasn't memory. It wasn't imagination. It was her. His mother. As though she were standing just beyond the darkness, her breath brushing against his ear.

The red deepened, expanding outward, and the black that surrounded him began to burn away under its suffocating light.

"Run, my boy… run."

The words didn't fade. They *dug in*, burrowing into his chest, clinging to the rhythm of his heartbeat until he could not tell if it was his own pulse or her voice keeping him alive.

The crystal pulsed again—once, twice—like a predator tensing before the strike.

He looked down.

The crystal of his mother, still shackled in his left hand, was trembling—not from his grip, but from something deeper, something resonating in the bones of the world. Its familiar blue flickered erratically, like a candle caught between breaths. Then, without warning, a single, piercing thread of blue light shot from it and *stabbed* into the heart of the red crystal before him.

The colors collided.

Blue and red swirled together in violent spirals, twisting around the deep green that still burned within his Sunspear. It was wrong. It was impossible. Every law of the Flow, every sacred tenet of wielders, screamed against what was happening.

For those fleeting seconds, he realized the truth.
He wasn't holding *a* crystal.
He wasn't holding *two*.

He was holding *three living crystals at once*. One green, One Dying blue and the new it was forming

The chamber reacted instantly. The gold-veined marble walls groaned, hairline fractures spiderwebbing across their surface. The white light of the room deepened into a storm of shifting colors, like the whole place was caught between three suns fighting for dominance. The Flow itself felt strained, stretched—as if reality was a tapestry and he was pulling three threads in opposite directions at once.

And then the visions came.

Not whispers. Not dreams. Visions that struck like hammer blows.

A colossal shadow loomed at his back, its form shifting, indistinct, but heavy enough to crush the air from his lungs. Chains bound his wrists so tightly that his hands were numb, the iron links thrumming with the same impossible green-red-blue light.

A cell surrounded him—stone walls slick with moisture, the air cold enough to bite.

And there… across from him… *me.*
My fingers clutched the bars, white-knuckled, my voice steady even though my eyes burned.

"I love you."

The words ripped something open inside him. Tears pricked his eyes, hot and blurring the vision. His throat closed, but his grip tightened around the crystals until his knuckles turned bone-white.

And then—the detonation.

It wasn't sound. Not really. It was force.
A concussive wave erupted from the crystal, so violent it *erased* the air for a moment. The golden inlays of the marble floor snapped like brittle twigs. The pristine white pillars cracked from base to crown. Hanging lanterns burst in sprays of molten glass.

The floating crystal—the untamed heart of this holy place—shattered. Not into pieces, but into blinding shards of light that burned like dying stars before dissolving into *nothing*.

The Flow's voice came into his mind, cold as deep water, final as a blade against the throat:

One wielder. One crystal. This is law.

In his left hand, the blue of his mother's crystal flickered weakly, like it was trying to hold on. Then it dimmed… guttered… and went dark. *Again.*

The great doors slammed open behind him, and soldiers stormed in, weapons drawn, eyes darting for an enemy that wasn't there. The aftershock still vibrated through the air, rattling the broken marble at his feet.

But there was only Apollo.

He stood before the empty air where the crystal had been, breathing hard, shards of marble crunching under his boots. One hand hung empty at his side. The other clenched the lifeless fragment of his mother's crystal, his knuckles still locked in that desperate grip.

And in the silence that followed, the soldiers did not speak.
None of them dared.

apollo emerged from the shattered heart of the temple like a shadow given flesh. His steps were

Apollo emerged from the shattered heart of the temple like a shadow given flesh.

His steps were slow, deliberate, each one echoing across the blood-stained marble. The soldiers stationed in the hall parted without being told, their eyes tracking him in silence. It was strange, almost wrong — grown men who had carved their way through the temple just hours ago now standing aside for an eighteen-year-old boy.

But it wasn't his age they respected. It was what they had just *felt* from inside those doors — the explosion that rattled their bones and the aura that clung to him now like a second skin.

When he stepped into the blinding light outside, the wind tugged at his cloak, carrying the scent of smoke and scorched incense from the temple behind him. The landing ramp stretched ahead, descending toward the staging grounds where the last pockets of resistance had already been silenced.

And there he saw them.

Zack stood in the open sun, the heat glinting off his polished armor. Around him, the remnants of the Axis forces milled in uneasy silence, their chatter muted as Apollo appeared at the top of the ramp.

The commander's gauntleted fist was clamped around the arm of the soldier who held the little girl. She was tiny against the bulk of the man's armor, her legs dangling in the air, bare feet kicking in vain. Her face was pale beneath the streaks of dirt and blood, her lips trembling but pressed tight as though she'd run out of screams.

When Zack noticed Apollo, his mouth curled—not in greeting, but in something sharper. He jerked the girl from the soldier's grasp like a farmer yanking a weed from the earth. She stumbled forward under his hold, a whimper breaking free before she clamped her jaw again.

Her crystal, a small shard no bigger than a fingerbone, hung from a cord around her neck. It caught the sunlight—a fragile glint of beauty in the carnage—before Zack's hand closed over it.

"I said *kill them all!*" Zack's voice cracked like a whip over the staging ground. "No prisoners!"

The order rippled through the soldiers, but none moved. Eyes shifted between Apollo and Zack. The heat from the sun seemed to press down harder, every breath heavy.

Apollo's voice cut through the stillness—quiet, but it landed like a blade point on bare skin.

"Leave her."

Zack blinked at him, incredulous, before a slow grin spread across his face. "Oh? Since when do *you* decide the orders?"

He drew his sword in one smooth, practiced motion, the metal catching the light in a brilliant arc. The girl tried to twist free, clawing at his armored hand, but his grip was unyielding.

"If you're not going to do it," he said, his tone laced with mockery, "then I will."

The hum of the Flow shifted—subtle at first, then unmistakable.

Apollo's hand moved almost lazily to his hilt, and in an instant, the deep green blade of his Sunspear roared to life. Its jagged edge burned with that same unnatural hue, light bending strangely around it. The soldiers nearest to him recoiled instinctively, their boots scraping against the dirt, their hands tightening on their weapons though they dared not raise them.

Apollo took a step forward, his shadow cutting across Zack's boots.

"I said… leave her. Or pay the price."

Zack stopped mid-breath. For a flicker of a moment, the smirk faltered. There was something in Apollo's eyes—not rage, not even defiance—but the cold, precise promise of death. It was the look of someone for whom killing was not an act of anger, but of inevitability.

The wind hissed through the silence.

Finally, Zack released her. She stumbled, catching herself awkwardly before Apollo knelt in front of her. His armor still carried the dust and blood of the temple, but his voice softened, its weight shifting from threat to vow.

"Nobody will ever touch you."

Her eyes, wide and rimmed red, searched his face for something—perhaps a lie, perhaps the truth.

He reached out, taking her hand. His grip was gentle, careful in a way that felt strange after the violence of the day. He rose, bringing her with him, and began walking toward the carrier.

Behind them, Zack's voice came, low and venomous:

"Wait until Markus hears about this…"

Apollo didn't even turn. The girl's hand was small and trembling in his, but she matched his steps, the sound of their footsteps carrying up the ramp toward the waiting steel of the ship.

Inside the carrier, the air was thick with the smells of rations, metal, oil, and sweat—the stale tang of a ship that had carried war in its belly for too long. Soldiers lounged on the steel benches bolted to the walls, some tearing open food packs with greasy hands, others clattering dice onto overturned helmets, the sound sharp against the hum of the engines.

Their laughter was loud—rough, brash, the kind that covered fatigue with bravado—until Apollo stepped through the hatch.

The girl was at his side, small enough that she could disappear behind his shadow. The noise didn't stop all at once; it thinned in a ripple, like a sudden wind moving through tall grass. The laughter faded into murmurs, glances traded over half-finished meals. No one spoke to him. No one spoke to *her*.

Not because of fear of the girl—but because of *him*.

There was something clinging to Apollo now, an aura born from the temple's fall, from whatever had happened behind those marble doors. It wasn't the scent of blood or smoke—it was heavier, older, and the men didn't want it too close.

He led her to an empty stretch near the viewport. She sat without a word, knees drawn up, her bare feet tucked under her. Her small hands gripped the torn hem of her tunic so tightly that the knuckles stood white. The viewport's pale light framed her in silver, making her seem even smaller.

Apollo crouched beside her, lowering himself until his face was level with hers. He searched for words.

Jaleon would have known what to say.
Jaleon would have leaned in with some clumsy joke, something harmless and warm enough to melt the ice from a child's eyes.

Apollo tried. His voice was softer than he expected, careful, like speaking too loud might shatter her. "What's your name?"

Her gaze lifted, slow and wary. She studied him with eyes too old for her face, the way a cornered animal gauges the distance to an open door.

"Elpis," she said at last.

The word struck him—not as sound, but as meaning. Like a single note of music played in a city long since gone silent.

Hope.

For the briefest moment, he felt it—a flicker of something untouched by war. Something worth protecting. It was small, fragile, and fleeting… but it was there.

By the time they reached the capital, the warmth Apollo had felt from Elpis's name was gone—smothered beneath the rumble of engines and the weight of what awaited him.

The carrier's ramp hissed as it lowered, the metallic groan swallowed by the roar of the gathered crowd. Families of soldiers surged against the barriers, their cheers jagged with relief and exhaustion. Mothers clutched children to their chests, wives and husbands waved frantically, fathers reached for the hands of their sons returning from war.

The smell was overwhelming—incense burning thick from the great braziers of victory, mingling with the brine of sweat, leather, and dust. Paper ribbons and flower petals drifted on the wind, sticking to armor still slick with blood that wasn't their own.

At the far end of the square, framed by banners bearing the Axis sigil, stood Markus.

The crown was new—gold filigree laced with black gems, catching the sunlight with each subtle turn of his head—but the authority in his stance was ancient and immovable. He had crowned himself king in their absence, and he wore the title like it had always been his.

The first he embraced was Zack. They clasped forearms like brothers, but when the crowd's view shifted, Zack leaned close, his mouth brushing Markus's ear. From where Apollo stood, he could see the faint tightening at the corner of Markus's jaw as Zack's venom spilled—a quiet, coiled poison in the shape of words.

Then Markus turned to him. The smile he wore was warm enough for the crowd, but Apollo could see the steel beneath it.
"Oh," Markus said smoothly, "you brought me a prize."

Apollo's reply was quiet, but it carried.
"This isn't a prize."

The air changed. Heavy. Close. As if the city itself had stopped to listen. For a long moment, the crowd's cheers felt far away, the sound muffled like a storm waiting behind the mountains.

That tension shattered when a boy—no older than ten—broke free from the crowd. He darted forward, weaving between armored legs and the hafts of spears until he reached Apollo. Without hesitation, the boy flung his small arms around Apollo's leg, clinging as if he were a fortress. His face was smudged with dust and sweat; his clothes worn thin from weeks of waiting.

In his tiny fist, he held a wildflower. Its petals trembled in the wind, a fragile defiance against the backdrop of war.

"Thank you, sir," the boy said, his voice cracking with emotion. "For bringing my father back. You're my hero."

The word struck the air like a spark hitting dry grass. Hero. Hero. HERO.
The chant began in scattered pockets, but in seconds it was everywhere—a tidal roar pounding against the white stone walls of the square.

Apollo's hand slipped into his pocket and found the cold, lifeless weight of his mother's crystal. His fingers curled around it, feeling its dead silence. And in that moment, something inside him broke—the last link of the invisible chain Markus had wound around his soul snapped.

He lifted his gaze over the crowd. Faces stared back at him—desperate, naïve, hungry for a story that would make the bloodshed worth it.

"A hero?" His voice was calm, but the chant stumbled and faltered.
"A hero?"

The word hung in the air, heavy as a sword above their necks.

"I am not a hero."

He took one step forward, closing the space between himself and Markus. Then, in a voice low enough for only the king to hear, he said:
"I am a killer."

When Apollo spoke again, the words cracked like thunder.
"No… no, no, no. Everyone is lying to you. This is not war. This is not great. This is a massacre!"

The crowd stiffened, whispers cutting through the silence that followed.

Markus's smile vanished. His jaw set, his eyes narrowing to hard, sharp slits.

"Come, Apollo," he said, every syllable an iron command. "You are tired."

But Apollo's reply was fire.
"I am not a hero. I am done. Do whatever you want—but leave Elaris out of your stupid war. Remove your troops… or I will force them out myself."

No one moved. The air itself seemed to freeze, the only sound the snapping of the victory banners overhead, their golden edges catching the light like drawn blades.

"I will walk here a free man," Apollo said, his voice carrying to the farthest balconies, "and if you try to take that from me… I will make you pay the price."

The two men locked eyes—the crowned king and the boy who had just dared to defy him before all of Axis. The crowd seemed to lean forward, caught between fear and awe.

Finally, Markus gave the faintest nod, his crown casting a shadow across his eyes.
"You can leave."

Apollo turned without another word, holding the flower in one hand and Elpis's small, trembling fingers in the other. Together, they stepped into the parted sea of onlookers. No one blocked their way. No one dared.

They watched him go—some in reverence, some in terror, all knowing they had seen something irreversible.

And behind them, Markus stood in his self-forged crown, sunlight glinting off gold and black, his gaze fixed on the boy walking away.

It would be remembered as the day the end began.

The Elarian Chronicle of the Silent Years

"Mark this well, reader: the boy was eighteen, yet his voice that day carried like the bells of Elaris in their prime. He named the slaughter for what it was, and before the false king's court he spoke truth in the language of fire. Those who stood there swore the air itself grew heavier, and that the Flow dimmed its light to hear him. From that breath onward, the king's crown was ash, though it still glittered in the sun."

As Apollo's figure vanished into the throng—the flower in one hand, the girl's trembling fingers in the other—Markus's smile never wavered, but his eyes followed him until the boy was completely gone.

When the last echo of the crowd's cheer faded, Markus's voice cut through the air like the strike of a gong. "Summon the commanders. All of them."

The messengers ran.

Within minutes, the war chamber was filled—brass-breasted generals, dust-stained field commanders, the scent of sweat and travel still clinging to them. They ringed the great obsidian table, its surface carved with the map of Axis and its conquests. Victory banners hung from the ceiling, the golden crown of Markus's new reign glinting in the torchlight.

Markus stood at the head. His tone was calm, measured, every word heavy with intent.

"Our troops will withdraw from Elaris," he said.

A murmur passed through the room.

"They were sent in the name of peace. Now, they wish to stand alone… so be it."

A grizzled general leaned forward. "And what of the boy? That… display in the square? His words were a stain on our victory."

Another commander scoffed. "Apollo is young. He will learn the mistakes of his tongue. Time will temper him."

Around the table, heads nodded in agreement—all except one.

Markus's gaze moved from man to man until it found Zack.

"Stay," he said. "The rest of you—leave us."

The others filed out, the heavy door closing behind them with a dull, final thud.

Markus poured two glasses of dark amber liquor, the bottle's neck clinking against the crystal. He slid one across the table toward Zack.

"You will travel alone," Markus began, his voice dropping low, intimate, "to Zhar. There, you will find a man named Jahan Bahar. You will give him this." From inside his cloak, Markus withdrew a sealed parchment, the red wax bearing the emblem of the Axis crown—and beside it, smaller seals, aged and cracked, belonging to men long dead.

Zack frowned, turning the letter in his hand. "What is it?"

Markus took a slow drink before answering.
"The enemy of my enemy is my friend. That letter explains, in… meticulous detail, that Apollo was solely responsible for the destruction of the Temple of Thyrix—that we, noble Axis, tried to stop him but failed because of his… dangerous connection to the Flow."

Zack's grin began to curl at the edges.

Markus went on, savoring each word.
"It also states—as sworn by the seals of the late senators — that the fall of Giirth was the work of the Order. Not Axis. Not my hand. All of it, tied to one man: Apollo of Elaris."

He leaned in, his voice now almost a whisper, but carrying the weight of iron.
"Elaris will have their precious freedom. And once the world believes their hero is a butcher… I will collect my prize. After all."

Zack laughed, the sound sharp in the enclosed chamber. "I'll see it done," he said.

Markus raised his glass. "To patience, Zack. The greatest weapon of them all."

The two men drank, the flicker of the torches throwing long shadows on the war table—shadows that seemed to reach far beyond the walls of the chamber.

From the Codex of the Silent Depths

"Beware the forging of false truths, for a lie sealed in blood may awaken what even the Firstborn feared. When the Flow is bent to bear the weight of injustice, its current turns black — and in its depths sleeps the oldest power. Those who rouse it will not see its hand, only feel its judgment."

"But Nana," the girl said, her small brow furrowing as she shifted closer to the firelight. "How do you know all this? You… you weren't there."

Old Valere smiled—not the smile of amusement, but of someone who had been waiting for the question. Her fingers, weathered and thin, paused in their slow weaving of the shawl across her lap. The firelight danced in her pale eyes, catching a depth that made the girl's words falter.

"My sweet child," Valere said softly, "when your connection to the Flow grows old within you… it changes."

The girl tilted her head. "Changes?"

Valere nodded, her gaze seeming to pass through the walls, through the years. "It ceases to be just the current that moves you forward. It becomes a mirror… and a window. In its depths, I can witness what has been, what will be, and what stirs this very moment. Time… loses its walls."

Her voice lowered, like a secret carried by the embers. "That is how I know everything that happened. In those days, I knew nothing. I was as blind as any other soul. But later…" She let out a long breath, almost a sigh. "Later, the Flow carried it to me. It came in pieces, in whispers, in dreams that felt too heavy to wake from. And so, little by little, I walked in their shadows—past, future, and present—until I understood."

The fire popped. The girl's eyes were wide, caught between wonder and unease.

"Does… does it still come to you? The dreams?" she asked.

Valere's gaze returned to her, and for a heartbeat, there was something sharp in it—something that belonged to a much younger woman who had seen too much.

"Always," she said.

As Apollo stepped off the carrier's ramp, the weight of the journey pressed on him like armor he could not remove. The wind caught the edge of his cloak, carrying with it the faint scent of metal, smoke, and the dust of a land left in ruin.

Elpis rested in his arms, small and silent, her thin frame trembling with exhaustion. Her head was tucked into the hollow of his shoulder, as if the world beyond that space no longer existed. Apollo tilted his head down, speaking softly so only she could hear.

"You will be safe here," he murmured, his voice steady but lined with something that felt like a promise to himself as much as to her.

The carrier doors ground open further, spilling a flood of sunlight into the hangar bay and outlining the figures who waited for him.
First, Serene—her stance tall, but her eyes carrying a thousand unspoken questions.
Then Jaleon—arms folded, a grin already forming.
Lux, calm and watchful as ever.

And, last… me.

Apollo's boots touched the familiar stone of home, and he moved toward Serene first. His steps were slow, deliberate, each one echoing faintly in the space, as though marking the end of something unseen. Despite the scar that still burned in his chest, his posture was unyielding.

When he stopped before her, the hardness in his gaze softened, if only for a heartbeat.
"Now I know your burden," he said. The words came low, carrying a weight that only she could measure. "And I forgive you."

He shifted Elpis gently into Serene's arms. The girl's small hands clung to the folds of Serene's robe, instinctively recognizing a presence that meant safety.
"Please…" Apollo's voice dropped even lower, almost a breath. "Protect her. Like you did with me."

Serene's composure faltered. Her lips trembled, and her eyes filled with tears that shimmered in the light. She drew the girl closer, holding her as if she were something fragile and irreplaceable.

"Thank you," she whispered. The words were raw, almost breaking in the middle. Before she could think to stop herself, she leaned forward and pressed her lips to his cheek—a brief, human moment in a world where such moments were rare.

Jaleon didn't bother with words.
One moment Apollo was standing there, the weight of Thyrix still clinging to him, and the next he was being crushed in a bear hug so fierce it nearly drove the air out of his lungs.

"Man," Jaleon grinned, stepping back just enough to look him over, "you got even shorter."

Apollo barked a laugh—the kind that came unexpectedly, cutting through the heaviness. "I knew you'd be here. I missed you. The other two aren't half as funny."

"Maybe," Lux called over with a smirk, "you're just not the funny one."

Apollo turned to him next. They clasped forearms first—the grip of comrades—before it shifted into a tight embrace, the kind that spoke of battles survived together, of trust that didn't need words. Lowborn and nobility, soldier and mystic—family in everything but blood.

Then his eyes met mine.

In his left hand, he still held the wildflower—its stem bent, petals crumpled, but stubbornly unbroken. I remembered his voice when he'd handed it over, the weight of those words that would echo in my mind for the rest of my life.

Apollo stepped closer, his hand lifting to cup my face. The warmth of his palm against my skin was jarring— this was a touch meant for reassurance, not for war.

"If thought were seeds," he murmured, his voice threading into me like the Flow itself,
"then for every moment you've lived in my mind, a garden would rise without end...
and I would walk it until the stars forgot their names."

The tears came without asking permission. I wrapped my arms around him, holding him as though I could keep him there, as though I could stop the world from pulling him away. I poured every fear, every relief, every unspoken thing into that embrace.

Jaleon, naturally, couldn't stand the silence for long. "Alright, alright, break it up," he grinned, tossing in some exaggerated wink. "You're making the rest of us look like we don't care."

Lux shook his head, smirking. "Jaleon, you've never looked like you cared about anything."

"Hey, I care!" Jaleon protested, clutching at his chest in mock injury. "I care deeply about my reputation for not caring."

Even Elpis, who had been silent and guarded since they'd stepped off the carrier, let out a small, shy laugh. It was quick, almost hidden—but real enough to be felt.

For the first time since Thyrix, the war felt… distant.

It was Jaleon who broke the easy laughter first.
The grin faded from his face, replaced by something heavier, and his voice dropped low enough that the others instinctively leaned in.

"There was a night," he said slowly, "when I felt it in my chest… like a spearpoint driving straight through me. And I felt you. Your emotions—rage, grief, something I can't even name." His eyes locked on Apollo's. "I don't know how, but I felt it, brother. What happened that night?"

The words hung in the air, and the warmth of the reunion seemed to cool by a few degrees. None of us answered for him—not Lux, not Serene, not me.

Apollo took his time before speaking. His eyes dropped, not in shame but in the way a man lowers his gaze before opening a wound.

When he finally spoke, his voice was steady, but there was iron beneath it.

"I killed the Senate."

Apollo's voice was low, but it carried like thunder rolling in the distance. "Not in justice. Not in strategy. I acted out of rage. They cursed my mother's name, and I… lost myself. The Flow was in me, around me, yet I could not master it. I became something I do not wish any of you to see."

He looked past us, as though seeing again the moment. "But even that—even my rage—is a lie they planted. They knew. They knew when they sent their armies to Kaith that day that my mother would die. And when she did, I took my revenge. I took their lives."

The words hit like the toll of a funeral bell.

"After that," he went on, "Markus claimed the throne of Axis. He crowned himself king over the blood I had spilled. Then he sent me to Thyrix, to rain down his justice on the Umber Temple. And there… I met the kindest soul I have ever known, and the greatest warrior I have ever faced. We fought. She defeated me—yet here I stand before you."

His gaze swept over each of us, lingering for a breath. "I could tell you the rest, every detail, every truth they've buried. But perhaps… that is for another life." His hand found the wildflower in his palm, the petals worn but still intact. "One thing is certain: Elaris is now free of Axis."

There was no time for words.
No time for the questions burning in our throats.

From the great steps of the temple, the Axis soldiers emerged.
They came in silence—no shouts, no drums, no clash of armor—only the steady rhythm of their boots striking the marble in perfect unison. Their formation was flawless, as if they were part of a single living machine. Even their eyes were fixed forward, unreadable, untouched by the chaos that had raged here only hours before.

The sun caught on their polished armor, throwing shards of light across the courtyard. They marched down the long causeway toward the carrier that had brought Apollo back, their shadows stretching long and sharp over the sacred stones.

We stood watching, the air heavy, almost brittle. The smell of incense still clung to the air, mixing with the faint tang of scorched metal. Somewhere, far above, the wind tugged at the torn banners of the temple, making them snap like distant whips.

One by one, the soldiers boarded the carrier. None of them looked at us. None of them spoke.

And then the last came.

Their commander—tall, austere, his cloak catching the light like molten gold—paused. His gaze found Apollo, holding him for a long, unreadable moment. There was no malice there, no pride, no visible victory—only something deeper, harder to name.

When he finally spoke, his voice was low, yet it seemed to carry to every ear in the courtyard.
"Let there be peace."

The words hung in the air like a benediction… or a warning.

Then he turned, his steps unhurried, descending toward the waiting carrier. The ramp lifted behind him with a hiss of hydraulics, and the vessel rose into the sky. Its shadow passed over us like the wing of some vast bird, and then it was gone, leaving only the echo of marching boots and the weight of a promise none of us could yet believe.

"You see, my child," old Valere said, his voice like stone smoothed by time, "the throne… it never belonged to the weak. It does not wait. It does not beg. It stands empty—daring, challenging—calling only those with the courage to take it. And to claim it, one must stain the earth with blood."

The firelight flickered in the child's curious eyes. "But why, Nana? Why not Apollo? Why not the one who fought?"

Valere's gaze turned distant, heavy with the burden of memory. "Markus knew the game too well. He could not let Apollo rise, could not allow the boy to have his moment. Apollo was never meant to wear a crown. In Markus's design, he was meant to kneel. To obey. To vanish into the nameless dead. But he did not. Every scar, every fall, every battle he endured—all of them became steps, stone after stone, leading him closer to…"

Valere's voice faltered.

"Closer to what, Nana?" the child pressed, her tone trembling with wonder.

Then the Flow stirred.

The air thickened, cold and electric. A whisper, faint yet cutting, slid between the cracks of silence—not sound, but presence. A voice, older than kings, carried on the current of eternity:

"Because the crown is not given. It is taken."

The child froze. Her breath caught in her throat. She clutched Valere's hand tighter.

Valere did not answer at once. His eyes, shadowed by memory, turned to the empty dark beyond the fire. He knew what the child did not — this was not merely a story, not merely an echo of the past. The Flow itself had spoken, carrying the remnants of battles, betrayals, and truths not yet done whispering through time.

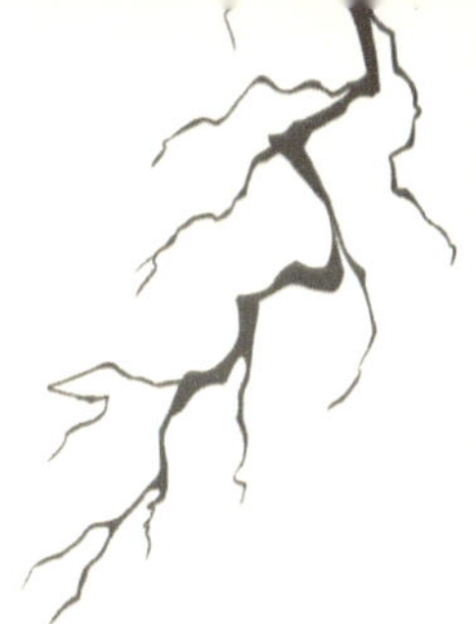

CHAPTER 21

The night found us at last.

The fires of the day—the noise, the weight of everything—had faded into the hush of starlight. The air was cool, carrying the faint scent of distant rain, and we were alone.

I stood before Apollo, my purple hair falling in loose strands across my face, catching the glow of the moonlight. He looked at me as though I were the only thing in the world worth seeing—and for that moment, I believed him.

I reached for him.
No hesitation. No words.
Our lips met, and the world dissolved.

It wasn't just a kiss—it was days of unspoken words, all the things we had endured apart, the battles fought and the ones still ahead. I poured everything I had into it—all my love, my longing, my defiance against a world that would tear us apart.

His hands found me, strong yet unshaking, one pressing against the small of my back, the other curling at my waist. I could feel every line of his palm, every callus earned through battles and blood. But here, with me, his touch was not war—it was sanctuary.

He kissed me back with the same fire, and I felt it in my chest, in my skin, in my bones. Sweet and bitter all at once—the taste of him was memory and desire, the sharp edge of survival and the soft ache of home.

I broke the kiss only to look into his eyes—deep, endless, burning with something more than the Flow, something older. And I saw myself there. Not as a warrior, not as a survivor, but as his. And he was mine.

The hours blurred.
We were a tangle of breath and heartbeat, of whispered words too quiet for the night to carry. We held each other as though letting go would be the end of us. The moon sank, and the stars wheeled silently above, witnesses to our reunion.

When sleep finally found us, it was not the sleep of exhaustion but of peace. He lay beside me, one arm around me, his face buried in my hair. My head rested against the rise and fall of his chest, listening to the slow, steady rhythm of his breathing.

I traced the faint line of his scar with my fingertips, feeling the story in it, and he tightened his hold on me in answer. No words. Just that.

We stayed like that until morning—bound together by the quiet truth that, for this one night, nothing else mattered. Night pressed close like velvet, and Apollo's arms were a quiet circle around me when the vision struck—the first I had ever tasted. It did not simply show me; it returned me to our first mission to Tessara. The air there had that metallic chill again, the drone of engines far below, and then the pressure—the unmistakable feeling of being watched.

Two eyes opened in the dark. Not eyes like ours: fathomless, lacquer-black, wet with malice. Their focus pinned us where we stood, but most of all it fastened on Apollo as if measuring him for a verdict. I felt the emotion before I could name it—rage, raw and ungoverned, a storm without a shore. It crawled over my skin like static, made each breath taste of iron.

Then the flashes came, stuttering frames of a film I couldn't slow: a corridor washed in violet emergency lights; a viewport smeared with frost; a lone figure at the end of a gantry, too still, too patient. He was a stranger I had never met, and yet he watched as though he owned the moment. Each flicker drew him closer until the vision snapped into a single, perfect clarity—his face turned toward me.

He smirked.

The expression was small, but it hollowed the world around it. When he spoke, his voice was a blade wrapped in silk—steady, almost amused, each syllable placed with surgical care.

"No worries, Purple. You will be judged."

The words didn't echo; they *settled*, like ash, in the spaces between my ribs. I woke with my heart loud in my throat, Apollo's warmth still around me, the room exactly as I'd left it—harmless, ordinary. I told myself it was nothing. I filed it with the other strange midnights: a trick of fatigue, a mind misfiring sparks.

But Tessara is patient, and so are omens. In time, I learned what the gaze belonged to, and why it preferred Apollo.

In time, I learned that judgments do not arrive with trumpets, but with a smirk and a promise you only understand after it's too late.

The first light of morning crept through the shutters, spilling across the tangled sheets. The air was still heavy with the warmth of the night before, the quiet rise and fall of Apollo's breathing beside me. My fingers were still loosely curled against his chest, feeling the slow, steady heartbeat beneath skin and scar.

The door creaked open without warning.

"Rise and shine—" Jaleon's voice was all mockery and cheer until his eyes actually landed on us. He froze mid-step, mid-breath. "Oh—oh, gods, no. Nope. Man, put some clothes on! I didn't need *this* burned into my soul first thing in the morning!"

I pulled the blanket higher over myself, biting back a laugh. Apollo didn't even flinch, just propped himself up on an elbow and gave Jaleon that infuriatingly calm stare.

From the hallway came Serene's sharp, unamused tone. "No matter what you've been doing, it's training day! Time to break our bodies again!"

Apollo swung his legs off the bed and stood, utterly unbothered.

Jaleon's hands shot up like a man fending off a wild beast. "Whoa, bro, seriously—pants. Now. There are limits to our brotherhood." His joking tone faltered as his eyes dropped, not to Apollo's face, but to the dark, jagged scar etched across his chest. His gaze lingered there, the humor bleeding from his expression.

Apollo noticed, grabbed his tunic from the floor, and pulled it over his head in one fluid motion, covering the wound without a word.

We dressed quickly and made our way toward the great hall, the echo of our footsteps bouncing off the stone walls. The smell of steel and oil was already thick in the air—the scent of another day's drills.

Halfway across the hall, Julius stepped out from a side corridor, his presence like a wall across our path. His eyes locked on Apollo, hard and unwavering.

"Later," he said, his voice low but firm enough to leave no doubt it wasn't a request. "You and I need to have a word."

There was no smile, no humor, just the promise of a conversation that wouldn't be easy. Apollo met his gaze for a moment, then gave the barest nod before we passed by, the weight of that unspoken reckoning following us all the way to Serene's judgment.

We gathered at dawn, robes draped loosely over our shoulders, crystals clasped firmly in our hands. The air was cool, sharp, and carried that faint mineral scent that always seemed to hum when training was about to begin. All of us were stripped down to the essentials—no weapons, no armor—only the crystals and our determination. All of us except Apollo. He, as always, carried something unseen, the presence of his mother tucked away in some hidden charm. It lent him an aura, quiet but unmistakable, like he was never truly alone.

Serena stood before us, spine straight, eyes sweeping over the group. There was something sharp and mischievous about her smirk when it came.
"Jaleon," she barked, voice ringing clear, "I hope you ate a *big* breakfast, because I am waiting to see your vomit!"

The group erupted in laughter before Jaleon even answered. He turned, fixing Lux with a crooked grin, and fired back:
"No worries, old lady. I'll throw everything up on Lux."

His eyes slid up and down Lux, mockingly appraising. "Man, even your training gear looks better than ours. Do you have a personal stylist or something?"

Lux's laughter rang easy, unbothered. Apollo's reply came quick, sharp with brotherly teasing:
"No. He's just nobility—not like you, the orange peasant who eats like an entire army."

That broke us. The whole group roared with laughter, the kind that doubles you over, even as Serena rolled her eyes.

"Attention!" she snapped, her voice slicing through the mirth. "Give me ten kilometers. After that, battle positions."

Without hesitation, we fell into stride. But this time, something was different. We weren't scattered, tripping over each other's pace. Every step landed as one. Our breaths fell in rhythm, the sound of our sandals striking the earth like a single drumbeat. For the first time, we felt like a unit, a pulse beating through many bodies but moving as one.

At the five-kilometer mark, the world shifted. Serena came at us out of nowhere, striking like a storm breaking over calm seas. One heartbeat we were running; the next, it was chaos.

Four against one—but it felt the other way around. She was fast, precise, and merciless, a predator toying with its prey. Each blow landed not just on our bodies but on our pride, and she was smiling—actually *smiling*—as she dismantled us one by one.

It wasn't punishment. It was a game to her. And we were the toys.

True to form, Jaleon went first. Serena met him not with strength, but with rhythm. Her sword flowed into motion, catching the edge of his strike just enough to turn it aside, the green glow rippling along the axe's fiery lines. Sparks scattered, emerald against amber. Jaleon grunted, muscles straining, but Serena moved like wind—slipping past his guard, her blade tracing elegant spirals around his brutal swings.

Every clash painted a picture: orange force against green elegance. Jaleon's movements were wild, heavy, and direct, but Serena's were fluid, weaving around him like a dancer shaping the tide of battle. Each time his axe slammed down, the earth shook; each time her sword sang through the air, it seemed to draw his power away, unraveling his fury into wasted momentum.

Then, with a twist of her wrist, Serena let the sword's green light flare—she slid along the haft of his axe, using his own strength against him. One breath later, Jaleon was stumbling, his mighty weapon thrown wide, his chest open. Serena stepped in, the tip of her blade stopping just short of his throat, the glow casting green shadows across his defiant grin.

"Raw power is loud," she murmured, her voice smooth as silk, "but flow… flow is endless."

Jaleon spat in the dirt, axe still burning in his grip. "Endless or not," he growled, "I'll break it one day."

Serena only smirked, drawing the sword back with the same fluidity as a wave returning to the sea.

Lux slipped in like a shadow cutting across water. His steps were crisp, precise, every motion angled with intent. Serena answered, her green blade flowing in curves, never rigid, always shifting like a river around stone.

He struck fast, feinting left—steel flashed—then darted right, his blade snapping forward with surgical sharpness. Serena met him, and for a moment the clash became a dance: blue light slashing in clean lines, green arcs weaving in spirals, each impact ringing like hammered glass.

Lux pressed harder, movements tightening, each strike quick as breath. Serena let him, her body bending and rolling with the rhythm, never breaking, never forced. Then she laughed—sudden, bright, mocking—and the flow changed.

Her sword curved beneath his guard, sliding along his strike like a ribbon catching wind. She turned, wrist snapping, and in a blur she caught him—a twist, a pull—and the ground met Lux before he knew he was falling.

Serena stood above him, green sword resting lightly against her shoulder, smirk sharp as the edge of her blade.
"Stylish," she said, eyes gleaming, "but style doesn't win battles."

Apollo stepped forward next. Calm as always, but beneath that calm was something else—an invisible heaviness that filled the air around him, the quiet echo of his mother's gift still clinging to his soul.

He did not charge. He did not strike first. He simply stood, waiting. The space between him and Serene stretched taut, like the breathless instant before lightning splits the sky.

Serene grinned—she always grinned when the fight began—and came at him first. Her strikes were sharp, fast, honed by years of discipline. Apollo met them without flourish, each movement deliberate, controlled. When their crystals met, sparks hissed and light splintered across the floor. For a heartbeat, it seemed evenly matched.

But then… something shifted.

Every time Serene's blade met his, she felt a resistance deeper than steel—as if the Flow itself recoiled from him, or through him. His eyes were calm, too calm, and in them she saw a reflection that made her grin falter: he wasn't fighting her. He was holding *himself* back.

The tempo slowed, heavier. His aura pressed against her like a tide threatening to drown the shore. And then— with the smallest opening, the smallest feint—Serene swept his legs and sent him crashing to the ground.

Gasps filled the hall. But Apollo did not stay down. He rose in one fluid motion, jaw tight, eyes burning. His weapon hummed with a strange, restless light.

Everyone thought he would charge again. That he would strike harder, faster, and push until one of them broke. But he didn't.

Apollo lowered his blade. His chest rose and fell with restrained breath, his knuckles white around the hilt. "I could go further," he said quietly, almost to himself. His gaze flicked over the hall, then back to Serene. "But if I do… I don't know what I'll become."

A silence spread, heavy and unyielding. Even Serene didn't press him—she only studied him, the weight of understanding in her eyes.

Then, without another word, Apollo stepped back. Not defeated. Not broken. Simply choosing.

He had not lost. He had quit—not out of weakness, but out of fear. Fear of the storm waiting inside him.

And for everyone who watched, that choice was somehow more terrifying than if he had unleashed it.

By then my heart was hammering, every beat a drum of defiance. The rhythm of our unit was breaking, unraveling under Serena's relentless mastery, but something in me refused to yield. I could taste dust in the back of my throat, sweat stinging my eyes, yet still I lunged.

But Serena *thrived* in chaos. It was her element, her symphony. She turned into my momentum, not against it, slipping around my blade as though the strike had been part of her plan all along. Her hand snapped forward, fingers like iron, clamping around my wrist.

The world spun.

She twisted—my body turned helplessly with hers—and in one fluid motion she hurled me sideways. I collided hard into Jaleon, his armor clanging, both of us tumbling into the dirt in a tangle of limbs and curses. The impact rattled my teeth, the breath driven from my lungs, dust exploding around us.

Serena stood above, unruffled, sword humming with emerald fire. Her smirk was a brand seared into my pride.
"Unity is only as strong," she said, voice cutting clear through the ringing in my ears, "as the weakest moment."

Jaleon shoved me off him, grumbling, "Next time, warn me before you try to kill me."

I coughed, rolling to my knees, chest burning, but even as shame threatened to bite, I couldn't help but see it—the truth in her words, the weight in her lesson. And still, beneath it all, the stubborn flame that refused to go out.

The training floor was still scarred from their clashes—dust hanging in the air, faint scorch marks tracing the stone, the silence after chaos. Then, Jaleon groaned dramatically from where he was sitting.

Jaleon: "Ugh. I think Serena broke my everything. My arms, my legs, my pride... even my axe looks embarrassed."

Serena (grinning, twirling her sword): "Your axe just realized it deserves a better wielder."

Lux (deadpan, adjusting his sleeve): "Honestly, Jaleon, you were outmaneuvered before you even swung. It was almost... educational."

Jaleon: "Educational?! She tossed me around like a sack of potatoes! That's not education, that's cruelty."

Apollo (leaning against the wall, smirking): "You're just mad because I lasted longer than you did."

Jaleon (pointing): "You didn't win either, you quit!"

Apollo: "Correction—I didn't lose. Big difference. Besides, I didn't want to hurt her."

Serena (raising an eyebrow): "Oh, please. If you had unleashed that storm inside you, half this hall would be rubble, and Lux's hair would finally look interesting."

Lux (snapping his fingers in mock offense): "My hair is interesting. It's called style, Serena. Something your footwork lacks."

Serena: "Says the man who ended up face-first in the dirt."

Valere (sitting cross-legged, sipping tea like none of this mattered): "Children, children… it was a delight watching you flail around. Like sparrows arguing which one flies higher while the hawk circles above."

Jaleon: "Are you calling me a sparrow, old man? Because sparrows don't swing axes this big!"

Valere: "No, you're more like a pigeon. Loud. Messy. Hard to get rid of."

The group burst into laughter, even Apollo — the tension of past days finally loosening in their chests. For a moment, war, politics, and Markus's shadow were far away. They were just five souls bound by something stronger than blood.

We were laughing.
For one fragile heartbeat, the world was nothing but warmth and breath. Our voices braided together, tangled with lightness—not as warriors, not as survivors, but as a family stitched together by fire and fate. The hall—once echoing with the clang of steel and the hiss of training—carried instead the rare song of joy.

Then the world ripped apart.

CHAPTER 22

The explosion did not arrive with sound, but with force. A living wall of fire and air slammed into us, tearing laughter from our throats. Time broke into fragments. My vision dragged into slow motion—each shard of stone, each ripple of heat, each gasp of surprise stretching into eternity.

My face snapped sideways, skin stinging with the heat of the blast. The sharp grit of powdered obsidian cut across my cheek, carried by the storm. The scent of burning air filled my nose—acrid, metallic, alive with destruction.

I was already on the ground before my mind could catch up. My ribs screamed with every shallow breath, pain spreading like cracks through glass.

Jaleon was on his knees, massive frame trembling, his teeth clenched in a snarl not of rage but survival. Dust streaked his shoulders, and the firelight danced in his wild eyes.

Lux was a shadow crumpled in the debris, his hand clutching at the floor. A thread of crimson trailed from his lips, staining his chin. He coughed once—the sound raw, wet—and spat blood into the shattered stone.

And Apollo—

He lay far from us, too far, fifteen meters across the fractured tiles. His body was bent, still, broken against the floor's jagged wounds. But I knew. I knew in my bones—he had thrown himself into the fire. The blast was meant for me, for us, and he had taken it all. His form had shielded me, shielded us.

Still as stone. Unmoving.

The hall that had felt like home was unrecognizable. Smoke curled along the edges of the broken obsidian. Fractures spread like spiderwebs across the once-perfect floor. The banners of Elaris sagged in ash. What had been laughter was now silence—broken only by the crackle of dying flame and the cough of those struggling to rise.

Serene was crouched on one knee, one hand braced against the fractured floor. Her blade was dimmed, the green glow flickering like the heartbeat of a dying star—but unbroken, unyielding, like the woman herself.

The temple of Elaris—once a monument of eternal order, flawless obsidian polished by centuries of devotion—was crumbling. The floor split open into jagged scars, black glass-like stone splintered and buckled under the violence of the blast. The towering stair, the pride of the temple, collapsed in ruinous heaps, stone steps tumbling like the bones of giants. Dust rolled down in choking waves, veiling the air in pale fog.

And then… the tide arrived.

Through the shattered gates, shadows poured forth. An endless sea of Umber warriors, their armor blackened and streaked with crimson sigils of fanatic zeal. Their banners—blood-red cloth daubed with the mark of their creed—whipped through the choking air. Their war-cries rose in unison, primal and merciless, splitting through the ruin like thunder.

They descended on the unarmed first. Acolytes. Healers. Children of the temple. Faces I knew. Names that lived in my childhood. I saw them fall in flashes of red steel and screams that turned to silence. The stones that had heard my laughter as a boy now drank their blood.

But then… behind them, the storm broke into silence.

He came.

Magnus Throne.

The nightmare of the Umber host. A name whispered with dread in every war camp, a shadow that haunted even the bravest generals. His mere presence bent the air itself, pulling all weight toward him, as if gravity had grown heavier.

He was a tower of flesh and will. Tall. Unyielding. His shoulders carved from stone, his stride measured, slow, deliberate—the walk of a man who had never known defeat. His eyes burned like twin furnaces: one of flame, one of iron, both promising ruin.

Strapped to his back was his crystal—massive, jagged, a shard of eternity itself. Unignited. Silent. He did not need its power, not yet. His silence declared louder than any words: *You are not worthy of my crystal. Not yet.*

The temple quaked with the sound of his approach, every step echoing like the toll of a war drum.

And then—above the screams, above the collapsing stone, above the storm of chaos—Julius voice cut through.

A single command, sharper than her blade, alive with all the fury of Elaris itself:

"BATTLE POSITIONS!"

My breath caught. My legs shook. Apollo lay unmoving, his chest barely rising, his body broken where it had shielded us.

Jaleon's rage ignited before his voice did. His axe roared to life in a blaze of orange fire, and with a bellow that split the hall, he charged like a beast unchained.

Lux, blood still on his lips, pushed himself up, staggering but unrelenting. Blue light flared from his blade as he threw himself forward, shadow trailing fire.

And me—I felt my legs move before I chose to. Something inside me woke, deep, ancient. My crystal flared, not weak, not trembling, but steady. Its color burned deep, alive, *mine*. For the first time, I was not chasing control. I was in control.

I turned to Serene. Her gaze locked to mine. No hesitation. No doubt. Only command.

Her word was simple, but it shook me like a second blast.

"CHARGE."
And so we did.
Not as warriors seeking victory.

Not as survivors clinging to life.
But as fire thrown into fire—
as mortals flinging themselves into the jaws of the storm.

Serene moved like a storm in human form.

Her emerald blade ignited, singing through the air in sweeping arcs. Each motion was poetry in violence, a choreography of death. She slid across the fractured obsidian, her footwork light as mist, her strikes sharp as thunder. One soldier raised a spear—Serene spun, green light severing shaft and throat in a single motion. Another lunged at her side—her wrist turned, her blade reversed, and he fell in silence.

There was no hesitation, no pause. Every swing flowed into the next, elegant, brutal, flawless. She carved through their ranks as though they were reeds before the river. Sparks leapt from the stone as her sword scraped, danced, rose again.

She was the temple's fury—Elaris itself taking vengeance.

Behind her came the roar.

Jaleon launched himself forward, leaping through smoke and falling stone. His axe blazed orange, a sunburst in the darkness. He landed with the force of an avalanche, the obsidian floor cracking under the weight.

The first line of Umber soldiers shattered. Shields splintered, bodies flew. Jaleon swung wide, each strike heavy enough to break not just men, but the will of those who faced him. His chest heaved, eyes burning with rage.

And when he locked eyes with Magnus Throne across the chaos, his voice carried above the war-cries:

"COME THEN!"

He broke through lines as though his axe drank their fear, splitting armor, cleaving pikes in two. He *was* the wall, the anchor, the unmovable force that no tide could drown.

Where Jaleon was thunder, Lux was lightning.

He slipped into the gaps, his blade igniting blue in flickering arcs. He was everywhere at once—a blur, a ghost. An enemy lunged—his throat opened before the strike landed. Another swung—their arm fell before the blade reached.

Lux moved with a precision so sharp it bordered on unnatural. His strikes were whispers of death, his steps the hush of wind over stone. The Umber soldiers never saw him coming—they only felt the cut, the cold, the end.

He danced through their ranks, his robe flickering with every sudden turn. To watch him was to see inevitability made flesh: the quiet certainty of a blade that never missed its mark.

And then there was me.

My legs moved before thought, before fear. The Flow surged, wild and deep in my chest. I leapt, landing beside Jaleon in the thick of the carnage, my crystal blazing a color I had never seen before.

The Umber soldiers came for me with malice—their eyes wide, their mouths spitting hate. They wanted me dead. They wanted me to bleed on the stones of the only home I had ever known.

And I met them.

My blade burned, my arms moved, and for the first time in my life I was not fighting against the Flow—I *was* the Flow. Each strike found flesh, each step found rhythm, each scream around me became part of the storm that carried me forward.

The first soldier's strike missed because I was no longer there. The second fell before he even finished his war-cry. I moved through them with clarity I had never known, with fire in my chest and fury in my soul.

I was no longer just surviving.
I was *fighting*.

And through it all, he watched.

He stood at the far end of the shattered temple, towering, unyielding. His soldiers died in rivers before him, but his crystal—jagged, massive, monstrous—remained sheathed on his back. Unignited.

His eyes cut through the battle, stone and flame in equal measure. He did not move. He did not need to. His very presence bent the air, bent the will of those who dared look upon him.

But before we were close enough, my eyes caught a sight that froze the breath in my chest.

There—at the broken obsidian steps of the temple — stood Julius. Tall, unyielding, the embodiment of discipline and silent command. Beside him was Jihn, the old warrior whose scars were older than most of our victories, and further back, our quartermaster, steady as the iron gears that kept our home alive. And behind them all — Elpis. The child. Her crystal already blazing with a defiance too great for her small frame, the blue light of it desperate, reaching for Apollo's fallen body.

It was then I saw it.

Julius drew his weapon. For the first time, the blade revealed itself to me. A deep yellow crystal, glowing close to gold. Not dull, not hesitant—perfect. Its edge carried the weight of judgment itself, a sword that seemed carved from the marrow of the sun.

Beside him, crimson lights sparked to life. Jihn's crystal stretched into the long haft of a spear, its tip glowing like liquid fire. And the quartermaster's crystal curved into the elegant frame of a bow—crimson strung with energy, the very air trembling as he drew the first arrow of Flow.

I had seen them many times as men.
But never—never—as wielders.

The bow sang first. Arrows of Flow split the air, streaks of red fire arcing into the enemy. One, then another, then a volley—precise, unyielding. But the Umber host did not slow. They came like a tide, fanatic eyes burning, ready to die if only to drown us in their sacrifice.

And then Magnus moved.

It was not with crystal. Not with Flow. But with something far crueler—simplicity. A dagger. Not forged in sacred fire, not carved by Flow. A simple blade of steel, crude and small in his massive hand.

He threw it.

Gods… he *threw it.*

The knife tore through the battlefield like lightning unchained, splitting past soldier and arrow alike. Its speed was inhuman, its aim absolute. In the blink of an eye, it pierced the quartermaster's chest—the heart struck true.

His crimson bow shattered into nothing.

The man who had armed us, who had fed us, who had kept us alive in the quiet moments between wars, fell without a word. His death came not with a blaze of Flow, not with the honor of duel, but with the cold finality of steel. A reminder that even in the age of gods and crystals, the simplest blade still kills.

And in that instant, I felt it.
The tide was turning.
But not for us.

Julius and Jihn charged. Rage carried them like fire given form. Julius was a wall of golden light, every strike of his blade precise and terrible. But Jihn—Jihn was something else.

He fought like a wild bear driven mad with hunger, each swing of his crimson spear desperate to tear through the Umber lines, desperate to reach Magnus and the justice that waited behind him.

He cut down soldier after soldier, his roars echoing louder than their war cries. His spear spun in wide arcs, scattering armor and flesh, his fury so raw it seemed unstoppable. He was a beast, a storm, a force of nature that none could withstand.

But then… fate.

Through the chaos, a smaller figure appeared before him. Ordinary. Almost laughably so. The man wore nothing but the plain steel and dull armor of a common soldier. His weapon was no crystal, no blazing mark of Flow—only a simple sword, unremarkable, unthreatening.

And that was the Umber trick.

For generations they had hidden their wielders in plain sight—dressing them as common foot soldiers, sending them across enemy lines as shadows disguised as men. To the careless eye, they were fodder. But in truth, they were executioners waiting for their moment.

And Jihn, in his fury, made that mistake.

He roared, striking with his spear, expecting the steel to shatter under its crimson blaze. But the soldier slipped low, faster than Jihn could correct. With a swift motion, he dropped the steel sword—and pulled his true weapon free.

The crystal ignited.

Light erupted in his hands, a gleaming edge flashing beneath Jihn's guard. The speed was merciless. One strike—a perfect, surgical line across the air.

And Jihn's head fell.

The spear clattered from his grip, crimson light guttering out. His massive frame collapsed to the shattered stone, silent.

For a moment, time froze.
The bear was dead.
The storm was broken.

And in the eyes of the Umber host, their fanatic fire blazed higher. The moment Jihn's body hit the ground, a silence, sharp as a blade, cut through the battlefield. And then Julius roared.

It was not grief. It was not even rage. It was fury sharpened into purpose. His golden blade ignited brighter than I had ever seen, its light burning through the smoke like a second sun. He surged forward, his stride hammering cracks into the obsidian beneath his boots.

The disguised Umber wielder barely had time to raise his crystal again. He struck fast, his blade snapping in sharp, deadly angles. But Julius was beyond precision now—he was wrath incarnate. His sword moved with brutal choreography, wide arcs of molten gold forcing the wielder back, each strike heavier than the last.

Steel rang against crystal. Sparks burst with every clash. The wielder tried to slip low, darting like a snake, but Julius pivoted, cutting his path off with a sweep that carved a scar through the stone floor.

"SERENE!" Julius's voice tore through the chaos, ragged with fury. "WITH ME!"

From the shadows of the melee, Serene responded— green light blazing as she cut her way toward him.

The Umber wielder fought with speed and deception, his movements sharp, sudden, meant to unbalance. He darted inside Julius's guard, his blade flashing for the throat. But Julius slammed the flat of his sword into the man's wrist, sending the strike wide, then turned the momentum into a cleaving arc that would have ended him—if not for a desperate retreating roll.

The two circled.

The wielder's eyes darted, desperate now, his strikes quicker, sharper, more frantic. Julius's movements, by contrast, were controlled fury. He absorbed the blows, parried with sparks of gold, each clash ringing like a war-drum, his sheer force pressing the enemy into tighter ground.

And then Serene arrived.

Her green blade spiraled through the chaos, weaving with Julius's gold. Their attacks began to overlap—a rhythm, a deadly duet. Serene cut high, Julius cut low. She spun left, he crashed right. Together they pushed the wielder back, back, step by step, until his footing faltered.

The wielder tried one last trick—a feint toward Serene, a sudden lunge at Julius's exposed side. But Julius had seen it before it began. He dropped low, his golden blade flaring like sunrise, and with a single, flawless arc, he cut through the wielder's guard.

The strike shattered the crystal.
The body followed a heartbeat later, falling lifeless to the blackened floor.

Julius stood over him, chest heaving, golden light dripping from his sword like liquid fire. He turned to Serene, his voice low but steady now:

"We fight together… or not at all."
The words left Julius's mouth like steel, strong and certain. But deep down, beneath that golden shine, it was a lie.

For he carried a shadow none of us could see then—a choice made long ago, a hunger that had festered into rot. He had betrayed us in secret, bartered away pieces of his honor for the clink of coin. And now he stood here, blade drawn, fighting shoulder to shoulder with us… but what for?

Was it for Apollo? For us? For the temple we swore to protect?

Or was it only for his purse, for the promise of riches that would bury the guilt of a man who no longer knew what side he stood on?

None of us knew. Perhaps he didn't either.

You see, child… coin is strange. It calls to the worst in men and corrupts the best. It blinds even the proudest warrior until he can no longer tell friend from foe, loyalty from betrayal.

And yet… in that moment, when the Umber tide surged again and the walls shook with the roar of their fanatics, Julius still raised his sword. He stood beside Serene, golden sun and green flame burning as one.

Together, they braced for the storm.
Together, they fought.
Even as the truth gnawed unseen at the edges of his soul.

But Magnus… Magnus was something else entirely.

When Serene and Julius charged, their blades lit like twin suns, Magnus did not even raise his crystal. With a flick of his wrist—almost lazy in its cruelty—he caught Serene in the Flow, twisted it like a child tossing a doll, and hurled her across the battlefield.

She slammed into the broken obsidian floor at our feet, the air rushing out of her lungs in a thunderclap of dust. All we could do was watch.

Julius pressed forward alone. And gods, in that moment he was the very embodiment of what a warrior should be—balance, precision, devotion carved into motion. His every strike was flawless, his golden blade singing arcs of justice through the air. To my eyes, he was perfection itself.

But to Magnus? It was nothing.

He didn't even ignite his crystal.
He shifted aside, step after step, each dodge effortless, like he was dancing through Julius's fury. Then he bent down, almost mocking, and tore a sword from the hands of a fallen soldier—a crude, iron thing, chipped and stained.

"I will kill you with this," Magnus said, his voice like iron dragged across stone. "You are too weak to warrant my Flow."

Julius roared, blood and defiance blazing in his chest, and struck. Golden light clashed against common steel—and still Magnus moved faster. He slipped left, his arm cutting like a shadow, and in one swift, merciless motion, Julius's arm fell.

The scream that tore from Julius's throat was not just pain—it was despair, fury, the collapse of everything he had carried for us. Blood poured in sheets from the stump, but still he stood, his remaining hand clutching his crystal, eyes wild.

"Let's make peace!" Julius gasped, tears burning his face, his voice cracking with the weight of his desperation.

Magnus laughed. A laugh that did not belong in any world of men. His smile was void, cruel and endless.

"Peace?" he hissed. "You dare ask for peace? In a moment, you'll be dead. You won't have eyes. You won't have a tongue. I'll put your head on a spike with two coins in your sockets, and the flames will know the truth."

He raised the void-sword, shadows trembling along its jagged edge.
"The fool Julius. The false priest who dared to fight Magnus—wielder of the void."

And in that instant, the world itself seemed to hold its breath.

The end came swift.

Magnus's steel blade swept across in a brutal, efficient arc. The black hair caught the dim light as the steel connected, and Julius staggered. For a heartbeat, time slowed. His yellow blade slipped from his fingers, sparks bursting like dying stars as it struck the obsidian floor. Then his body followed, crumpling into the cracks, blood flowing where once brilliance had burned.

The golden glow faded, guttering out like the last flame in a storm.

Silence struck us all.

Magnus Throne stood tall, unbent, the storm of battle raging around him as though it were nothing more than wind in a field. His steel blade dripped with the blood of Julius, but it wasn't enough. Death alone was too merciful for a man who had dared defy him.

With deliberate slowness—as if forcing us all to witness—Magnus bent down, his massive hand closing around Julius's head. The glow of the fallen crystal guttered out beside the body, leaving only silence and despair.

Then, in one swift motion, he swung his blade again.

The sound was sharp, final.

The head of Julius—once the golden flame of Elaris, once the man who swore to fight with us or not at all—was severed cleanly from his shoulders. His body collapsed into the dirt, lifeless, as Magnus lifted the head high by its dark hair.

We screamed. Serene's voice cracked into a roar, Jaleon bellowed in broken rage, Lux cursed through bloodied lips, and I… I could only watch, my stomach hollow, as if my soul had been torn out.

But Magnus was not finished.

He strode to the nearest broken spear jutting from the obsidian floor, its shaft cracked but upright. With the cold efficiency of a butcher, he rammed Julius's head down onto the point.

The spear pierced through, lifting the face of our brother, our leader, into the air above the battlefield. His lifeless eyes stared out across the temple—a grotesque statue, a trophy of defiance turned to ruin.

Magnus planted the spear firm in the ground and stepped back, his abyssal gaze sweeping over us all.

"Look well," his voice thundered, low and merciless. "This is the fate of those who dream of crowns. This is the fate of those who think themselves worthy to stand against me."

The army of the Umber roared their approval, their red banners thrashing in unholy triumph. And we… we stood paralyzed.

For Julius was no longer simply dead.
He was a warning.
An effigy of despair, meant to break us before the next blow would even fall.

The banners of the Umber host billowed like blood aflame, their soldiers screaming oaths of zealotry, but all of it vanished when his gaze fell upon me. My breath caught. I had seen this before—not in life, but in my dreams, visions that had stalked me like a curse. And now here he was, real, flesh and blood, heavier than stone, sharper than fire.

His eyes pinned me, and his voice—deep, absolute, a sentence carved into the marrow of the world—broke me open:

"I told you… judgment will come, purple."

My knees nearly buckled. The Flow within me recoiled as though struck. But Jaleon's roar tore through the terror.

"TO HELL WITH YOUR JUDGMENT!" he bellowed, igniting his axe until it blazed like a second sun. He charged with the fury of ten men, weapon swinging down in an arc meant to cleave the earth.

The impact shook the temple. Magnus caught the haft of the axe in one hand. One hand. The shockwave blasted Umber soldiers aside like rag dolls. Jaleon gritted his teeth, straining, muscles tearing against the immovable wall before him.

Then Lux was there, darting in like a streak of lightning, his blue blade flashing for the throat. "While he holds you—!" he hissed. But Magnus tilted his shoulder, brushing Lux aside with nothing more than the sweep of an arm. The air itself roared as Lux was hurled backward, tumbling across shattered stone. He landed on his feet, spitting blood, and charged back in without hesitation.

Serene was already moving. Her green blade flowed like a river, weaving between their fury. She struck where Magnus opened, parried where his counters fell, binding their rhythm together.

"Stay on him!" she cried, her voice fierce. "Don't give him breath!" Her sword flashed in elegant spirals, catching the edges of Magnus's force, deflecting strikes that should have crushed bones.

But Magnus didn't yield. He didn't even ignite his crystal. He fought with raw power alone, every motion vast, unstoppable. When his fist struck the floor, the obsidian cracked like glass, chunks of stone blasting into the air. When his arm swept across their line, a wave of pressure threw soldiers and acolytes screaming into the shadows.

Jaleon roared again, leaping high, axe raised above his head. "DIE, MONSTER!" He swung down with a blow meant to break mountains.

Magnus's hand shot up, catching the haft mid-swing. His other palm slammed into Jaleon's chest—a thunderclap of force—and Jaleon was hurled across the hall, crashing into a pillar so hard the ancient stone groaned and split.

"Jaleon!" I screamed, but my voice drowned in the chaos.

Lux pressed harder, faster, his blade slicing for arteries, tendons, ribs. "You're not untouchable!" he spat, each strike clean, merciless.

Magnus turned his head slightly. Just slightly. His shoulder rammed into Lux with the weight of an avalanche. Lux spun through the air, blood spraying, his sword clattering across stone. Still, he rolled back to his feet, eyes blazing, refusing to quit.

Serene alone faced him now. Her sword danced in arcs of green fire, striking from above, below, sideways, a tide of endless motion. She ducked beneath his swing, rolled up his arm, and carved for his back. For a heartbeat, it looked as though she had him.

But Magnus moved faster than anything his size had the right to. His hand caught her mid-spin by the wrist. He lifted her like nothing, then slammed her into the fractured floor with such force the ground quaked. Dust and blood rose in the same breath.

Pinned beneath his grip, she still slashed upward, her blade grazing his cheek and leaving a thin line of fire across his skin.

Magnus did not even flinch. He looked down at her, and in that calm voice that crushed mountains, said: "Still flowing. Still nothing."

And me—I stood frozen. My friends gave everything. Jaleon's fury, Lux's precision, Serene's endless flow. And still, they were breaking. Not because they were weak, but because he hadn't even begun.

Magnus had not drawn on his crystal.

And I knew what they didn't: when he did, the temple would not survive the night.

Jaleon was breaking.

Blood streamed from his mouth in thick, red threads. Each cough rattled his chest like broken glass, and when he stood, his ribs shifted visibly beneath the strain. His axe trembled in his hands—not from weakness, but from rage, from a fire that refused to die even when the body begged to collapse. His pride, his ego, his very will—all of it had been shattered against Magnus Throne.

And still… he rose.

With a roar that cracked the dust-laden air, Jaleon lifted his double-headed axe. It ignited, no longer a weapon but a beacon. The orange blaze was pure now, untainted by fury, honed into raw, unyielding desire. It wasn't vengeance. It wasn't pride. It was the will to win.

He charged.

The ground shook beneath his stride. Every step carved fractures through the obsidian floor. And then his axe came down—once, twice, again—strikes that were like mountains collapsing, like storms breaking against the sea.

Magnus—for the first time—faltered.

He stepped back, boots grinding across the fractured stone. His forearms rose to meet the blows, his great body twisting and turning as Jaleon rained down relentless force. Sparks burst with every impact. Dust clouds erupted with every crash. The temple roared with the music of war.

"YES!" Jaleon bellowed, his eyes wide with fire. "BEND, GIANT! BREAK!"

And for an instant, it looked as though Magnus might actually yield. His feet shifted, his shoulders dipped, his great chest rolled with the strain. Jaleon drove harder, his swings fueled not by muscle now, but by the very flame of his soul.

But then—

Magnus's voice cut through the storm, deep and steady as a god's decree:
"Enough… child."

In one smooth motion, he ducked beneath the sweeping arc of the axe. His massive frame blurred with speed no human should own. He surged upward—his fist slamming like a hammer into Jaleon's shattered ribs.

The sound was sickening. Bone crunched. Air fled Jaleon's lungs in a single, strangled cry. His axe faltered, flame flickering.

Before he could stumble, Magnus's hand clamped around his throat. Fingers like iron closed, lifting the titan of our unit as though he were nothing but a ragged doll. Jaleon kicked, his axe flaring wildly, but the blaze was dimming, its light guttering with every second that Magnus's grip stole his breath.

I could see it.

The life of the weapon—the fire of his will—fading. The orange glow sputtered, trembling as Jaleon's arms clawed at the hand crushing his neck. His face turned red, then purple, veins straining as he fought against the inevitable.

Magnus brought him closer, eye to eye. His voice was low, like stone grinding against stone:
"You thought you were the storm. But I... am the mountain."

The axe's light flickered once more—then dimmed, as though the Flow itself mourned what was about to be lost.

And I—frozen, helpless—watched Jaleon's fire die in Magnus Throne's grasp.

Lux struck like a shadow tearing through flame. His blade swept low, fast and precise, catching Magnus at the joint of his armor. For the first time, the giant staggered—metal groaned, split, and shattered as Lux's strike carved through the plating and bit deep. Sparks flared. Stone cracked beneath their feet.

Jaleon tumbled to the ground, freed from that crushing hand, but broken and bleeding. His axe flickered weakly by his side, its glow trembling with his pulse. His voice was wet with blood, but alive.

Lux dropped beside him, one hand steadying his brother, his chest heaving. "Stay with me, Jaleon," he said, eyes never leaving Magnus. His voice was steel. "I will die before I let you fall."

But Magnus only turned his head slowly, like a beast inconvenienced, not wounded.

And then—he drew it.

The crystal tore from his back with a hiss like screaming metal, the air itself trembling as though the world resisted its birth. From the jagged shard coalesced a blade—crooked, uneven, fractured like a nightmare given form.

And black.

The forbidden color. Void.

Its presence sucked the breath from my lungs. It wasn't a weapon; it was absence made steel. It drank the light around it, casting long, unnatural shadows that stretched and writhed across the shattered temple floor.

And then came the whisper.

Not words, not sound—but an echo that slithered into the marrow of bone. A chorus of voices, thousands of them, crying, wailing, begging. Dying. My ears rang though there was no noise. My heart quailed as though every soul the blade had ever touched was screaming inside me.

Lux froze. His body locked in place, sword hovering uselessly mid-guard. His chest rose and fell in ragged bursts, every instinct screaming at him to run, but there was nowhere to run. I saw it in his eyes: not fear of dying, but the awful certainty of death itself. He wasn't looking at Magnus anymore—he was looking into the abyss, and the abyss looked back.

Magnus's lips curved into something colder than a smile. A verdict.
"You run on speed and precision," he said, each word a rumble that shook the broken stones. "But the void runs faster. And the void misses nothing."

And then—the black blade struck.

It did not swing; it *descended*. A guillotine of shadow, swallowing light as it fell. The air split around it, cracks of darkness spiderwebbing across the air itself. The temple shook as if recoiling from the strike. Dust lifted in trembling waves.

Lux barely managed to move. His sword came up, arms straining, sparks screaming as crystal met the void. The clash wasn't sound, it was silence—a vacuum that devoured the noise around us. The impact hurled him back, his body crashing against fractured pillars, stone erupting in a plume of dust and shards. His blade was still in his hands… but cracked, bleeding light.

And Magnus advanced, step by step, as if nothing in the world could stop the void in his hand. Lux was down, buried in shattered stone, blood streaking his mouth. His sword, cracked and bleeding light, trembled in his grip as though it wanted to give up when he did not. Magnus's void blade lingered above him, humming with whispers, drinking the air, promising the final strike.

And then—she moved.

Serene.

She was fury, she was grace, she was the Flow given flesh. Out of the dust she emerged, her blade already in motion. A streak of green brilliance cut across the black. The impact thundered, sending a shockwave through the ruined hall. Where Magnus's void sucked light away, Serene's crystal poured it forth, like a river spilling against a starving desert.

For the first time—he paused.

Magnus tilted his head, eyes narrowing, pressure grinding through the air as though his very presence was testing her resolve. Their blades ground together, void against flow, black against green. The floor beneath them cracked deeper, veins of obsidian splitting under the strain.

"Stay away from him!" Serene's voice wasn't a shout— it was a command. Her eyes blazed, her stance flawless, every movement precise as if the Flow itself balanced on her shoulders.

Lux coughed, forcing words through the blood in his throat. "Serene—… don't—"

But she didn't falter. She *leaned in*, blade pressing against Magnus's void-sword, sparks of green light flaring each time the abyss tried to swallow her river whole.

Magnus finally spoke, his voice low, rumbling through my bones:

"Your rhythm is flawless. Your courage, bright." His black blade twisted, inching closer, grinding against her strength. "But rivers end… and the void does not."

She pushed harder, teeth gritted, refusing his truth. "Then I'll *break* the void before I let it take them!"

Her green light flared—a surge of flowing arcs, weaving in spirals around his void strike, forcing him one step back. It was small, but it was something. It was resistance.

For the first time, Magnus blinked.

Serene's blade sang against the void, arcs of green weaving like rivers against black hunger. Each clash thundered, each step carved ruin into the obsidian beneath them.

Then Lux rose. Bloodied, breath ragged, but his eyes still sharp. He staggered forward, sword dragging in the dust before snapping upright, blue light flickering alive once more.

"I said I'd die before Jaleon," he rasped, voice trembling but iron at its core. "So I'm not dying here."

He slipped past Serene's shoulder like a shadow, darting in with surgical precision. His strikes weren't wide, weren't brute — they were threads of lightning, stitching themselves around Serene's sweeping flow. Where she held the void at bay, he sought the openings — a wrist, a shoulder, the cracks in Magnus's jagged armor.

Magnus caught his blade on the void-sword, sparks of black fire spitting between them. "Fast," he muttered, almost amused. Then with one twist of his arm he nearly flung Lux across the hall again — but Serene was there, sword spiraling upward, forcing Magnus to lift his guard.

And in that gap—the ground shook.

Jaleon.

Bleeding. Coughing. His ribs shattered, his tunic split open. But Jaleon was not broken.

He dragged himself forward like a storm crawling back to life, his body a ruin yet his spirit unyielding. His axe blazed orange—not just flame, but a sun torn from its sky, brighter than fury, brighter than any mortal fire. His roar shook the ruined temple, rattling my very bones as he charged.

And with blood in his throat, he bellowed: "Nothing? My attacks mean NOTHING to you?! Who decided that?! Will your void devour my pride too—leave me with NOTHING?! Who decided that? WHO?!"

The strike came like a mountain falling. His axe hammered against Magnus's guard, the impact booming like thunder. And for the first time—the titan gave ground. His boots skidded, cracking obsidian beneath each retreating step, the void itself straining under the weight of Jaleon's will.

"ENOUGH!" Magnus's voice ripped the air, an earthquake given sound. His free hand lashed out, a tidal shockwave of raw Flow exploding outward. Serene was hurled back, her body sliding in a spray of fractured stone. Lux was flung aside, coughing blood.

But Jaleon—Jaleon held.

His axe bit into the void-blade, locking it in place, sparks of orange and black clashing in violent bursts. His feet ground trenches in the floor, his teeth bared in defiance as every vein in his neck burned with fire.

"Break!" Jaleon howled, rage and despair forged into one unyielding roar. "I'LL BREAK YOU!"

And for one heartbeat—it looked as though he might. The void strained. Magnus's expression flickered.

That was when Serene surged back into the fray. Her green blade carved spirals of liquid light, flowing around Jaleon's brute force. Each arc bent Magnus's defense tighter, weaving grace into fury. Lux darted between them like wind incarnate, his blue strikes sharp, surgical, slipping into the narrow seams of Magnus's guard.

Together—green, blue, and orange—they became a storm. Three rivers of Flow crashing as one against the abyss.

But Magnus only smiled.

He planted his boots. His void-sword pulsed, shadows swallowing the air itself. His voice was calm, merciless, inevitable.

"Three rivers," he said, eyes burning black. "But all rivers… end in the void."

And then he struck.

Then the whispers rose louder, the abyss itself stretching from his blade. Shadows swallowed their light. And I, frozen, could only watch.

Magnus had had enough of play.
I felt it the instant he shifted, like the air itself warning me of what was about to come. His stance—once loose, almost taunting in its arrogance—snapped into a posture of pure inevitability. One step back, heel grinding against fractured obsidian. His void-sword lifted, jagged edges catching no light, because the blade *consumed* it.

And then his eyes—
Gods, his eyes.

They bled into rivers of shadow, spilling black Flow until his gaze was nothing but pits of endless night. It wasn't just sight. It was gravity. To meet his stare was to feel pulled inward, like your very soul was being dragged toward an abyss that would never end.

Then the storm broke.

The Flow poured out of him, spilling like a dam shattering. Not a stream. Not a wave. A deluge. Black torrents split the air, weaving left and right, crashing against the shattered walls. The temple of Elaris groaned like a dying titan, ancient stone quaking under the weight of his aura.

And then he moved.

One sweep of his arm. Nothing more. But the void answered.
The blade cut forward, and the strike did not stay with him. It leapt outward, a crescent of darkness born from the void, tearing across the chamber. It hissed like flame, but colder than any ice, traveling faster than arrows. Where it passed, stone didn't crack—it unraveled, sheared away as though reality itself couldn't stand against it.

For a breath, I swore the very sun dimmed. The void's aura stretched so vast, so suffocating, that light itself seemed to falter.

I turned my head—and saw despair.

Serene, the fury of our temple, the unbreakable, had cracks in her eyes. Her lips parted, but no command came. For the first time, I saw her faith shake. She stared at Magnus like a mortal staring into the jaws of a god.

Lux… Lux was a ruin. Blood soaked through his tunic in dark rivers, his knees trembling with every breath. His blade hung in his hand, but his arm shook too violently to raise it in time. His face was pale, every ounce of speed that once defined him stolen away by exhaustion and wounds.

And Jaleon—
Gods, Jaleon looked like death itself had already taken him, yet refused to let him fall. His chest heaved, every breath bubbling with blood. His ribs were broken, his shoulders sagging. The once-roaring flame of his axe now guttered, its orange light flickering like a dying ember. He was still upright, but only in defiance of inevitability.

And me?
I felt the terror boiling in my chest. My heart pounded so violently it hurt. And yet… my legs refused to run.

And so I stepped forward.

Every muscle screamed at me to stop. My ribs ached, my lungs burned, my body knew it could not endure more—but I moved anyway. Because they weren't just comrades. They weren't just allies. They were my family. Jaleon, Lux, Serene… and Apollo. I would not let them fall while I still drew breath.

I raised my blade. Fear burned inside me, a wildfire I could not contain. And from that fire, my crystal answered. Purple light erupted, not as a blade, not as fury—but as a shield. The Flow bent and wrapped itself around me, trembling, alive. It was not the shield of a master. It was raw, desperate, forged of instinct and terror.

The void struck.

Magnus's wave of shadow crashed against me, a tide of death that sought to unmake all it touched. My shield screamed, shuddered, threatening to collapse—but I held. My knees dug into fractured obsidian, my bones rattled like brittle wood, and still I held. For one impossible breath, I stood between the void and my family.

And then I screamed.

It wasn't a cry of rage. It wasn't even courage. It was everything inside me—fear, defiance, grief, love— poured into sound. My scream shattered the silence, and I hurled myself forward, purple light blazing, crashing against the endless black. Justice against void. Family against doom. For a heartbeat, the temple belonged to me.

But a heartbeat is all it was.

Magnus swayed aside with the grace of inevitability, his void-sword waiting for me as though the abyss itself had stepped to meet my charge. His lips curled in a cruel smile.

"Little flame," he murmured, voice heavy with contempt, "you burn so brightly… only to die faster."

The blade blurred left, then thrust forward—jagged, crooked, merciless. It pierced through my right shoulder, the impact like a lightning bolt tearing down my spine.

Pain. White-hot, blinding, merciless pain. My body lifted from the ground, impaled on his void-born weapon. Blood burst from my mouth in a red arc, splattering the broken stones below. My fingers spasmed, my sword slipped free, purple light guttering out as it struck the floor.

For a heartbeat I dangled there, pinned on his blade, staring into his abyssal eyes. And in those eyes I saw it—my death, cold and inevitable.

With tears flooding my vision, I turned my head. Through the haze of agony, I saw Serene. My sister in battle. The fury of the temple. Unbreakable. And now her face cracked with horror.

"I'm sorry," I choked, voice torn to shreds, each word dripping blood. "I'm sorry… I'm weak."

Magnus wrenched me free like I was nothing, casting me aside. My body struck stone, pain searing through every nerve. Darkness clawed at the edges of my vision, heavy, choking.

And then—Serene's cry ripped through the temple.

Not a command. Not a leader's voice. Not even a warrior's roar. It was raw, broken, desperate.

"APOLLO! PLEASE—DO SOMETHING! Don't run now!"

Her scream wasn't strategy. It wasn't order. It was prayer. It was the last plea of a sister who had run out of strength, hurled toward the one who still hadn't risen.

A cry for salvation.

Apollo was in the dark.

Not unconscious—no. He had fallen deeper than the world of flesh. He drifted within the Flow itself, swallowed by shadow, weightless, endless.

Around him, whispers slithered like currents, ancient and hungry, pulling him further into silence. Each one hissed of surrender, of letting go, of becoming nothing.

And then—her voice.

His mother's. Gentle, trembling, desperate.
"Run, my boy. Please... run."

She stood there in the abyss, a shape of light amid endless black. Her hand, luminous and shaking, reached for him through the veil. Every part of him longed to take it, to collapse into the comfort of her embrace, to escape the weight of blood and battle.

But then another sound broke through—sharp, ragged, *alive.*

Serene.

Her voice wasn't memory. It wasn't dream. It was here, now. Her scream shattered the silence like a blade through glass:
"APOLLO! PLEASE — DO SOMETHING! DON'T RUN NOW!"

It hit him harder than any wound. A plea, but not for herself. For them all.

The darkness cracked.

A fissure split the void around him, light bleeding in like dawn tearing through storm clouds. The whispers recoiled, hissing, as if burned by the force of her cry. The weight of surrender collapsed in on itself, and Apollo's heart—which had felt still for too long—thundered.

His eyes opened.

The world returned in fragments. Dust motes glowing in shattered light. Heat licking his skin. His chest rising with fire. Pain, real and consuming, dragging him back into the living.

And above him—Elpis.

Her hands pressed against his shoulders, shaking him, eyes wide with terror and tears. Her lips moved, her voice quivering, but he couldn't hear her words over the roar of blood in his ears. Behind her, a soldier loomed, blade raised, the death of innocence only a breath away.

Apollo moved.

It wasn't speed. It wasn't reflex. It was inevitability.

One moment he lay broken—the next, the soldier's body was *gone,* ripped apart in a storm of pure force. Bone shattered, steel twisted, flesh evaporated in the torrent of his awakening rage. Nothing remained but a red mist dissolving into the chaos.

Apollo rose.

And the temple *answered.*

His crystal ignited—not in the clean blaze of power , but in a violent eruption of **deep green.** The light wasn't smooth, wasn't perfect. It cracked outward in rough edges, shards of brilliance like an emerald shattered and reforged by fire. Where others' blades sang with refinement, Apollo's *roared* with defiance.

His sword formed slowly, piece by piece, jagged and uneven as though the Flow itself struggled to contain his power. Its edges were crooked, raw, alive—a weapon born not of elegance but of *will.* Every fracture in its surface glowed with that searing green, pulsing like veins through stone, each heartbeat echoing his rage.

The hilt was scarred, rough to the grip, yet unbreakable— as though it had been forged not by smiths but by the earth itself. The blade stretched long and uneven, not symmetrical, but there was a *truth* in it, an honesty.

It looked wild, untamed, like a mountain ripped from the ground and sharpened into fury.

And gods, it was strong.

When he raised it, the Flow bent toward him, streams of green arcing into the jagged weapon, filling its cracks with violent light until the air itself seemed to fracture. Every soldier froze at the sight, even Magnus's void dimming, recoiling for the first time.

It wasn't a polished blade. It wasn't pretty. It was a *judgment given form.*

And when Apollo swung, the sword screamed like the breaking of chains—a sound raw and terrible, yet beautiful in its defiance.

Every one of us felt it.

Even sthrough the haze of blood and broken breath, through cracked ribs and torn muscle, we felt his return. It wasn't sight that told us. It wasn't sound. It was in the marrow, in the very rhythm of the Flow. Apollo's presence pressed against the battlefield like a second heartbeat, heavy, unrelenting, impossible to ignore. The temple shook not with stone, but with certainty.

Apollo bent down, his breath ragged but steady, his arms closing protectively around Elpis. For a moment the world seemed to vanish—no screams, no steel, no void. Just the two of them.

He pressed his lips to her cheek, a gesture soft and trembling, so at odds with the storm raging behind him. "No one will hurt you," he whispered, his voice breaking yet unshakable. "I promise."

Elpis clung to him, her tiny arms wrapped around his neck, her crystal still faintly glowing blue. She held him not out of fear, but out of love—as though she believed that promise completely, as though Apollo himself was the shield of the world.

But over her shoulder, his gaze locked on Magnus.

The titan of the Umber host was moving, blade raised, eyes of black fire fixed on us. Death was already coming.

Apollo's face changed.

The boyishness, the hesitation, the doubts—gone. What stared back at Magnus now was carved iron. A calm colder than the grave. Eyes burning with emerald light, jaw set like stone.

When he spoke, it was not sound. It was law.

"Run."

The word crashed through the battlefield like a command written into the Flow itself. Elpis's body jolted, her feet moving before her mind could resist, as though even the earth beneath her had obeyed. She slipped free of his arms, running, but not away from him—running because he had said it, because he had made it truth.

And Apollo rose.

Then—he was gone.

Not running. Not leaping. *Gone.* Distance collapsed. Space folded. Apollo broke the covenant of ground and time. One instant he was with Elpis, the next he stood before Magnus, his form a streak of emerald fire cutting across ruin. His very steps seemed to burn paths into the fractured obsidian, green afterimages trailing like ghosts of judgment.

And then came the strike.

The clash was not a sound, but a world ending. Green fire against black void. His jagged, uneven sword—pulsing, alive, fractured yet unbreakable—slammed against the forbidden blade.

The impact tore through the temple: obsidian split apart in jagged lines, shattered stone rising into the air as though gravity itself recoiled. The red banners of the Umber horde ripped from their posts, snapping into the storm. The very air blazed white, stripped of color by the violence of their collision.

For the first time, Magnus's weapon faltered. The void, eternal and merciless, recoiled as though caught by doubt. Its whispers stuttered, its shadows warped, uncertain before the deep green that burned with something stronger than despair.

Magnus's eyes narrowed, his body straining, black aura spilling like blood. But Apollo—silent, burning, relentless—pressed forward. Each movement was a hammer, each breath a command. Where the void sought to consume, Apollo's flame carved a path through it, raw and unyielding.

And for the first time, we believed.

The battlefield stilled as if the world itself leaned in to watch.

Magnus Throne stood, his jagged void blade whispering its chorus of despair. Shadows curled at his feet, bending light, bleeding reality. His blackened aura spread like a storm devouring the edges of everything.

Apollo, opposite him, was fire forged from silence. His deep green aura rolled out in waves, steady yet alive, the jagged edges of his uneven sword humming with a low, resonant thrum. Where Magnus was void, Apollo was growth and life—fractured, imperfect, but unyielding.

The temple itself became their stage.
I will never forget that moment.

The battlefield stilled—not because the fighting ended, but because even death itself leaned closer to watch.

Magnus Throne stood like a mountain carved of shadow. His void blade hummed, crooked and jagged, whispering despair into the marrow of all who dared to listen. Around him, the temple bled darkness — stone groaning, banners snapping, the very air warped by his presence.

And then there was Apollo.

I felt him before I saw him. His aura—green, deep, alive—spread like wildfire across the broken floor. Not smooth, not perfect. His blade was jagged, uneven, rough-hewn like it had been forged by the earth itself. Yet it pulsed with power, undeniable, raw.

I was broken, bleeding, lying in the dust—but when I looked at him, I believed again.

Magnus moved first. One step, one swing—and the void lashed forward, a crescent of black tearing through the temple floor like an arrow of death.

But Apollo—gods, Apollo—blurred into motion. His steps bent the Flow itself. He was here, then there, folding distance like cloth. In a blink he was inside Magnus's strike, his jagged green blade hammering upward.

The clash was thunder made flesh. Green fire against black void. The temple screamed. Tiles split, banners ripped apart, the air itself ignited white.

For the first time, I saw Magnus hesitate. His blade—the void itself—recoiled.

What followed was no fight. It was a storm.

Magnus struck in arcs vast enough to break the world. Every swing of his void blade ripped new scars throusgh stone and air, darkness leaping like arrows across the hall.

Apollo answered not with grace, but with rage. He weaved through the void arcs, jagged blade striking in wild, brutal counters. His movements weren't clean like Lux's, not flawless like Serene's. They were raw, imperfect—but they worked. They landed.

Steel screamed against void. Sparks and shadows rained down like twin storms colliding. The ground cratered under their steps, each strike carving deeper into the temple's bones.

I could only watch, breathless, heart hammering, as gods clashed before me.

Then Magnus roared. He slammed his blade into the ground, and void exploded outward in a dome of annihilation.

The blast hurled Apollo back. I thought it finished him—but he rose. Silent. Calm. His green aura flaring brighter.

Magnus sneered. "Run my boy Run" Like he knew

Apollo's reply was low, cold, carried on the wind: "I am not running."

And then he charged.

They met again in a fury of motion too fast for mortal eyes. Apollo vanished, reappeared behind Magnus, his blade crashing down like lightning. Magnus twisted, caught it—sparks and shadows screamed.

Apollo cut low, scoring Magnus's thigh with emerald fire. Magnus answered with a brutal knee, slamming into Apollo's ribs, lifting him from the ground. Apollo twisted midair, landed hard, rolled, came up slashing.

Their blades locked. Black void against jagged green. Their auras collided, battling for dominance—one devouring, one defying. The hall cracked, stone falling from the ceiling.

Magnus leaned in, voice a growl:
"You burn bright… but I am the end of burning."

Apollo's teeth clenched, his legs buckling. And then—his aura flared. Green fire roared out, violent, untamed, the jagged blade screaming like it was alive.

And Magnus… for the first time… stepped back.

Just one step.

But it was enough.

The void had hesitated.

For us, it felt like hours.
Every strike, every scream of steel against void, stretched the air into eternity. But in truth—it was only minutes. Minutes in which gods and monsters traded blows

through mortal vessels. Minutes where the fate of all who breathed hung suspended on two men's shoulders.

Apollo and Magnus. Green against black. Rage against void.

The Flow bent around them, no longer gentle streams or currents but a hurricane, a living storm of colliding wills. It did not move around Apollo and Magnus—it *obeyed* them, surging, tearing, shrieking as if the very essence of the world had been weaponized.

Every clash was a catastrophe. Obsidian shrieked beneath their feet, cracks spiderwebbing outward like veins of lightning. Pillars groaned, split, and toppled into clouds of dust. Banners ripped free of their poles, igniting in green or vanishing into black as energy tore the air apart.

Magnus struck first.
His void-blade screamed through the air, jagged arcs of annihilation bursting outward like arrows of midnight. Each swing loosed a crescent of darkness that shredded the floor and smashed statues into glass-like shards. Nothing survived his swings—they weren't strikes of a weapon, but pieces of nothingness unleashed, hungry and merciless.

Apollo did not evade. He met him head-on.

His jagged green blade—crooked, raw, uneven—burned as though carved from the world's roots. Sparks of emerald fire bled from it, each drip hissing as if it ate through the air itself. He swung with brutal fury, no elegance, no restraint, each movement powered by the weight of his scars, by rage and defiance.

The two blades collided—and the temple screamed.

The impact shook the air into shockwaves that rattled my teeth even across the hall. Green light erupted against void, and the clash detonated into an explosion of dust and shattered stone. Their forms blurred— Magnus a storm of black crescents, Apollo a streak of jagged emerald arcs, each blow colliding with force that threatened to unmake the world.

Magnus pressed low, sweeping with one brutal horizontal slash that split the obsidian floor into two trenches. Apollo vaulted over it, twisting mid-air, his green blade carving downward like a falling star. Magnus spun, steel meeting emerald, sparks cascading in sheets of green and black flame.

Their choreography became something beyond battle—a duel of philosophies.
Magnus fought with inevitability, his blade always straight, always heavy, every strike designed to erase. Apollo fought with chaos. His blade moved jagged,

unpredictable, swinging with the desperation of a boy who had broken past the Flow's limits and was now burning himself alive to prove he could stand.

Each strike cost Apollo blood. Each collision cracked bone, tore muscle, ripped him apart. His hand split at the knuckles, his ribs strained, and still he struck, driving Magnus back step by step.

For the first time in my life, I saw Magnus Throne stumble.

And still, he smiled.

But then I saw it. We all did.
Something was wrong.

The Flow bends to emotion, but it is bound by flesh. And Apollo… Apollo had broken past that binding. His body was no longer vessel, but prison—and the storm inside him was breaking free.

With one monstrous strike he shattered Magnus's guard. The void-sword itself staggered back, flinching as if uncertain. But the cost—gods, the cost.

His wrist snapped under the force. I heard it, a wet, cracking pop that turned my stomach. His hand broke, skin splitting, bone tearing through knuckle. Blood sprayed with every impact, not from Magnus's blade, but from Apollo's own power turning against him.

Still, he raged.

His ribs groaned and split like branches under lightning. His shoulders tore open under the recoil of his own swings. His skin blistered and cracked as if the green fire inside him sought escape, carving him alive.

And his eyes—gods, his eyes—blazed like two emerald infernos. No longer pupils. No longer human. Just rivers of Flow pouring where no man should survive. They weren't eyes anymore; they were the gaze of a force that had outgrown its cage.

And yet—through ruin, through the collapse of his own body—he struck.

Apollo's jagged blade rose one final time, green fire howling around its broken edges. His arms shook, torn ligaments screaming, ribs shattered like brittle wood. Every inch of him bled. Every breath came with a sound like glass breaking in his chest. But he didn't stop. He couldn't.

The blade came down in a storming arc, a comet born of agony and unchained will.

The impact landed.

The sound was not steel on steel—it was worlds colliding. The air buckled, the obsidian floor detonated into splinters, the banners of the Umber host ignited in green flame.

And Magnus Throne —the nightmare, the unbreakable, the one who strode with void on his back—staggered. His right shoulder cracked beneath the force. Armor shattered into shards that skittered across the ruined hall. Bone splintered with a sound that echoed even louder in my chest than the clash itself. His body reeled, thrown back half a step, then another.

For the first time, he faltered.
For the first time, his eyes widened.
The void itself flinched.

And there was Apollo.

Standing over him, broken beyond repair. His body a ruin. His blood pouring in rivulets down his arms, dripping from torn skin, staining the fractured green crystal in his grip. His breath came ragged, hollow, but his stance was unyielding.

Green flame hissed around him, not a soldier's aura—
but a dying star refusing to go dark.

And I realized—we were watching the impossible.
A man who had shattered himself into pieces, still
standing tall enough to strike down a god.

Apollo stood above him.

Magnus—breaker of kingdoms, the terror of the
Umber banners—was on one knee, his great void-sword
trembling to hold its shape. Around us, the battlefield
had gone silent. Even the cries of the horde faltered, as
if the Flow itself demanded they bear witness.

And Apollo… gods, Apollo was no man in that moment.

His jagged green blade burned brighter than any star
I had seen, but not in a steady glow. The Flow was
bleeding from it, dripping in thick, glowing rivulets
that hissed as they struck the stone. Each drop left a
molten scar across the obsidian floor, rivers of green
fire spreading like veins through the ruin.

His body was shattered—ribs cracked, flesh torn, his
arm bent at a grotesque angle—yet he stood. Tall.
Relentless. His presence was not carried by strength
of bone or muscle, but by something deeper. By will.
By rage. By love.

And then he spoke.

Not to Magnus.
Not to us.
To the world itself.

"I—HAVEN'T—LOST—YET."

His voice was not sound. It was verdict, decree, a hammer striking marrow. The words rolled over us, rolled *through* us, pressing into bone, into blood. Even the broken pillars quivered as though forced to listen.

His sword dripped again.
Hissss.
Another river of green flame spilled from the jagged edge, carving deep scars into the obsidian floor. Each drop seared like molten truth, alive, defiant, endless.

Apollo leaned forward, his body broken, but his emerald gaze—gods, his gaze—was fire carved into stone. It cut straight into Magnus. And for the first time, *for the first time,* the tyrant of the void faltered. In those abyssal eyes, for the briefest heartbeat, there was fear.

But Apollo wasn't seeing Magnus.

In front of him, rising from the torrent of Flow, a shadow took shape. It moved with him, struck with him, fought beside him. For the first time, he was not alone in the storm. Behind that shadow—her. His mother. Her hand reaching, her voice trembling as the void cracked with her words:

"Why didn't you run, my boy?"

His chest heaved, blood bubbling on his lips. His answer was madness, grief, defiance all at once.

"SHIT—SHIT—SHIT!"

He swung his leaking blade toward *us*—toward Serene, toward Lux, toward Jaleon, toward me. We were broken, bloodied, crawling on the edge of death. But alive. Still alive.

And in that moment, with Apollo's body unraveling, his blade dripping rivers of Flow, his eyes burning emerald fire—we believed. Even Magnus believed.

But Apollo was already finished. His body was tearing itself apart. Still, he roared into the storm, not at us, not at Magnus, but to the shadows that only he could see:

"THIS IS BULLSHIT! BULLSHIT! — I WANT MORE POWER!"

The temple froze.
Magnus froze.
We froze.

For the first time, it was not the void we feared—it was Apollo.

His body—gods, his body was nothing but ruin. The Flow he had commanded, the storm he had unleashed, was not meant to be borne by mortal veins. His skin cracked like glass, green light spilling from the seams. Blood and Flow bled together, a river of red and emerald dripping into the shattered temple floor.

The jagged blade in his hand faltered. What had been a torrent of unstoppable force guttered like a dying flame, green fire coughing in sparks before dimming into smoke. His arms, torn and trembling, hung limp at his sides. His legs buckled, bones too broken to hold him.

But before he fell, we all *knew*.

If he had lasted one more minute—one more heartbeat of rage, one more swing of that leaking blade—Magnus would have fallen. The nightmare of the Umber host, the breaker of kingdoms, would have been broken himself. Even Magnus knew it. His abyssal eyes—wide, shaken, disbelieving—told the truth.

And then Apollo collapsed.

He fell not as a man bested, but as a star burning itself to nothing. His body struck the obsidian in a spray of green fire and blood, the sound echoing like the last toll of a bell. The Flow around him unraveled, fading back into silence, leaving only ruin in its wake.

The duel was not won.
The duel was survived.

We, the broken remnants of the temple's defenders, still breathed because he had given everything. His storm had not slain Magnus Throne—but it had shown him fear. It had scarred him. It had reminded even the void that something greater than darkness could burn in this world.

And Apollo lay amidst the wreckage, broken, destroyed, consumed by his own fire.

Apollo's sword was fading.

The jagged emerald edge, once a storm of fire and fury, now dimmed to embers. Green light dripped from its cracks like dying stars, until even that guttered away. The weapon lay heavy in his limp hand, more ruin than blade.

And yet… I saw it.

No one else did. In the corner of his shredded tunic, from a pocket near his heart, a single glimmer stirred. A stripe of blue. Small, faint—but alive. It shimmered once, wrapping him with a whisper of care, as though the Flow itself sought to cradle him. Then, as quickly as it appeared, it vanished.

I wanted to reach for it. To ask what it meant. But I had no strength. And it no longer mattered.

We were defeated.

The silence was broken by Magnus Throne's voice— firm, commanding, immovable.
"Take them."

The remnants of the Umber horde advanced. Not in triumph. Not with mockery. With something closer to reverence. Bloodied as we were, broken as we lay, they did not drag us like spoils. They carried us like fallen champions, as if even enemies could not deny what we had done.

I felt their gauntlets close around my arms, my legs. My body resisted, but only for a moment. There was nothing left to give.

They put us into their carriers—all five of us. Serene, her fury silenced. Lux, barely breathing. Jaleon, more blood than man. Apollo, crumpled and drained, yet still a storm even in stillness. And me, too weak to lift my blade again.

The last words I heard as the obsidian temple faded from view were Magnus's—steady, cold, absolute. "Heal them."

Not mercy. Not kindness. Command.

And through the blur of my vision, as darkness reached for me, I saw her.

Elpis.

She was crying, her face streaked with fear, with grief, with something deeper I could not name. My thoughts clung to her even as my body caved, even as the world folded into silence.

What will happen to her?

It was my last thought before unconsciousness took me. And so we, defenders of Elaris, fell not into death—but into the hands of the enemy.

To be continued …. May the flow guide you .